# Without Warning

Vic Broquard

Broquard eBooks.com
103 Timber Ln
East Peoria, IL 61611
author@Broquard-eBooks.com

Artwork by Crooked Willows Studios

For Morgan and L. Ron Hubbard

# Table of Contents

# Chapter 1 A Strange Meeting

Early Friday morning came announced by a loud alarm clock. Zed groaned as he rolled out of bed. Zed Osmund's passion in life was simple: brew a hot cup of coffee for those heading to work in the early morning hours. He dreaded the coming weekend. Cat would be closed, and the downtown business section would be deserted. There would be no point in opening his Hot Brew stand on Main Street. No customers, no friendly people to drop by and chat.

Staring into the bathroom mirror, Zed growled to himself, "Okay, I admit it. I dropped out of junior college last year. All that book studying left me bored." He felt as though he were answering his father's angry questions. He'd gone one year at his father's insistence. After all, dad was a very successful engineer, but he had been transferred to Houston last year, and Zed's mom went with him, as well as his sister. This time, Zed had refused to move. It was not that he was in love with the River City. No, rather he was tired of all the constant moving from city to city that his family had to do. Peoria marked the tenth city that they'd lived in during his young twenty years. When they left, although he promised his folks that he would go to college, he'd changed his mind. "I've a right to do that, you know," he growled at the imagined face of his father in the mirror. Zed always got a little antagonistic when talking about such things.

After walking out of junior college, Zed spent weeks looking for a job. Unable to find anything that he could see himself doing and with the economy now gone to the dogs, just as his money was running out, Zed got lucky one night at the Paradise, the local cassino, winning twenty grand. He then spent most all of it on his truck stand, the Hot Brew. Essentially a converted Ford, the bed supported a stainless steel coffee kiosk. One side opened to the sidewalk — his window into the wide world. By six a.m. Zed had already parked in his usual spot with three pots both hot and ready. "God, I love this job," he muttered to himself as he slid the stainless steel side up, ready for business.

"Morning. Your regular?" he asked cheerily. A tall, thin man, wearing what must be a three hundred dollar suit and carrying a fine, black leather briefcase, walked up. His solemn face with sleepy eyes brightened up as he approached.

"Yes, decaf mocha."

"Looks like it might rain later today. Not good for the Chiefs, eh?" Zed chatted, fixing the man his brew. He used only the finest cups, whose lids could not come off easily, not even if the cup was dropped. After all, the man wore an expensive suit; a coffee spill was not an option. Zed knew that this man also knew this too and this was probably why he dropped by every morning on his way into the Corporate Headquarters building. Once he had given Zed a ticket to the Chief's game, a box seat no less.

"Thanks, keep the change. Glad you are out and about at this god-forsaken hour. Yes, Channel 31 said there's an eighty-five percent chance of rain later today. Catch you Monday," he replied and left with his brew, accompanied by a momentary smile on his face.

"My usual, Zed. I'm in rather a hurry this morning," a young woman in a smart business suit said, hastily filling the void left by the man with the suitcase.

"Coming right up. You look a bit rushed, but think about sipping this mocha five minutes from now," Zed suggested, handing her the tall cup. She always took the extra large cups. The worry lines vanished; a smile pursed her red lips, a sparkle returned to her eyes.

"Already anticipating it, Zed. Thanks. Cya on Monday." She pivoted and hastily headed across the street, pushing the Don't Walk light just a bit.

A short, pudgy man stepped up, "Hi Zed. How's it going? Latte please. Going to rain today."

"Coming up. Hope you brought your umbrella. Doing just fine this morning. Yourself?"

"Oh, my arthritis is acting up. Always does just before it rains."

"Well, the coffee will warm you up."

He smiled, "Sure does. Don't know what we all did before you opened up here."

"You all had to go out of your way to catch Starbucks, I'll wager." The man smiled and took a sip of his coffee before moving off, revealing a tall, thin woman standing up against the plate glass window of the building before this side of his stand. She was looking straight at Zed. Her sky blue eyes met his, but another customer moved up, blocking his vision.

For the next hour, Zed caught occasional glimpses of this woman between eager, rushed customers. She had long black hair with bangs down to her eyebrows, the rest falling to her shoulders, giving her face a roundish, pixie-like appearance. Wearing jeans, sneakers, and a bright, multi-colored, tie-died tee-shirt, she looked out of place among these professional men and women scurrying into the many nearby buildings. For the next two hours, Zed caught glimpses of this mystery woman in the background. Always, she was observing him as he interacted with his steady stream of early morning customers.

Around seven-thirty, the predicted June rains came, along with the necessary umbrellas. A harried middle aged woman stepped up to the stainless steel counter, rain pouring off of her pink umbrella. "Three today, Zed. Running late," she said, fumbling with her purse.

"Ah, a third arm would be most useful now," Zed teased her, bringing a grin to her face. "Here, I'm putting in an extra one. On the house. Make someone's morning," he suggested, handing her the small carrying bag, one that would not disintegrate if it got wet.

"Thanks! I'll do just that. Keep the change. In a rush. Cya on Monday," she replied, moving out into the downpour once more. Just as another man moved to take her place, Zed caught a glimpse of the mysterious woman. She was still watching him closely, though now she was getting drenched, but she seemed not to notice the downpour. What was this strange woman doing? Why was she watching him, he wondered.

Around eight, the last customer left, running across the street, very late to work this morning. Zed peered out from his kiosk. Except for this soaked young woman still leaning against the glass pane, the street was empty of foot traffic. "Oh hell," Zed thought to himself. "Miss? You want a free coffee? You are getting drenched. On the house. I'm about to close up," he called out.

She looked up and down the sidewalk. Seeing no other pedestrians, she glided effortlessly up to his silvery kiosk. "Hi, I am Miranda Whitney. Thanks for the offer, but I prefer tea. I seem to be a bit wet," she replied, leaning slightly inside the window so that the tiny awning shielded her face from the steady downpour. Her enchanting voice and her sparkling eyes captivated him.

Zed felt strangely attracted to her, perhaps because she was now soaking wet. "Saw you watching me for the last couple of hours," he said, totally unsure what to say to her. He could only think of the obvious. She wasn't wearing any makeup like all of the other women who had stopped by for their morning coffee. He couldn't bring himself to just outright ask her why she had been standing there watching him for two hours, especially once the downpour began.

"Yes, I was observing you. You have quite a rapport with your customers. I like that. Say, are you finished here?" she asked.

"Yes, all done until Monday. Somehow I have to survive the long weekend. I wish Monday morning were here." Zed felt a pang of sympathy for this woman who had gotten completely drenched for no other apparent reason but to observe him this morning. Without thinking much about it, he asked, "Say, can I give you a lift somewhere?"

"That would be very kind of you. Yes, could you drop me off at my place on the bluff? I take it that you love coffee?" she asked.

Zed chuckled. "Not really. I prefer a good cup of black tea, as a matter of fact. Hop in the cab. I got to close up back here. Join you in a bit." She flashed him a big smile and did as asked. Quickly, Zed closed his stainless steel window and shut down the three pots. I guess there is no harm in dropping her off at her house, he thought. Two minutes later, with everything secured, he stepped out the back door into the rain. Hunched over as if the falling rain would somehow clobber him, he made a dash to the driver's door.

"Sorry about getting your seat wet," Miranda apologized as he entered dripping water onto his seat and steering wheel.

"No problem. Neither my trusty truck nor I melt in the rain. Where to, Miranda?" he asked as he started it up. The rain fell harder than ever and his windshield wipers barely opened a momentary window onto the street.

"Bluffs. Take Main to West High to West Moss. Thanks for giving me a lift. I walked down here this morning. It was a pleasant walk then, but going back isn't going to be. Sure is hard to see isn't it?"

"No kidding. Wipers are flying off. Well, go slow enough and I can sort of see." Miranda wisely said nothing more, allowing Zed to concentrate on driving. Visibility was but a few feet ahead in this downpour, which had now turned into a thunderstorm of some magnitude. The voluminous booms seemed magnified in the compact cab of the truck. Zed had to concentrate on driving, not his mysterious passenger.

"Here we are. This is it. Turn in here," Miranda pointed out. Zed could scarcely believe his eyes. They entered a driveway between two large stone lions. Ahead was an old Mediterranean style mansion, sitting high on the edge of the bluff overlooking the heart of the city.

"Wow! Some place you have here!" Zed exclaimed, more that a little awed with the sight before him.

"Mom and I like it. Please, come inside. Let me fix you a hot tea while we dry off. You do have time for a chat, don't you?" she asked in a demure tone of voice. How could he possibly refuse? Besides, he had nothing to do but kill time until Monday morning came at long last. Yes, he was intrigued by this attractive woman. She was not wearing a bra, he noted as they stopped and he looked at her. Her soaked tee-shirt left little to his imagination.

"I'm yours, at least until Monday morning," he found himself replying lamely and wishing he'd kept his mouth shut. He got out and followed her into the huge ornate entryway, where at last the pounding rain ceased falling on them.

Once inside, Zed found himself unable to say anything more than, "Incredible! Wow!" He'd never been inside such a mansion before, let alone seen such craftsmanship, such woodwork, such paintings, such sculpture.

"Look around. Back there is the sitting room. It has a great view. Be back in a minute. I've got to get into some dry clothes. Make yourself at home, Zed," Miranda said softly, before ducking down a side hall.

He did as suggested, staring at the impressive sights, which demanded his attention. For the moment, he forgot caution and why would this woman be standing for hours watching his small business. Zed found himself drawn into the sitting room almost at once. Here a large bay window poked out over the bluff. Giant picture windows framed with luxurious red velvet curtains called to him. He stood and stared out at the view. Streaks of lightning arced through the space before him, while down below him the city's heart sprawled. He felt as if he were some god looking over his city from a heavenly cloud.

"Impressive isn't it?" the soft voice of Miranda registered in his mind, bringing him back to the present. He turned and saw her standing in the doorway. She wore almost the same style clothing as before, only the tie-died tee-shirt was not quite the same. Her black hair was still quite damp, however. "Don't you feel like you are some god on high looking down? I always do. This is my favorite room in the house."

"How did you know that's what I was thinking? Well, it is certainly spectacular here. Incredible beyond words. I've never seen anything like this before. You must be rich," Zed replied, still very much in awe.

"Come on. This way to the kitchen. I promised you a hot cup of tea. It's surprising that you prefer tea over coffee, Zed. I admit that I'm a little surprised," she prodded slightly as she led him into their large, spotless kitchen. The ceilings were quite high and various pans hung down from the ceiling. A large rectangular, marble workspace counter sat precisely in the center of the room. She opened a cabinet, revealing numerous teas.

"Ignore those. They are mom's green and herbal teas. Pick whichever one you want. I've got them arranged in order. This shelf is all black teas; this one is oolong," she indicated.

"Hey, you have Prince of Wales! Great. I'll have that one, please," Zed replied, seeing the familiar black tin with white lettering on it. He watched her as she set about making the tea. She was attractive, no doubt about that. Why had she been watching him for two hours this morning? Zed couldn't get that curious detail out of his mind. He knew that he had never seen Miranda before this morning, not even at the junior college. Had she seen him somewhere? That must be it, he decided, but then wondered why she would have been watching him for hours. It did not make any sense to him.

Before long, the two sat down across from each other on either side of the counter. "How come you sell coffee in the early morning hours and you don't really like coffee?" Miranda began their conversation. Her eyes never left his, and he found that she was a very good listener. Before long, he was telling her his whole life story!

"I like to help people. I bring a smile to their faces each morning. That's why I am doing it. I sort of break even. I'm not really making more money than I need to pay the bills. But that's not the point. I get a whole lot of satisfaction from just helping in so simple a way, you know. I bring smiles to otherwise dreary faces. That's why I can't wait for the next morning. I hate the weekends, nothing to do except wait until Monday comes around again."

"That is both fascinating and a rewarding thing to do," she acknowledged.

Somehow he felt that he ought to really be honest with her, though he didn't know why. She was a total stranger, after all. "Yes, well, it was the only job I could find that I halfway liked. I dropped out of college, you know. Couldn't stomach all that book learning. Boring. Dad's an engineer with Cat but he keeps on getting transferred all over the country. We've never lived in one place more than a couple of years. He got transferred again last year and this time I refused to go with him, mom, and my sister down to Texas. I know that I promised him I'd go to college, but what the heck. It's my life now," he admitted. Again, he wondered why he was telling her his private thoughts. Surely she would not have the slightest interest in them. Perhaps it was that he had no other idea of what to say to her. Well, there was some truth to that, he mused. He seldom had gone out on any real dates before now.

"Yes, that it is. I understand about college. Haven't gone myself either," she admitted. Somehow this tiny morsel of herself felt like a perfect thing for him to hear. A kindred spirit, perhaps, he thought.

He continued chatting, "I did hit the jackpot over on the Paradise last fall. Won twenty grand. That's when I decided to buy my truck and sell coffee to folks. I'd seen so many somber faces heading in to work. I wanted to bring a bit of happiness to all of them, if only for a few minutes."

"Yes, I could see their reflections in the stainless steel sides. You are definitely being successful at putting a smile on their faces. Good feeling. I bet you aren't easily surprised," Miranda suggested. She felt encouraged that he was so readily talking about himself. Emboldened, she added, "I mean, I bet you have seen all sorts of strange things and happenings out there on the street." Miranda decided to test Zed a bit. In fact, she was quite desperate. Her search for someone who might be able to help her had met with utter failure for over two weeks now. Only yesterday, she'd spotted his truck and had decided: what the heck, give him a try. Already, she'd tried all of her so called friends and met with dismal failures with each. She now had no other choice but to try total strangers. Yes, Miranda was desperate.

Zed couldn't resist the nudge. "Oh, I suppose so. I don't get easily riled, if that's what you mean. I was nearly broke after dropping out of college. Some said that I was being too picky about finding the right job to earn money. I didn't get riled, instead, somehow I won big at the gambling tables, though I do have to admit, Miranda, I have no idea what I did there that night. I had never been gambling before then, only that once. I haven't gone back. I figure that it's there when I really need it." Zed chatted on, describing several chance encounters, including a guy who tried to rob him. Instead, Zed had just given him a coffee, which confused the man completely.

Miranda observed that Zed had the right attitudes. He certainly wasn't carrying along emotional baggage that would defeat him. He wasn't out to make a fortune or even gain personal fame. Rather his desire to help others seemed to be his strongest characteristic, she thought. If she wasn't so desperate just now, Zed was certainly worth knowing better. He was a bit shy around women, she noted, but kind-hearted. Still, she was desperate. Her mother had been missing for over three weeks now, and two of those she had lost while testing all of her friends and acquaintances, none of which had panned out. That he had been lighthearted about being nearly broke and had then won big at the Paradise tended to make her think that perhaps Zed was not so heavily in agreement with the physical universe as were all of her friends.

Zed chatted away, but continued to look Miranda over. He felt attracted to her, her face, her hair, her eyes, all commanded his attention. No, it was more than physical attraction; there was something deeper with Miranda. He knew that he was doing most of the talking, telling her his life story, more or less. Still, she was keenly interested in listening to him, he noted, wholly unlike so many other women his age. What did she really want from him? Why had she stood for hours watching him sell coffee this morning, especially after the rains came?

Wait! He'd seen the look that every so often appeared on her face. Yes, he'd seen it before. She needed help with something! That had to be it. She was in some kind of trouble and was looking for someone to help her out of it. He'd seen that facial expression before — okay, maybe it was not so much a "look" as a "feeling" that emanated from her.

He'd finished his tea and decided to see if she would talk to him about herself. "So I couldn't help noticing that you were watching me all morning, ever since shortly after I opened the window. How come?" Well, Zed thought that had come out entirely too bluntly and he inwardly cursed himself for not having more tact.

"Yes, I was watching you." Miranda reached a decision. She could not say more about it. She could not answer his direct question without revealing far too much — not without knowing more about him. She decided to put Zed to the acid test. She hated not being forthright and honest with people. If he passed, then she could at last stop avoiding his questions and answer him truthfully. If not, well, she could be polite about a little lie. "Say, would you like to see my room?" she asked.

Zed flushed. What was she asking? Was she making a subtle hint for a romantic interlude? He'd only just met her. Yes, he was attracted to her, but still, he knew nothing about her at all. He decided to let her know just where he stood, to be up front with her. "I'm sorry, but we've just met. I don't do casual sex, if that's what you mean, Miranda. Besides, your mother might return."

Miranda crimsoned. In a flash, she realized that what she had asked sounded like a proposition and that it had been so interpreted. "I'm sorry, Zed. I didn't mean that quite like that. I don't do it either. Mom's not going to be back." She dare not reveal more about her mother, not just yet. She knew that she'd gotten herself into a bind. How do I get out of this one, she wondered. "I meant that I'd like to show you my room and my things. All this stuff you have seen is really mom's, not mine. I wanted to share a bit of me with you." She flushed even more so, realizing how this must sound to him. "You know, a bit about who I am — not the other," she added hoping that he'd catch on and not take her last statement the wrong way.

Zed felt a bit of relief. Miranda was not after getting him into her bed. He relaxed, "Ah well, then in that case, I'll take your head. I like your head. That's a fine bit to share." He grinned, signaling that this was a tease.

Miranda picked up on him instantly, a big grin replaced her serious mien. "Good one, Zed. Sorry, I can't seem to disconnect it right now," she countered his tease, before asking, "Do you like early Jethro Tull or early Pink Floyd?" She decided that the optimum way to proceed was to segue into a reason to go to her room.

"Sure, Locomotive Breath is something else. I'm not too in to the more modern rock. Perhaps all of the artists have lost their creativity," Zed suggested.

"Way cool, Zed. I've an autographed copy of Aqualung in my room. Ian signed it for me when I was at one of their concerts in the Quad Cities. It's in my room. My stereo is there too. Mom is not into rock; she's into symphonies and all that. Come on. I'll show you. I hope you don't mind too much pink. I've got pink walls," she teased him. He rose and followed her out of the kitchen and down a long hallway to her bedroom, hopeful of learning a bit more about this strange young woman.

She opened the door and called out, "Play Locomotive Breath." She had a voice activated stereo system, Sync probably, he concluded.

However, she actually did not have to vocalize her request; she could just activate the system directly and faster without using words. She used her voice to make it fit better into Zed's frame of reference. He was about to be surprised anyway.

Pink flooded the color sensors in his eyes, momentarily blinding him. He'd never been in a room so entirely pink before. The floor just before them was sky blue and a chandelier rose up from the center of the floor, as if it was the ceiling. Zed blinked twice, but the light stayed put, rising upwards. "Like this," Miranda called out. She took a step inside, while holding onto the door frame. She pivoted her body upside down and landed on the roof of her room, where there seemed to be a lot of objects, a bed, stereo, books, and closets — apparently all upside down!

Zed froze for a moment, trying to grasp what he was seeing! Her ceiling was her floor! There she stood seemingly upside down to him, her feet on the floor, or ceiling rather. Her hair fell to the floor as normal, only it was upside down somehow. How could this be? "Come on in," she invited.

He put his hand on the doorframe as she had done and took a hesitant step into the room. At once, he believed that he had begun to fall upwards towards the floor. Only at the last second did he finally grasp that he must be falling and managed to only get partially twisted around, landing solidly on his butt. "Ouch."

"Here, let me help you up. Most people have trouble getting in here. Mom certainly does. So what do you think of my room?" she asked. Zed was now in her final test. How would he react to a total disagreement with the physical universe? Her friends had all freaked out, every one of them.

"Dunno. My feet seem pulled to the floor firm enough." He looked up at the ceiling, which he believed had been the floor. He added, "Well, if I forget about coming in here and just focus on the room, it seems normal like, except for the overwhelming pink. You must like pink a whole lot. Can I sit on your bed?" Just now, Zed felt slightly nauseated and really needed to sit down. His mind was swirling, trying to grasp the largest shock of his life. What kind of illusion was this room?

"Sure. Why?"

"I want to see if I fall up and hit the ceiling," he replied, unwilling to divulge just how totally disoriented and spooked he was. He plopped hesitantly on her bed's pink quilt. He bounced as if he was on a normal bed. Satisfied, he took a deep breath and said as calmly as he could muster, "Well, I have to admit, Miranda, this is the strangest room that I have ever seen. How come everything seems upside down? Can't be magnets. I don't have any metal on me, except my buckle. I don't feel any forces on me, except gravity which is pulling me down, er up I guess. How'd you do this? This is incredible! This is unreal!"

"I made it seem that gravity is upside down in here. I am different and I wanted others to know that I am me and am different. Drives mom nuts, though. Dad just laughed. He died about a year after we redid my room like this — been eight years ago now." Miranda began to relax for the first time. Zed was not freaking out. Well, he was showing signs of stress, but was handling it incredibly well, she thought. Hence, she began to reveal a bit about herself to him.

"I'm sorry. I didn't know that he'd died." Zed said consolingly. Damn, he thought to himself, I hope that she doesn't start to cry or anything. I don't think that I can handle much more just now. Focus, Zed, focus.

"Thanks. Oh, here's my pride and joy." She handed him her Ian-autographed album cover.

"Way cool indeed! That's worth keeping," Zed admired it. He saw the scrawling signature, probably made with a felt pen, he thought. The driving part of the song now flooded the room and he could not help but compliment her, "Excellent sound system. It sounds very real. I caught one concert once; they played in Chicago when we were living there. So did you just take the album backstage and he signed it?" While he would never want to get some rock star's autograph, he respected those who did, especially girls. He knew that his sister would be wild with excitement over seeing it.

"Yes, I paid a fortune to get the backstage pass and a minute with him. He's cute, but awfully old now. I'm not sure that I really dig his later releases though. For my money, they don't have the same punch, but artists evolve too, I guess," she replied. Miranda could scarcely conceal her enthusiasm! Zed had not freaked out at all and was quite calmly enjoying this most unusual experience! He had to be the one! He just had to be!

"Cool." He laid back and looked up at the ceiling. If he forgot about entering the room; it all looked and felt normal. He latched on to this point of view. Gazing at the sky blue ceiling, he added in a mused fashion, "You know, I think that you ought to add some stars on the ceiling. You can then lie down and look up at them as if you were outside at night," Zed suggested.

She flushed, "You saw them?"

"Huh?"

"Lights out," she commanded, though she actually carried out the command herself. She could explain this again as voice activated switches. At once the lights went out and sparking stars dotted the ceiling, which once had been the floor.

"Wow! Yep, this is super cool, Miranda. Now if they only moved around some," he suggested.

She turned the lights back on. "Voice activated stuff, right?" he asked. "I've seen commercials for these kinds of things in cars, expensive cars, that is."

"Yes, voice activation," she lied effectively, just as she had done many times before.

This has to be an illusion, Zed thought. This cannot be real. Gravity pulls things down, not up. This cannot be real. Then a wave of fear arced through his stomach. Had she slipped him some drug? LSD perhaps? How could he have been so foolish? Allowing an unknown woman to invite him, a total stranger, into her home and serve him tea — foolish beyond words. Had she slipped him something? Why was she inviting him into her bedroom of all places? Was she out to seduce him? So far, Miranda made no such moves, rather the contrary. She'd made no sexual moves, not even flirting. Why was she doing this to him? Zed's mind raced down many paths of explanations, but none wholly fit with the circumstances. The only effect that could be explained was the voice activation of her stereo and the lights. He'd heard of such electronic devices. Some were in popular children's toys.

Think, man, think! He forced his mind to shift into high gear. No, I cannot be drugged, he thought. I'm not dizzy, spacey, or anything. I was feeling perfectly normal up until she opened her bedroom door. There could not have been anything in my tea; it would have hit me sooner. Besides, I feel fine right now. If I was drugged, I think that I would somehow feel differently. Zed had never downed anything harder than an aspirin.

Gravity was down, not up, as her room suggested. This whole thing just could not be "real." His mind could come up with no other logical explanation. At last, the song ended and he spoke firmly, "Miranda, this cannot be real. It has to be some kind of illusion!" He said it with a firm conviction and full intention. There could be no other rational explanation; it had to be some kind of elaborate illusion.

The instant that he uttered his conviction, he felt something change about the room, though if you asked him what, he could not have said. Everything still looked the same as it had since he entered the room. Yet, he sensed something had changed somehow, and he looked around trying to pinpoint it. Well, everything was not the same. His eyes finally landed upon Miranda, her mouth was gaping, her eyes, quite startled. That was different.

Miranda was shocked. His simple statement had completely canceled her illusion spell. Only her mother and late father had ever been able to completely wipe out one of her illusions so completely and so quickly! As far as her test was concerned, Zed had not only passed, but he was far beyond anything that she had ever dared dream to find. For the first time in her life, she was completely shocked herself. She was only vaguely aware that her mouth was wide open. Her mind was trying to grasp the significance of this wholly unexpected event.

How long had she stood there gaping? Seconds, minutes? At last, she found her voice. "Yes, Zed, part of it was an illusion which you not only saw through it but also canceled it. What you are now seeing is really my room. Here, I'll open the door." She moved quickly and opened the very door through which they had entered. Zed looked out to the hall. Now everything seemed normal. Her floor was a highly polished wood, a continuation of the wooden hallway flooring. Still, her walls were vivid pink, the bed, stereo, and other items were as they had been, only they were on the real floor and not apparently hanging upside down from the ceiling as he had thought he had seen at first.

"Zed, I am very sorry to have done that to you, but I was testing you. I had to do it," she finally began to level with him.

"Testing me? How? Why? What are you talking about? Why me? Why were you watching me all morning long? What's going on here? Is this really your home?" Zed finally stopped, although he still had a lengthy list of more questions. He sheepishly realized that he'd asked a whole bunch already.

Ding. Dong. From a distance, a doorbell rang, breaking the momentary silence. "Oh, that'll be the Domino's pizza man. I'm starving. Zed, will you get the front door for me? There's a twenty lying on the small ledge to the left of the door. I ordered three for five dollars. Give it all to him. I'll fix us some sodas in the kitchen. You do like pizza don't you?" Miranda hastily explained and asked, thankful for a very short reprieve. She knew that she was facing some very tough questions which she had to answer honestly, if she were to have any chance at all in enlisting Zed's help.

"Wow. I am hungry; it's close to noon. Okay, I'll take care of it. Got any Cokes?" he replied, as the two headed down the long hallway. He was determined not to get sidetracked by pizza. He wanted answers from this woman, understandable answers, answers that made sense. This had been the strangest morning he'd ever experienced.

# Chapter 2 Explanations

When Zed brought the three boxes into the kitchen, Miranda had already gotten the Cokes out along with a pile of napkins. "I ordered three kinds, take your pick. I like all three," she said. Zed checked them and settled for the sausage and double cheese. Again, the two sat across from each other.

"Okay, I owe you a lot of explanations, Zed. Please, hear me out all the way before you judge me," Miranda began, pleadingly. She'd found in him far more than she had ever hoped for but now sensed that she might have blown any chance that she had in eliciting his help. Still, her explanation had to be carefully constructed, totally honest, but done in such a way that Zed would be able to understand it. If not, she knew that she'd only find him walking out the door on her.

"I'm going to start at the beginning, Zed. First and most importantly, man is a composite being composed of four parts. Our physical bodies here are just carbon-oxygen based engines that use food for fuel, pizza at the moment. We have a somatic kind of mind that runs our engines, that is, our bodies, which handles breathing, heart beats, digestion and the like. We all have minds which we use to pose and resolve problems and such. Then, there is the real person, the "I," the personality, the spiritual being. It is us, the spiritual beings, we who are aware and alive and animate the physical body."

"Look, I'll show you. Close your eyes and see if you can get an image of your fancy truck." Zed nodded. "Okay, that image is in your mind. Who is looking at that image?"

"Well, I am; someone has to be looking at it and seeing it," Zed replied, opening his eyes. "I never looked at it this way. I am the one doing the looking. So this is me, eh?"

"Yes, we beings are not made of any physical universe stuff, no matter, no energy, no space, no time, none of it. Yet, we are natively extremely powerful, though often we believe that our bodies have power and that we do not," Miranda tried to explain, but felt an increasing frustration over how on earth she was going to be able to make all this understandable to him. To her, this was all second nature, always had been.

"I am not into all this religious stuff," Zed admitted. He declined to add that he was beginning to think that Miranda was some kind of a religious nut. Yet, he could see what she meant by man being composed of four parts. What intrigued him was just who and what was he? Zed had just realized that it was he and he alone who was looking at his mental image of his truck. Until this moment, he'd never given such things any thought at all. Was she right? He didn't seem to have any weight or energy; it was just himself looking at the image in his mind.

"Well, I am not either," Miranda hastily added, sensing that she had somehow misled him. "The 'praise the lord and pass the plate fellows' are just con men after your money. History is replete with crimes, hatred-inspired wars, and intolerance fomented by many organized religions. Forget them, I say. No, Zed, I am talking about who and what you and I really are. You are the one looking at the image of your truck in your mind. I'm talking about the real you."

Zed visibly relaxed and took another large bite of his pizza, washing it down with a swill of Coke. Miranda had defused his apprehensions, but he still had no idea what she wanted. Why, remained as elusive as ever. "Well, yes, I am seeing my mind's image, so I am here doing the looking,

Miranda, but I don't seem to have any real substance, if you follow me."

Maybe this wasn't going all wrong after all, she thought, relaxing slightly. She too ate another big bite before continuing. "Yes, we are not made of physical universe stuff, Zed. In terms of matter and energy and space and time, we are not composed of any of those things. We are immortal spiritual beings who are living for a time in these bodies. I know that you may not believe all of what I am about to say, but here goes anyway. We beings, while not of the physical universe, are capable of creating all four of the universe components, that is, matter, energy, space, and time."

"Let's look at the one thing which is the most important factor that happened with my room. Reality. Zed, what is reality? It is simply agreement. When we all agree that something is, then it is. Take your customers, for example. You and they all agree that you are there each morning selling coffee. And so it is. Yet, what would happen if a guy came along and started telling everyone that you were selling monkeys out of your stainless steel kiosk?"

Zed chuckled, "They'd laugh and say he's crazy. Oh! I see, he is not in agreement with the rest of us, is he?"

"No he is not agreeing with the rest of you. Now wouldn't you feel a bit funny having him around, being around him, if he constantly harped about all the monkeys there inside your kiosk?"

"No kidding, it'd be spooky. Probably have to call the cops and have the crazy man taken away or something," he admitted.

"Indeed. This goes deeper Zed. When you won all that money, right after that, didn't you get the idea to have your coffee stand?"

"Sure, I sat back and mused for several days, Miranda. That is, after catching up on my bills. I looked at my future and saw that I wanted to sell good quality coffee to these professionals heading into their offices each early morning. I saw this as a way to brighten up their days a little bit," Zed replied honestly.

"Cool. You began making what engineers call a mockup of your future path. Did you not get an idea of what you wanted in the way of your truck too?" she asked, knowing that he must have done so.

"Sure did. I looked over a number of possibilities and decided on this very one. Oh, I see what you mean, well maybe. I sort of put the truck and my selling coffee to them into my future."

"Yes, and then you worked to get others to agree with your ideas. You got the truck, made coffee, and began selling it. You made it real not only for yourself, but also for everyone else," Miranda explained.

"Maybe I am seeing what you mean. I created my own mockup, my own illusions of what I wanted to be in the universe and then brought it into being. Is this what you are alluding to?" he asked.

"Precisely. Reality is nothing more than an illusion. Yes, it a solid, strong one, because we all agree on it. Everyone is in solid agreement that our house is here, that your truck is on our driveway. Yet, it still is an illusion in the final analysis. That's what I did with you when I took you into my room, Zed."

"Huh? I don't follow you. Your room was upside down," Zed said, confused once more.

"I created an illusion of my room being upside down and was able to get you to agree to it as well. Thus, you also saw it as upside down. However, Zed, before too long, you saw right through my illusion."

"Well, I just found too many reasons why that could not be happening," he suggested an alternative.

"Of course, you did. As a result, you were able to break your agreement with me about what was happening. Poof! There went my illusion's agreement. You passed my test. Only my mother and deceased father could ever do that — break their agreement with my illusions after I had gotten them to agree with me in the first place," she admitted. She looked terribly humbled, he noted, not at all what he had expected. Her eyes looked downward at her box of pizza.

However, one phrase stuck in his mind, registering like a hammer: passed my test. "Wait, what test? What's going on?" he asked, slightly annoyed. Under other circumstances, he knew that he would have been quite antagonistic. He hated tests. He'd had to deal with new teachers at new schools nearly every two years since first grade. Each school had their own ideas of what ought to be taught to what grades. Transferring every two years or so had taken its toll on him.

Miranda had no choice now but to come right out with it. She could see no way to skirt it any longer. "Mom is missing, and I have been looking for weeks for someone to help me go in search of her. I know that she is in mortal danger. I hope and pray that I am not too late. Zed, you are the first person that I have found who could possibly help me. I know that you don't even know me, let alone my mother. There is no reason why you should even want to help me, especially when you hear just how awfully dangerous even searching for her is going to be. Yet, Zed, I am ready to beg you to help me with this. I'll offer you whatever you want: money, a job, a house." Her voice faltered and her voice barely a whisper, she added, "Even me."

"Damn it Miranda, why didn't you just ask me to help you find your mother in the first place?" Zed answered. While he had no real idea just why all this weird test was needed or even what it remotely signified, he felt annoyed and bothered with her total lack of directness. Beating around the bush always turned him off. Okay, he realized that his sister always used such means to get him to do things for her. It was her control mechanism over him, and his annoyance stemmed from his sister, not Miranda, who he saw was now fighting back tears.

Damn, he was being too harsh with her, causing her to cry. Her mother was somehow missing and for whatever reason she felt that she needed someone else's assistance in finding her. Instead of lending a sympathetic ear to her very real plight, here he was being somewhat antagonistic with her. "I'm sorry. Miranda, I will be glad to help you try to find you mother." There, he agreed to do it. He prayed that she would not begin to actually cry.

Miranda fought hard against her watering eyes, slinging one finger beneath first her right eye and then her left eye. She was not wearing any eye makeup, though for an instant, she had the image of showing Zed some ugly black streaks seeping down beneath her eyes. "Thank you, Zed, but you should wait until I tell you what happened to her and what you are getting yourself into before you agree to help me."

"I'm all ears. Tell me about it," he said softly. Indeed, his curiosity was roused. Had someone kidnaped her? Had she taken some trip and gotten lost? Why hadn't she just called the police?

"It has to do with this house. It was built back in 1805 by Able Montford. He was into what the locals called back then Black Magic. People have to put a label onto things that they don't understand. That way, they figure that they have a way to grasp it. Anyway, it all started about six weeks ago. Come on. I have to show you." She rose and took his hand in hers, leading him out of the kitchen.

Her hand felt soft and gentle, but firm. Zed felt a tingle throughout his body, a sensation he rather liked. This time, they went the opposite direction down the hallway. "Here is our study; it's in here." She led him into an elegant room. Reddish, highly polished mahogany furniture complimented the matching curtains and woodwork around the huge windows. Book cases lined two walls. He didn't get a chance to see just what the book titles were, however. His attention was called to the entrance beside them. Some construction was underway by the left entrance to the room.

"Mom decided that we ought to widen the doorway here. She wanted to let in more light and air to the room. She loves to come in here and read each night. As you can see, the workers began by knocking out this wall section here. It turned out to be hiding a small enclosure. It's six feet by six. Someone in the distant past boarded up this small space. Now we know why they did it."

Zed saw where the workers had knocked out two of the walls that had entirely closed off this small space. However, on the far wall of this tiny space a sheet now hung, hiding something from view. Obviously, they had uncovered something, something that had remained secret for over a hundred years. He felt her hand trembling slightly and guessed that it was not something pleasant nor valuable that lay covered up by the sheet.

"Before I uncover this, I have to tell you a bit more about life or this will be meaningless for you. You see, Zed, there are other universes besides this physical universe. Each one of us has the potential to create our own universe and even to share it with others. But mostly we are so totally engrossed in this universe that we've forgotten all about how to make our own or that we can even make them. Authors still do, though, mockup or create universes in their stories."

"Anyway, we uncovered something that perhaps ought to have remained hidden or perhaps even destroyed. It's Montford's Portail Mystique d'Univers. It's a portal or entrance to the Black Magician's private universe. When I pull the sheet away, whatever you do, do *not* lean into it or you will be sucked away into that universe." He detected traces of fear in her voice. Even her hand, which still held on to his, no longer had that firm, resolute grip. None of this made the slightest sense to him, but he could tell that she was afraid of whatever was behind the sheet. He guessed that she had probably put the sheet over it herself.

She pulled it off, revealing what appeared to be a miniature doorway, perhaps two feet tall. Wooden doors with door knobs that appeared to be centuries out of style beckoned. Large, black, gothic letters formed an arc over the doors proclaiming Montford's Portail Mystique d'Univers. Below the doors in red gothic letters but much smaller the phrase read: Enter ONLY in Pairs.

"What is this thing?" Zed finally found some words to say. He'd never seen anything quite like this before, a pair of tiny doors somehow embedded in a side wall. It made no sense to him at all. No one could possibly get through those doors. Well, perhaps a small baby might fit, certainly not an adult. And what did this have to do with her mother's disappearance? The longer he was around Miranda, the more confused he became, the more questions he had about her.

Miranda's voice lowered, "When the workers discovered this, mom stopped the construction project. She began researching Able Montford, who built this house and this magical portal. She claimed it was the find of the century. Three weeks ago, when I went out grocery shopping, she opened the doors and went into it. For days, she and I argued about using it. I was dead set against it, but she wanted to see what and where it led. Mom let her curiosity get the better of her. I came back and discovered that the doors were opened and mom was gone. That was over three weeks ago now. I just know that she is in really big trouble, because she violated what it says, to enter only in pairs. She went in there alone. I just know that mom's in horrible trouble, if not dead." For the first time, Miranda actually vocalized those words aloud. Tears welled up in her eyes, though she fought hard to keep the wave of emotion from creating a physical effect.

Damn, she's crying, he thought to himself. Oh hell. He did the only thing that he could think of doing at the moment. He pulled her body into his, slid his free arm around her back and pushed her head onto his shoulder. She responded. Both her arms encircled him and grabbed him in almost a vice grip! She finally allowed herself to cry, releasing three weeks of pent up grief, loss, and constant worry. Zed found himself patting her back gently, though he had no idea what to say and so wisely said nothing.

After her sobbing died down a little, while still holding her against himself, he led her back to the kitchen. Give her time to recover, he decided. "We'll find a way to rescue her," he said lamely once they were back with their pizzas and Cokes. She had pulled away and was wiping her eyes, embarrassed that she had so totally lost control, especially in front of Zed, whom she'd just met.

She sat back down and picked up another piece of pizza, though she really didn't feel much like eating just now. Miranda forced herself to take a bite, if only to give herself more time to recover. At last, she found her voice again, thought she had to fight to keep her tone even, "Thanks. I have no right to ask you to help me, Zed. You have no idea what you are getting yourself into with this stuff. You are not trained or even knowledgeable, but you are the only one whom I have been able to find in two weeks who even remotely has any chance of helping me with this. I know that you don't know anything about all this spiritual stuff. Call it magic or black magic or witchcraft. Heck, you can even think of me as a witch if that will help you cope with all of the incredible things that may well happen if we enter that Portail Mystique d'Univers."

"Would that help me?" he asked, knowing that was about the lamest thing that he'd said all day.

"Probably not, but you would at least have a label for it," she admitted.

"Do we need to use magical spells and incantations and things like that? I used to play a lot of Dungeons and Dragons when I was in high school. Have you got fancy spells to use? Do I need to take along swords or guards and wards?" he asked, his imagination suddenly sparked, recalling his many fantasy adventure games that he used to play every weekend.

That brought a smile to her face. "No silly, there aren't any such things, though you might think so. Minds will do anything to come up with a logical explanation for something unknown that it observes. People see strange, unknown lights in the desert sky and immediately assign them to UFOs. No, here everything that happens is something directly created by one or more of we spiritual beings and is agreed upon by ourselves and/or others. But if it helps, you can think of me as a witch with magical spells, if you like." Miranda conceded the point. He was going to get his mind blown. Of that, she had no doubt. Still, if it helped him orientate himself by thinking of her as a witch with spells, then so be it.

She decided to add a bit of caution. "Look, on earth, most of us have long ago abandoned our own personal universes in favor of this physical universe here. We've gone from a near infinity of our own created universes down to nearly nothing, while the physical universe here has gone from nothing to a state of nearly all that there is. If you come with me into this portal, we will be stepping out of our comfortable, predictable physical universe into someone else's universe. Lord knows what we will find there. I am more than a little scared of it. Mom was way too foolish to go it alone."

"You think that she has been hurt or something? Shouldn't you take this to the police?" he suggested. "Don't the authorities know how to deal with something like this?" This whole thing was sounding weirder by the minute. Yet something must have happened to her mother. Who ever heard of other universes anyway? Maybe this young woman was a psycho case. Still, the visit to her bedroom had been quite unsettling, otherworldly perhaps.

She sighed. "You still don't understand. The police only know how to stop things. They are masters of using heavy, physical universe force to stop all motion, all action, subdue people, vehicles, and things. The cops would not last one minute in someone else's universe, where the ability to start and change according to new rules play a major role. Besides, they would not believe a word of what has really happened. They'd think that I was crazy or something and go off looking for mom around Peoria or Illinois. I assure you, Zed, she's not even in this universe anymore. Trust me, Zed, if you come with me through that portal, the instant you do you will know what I am saying is true."

Was she crazy or was she for real? Would this be the strangest trip imaginable? Zed couldn't help wondering if Miranda was not just a little off. After all, very little of what she was saying made the slightest sense. Well, she was convinced that her mother was gone. He'd just have to take her word for that. He had said that he would help and he knew that he would, whether or not she was off her rocker. Zed was a man of his word. After all, what else is there if you do not follow through on what you promise?

"Hey, I promised that I would help you find your mom. I keep my promises, Miranda. What does your mother look like? Got a picture of her?" he asked, getting down to the real business.

"Rose, her name is Rose. Here," she pulled a photo out of her billfold and handed it to him. Zed guessed that she must be in her fifties. A hint of grey streaked her otherwise long black hair. He smiled, Miranda wore her hair very much like her mother, bangs down to her eyes while letting the rest fall straight to her shoulders. Well, if she still looked like her picture, he thought that he could now recognize her.

"Okay, when do we begin? What stuff should we take with us? Tents, sleeping bags, water, food, cell phones?" he asked. He didn't ask how long this fanciful trip might take, mostly because he was afraid of how she might answer.

"Just ourselves, Zed. I don't know how to thank you for lending me a hand with this. I owe you big time. I'd better lock up the house while we are gone. Do you need to lock up your truck? It should be safe here in this neighborhood," she asked. The relief on her face was very apparent to Zed, and he took some comfort in that. She stowed the uneaten pizza in the fridge and quickly raced around the mansion locking the doors. He grinned; she certainly was eager to go after her mother. Well, he admitted to himself that he would be too, if it was his mother who had disappeared.

# Chapter 3 It Begins

Zed and Miranda stood before the small wooden doors. She removed the sheet once more. Miranda didn't say anything for a minute, just staring at them. Perhaps nothing at all will happen, he thought, but then decided that was unlikely. Why should he think so replaced that notion. Such things cannot be real, he answered himself. Magic is just illusion. He'd heard that somewhere before. Why is she looking so worried, he wondered? This, he had no immediate answer for — at last his mind was blank.

Both wore jeans, a tee-shirt, and sneakers, though hers were designer-made and probably costly, he judged. He'd asked her if they ought to take along some food, water, camping supplies, flashlights, and perhaps something to protect themselves, such as an axe, which could be used to chop wood for a campfire if the need arose. "Where we are going, we will not need any of that," she had replied. Again, Zed just could not imagine how this could be so. None of this made any sense at all. People only speculated and imagined the existence of alternate worlds, for alternate worlds could be the only explanation that could fit with what he'd been hearing from her. Of course, such do not exist, he finally concluded, his eyes finally focusing on Miranda as she gazed at the small doors. Nothing is going to happen at all, Zed concluded at long last, and he relaxed, prepared to console her when she too agreed with that.

Breaking out of her reverie, Miranda became animated once more. Whatever spell the doors held over her seemed broken. "Okay, I'm ready to face this. Take my hand. Don't let go. I will see that we arrive okay." Zed's hand found hers and grasped it firmly. A faint smile pursed his lips; he rather liked holding her hand. Perhaps when this was over. . . he mused.

"When I open the doors, all you need to do is to look through them and lean towards the opening. Here we go," she stated, steeled in determination. With her free hand, she opened first one and then the other. At first, Zed saw nothing at all.

Just as he was about to console her about it, he thought he saw a yellowish glow emitting from the blank wall revealed by the now opened doors. He felt a magnetic pull on his body, as if some invisible hands were reaching out to him, pulling him gently towards the opening. He felt Miranda leaning, following the pull and he followed her lead. Slowly, the yellowish glow grew stronger and brighter. As it did so, the world around him grew dimmer and dimmer; the walls, floor, and ceiling began to disappear!

Suddenly, he appeared to be in an empty void! He felt the strangest sensations. Falling! Yes, he was falling down. Images of the sperm whale that materialized above a planet and began to fall down towards its surface and certain death in the movie Hitchhiker's Guide came into his mind. He felt his body spinning head over heels, around and around, now yawing, now rolling, now pitching in some kind of three dimensional fall, all wildly out of control. Panic rushed over him with only Miranda's solid grasp on his hand keeping him from acting on his terror. Still his free arm flailed around in all directions in a vain, useless attempt to regain some sense of stability, some sense of orientation.

"Pretend that you are descending the basement stairs!" Miranda yelled out loudly to Zed. He saw that she was moving her legs as if she was going down a flight of stairs. Her action was beginning to stabilize her fall, but in doing so, the force nearly ripped her hand from his! Frantically, he tried to duplicate her motion, but in a three dimensional spin, how do you go down a flight of stairs? With a force of will, Zed demanded his legs cooperate, step down, step down. To his utter amazement, the action began to have an impact upon their free-fall.

After a bit of struggling, he matched her descending leg motions and finally the two stabilized. To his amazement, their wild free-fall now seemed more like an ordinary descent into some unknown basement! At last, he gathered enough courage to tilt his head downward to see where they were heading. A vast patch of green appeared to be moving rapidly towards them. With a bit of will power, Zed finally became oriented. Now they did indeed seem to be descending a set of stairs onto vast grasslands, though it was an invisible stairs.

Bits of brown appeared and Zed finally recognized what appeared to be trees surrounding the open rolling grasslands. They were headed into a large clearing among the trees. No wait! There was something white appearing now, growing larger by the minute. Ah, a table with a white table cloth came into view. Their trajectory would land them close to the table. Satisfied that they were not about to smash into the ground becoming fresh meat, Zed began to relax slightly and wondered how many more downward steps would be needed to reach terra firma and if his knees would hold out. He felt as if he'd taken a hundred steps down, maybe more.

Wait. Figures. He saw three figures sitting around the rapidly approaching table! Strange figures! He blinked twice, heard voices, and landed on the ground. He lost his grip on Miranda and tumbled head over heels. She, however, landed on her feet.

"Ah look! Two more balloons are landing, but then I am never right," an apathetic tortoise named Albert Rose exclaimed, his head pivoting and looking up at the two forms rapidly descending towards their table. He was sitting precariously on a rock sufficiently high so that his head could reach the straw coming out of a tea cup sitting at his place on the table. The three were taking high tea when the two balloons decided to descend upon them.

Beside him, a squirrel sat on a chair while resting his feet on the tortoise's shell, much to Albert's annoyance. "I say old man, you are right, though that cannot be, cause, as you yourself always say, 'you are always wrong.' Therefore, they must not be balloons. What say you, Herr Adelstein?" He fidgeted nervously on his chair, knowing that he dare not be wrong, and certainly not now, not with two balloons landing uninvited beside their table — not that it would have made any difference to him had they been invited. Everyone knows that a squirrel cannot ever dare to be wrong, not ever. Certainly Sir Thomas d'Lyons knew this instinctively.

The rabbit glared at the two. "You are totally and completely wrong, wrong on both counts, Sir Thomas! When you said that he said that you are wrong, do you mean you or he? You see, you have it all wrong yet again. You are wrong, wrong, wrong!" Herr Adelstein pounded his clenched fist on the table nearly spilling his tea cup. Three sets of spoons bounced into the air momentarily before resting askew beside their cups. "Besides, if Albert is always wrong, then we can conclude that indeed we are not seeing anything at all landing on the grass interrupting our tea or that they are not balloons. I suggest that we are not seeing anything at all. Let's resume our tea. More tea, Albert?" He reached for the tea pot, completely ignoring the fact that at that very moment two balloons or whatevers had just landed not four feet from himself and his two friends. Well, one landed, the other fell and executed some strange rolling motions.

"See, I told you that I am always wrong. The balloons are not in the sky any longer," Albert muttered, agreeing with his two friends. "I would like more tea, Herr Adelstein. Yet, if I am always wrong, then perhaps I actually don't want more tea after all. Could that possibly be?" The tortoise looked slightly perplexed, but was content to ignore the balloons which he had just seen landing nearby. "Hum, yet if I take that approach, that I would like more tea, but really meaning that I do not want more tea, and if I am always wrong, then would that not suggest that indeed I really don't want more tea, which I said that I do want more tea?"

"Oh Albert!" Herr Adelstein exclaimed totally exasperated with his friend. "Will you please make up your mind? More tea or not? Can't you even make one decision?"

"Herr Adelstein, please have some compassion for dear Albert. You know how difficult life is for him when he knows that he is always wrong," Sir Thomas begged nervously. Herr Adelstein's anger had quite flustered him, and his hand shook rather violently as he held his own tea cup out, while the rabbit attempted to pour more tea into his cup. "Besides, this must be very important, Herr Adelstein. After all, two whatevers have just landed beside us. We must not be wrong. All manner of ill may befall us if we do not get this right. Are they or are they not balloons? You see, the two whatevers are at least as big as we are. Now if they were tiny mice, I would not be worrying, you see." His hand shook so badly that he had to use both hands to sit his cup back down on the table before himself. Nevertheless, a bit did spill; a dark stain crept outward from the bottom of his cup, marring the otherwise spotless tablecloth.

"Now see what you have done, Sir Thomas!" Herr Adelstein growled. "You've ruined our tablecloth." This only made Sir Thomas all the more edgy. "I said nothing has landed beside us. Let us drink our tea."

"Can you position my straw closer, please?" Albert asked humbly. His head was just an inch from being able to reach the fresh cup that the rabbit had sat before him. Begrudgingly, the rabbit complied. "So no balloons have landed. Okay. I agree. But, Herr Adelstein, you know that I am always wrong. Doesn't that mean that two balloons have actually then landed?" the tortoise asked. The rabbit threw his hands up in utter disgust and finally turned to face the newcomers.

Miranda saw a brownish rabbit that stood at least six feet tall. He wore an immaculate, dark brown, business suit with what must have been a white, starched shirt. A black bow tie and cummerbund rounded out his apparel. His very long ears rose slightly before flopping over. As the rabbit rose from his seat, Zed finally joined Miranda, staring blinkingly at the rabbit.

Seeing Herr Adelstein rising, Sir Thomas quickly took his feet off of the back of Albert and jumped hastily to his feet, daring not to be wrong, following implicitly the rabbit's lead. He stood just under six feet tall. He wore a black suit with a white shirt, very similar to the rabbit's. However, his tie was a ghastly paisley, a bit too long and far too wide at its bottom. Hastily, he ran his hands over his head, smoothing his top hair.

Albert, free at last from being the squirrel's foot stool, wiggled with some effort and at last slid off of his rock, his enormous feet finally reaching the ground. He wore a greenish tie around his neck, but no suit. His shell was azure with flakes of silver sparkling in the sunlight, although at the moment, had anyone cared to look into the sky, they would not have seen the sun itself, though the sky was perfectly clear. A bit more wiggling and Albert finally stood on his rear legs, facing the whatevers. His eyes stared long and hard at the two.

"Excuse us, please. We didn't intend to disrupt your tea," Miranda politely began the conversation, acting as if it was no surprise to her to be standing beside a six foot tall rabbit, squirrel, and tortoise. Zed just gaped in complete disbelief. "My name is Miranda and this is my friend Zed."

Herr Adelstein rose to the occasion. In a harsh tone, he replied, "Well, Albert, indeed you were *quite* wrong. These are most definitely *not* two balloons which have come down from the sky to interrupt our tea. I am quite sure that balloons have *never* been known to talk."

"Gosh, Herr Adelstein," Albert mused, "are you really certain of that detail? Perhaps they are a new type of balloon that we have not seen before. But then, you know that I am always wrong."

Whispering to the rabbit, Sir Thomas said very nervously, "They are as b-big as us!"

Miranda picked up on his fears and hastily added, "We mean you no harm, Mr. Squirrel."

"Sir Thomas d'Lyons," he politely and rightly corrected her.

Herr Adelstein even more hastily interrupted him, rather testily, "He takes offense to being called a squirrel. The word has some rather unpleasant connotations, you see." He stared at Miranda and then Zed, before adding in a growl, a big frown creased his forehead, "So are you talking balloons or are you not? You cannot dismiss the fact that you floated down from the sky like balloons!"

Zed grinned, "Sorry, sir. We are most definitely not balloons. We are humans. And I must admit that you three are the largest rabbit, squirrel, and tortoise that I have ever seen. How is it that you can talk? Such fine suits you are wearing."

Herr Adelstein put his hands on his hips, extremely annoyed. "Of course we three can speak! You must be idiots to think otherwise! What exactly is a 'uman anyway?"

"Of course my suit is a fine one!" Sir Thomas added. "I must look my best and proper at all times, if I am to be right, and I don't dare not be right, you see. Now Albert here, he doesn't have to worry so much; he can just retreat into his hard shell." He looked at his friend and added, "See, Albert. You were wrong again. These are not balloons, but 'umans, whatever that may be."

"We are people," Miranda attempted to explain and then gave up that line altogether. "My name is Miranda Whitney. This is Zed Osmund. We're pleased to meet you." She guessed a bit of politeness would be the best approach.

"Well, you most certainly cannot be people, because we are people, and you don't look a *thing* like us!" Herr Adelstein stated flatly. "However, we *are* civilized. I am Herr Petr Adelstein. My friends, Sir Thomas d'Lyons and Albert Rose, though we may not be so pleased to meet you. *That* remains to be seen." The three bowed to the two.

Still, Sir Thomas was quite nervous. He kept fiddling with his tie, though he didn't even notice that he'd quite twisted it around his fingers. "Perhaps we best offer them some tea, perhaps. Don't you think that we should, Herr Adelstein? You know that we cannot afford to be wrong about it."

"I suppose that you are right, Sir Thomas. Although we have no idea what these 'umans actually are, at least we can show them that we are highly civilized and refined. Please, Miranda, Zed, have a seat and join us. We were just about to have another round of tea." He gestured to the other side of the table, intent upon putting some distance between the two 'umans and themselves.

Poof! Two chairs suddenly appeared. Zed blinked and swore they were not there a moment ago. He and Miranda headed around the table and gently felt them. Zed tested them to see if they were actually real. Poof! Two more cups, spoons, and napkins appeared beside the two, placed perfectly upon the spotless tablecloth, now stained slightly near Sir Thomas' cup. While the two sat down, the squirrel and rabbit did so quite formally, while the poor tortoise struggled to get back up on his rock once more. Once in position, the rabbit had to adjust his straw for him again. Dutifully, the rabbit poured what appeared to be strong black tea into the two cups.

"I do hope you like it black," Sir Thomas began to fidget once more. "I'm afraid that we are out of sugar and milk at the moment."

"Are we out or did we forget them again?" Albert asked quietly. Herr Adelstein ignored him completely, but stared at the two newcomers with a steely eye. Zed sensed that the rabbit certainly did not trust them at all.

"Ah, excellent tea," Zed said, hoping to start the conversation fresh. "Might I ask just where we have arrived?"

"Uh, that's rather obvious, it seems to me," Albert answered in his slow, drawn-out manner. "You are here by our tea table. Since I am always wrong, perhaps we are not here either. If so, I wonder where we actually are?" He looked terribly puzzled; somehow his straightforward answer had led him totally astray once more. He took a sip of tea to forget about it.

"Yes, I'm thankful that we did not land on your table and spoil everything for you," Miranda opted to be polite once more. "I believe that Zed wishes to know is what is the name of this land, this country and perhaps where it is located, that sort of thing."

Sir Thomas fidgeted once more and whispered to Herr Adelstein, "They must be lost. Could that be it?"

The rabbit looked totally exasperated, as though this was more than he could possibly bear. He did reply though, "Malbon. This land is called Malbon, obviously." His whiskers twisted and waggled as if he found this beyond belief. "Where do you come from that you do not even know the name of our land?" He again took a defiant attitude towards the two.

"We come from a place called Earth," Miranda replied, trying hard not to further offend the rabbit, "though I expect that you have never heard of our land."

Herr Adelstein tweaked his nose, as if to say he didn't, but Albert spoke instead. "Do all of you 'umans float like balloons? I think that must be fun, but then, as everyone knows. I am always wrong about such things."

"Er, I don't know, Albert." Zed spoke up. Somehow he felt more comfortable talking to a tortoise than to an enormous rabbit or squirrel. "I've never floated like a balloon before this time — coming here, Albert. At first, it was awfully scarey, you know, a horrible feeling of falling to my death and all that. Miranda got me to taking steps down, as if I were going down some stairs. After that, it got to be fun. Say, are there many of you here in Malbon? Any cities or towns? Any humans like us?" He thought this might be a key piece of information to learn quickly.

"Ants live in the cities. I am sure that you don't want to go there!" Sir Thomas squeaked, suddenly shaking more than normal. His tea cup spilled even more. The dark stain spread noticeably now, and the rabbit glared even harder at Sir Thomas, whose hands began to shake even more so.

"Now see what you have done? All this talk about ants has totally shaken up poor Sir Thomas! We'll have to have a clean tablecloth now!" Herr Adelstein growled and waved his right paw. Poof! The white tablecloth vanished, replaced by a new one. "See if you can keep your tea inside your cup, this time, Sir Thomas. You know that I get tired of replacing it. Next time you have to replace it."

The squirrel looked mournfully at the ground. "Yes, Herr Adelstein. I will be more careful. You must warn them about the ants, though. Please. I am afraid that if I do, I will spill the rest of my tea."

"Ants! Brrrroooooogggghhh!" Herr Adelstein's tall, furry body shook with violent passions, of which fear was primary. He shook his head from side to side, as if somehow the very idea of ants would be thrown irrevocably from his mind. "Ants, oh, terrors of terror! Let's not talk about them, shall we? Have some more tea," he hastily changed the topic, refilling Albert's tea cup twice to overflowing. Zed watched as Albert's cup managed to somehow grow taller as the brown liquid continued to rise.

"Ah, Herr Adelstein, my cup runneth over," Albert whispered, as if the guests might not be noticing.

"Oops," the rabbit flushed, noticing that his friend's cup was now twice as tall as everyone else's cups.

"Quite understandable, quite," Sir Thomas apologized for his friend. "Here, I'll fix it for you, Albert." Poof. The excess tea vanished as Albert's tea cup returned to the same size as everyone else's cup, excepting for the straw, of course. The tortoise looked pleased and smiled to the rabbit.

Again, Zed was mystified by the growth and then shrinkage of the cup and tea. Miranda decided to try another approach. "Say, isn't this a bit strange? I mean back home when we have a picnic we either have it in our backyard or go to a park. Is this place here a park? Are there others about enjoying this beautiful day?"

"What precisely do you mean by *this* beautiful day?" asked Sir Thomas, growing slightly worried again. These balloons calling themselves 'umans, he found a bit unsettling. After all, it isn't just anytime that you have strange, foreign bodies that speak falling from the sky interrupting your tea.

"It's a fine day, bright, sunny, not a cloud in the sky. Perfect for a picnic, don't you think?" she hastily explained, failing utterly to see how this could be upsetting the squirrel. Then she noticed that although the day was indeed bright, she could see no sun in the sky at all! Zed saw her looking up and followed her gaze, wondering what she was trying to see. Then, it dawned on him, no sun! What was making it seem like it was a sunny day? He caught Miranda's barely perceptible glance and wisely said nothing about it.

Seeing Sir Thomas becoming even more agitated, Albert answered instead. "Well, it is a fine time for tea which is why we were having ours just now. Day is always present. The world is always as you see it now. How can it not be? You must come from some really weird place, but then I am always wrong on things that are important. Perhaps this is not important, in that case I might be right, but I never know, you see, since I am always wrong."

"You mean, Albert, that it does not get dark when it is time to sleep, to go to bed and rest?" Miranda asked point blank. Even though the squirrel seemed to be still agitated for unknown reasons and the rabbit continued to stick his nose in the air as if this was all just some insanity talk, the large tortoise seemed unmoved by it all.

"Dark? What is that?" he asked.

"You know, when the day goes away and the sky is dark. You can't see anything then, time for sleep," she tried to find a non-threatening way of explaining herself.

The squirrel nearly fell off of his seat! If he was shaking before, now his whole giant body seemed to convulse uncontrollably. Herr Adelstein almost dropped his tea cup and glared angrily at her. Albert seemed unplused by it all. "Oh, you must mean when the end of the world comes. It is said that when the light goes away, the world shall come to an end, but then I am not a philosopher, merely a humble tortoise. We rest in our houses when we get tired. Don't you rest when you get tired?" he asked, becoming curious about these two. Perhaps they did not need sleep as he and his friends did.

"Oh yes, we sleep about eight hours each day, er, I mean about eight every twenty-four hours," she replied.

Albert seemed relieved to hear this. "Ah that is good then. So do we. I just pull myself into my house here. I carry mine with me everywhere I go, much simpler this way. Now my friends here, they have to build their houses every time they get tired. Too much trouble, I say, but then they like their fancy houses. Me, I like it simple." A quizzical look appeared on his face. "Say, might I ask, when you were up there falling down to us, you didn't by chance see these others that you were referring to a bit ago did you? I don't expect that you could see the ant army, though. However, if you did, please don't mention it. Sir Thomas is quite scared of them; they are an army you know. Vicious, voracious eaters. I keep telling Sir Thomas that he ought to get a hard shell like mine. Then he would be safe from their attacks." Poor Sir Thomas. At the mention of ants again, he fell completely out of his chair. He rose shaking so badly that the rabbit had to get out of his chair and pick up the squirrel, depositing him unceremoniously back into his chair.

"No, we saw no one around but you three. I do believe it is quite safe here," Miranda decided to attempt to calm them down. Just what was this whole ant thing about anyway? She was now very curious, but knew that she dare not ask more.

"Well, that is why we chose this location after all. Isn't that right, Herr Adelstein?" the tortoise looked for confirmation, again somewhat unsure of himself.

"Yes, of course, Albert!" Herr Adelstein replied testily, having adjusted his suit coat before sitting back down. "All this talk has chilled my tea. Time for a fresh pot, don't you think?"

"I'm rather hungry," Sir Thomas squeaked meekly. "Perhaps we should dine now instead."

"Yes, I suppose so," the rabbit declared somewhat more pleasantly. "What do we feed our guests, eh Sir Thomas? I bet that you did not consider that when you made your suggestion."

"Of course, you are right as always, Herr Adelstein. I had not thought of them. It is proper that we offer our guests something to eat, that is, if we are going to dine. It is impolite of us to eat in front of them, isn't it? I know I dare not be wrong about that!" Sir Thomas replied, his nervousness having settled down. Perhaps it was merely that his stomach was more in control of his body than his fears.

"Hey, don't worry about us," Zed spoke up. "We just ate before we came. Honestly, we are not hungry. Why don't you just go ahead and fix yourselves your meal. We are quite happy with our tea."

Just then, the ground began shaking! "Oh no!" shrieked Sir Thomas. "The Enforcers are coming. Quick! Hide!" Poof! A large white house appeared. Made of oak clapboards and nicely stained to bring out the wood's fine grain appeared not five feet from the squirrel. Sir Thomas dove off his chair and bolted through his front door in a flash. Poof! The house and squirrel vanished completely and then reappeared for an instant. Poof! The table, tablecloth, and tea cups vanished, leaving Zed and Miranda quite startled. Poof! The squirrel's house vanished once more as a thundering noise could now be heard.

"Oh dear, oh dear. The Enforcers are at it again," Herr Adelstein declared, a touch of worry in his voice. "You will have to excuse us." Both Miranda and Zed had now arisen and poof, their chairs vanished as well, leaving no sign that a moment ago there was a picnic in progress. "Here you go, Albert," the rabbit stated dryly. Poof. A small stream appeared, along with several large rocks. The rabbit turned to the two, "Run, if you can. Fly, if you can. If not, it has been fun having you for tea. Bye."

Poof! Another large house appeared. This one was a bit rustic, something reminiscent of an old English cottage. Ivy covered its red brick walls. Brown curtains lined the edges of two front windows. The rabbit bowed to the two and ducked inside. Poof! His house also vanished.

Albert struggled to get himself down from the boulder on which his bottom had been precariously balanced. "Ah, that's better. Nice friends, don't you think? They've made me a perfect spot to hide. If I were you, I'd vanish as well. No telling what the Enforcers want. It's happened before, you know, balloon falling from the sky. Enforcers came then too. After they were gone, we discovered that the other balloon was also gone. I suppose that the Enforcers got her too, but then perhaps not. I am never right about important things, you know."

"What? Another one of us appeared? Did she look like this?" Miranda exclaimed. Could her mother have also met these three? Why had she not asked them immediately or shown them her mother's picture.

"Better hurry up, Miranda. I can see large forms coming our way," Zed cautioned her. He didn't like the sound of their name, Enforcers. Besides, they must be incredibly powerful to make the ground shake so far in advance of their position. She showed Albert the photo of Rose.

"Yes, that would be the other balloon. I have to hide. See you when it is safe again. That is, if you are still here," Albert replied. He slid into the stream and submerged, becoming indistinguishable from the several other boulders that lined the stream.

"Wow! Mom was here," Miranda gushed. "Now we are making progress! I wonder where she went next?"

"Miranda, what are we going to do? This situation sounds dangerous." Zed continued to look towards the oncoming riders, if riders they were. They were still a good distance away and he just could not make out who or what they were. Clearly, the three locals were terrified of these supposed Enforcers. "I wonder what they did with your mother?"

"I think that we are going to have to wait for them and ask them about mom. Perhaps we will be all right. I can't see us as being any kind of threat here. After all, we are just looking for my mother, who we now know was here."

"Okay, but we'd better not tell these Enforcers about Albert there. We can say that we are following her footprints, her trail, and apparently, she ran into them around this location," Zed suggested.

"I wonder what they enforce?" Miranda asked, but turned to face the oncoming Enforcers as well. Instinctively, her hand found his and they held to each other tightly.

"Elephants! I'll be," Zed exclaimed, as a half dozen, large, grey elephants came charging into view. Soon they were close enough that Zed could read the banner that was affixed to their heads, "Enforcer." The group slowed down as they neared and most definitely took note of the two standing beside the stream and boulders, one of which was Albert, of course.

They halted before the two. The one at the head of the pack spoke, "Well, what do we have here? Outsiders again, eh? Surround them boys; we don't want them to escape!"

"Hello, I am Miranda, and this is my friend, Zed. Why would we want to escape? Escape what? I'm sorry, we are just visiting here." She sounded as polite as she could be, though she wanted desperately to ask about her mother.

"Outsiders!" the deep, bellowing voice replied antagonistically. "Don't you know that practicing magic without a license is against the law here in Malbon? We are going to have to arrest you and bring you before the Court of Illegal Magic Use!"

"I'm sorry, but we don't know how to practice magic or anything else like it," Zed protested.

Several elephants laughed, though he had no idea why. The leader replied with a biting tongue, "Yes, yes, that's what they all say! You got here didn't you? That's magic, idiot. It is against the law to practice magic without a license. Arrest them."

"Excuse me, sir," Miranda interrupted him. Since he was dead set on arresting her anyway, she might as well ask about her mother. "Several weeks ago, did you arrest this woman somewhere around here? She is my mother and we are trying to find her. We think that she is lost or injured." She held up the photo of Rose.

"Well, that is easy enough to discover," he said. "Roscoe, Roscoe Small's my name. Let's see." Poof. A large scroll appeared before the pachyderm's head, floating in the air. As he looked at it, he asked, "Name of apprehendee?"

"Rose Whitney," Miranda replied sounding a hopeful note. While the two watched, a rather lengthy list scrolled by the Enforcer. One end of the scroll continued unwinding, while the other wound up the listing, all while floating in midair. "Ah yes. Convict Rose Whitney. Convicted of practicing magic without a license twenty-one days ago. Sentenced to the Ant Farm."

"Thank you. Can you take us to this Ant Farm? We want to find my mother, Roscoe," Miranda asked.

All six laughed heartily, shaking the very ground beneath their feet! At last Roscoe answered her, "As soon as you are convicted, you'll be taken there soon enough. Of course, you'll wish that you had not been just as soon!"

"But we haven't practiced any magic ourselves," Zed protested.

Antagonistically, Roscoe replied, "Well, you had better be right about that! Of course, we are right, always, but if you know what's good for you, you had better be right. That's all I'm going to say. Now you are hereby arrested. Say, by chance have you encountered a rabbit and squirrel? They go by the names of Herr Petr Adelstein and Sir Thomas d'Lyon."

"Er, no Enforcer Roscoe," Miranda lied, hoping that the elephant couldn't tell that she was. "What are they wanted for? Murder, thievery?"

"Oh far worse than that!" Roscoe exclaimed. "Practicing Magic without a License! Okay. Arrest time." Poof! Zed found himself sitting on the back of one of the elephants. His arms were tied behind his back. A rope was fastened to each foot and encircled the belly of the pachyderm guaranteeing that he could not possibly fall off. His legs were spread wide apart, most uncomfortable. Poof. Miranda found herself similarly placed on Roscoe's enormous back, tied up as well.

"I say, you ought to have a more comfortable box or seats on your backs," Zed commented.

"Oh don't be silly! You are being arrested, not dined as some dinner guest!" Roscoe taunted.

"You seem to be enjoying your job," Zed growled, not liking the way this was unfolding.

"Of course we like our job! Ours is the most interesting job in Malbon! Stupid strangers. Okay, boys, to the Court of Illegal Magic Use! Pronto!" Roscoe barked out his bellowing orders. At once, the group began their thunderous passage over the grasslands.

The ground thundered beneath their giant feet; wind of their passage blew Miranda's hair behind her. Zed kept bouncing on the back of his elephant. "I say, bumpy ride. Ouch. Is torture part of your arresting methods?"

"You are being arrested, not coddled. What did you expect? Using Magic without a license is a really, really bad crime here in Malbon. Didn't you know that?" the elephant trumpeted hostilely. "Well, you darn well ought to have known that in the first place."

"How? We are not from Malbon," Zed protested.

"We are not the Court," he replied testily. "That's for them to decide. If you are not from Malbon, and any fool can see that you are not, you got here, didn't you? That's magic in our books. Now shut up! We are obviously right."

More bouncing later and Zed had had enough. "Oh this is completely preposterous!"

Poof! Zed appeared completely free, standing on the grass. The startled elephants planted their enormous feet and skidded to a complete stop. Poof! Miranda appeared beside Zed, both rubbing their wrists. "Thanks," she whispered.

Roscoe whirled his massive body around, clearly very angry. "I've a notion to squash you right now and forget this arrest! You are quite wrong to continue to add to your crimes! Well, it will do you no good. Behold, the Court of Illegal Magic Use!"

Poof! A barrister complete with white wig suddenly appeared, along with a complete English looking court. Zed blinked; the barrister was a six foot tall monkey, dressed in formal court attire! At the bench was the High Judge, also wearing a white wig, which looked utterly ridiculous, Zed thought, considering the judge was a snake.

His Honor was at least seven feet long or tall, depending on how you looked at him. He stood upright. His girth was quite large, perhaps two feet, except near his middle where a roundish ball appeared. Zed didn't want to know what he'd had for lunch, for it had to be big.

The barrister read off the charges in a loud, but bored manner. "Hear yea, hear yea. The official charges are practicing magic without a license." Roscoe whispered something in the monkey's overly large ears. He cleared his throat and amended the charges, placing extreme emphasis on the first word, "Repeated practicing of magic without a license, Your Honor." The barrister straightened his robes and sat down on a chair which suddenly appeared behind him.

All eyes turned to the judge, who looked slightly annoyed, though not at the two accused. "Darn, I have indigestion once again. That darn pig anyway." He let out a huge burp; the smell almost knocked Zed out. "Excuse me," the huge snake said slightly apologetically. "Let's get this over with quickly. Accused will rise and address this High Court. How do you plead?" the snake said very bored with the proceedings. He'd overseen hundreds of similar cases and was frankly tired of the whole thing.

"Not guilty," Zed spoke for both of them.

The snake's eyebrows rose slightly. He appeared slightly annoyed with Zed. "Oh come now, the charges are quite clear. You can't possibly believe that you are not guilty," he said gruffly.

"Of course we are not guilty," Zed added. "We are not from Malbon; we've only just arrived. Neither of us knows any magical spells at all. Don't we get to present evidence in our own defense?"

"Oh why bother?" the snake said irresolutely, annoyed that the proceedings had gone on this long already. He let out another belch; the darn pig was annoying him even now, although it was obviously quite dead. "Clearly, I can see that you are here. Obviously that required magic. Any imbecile can see that! Come, I must be fair. I certainly don't want anyone accusing me of not being fair. State your names and I will consult the ledger." Poof! A giant scroll with ornate cylinders on each end appeared hovering in space before his eyes. Poof! A pair of black rimmed spectacles appeared before his eyes.

"Miranda Whitney and Zed Osmund," he replied. "We are looking for Miranda's mother, Rose Whitney." He added that last in hopes of getting a bit more information for Miranda. As they watched, the scroll began unrolling from one cylinder and rolling up on the other. Zed nearly laughed as he watched the snake's eyes moving rapidly from side to side as he read the names on the list. When the scrolling ceased, poof, it vanished as did his glasses.

"Names are not on the official registry. Guilty as charged."

Zed grinned, an idea formed in his head. "You honor, I believe that you missed them. If you will please look again at the very bottom, I'm sure that you will see our names there." Poof. He intended that they would be there, along with those of the three with whom they'd just had tea!

At first, Zed thought the snake might just explode, physically, that is. His cheeks puffed up twice their normal size, but then he knew so little about snakes. Perhaps his mouth did that anyway; after all how could he have possibly eaten that huge, well whatever it was that formed the huge ball shape in his middle. "Preposterous! I never miss a thing," the judge replied. He burped this time, and the poor barrister fell over backwards off his chair, having taken the blast of noxious fumes full in his face. He scrambled to his feet and tried to reposition his wig which had fallen off his head. Zed suppressed a laugh.

"Oh, just so we can get this infernally long trial over with sooner, I'll grant your request." The judge did as Zed asked. "What? How can this be? Why, I've never missed reading a name yet!"

"Perhaps it is because of your indigestion," Zed suggested politely. The snake's eyes bored into his, as if he were going to blast him with some kind of ray beam.

"Well, you got away with it this time. Don't let me catch you in my court again. I won't be so tolerant of you next time. Case dismissed." A large gavel materialized and came pounding down on a desk that suddenly appeared. Both vanished after the gavel pounded on the desk, making a loud bang.

"But Your Honor," the barrister protested, "their names are not on our Official Lists."

"That's your problem, not mine," the judge groaned.

"Excuse me, but can you tell us what happened in the case of Rose Whitney?" Zed insisted.

"The barrister can handle that. I am going to have a wee lie down now. All this court business has tired me out something terribly. Court is adjourned." With that, the snake vanished, leaving behind a puff of smoke.

"Oh this is wrong, this is so wrong, I just know it is very wrong. Your names are not on the Official List. Oh dear me. I shall have to investigate this further," the monkey exclaimed, nervously.

"While you are doing that, could you please consult your records and tell us what happened to Rose Whitney?" Zed insisted, wondering if he ought to pretend to be angry with the barrister or not.

"Well, that is easily handled," the monkey replied, donning his glasses for the first time. A green scroll appeared in his hands. and the paper flew by at an alarming rate.

"How can you read so fast?" asked Zed. Perhaps the monkey was a speed reader; still, he would have to be reading at least a thousand words a second to keep up with the speeding scroll!

"Ah. Yes, here we are. Rose Whitney. Convicted of using magic without a license. Sentenced to life in the Ant Farm. There, now I will get on with my investigation. Good day. I hope to have you rearrested soon." He glared at them and then vanished, leaving the two standing beside the elephants.

Zed turned to Roscoe. "Say, can you direct us to the Ant Farm where they took Rose Whitney, please?"

The huge pachyderm laughed so hard that the grasses shook rather violently. "Idiots. I will enjoy rounding you up a second time, when the Honorable Barrister issues the warrants. The Ant Farm is that way. Just start walking and you are sure to run into it. Of course, you will never leave there alive." He began laughing and the other elephants joined in, as if this was the funniest thing that they had ever heard in their lives.

Miranda took Zed's hand and led him off in the direction that Roscoe had pointed. When they were out of earshot range, she said, "Wow, you handled that well! Thanks. I would not have thought to put our names on the official list."

"I put Albert's and the others on there too. Don't know if it will do them any good, however," Zed explained, a wry smile on his face. Miranda giggled and squeezed his hand. Zed liked that more than he cared to admit just now. They continued their march across the rolling grasslands of Malbon.

"I wonder how far we have to walk?" Zed soon asked. The land all around them appeared pretty much the same. Trees were scattered here and there among the rolling hills. Tall grasses abounded. The terrain looked much the same in all directions. Worse, they had no real distant point towards which to head. "We might end up walking in circles," he added.

"I see what you mean. Perhaps we ought to decide that we have arrived at the Ant Farm," Miranda suggested.

"Huh?" Zed asked confused.

She stopped and faced him, looking him squarely in his eyes. "Silly, together, we agree that we have arrived at our destination. That's all. Come on; give it a try," she teased him with a coy smile. He smiled back and the two stated together that they had now arrived at the Ant Farm.

"Well, I'll be!" Zed exclaimed, followed by a shocked cry at the sight before his feet, "Oh no. Miranda!" Thousands of bleached bones and skulls lay scattered about the ground. Grasses growing up out of eye sockets gave a surreal view to the grave yard, for surely that must be what this was. Miranda let out a squeal.

In order to continue, they had to walk over the sea of bones. Crunching sounds accompanied each hesitant foot step as the two attempted to cross the wide expanse of brittle bones, which seemed to stretch out as far as they could see. Both steeled themselves and continued, neither daring to think the horrible thought that some of these could well be the bones of her mother! After what seemed an eternity, they finally reached the other side of the sea of bones and spotted the ants.

As far as Zed was concerned, these black ants looked like normal carpenter ants, and more importantly, they were the right size, perhaps a half inch long. A long line of them carried bits of grasses high over their heads moving in the same direction that they were heading. One ant that was not carrying anything looked up at the two forms and shocked the two by speaking quite unexpectedly, "Hello. Please be careful of my workers here. What are you doing here? Can I help you? Have you lost your way? The elephants haven't brought you, so you must not have been sentenced to our Ant Farm for crimes. Tom's the name, Thomas Longleaf."

"Hello. I am Zed Osmund and this is my friend, Miranda Whitney. Pleased to meet you. We will be careful of your workers. Say, that was an impressive pile of bones back there. I take it that the ants devour those who get sentenced to the Ant Farm." The bones had made an indelible impression on him. Zed was slightly nervous, though relieved to see that the ants were not giant sized as well. Had they been as large as the rabbit and squirrel, Zed would have been very nervous indeed!

Tom laughed heartily. "Ah, you saw them, well good. It took us a long time to get all of those bones carted there. My, what a project that was! Well, Zed, we had to do that. You see, not everyone is as careful as you both are being. In the past, we had so many of you giants trampling our workers. Why in just one day alone, we lost two thousand workers! We had to do something. I admit, our queen's plan has really worked. Those bones have placed great fears in the minds of all those in Malbon. Indeed it has. Now, none dare come anywhere near our colonies. Terrific plan, don't you think?"

"Why, I'd say positively brilliant plan. From those that we've met, I will back you on the results. Some are absolutely terrified of coming anywhere near here," Zed agreed with Tom.

"Indeed, it has been most successful. We were definitely right in putting up that barrier, but then, they were right too; our workers are so very small compared to the others. We are hard to see. So in the end, we are all more or less right, you see. Still, the bones have kept us from suffering catastrophic losses of our workers."

"So you don't really eat the prisoners who are sent to the Ant Farm?" Miranda asked, wondering what did happen to those who were sent here. She was, of course, thinking about her mother's sentencing to the Ant Farm. That some of those bleached bones were not her mother's was what she desperately wanted to verify.

Tom laughed, "Of course not, we are vegetarians."

"Say, how come you guys are not giant-sized, like the rabbit and squirrel that we saw?" Zed asked, curious to find that the ants were not enormous. The way that Sir Thomas had been talking, Zed had imagined the ants were also monstrously large.

Again, Tom laughed, "Ah, big folks." Poof! Tom appeared to be as tall as the two; his body was over six feet long. For a second, Zed felt a rush of anxiety. Tom looked awfully scary this large. "Look, if I was this big, how big would the grass have to be for us to eat? Why, unless you want the grass to be seven feet tall everywhere, we ants had better stay our size." Poof! Tom returned to his original size.

"Point well taken," Zed agreed, relieved to see Tom reduced in size once more. "Say, we are looking for Miranda's mother, Rose, who was sent here as a prisoner for practicing magic without a license. By any chance have you seen here?"

Tom shook his bulbous head, "No. Sorry, you are the only to giants that I've seen in some time. My job is to keep the workers in line and make sure they don't get into trouble."

"What do they do with the prisoners who are sent to the Ant Farm?" Miranda asked, still worried. She might not have been eaten, but still where was she? Imprisoned somewhere around here?

"Don't know myself. Have to ask the queen's guards. Follow us; we are heading there now with this load of grass for the queen's staff. She's the most important person in our world, you know, the queen, I mean. Don't you have a queen in your place?" Tom asked.

"Well," Miranda tried to reply, but then thought about how she could explain our president. "Sort of. Do you suppose that she will see us?" That seemed a more important fact to discover at the moment.

"Probably not. She is awfully busy, but her guards will see you. I'm sure that they will be helpful, if you don't go squashing any of us before then," Tom suggested.

They walked on in silence for a time. Zed thought that he ought to make polite conversation. After all, it wasn't every day that he had the opportunity to chat with an ant. However, he couldn't figure out anything to ask. He'd never given ants much thought in his life. Now if he had been the professor at the local junior college who often took summers off to go to far flung places on Earth to study ants, why, he assumed that he would have zillions of questions for Tom. Ants were ants to Zed, ah well.

Suddenly, he noticed that the line of workers was now descending down a hole in the ground. A mound of small dirt clods rose up making their hole appear to be a miniature volcano. Three mail clad ants holding long halberds suddenly appeared and then poof! The three appeared to tower over Zed and Miranda. "Halt! Who goes there?" one guard bellowed in a deep voice. "We've no notice of new prisoners."

"Hello. We are not prisoners," Zed quickly spoke for Miranda. "We have come looking for Miranda's mother, Rose, who was sent here as a prisoner for practicing magic without a license."

"Oh, well, that's better," the guard replied. Zed noticed that his uniform was red with bright yellow stripes. His chain mail rings tingled as he moved slightly, trying to keep his balance on his rear legs. The red and yellow shone through the grey rings of the mail. He looked an impressive guard, though the viciously sharp halberd kept attracting Zed's attention.

"Have you seen her? Is she being held prisoner around here somewhere? Could we possibly see her?" Miranda asked, hoping that at last they could at least see her and make sure that she was all right. She was also wondering how she might rescue her from this Ant Farm. Was she being held somewhere far underground? Perhaps in one of the many tunnels there?

"Yes. No. No," the guard replied in a machine gun fashion, mostly devoid of any recognizable emotion, which only added to her confusion and worry.

Zed was about to step in and ask "Why," when the guard finally gave a laugh. "Ho, ho. Sorry, just playing with you. Yes, yes, she was sent here. No, we don't really keep prisoners here. What could we possibly do with giants? You taste positively awful, and you are an extreme danger to our colony if only because of your size. We refuse to adopt larger forms you see, not unless they enlarge all of the grasses as well and maybe the trees too. In the past, we did petition the court to do just that, but they rejected it, saying that they would then have to enlarge themselves accordingly. Guess we are both more or less right on that one. Ah well. So, no, she is not here. We sent her on her way on the Malbon Express. Thus, no, you can't see her because she is not here."

"Malbon Express? What's that?" Miranda asked, relieved that her mother was not being held prisoner here, but worried about where she might now be.

"The train. Haven't you heard about the steam train? No matter. If you want to find this Rose person, then you need to get on the Malbon Express," the guard offered, just a bit too willingly, Zed thought. He rather felt that the guard was trying to get rid of them quickly. Well, perhaps so, after all they had to be very careful where they placed their feet. So many ants were about, it was hard not stepping on one.

"Thank you. Where do we find this train?" Miranda asked, resolved to follow in her mother's footsteps.

"I will get you aboard. However, you must give me your word that you will not come back here. Too much risk of squashing our workers, you see," the guard explained.

Both Zed and Miranda hastily agreed. Poof! They now stood on a train station platform before a long set of cars, reminiscent of the 1800's. Far up front, great clouds of black-grey smoke billowed from the antique steam engine. Curiously though, the two did not see any other passengers on the platform. "Here you go. Inside with you now," the guard said. Poof! The two found themselves inside a car, just as the train began chug-chugging away from the platform. Neither got the chance to say thanks to the guard.

# Chapter 4 The Malbon Express

Zed and Miranda found themselves in their own private car. All of the windows, of which there were many, were painted black. Yet, each window had a nice pull string shade, which was raised at the moment. Six plush leather, red bench seats, three on either side of the aisle, beckoned, while the front half of the car was open space, apparently for stretching their legs. Velvet red curtains adorned the sides and a plush red carpet felt soft beneath their feet. Golden lanterns hung every three feet along the sides providing a soft illumination and giving a warm glow to the car.

Another time, another circumstance, Zed thought that this would be an elegant, royal trip. Luxurious was indeed the atmosphere, regal perhaps. Just then, Zed felt something wiggling in his right pocket. Miranda likewise felt a strange motion in her left pants pocket. Both involuntarily started to scratch their itches, while taking in their most unusual surroundings. Pop! Zed's hand touched something furry! He looked down and saw Herr Adelstein's head sticking out of his pants pocket! "Huh?" he exclaimed totally surprised to see the rabbit's enormous head protruding from his pocket.

"It's safe, Sir Thomas; you can appear now," Herr Adelstein called out. Poof! The six foot tall rabbit suddenly materialized in front of Zed. Poof! Sir Thomas appeared in front of a very surprised and amused Miranda. The rabbit carefully pulled a very, very tiny Albert from Miranda's hair. "Sorry, had to put Albert in your hair," he said in a matter of fact manner, and then sat the very, very tiny tortoise on the floor and, poof, the tortoise grew to his normal size once more.

"What is going on?" Miranda asked, slightly confused and fingering her hair back into order, though it really wasn't all that messed up. "Where did you come from?"

Albert looked slightly embarrassed. Sir Thomas fiddled with his trousers, leaving the explanations up to Herr Adelstein. The rabbit cleared his throat, "Well, we wanted to thank you for getting us licensed to practice magic."

"Oh, my doing," Zed grinned. "I added our names to the official scroll and then added yours too. I hope that you don't mind. I thought it was the thing to do," he chuckled at his deviousness and creativity against the "establishment." The three bowed to him.

"Go on, tell them," Sir Thomas whispered slightly nervously, stepping from foot to foot, as if he might become glued to the floor of the train if he stood too long on one foot.

"It's all Albert's fault," the rabbit growled. "He said that it was best if we *didn't* tag along with you to see what happened to you, but then, as we all know, Albert is always *wrong* on the important things. So that meant that we really *ought* to tag along with you to make sure that nothing harmful happened to you 'umans."

"But oh my dear, goodness me!" Sir Thomas interrupted the rabbit. "We nearly fainted when we heard you crunching over all of those bones. Oh my yes. So many have died. Their bones — oh, it is just too horrible to say."

"Don't fret so, Sir Thomas," glared Herr Adelstein. "You heard Thomas ant say that they did not eat us."

"But everyone says that the ants eat every particle of flesh off of you, leaving stark white bones!" protested Sir Thomas. "Everyone knows that! We heard the crunching of the bones!"

Zed chuckled, "Sometimes what everyone knows isn't so."

"So, so, so you believe him? Ants don't eat us?" asked Herr Adelstein, still a bit uncertain of the outcome.

Albert scratched his head with his foot. "Everyone knows that the ants eat us down to our very bones, but now the ants don't eat us to our bones. Well, which is it?"

"Just because everyone says something is so doesn't make it so," Miranda explained patiently. "You are all so big that one mis-step on your part could squash hundreds of their fellows. They are just trying to protect themselves from your big feet, you see."

"Well, I can see that," Albert said, looking beneath each of his feet to make sure that no ants were stuck to them. Perhaps he had squashed some and had not realized it; then again, perhaps he had not.

"Harrumph. Well, why don't they put up a sign or something," growled Herr Adelstein. "Anyway, here we are and where are we going?"

Zed laughed, "We haven't the foggiest notion where we are going, only that Miranda's mother was put on this train some weeks ago. I guess we get off wherever she got off. Nice to have you along." The rabbit bowed; he seemed pleased to hear this.

Just then, they heard footsteps coming towards the door of their car, and the three guests immediately vanished from sight. Poof! All except Albert, who was once more shrunken down to barely an eighth of an inch across. He quickly scooted beneath a seat where he would not be stepped upon by errant feet. The door opened and a man wearing a tuxedo-style conductor's uniform entered. He carried a large golden punch in one hand and a pile of ticket stubs in the other.

Dryly, he said, "Ticket's please."

Zed looked at Miranda and she grinned back. "I'll handle this," she whispered. "I'm sorry. The ants just put us on the train. They didn't give us any tickets. If we need tickets, where do we get them and how much do they cost?"

He raised his eyebrows; his eyes seemed to bulge out. Zed couldn't quite ascertain whether this was a good or bad reaction, only that it was unexpected. The man had an enormous handlebar moustache, perfectly in place. His hair was immaculate. "Well, five stowaways, I see. You get tickets at the station, which we have already left some time ago. Well, no problem. One must be always ready to adjust to changing situations. Yes, that we must. Like I always say, adapt to what you are facing."

He waved his tickets and the golden puncher, and then continued, "Now then, you have no tickets for the Malbon Express. Since you have none, then you are going to have to work this trip. However, this is a very high class Express! I don't know where you come from, but it must be a heathen place if you wear such rags for apparel. This will never do, not in a trillion years. You both must be properly attired. Now let's see what I can find for you to wear."

Poof! New clothes appeared on both. Zed now wore an elegant, light blue tuxedo with twin tails, reminiscent of the 1850's while Miranda wore a matching ball gown, flaring out with numerous petticoats. Both looked at each other and grinned, pleased with their new look. Poof! A pair of hats appeared on their heads. Identical light blue hats were cylindrical with flat tops, about four inches tall. Sewn on the front side just above the tiny brim was an official Inspector's badge done in gold and black.

"Ah, there, now you both look official. During this trip, you are both appointed Malbon Express Detective Inspectors. As such, you will be charged with solving any crimes committed during the trip. Now then, your sleeping quarters are in this car." He demonstrated the pull down sleeping compartments stored overhead and which opened into the front half of the car, their leg stretching area. "Now, way up front behind the engine is the dining car where meals are provided at your convenience. That is to say, there is no set time when meals are served, though a bell will chime at the proper dining times. Of course, you are not required to dine just then, though it would behoove yourselves to make the acquaintance of the other passengers, just in case a crime is committed. If you need me, just pull on the cords at the sides of the cabins." He bowed, pirouetted crisply, and headed out the door. He turned and added, "Oh yes, this is the last car on the train."

"Detectives?" Miranda said curiously as the door shut.

"Perhaps we won't have any crimes to solve. Say, are you any good at doing that?" Zed asked, slightly worried. After all, thus far nothing seemed as it ought to seem.

"Crimes? Oh dear me," the voice of Albert squeaked from his hiding place in beneath the seat. Poof. He appeared his normal size; his face twisted in fear. "I don't like crimes. They mean someone has gotten hurt. Oh dear me."

Poof. Herr Adelstein's head with his flopping ears appeared. His eyes surveyed the cabin rapidly, as if ensuring that it was safe. Poof. The rest of his six foot frame appeared. "Oh I do feel so much better now that Herr Adelstein is here," Albert added.

"Is it safe?" whispered a fearful Sir Thomas, whose body was still nowhere in sight. His disembodied voice rather startled Miranda and Zed, who glanced around the cabin, unable to locate the squirrel.

Poof. Sir Thomas appeared, looking very worried indeed. "Crimes? Crimes? Oh my goodness! What have we gotten ourselves into this time? Herr Adelstein, I told you that this was not a good idea."

"Well, you know that Albert is always wrong," Herr Adelstein countered hostilely. "So if he says that a crime will be committed, we can count on one not being done. So I say that it is safe. We should sit back and enjoy the ride. So where are we going?"

"Er, Miranda, we forgot to ask him that," Zed pointed out. He was reluctant to pull the conductor's cord. Perhaps they would soon arrive and get on with their search for her mother.

"Maybe the tickets will say," Miranda replied. "Say, I have five tickets. How did he know that you three were with us? I thought that you three were well hidden." The rabbit shrugged his shoulders. Sir Thomas only found this even more startling and his legs began shaking, his knees knocking together, pounding out a percussive rhythm. While she found this sound slightly unnerving and almost annoying, Miranda chose to ignore it and studied the ticket stubs. "Ah, here we go. Our destination is a place called Sagacity. Now that sounds hopeful." A place of truth, sound judgment, and keen foresight ought to be a refreshing change, she thought.

Bong! Bong! Bong! A loud alarm sounded in their cabin, the kind of noise which one wishes that he or she could ignore but simply couldn't. "Oh no! I am wrong again. Crimes! Oh dear me!" moaned the turtle. Worse, a red light just below the alarm began flashing "Murder."

Sir Thomas' legs rattled together so hard that the giant squirrel completely collapsed onto the floor, landing squarely upon the hard shell of Albert. "Crimes! Murder!" squealed Sir Thomas.

"Yes, I am afraid that you have landed upon me once again, Sir Thomas. Herr Adelstein, can you help Sir Thomas off of me? I want to shrink and disappear before someone kills me," Albert said with a barely perceptible rise in emotion. "Besides, Sir Thomas is tickling me with his shaking."

Herr Adelstein hastily pulled the befuddled squirrel up, nearly jerking his arm off. "T-t-thank you. Oh my, oh my. Murder. Herr Adelstein, someone has been murdered. Are we next? I can't help thinking that there must be something terribly important that I have entirely forgotten to do before I get murdered. Besides, I am too young to be murdered. Don't you think so, Herr Adelstein? Please tell me that is so," the squirrel pleaded with the rabbit, who grimaced and adjusted his hat and coat.

Miranda could see that the rabbit was stalling, thinking rapidly. She spoke hastily, "Friends, the murder has already occurred, so I am perfectly confident that all three of you will be perfectly safe. Besides, who would want to harm such a fine trio of friends?" She flashed them an encouraging smile while poking Zed and nodding her head his way.

"Oh, yes," Zed finally caught her intention. "Yes, the murder is done, so you are now safe. Ah, here comes the conductor now. I bet that Miranda and I are going to be summoned to play detectives. You three can tag along with us if you want to."

"Oh please," begged Albert. "I feel so safe around you, Zed."

"Oh no!" Sir Thomas exhaled in a gush, very nearly falling down a second time.

Angrily, Herr Adelstein barked, "Now what is the matter, Sir Thomas?"

"Albert! He said that he feels safe around Zed," Sire Thomas squeaked.

"So?" Herr Adelstein growled, failing utterly to see the squirrel's point.

"You know that he's always wrong. That means that we will be in deep trouble if we go with Zed, even though I do want to go with them. I am terrified of being left in this car alone. Why, there is a murderer onboard this train. He might come into this car and kill us," Sir Thomas explained, his voice shaking nervously.

Miranda tossed her long black hair back and adjusted her light blue, cylindrical hat with its official gold and black Inspector's badge. The tuxedo clad conductor with his enormous handlebar moustache and immaculate hair stepped solemnly into the room. "There has been a murder in Compartment Six. Your services are needed at this time. If you will follow me, I will take you to the scene of the crime." He saw the three companions and added in a disgusted tone, "Are they coming as well?"

"Yes, if there is truly a murderer on board this train, then I want our friends to come with us for their safety," Zed stated flatly.

"Very good, sir," the monotone voice of the conductor replied. "This way then." He led the way out of their compartment.

Miranda put her arm around Zed and whispered, "In this dress, I need a bit of support. Hope you don't mind."

"Not at all," he smiled, glancing at her charming face. Herr Adelstein fell into line behind them, marching as if he were going off to war. Thump. Thump. Thump. His feet marked his passage. Nervously, Sir Thomas followed behind him, glancing over his shoulder continuously, as if the assassin might appear at any moment. Albert merely waddled along behind the squirrel, shaking his head and trying to decide if he had been right or wrong about this murder.

Soon they were navigating a long, narrow corridor with many compartments on either side. Most of the doors were opened now and various people called out. "Have you caught the murderer yet?" "Are we going to be safe?" "I want to talk to your boss!" "How dare you allow a murderer onboard the Malbon Express!"

"Are we next?" an obviously frightened elderly woman asked as the conductor passed by her compartment. "Mrs. Doubttree here is elderly, you know."

"I'm sure that you will be perfectly safe, Mrs. Hanna. If you will please remain in your cabin, these are the official Malbon Express Detective Inspectors. I assure you, ma'am, they will solve this crime before we get to the station." The conductor's bored tone did little to console the elderly woman though.

"Ah, here we are. Compartment Six. Nothing has been disturbed. Countess Vanessa Graves here found the deceased's body. They were sharing this compartment," the monotone voice explained. "You may also use the compartment across the hall, Number Five, if you need. When you have solved the murder, summon me. If you need anything, pull the cord. I must see to the other passengers. This is causing a bit of a row, if you hadn't noticed." He turned and left the two standing at the open door to Compartment Six.

Zed peered inside with Miranda still on his left. Herr Adelstein poked his head in below his right shoulder, while Albert craned his neck outward looking between the legs of the rabbit. Sir Thomas frittered nervously with his suit coat, muttering about whether or not he should look too. "Is there really a dead woman in there?" he finally asked, breaking the silence.

The compartment was large enough to sit six passengers. A pair of facing leather couches held the two occupants, while a suitcase was plainly visible in the overhead bin. On the right sat the lifeless body of an elderly woman. On the left looking straight at the pair was a young woman, probably in her mid-twenties, Zed thought. Although he ought to have been looking at the deceased, he could not take his eyes off of the countess.

Countess Vanessa Graves wore a light blue satin gown. Tight-fitting, it hugged her bounteous curves down to her knees where a hint of her white slip could just barely be seen. Zed had never seen a woman with so well an endowed bosom, an incredibly thin waist, and swelling hips. Curvaceous? Incredibly so. She wore black nylon stockings with enticing back seams. Her matching light blue stilettos were at least six inches tall, Zed noted. His eyes slowly rose upwards from her feet past her thin waist and enormous bosom, at last gazing upon her head. He saw that her blue eyes perfectly matched her dress and heels. Her face was oval and unblemished. Her eye lashes were overly long and heavy with mascara. She wore a dark blue eye shadow that lightened to a light blue. Her thick lips were cherry red and matching her fingernails, which had to be three inches long at least, he noted. Her hair was brown with a hint of red in it, wavy, lustrous and full, falling to the small of her back. A pair of long, gold, dangling earrings held four blue gemstones each, matching her ensemble perfectly.

Countess Vanessa Graves was the most beautiful woman that Zed had ever seen. When his eyes finally met hers, she spoke coyly, "Well, it is about time that someone has come to rescue me. I've had to sit here with that dead woman forever, it seems. Countess Vanessa Graves." She extended her right hand with its long talons to Zed, who flushed, but took it. She ignored Miranda entirely. She took Zed's hand securely and pulled, steadying herself as she rose onto her tall heels. "Please, allow me to hold onto you, Detective. These heels are not made for the eternal jostling of this train. There, that's better. And you are?" she fluttered her long eye lashes seductively, a disarming smile spread across her cherry lips. This close, Zed could smell the odor of flowers coming from her, but he had no idea what kind, only that this woman smelled as elegant as she looked.

"Er, Zed. My friend, Miranda," Zed's voice sounded distant to his own ears.

Miranda was not impressed with the countess and quickly spoke up. "So you found the body. How long ago was it? Were others in this compartment when it left the station? Who was the woman? Did she seem worried or anything? Come on, Zed, snap out of it. We have to solve this murder." Miranda definitely was growing annoyed with Zed, who seemed to be under some kind of trance. The countess has definitely overdone her makeup, she thought, so impractically dressed!

"I believe that she said her name was Mrs. Whitehall. Please, Zed, can you escort me to the empty compartment? It is *so* unnerving to be standing here beside a dead woman," Countess Vanessa asked coyly, again flirting openly with Zed.

Hastily, the others moved back a bit and Zed, still holding onto the shapely woman, helped her navigate the short distance into the neighboring compartment. Once there, she saw down and crossed her legs, dangling her enticing hose covered legs and heels before Zed. Vanessa continued to completely ignore Miranda. "I saw nothing amiss. She did not speak a word to me."

Becoming more annoyed with the countess, Miranda asked, "So how do you know her name then?"

Without taking her eyes off of Zed, she replied slowly, "If you will look at her suitcase above her, you can read the tag as well as I did. Mrs. Whitehall. Oh Zed, do you suppose that you could send her to fetch me a glass of water?"

Zed wanted to do just that, feeling an overwhelming urge to do absolutely anything this gorgeous angel might ask of him. However, Albert chose this moment to break her charm spell over Zed. "Oh dear me! It is a dead human, isn't it? But then, I am always wrong, so maybe she isn't dead or she isn't a human or maybe both. Zed, this is so hard for me to get it right. Which is it?"

"The woman's dead, Albert! Can't you see that?" Herr Adelstein growled angrily. "She looks like a 'uman to me. I wonder if she came down from the sky like these two did? Perhaps, she landed too hard and that's why she died. Perhaps there hasn't even been a murder, Albert."

"Countess Vanessa, if you will excuse me a minute? I had better take a look," Zed said as the woman's spell over him suddenly vanished. "Duty calls. I am supposed to be the detective, countess. Back in a minute."

"Oh, if you *must*," she replied feigning dejection. "But promise me you will come sit with me when you are done."

"Yes, countess. Come on; let's take a look at the body," Zed suggested.

Once in the compartment, Miranda whispered, "The countess is quite attractive, bit overdone on her makeup and her heels — so impractical. Still, I suppose that is what is expected of a countess. Zed, focus. We have to solve this before someone else is murdered."

"This doesn't make any sense. I don't know what came over me. Yes, she is a knockout. This murder, I mean, doesn't make sense," Zed replied, growing even more embarrassed and flustered, repeating himself.

Miranda tossed her hair back and said, "Well, on the CSI shows, they first have to determine COD, Cause Of Death."

"That's plain as day," Herr Adelstein broke in. "Anyone can see that you 'umans are not supposed to have holes in your heads."

"She's been shot," Miranda concluded. "But did anyone hear a gunshot?"

"What's a gunshot?" asked a nervous Sir Thomas. "Ought we be worried about a gunshot?" Zed and Miranda both saw what appeared to be a bullet entry point in the elderly woman's forehead, right between her eyes.

"Have any of you ever heard of a gun? It fires bullets," asked Miranda, trying to be helpful to the three. From their blank looks, she had her answer. "We should check with the neighboring compartments and see if anyone heard any loud noises, Zed."

"Yes, I suppose so," he replied a bit hesitantly.

"Allow us to help," Herr Adelstein insisted. "This is exciting, isn't it, Sir Thomas?"

"Well, I don't quite know if it is a good exciting or a bad exciting," the nervous squirrel replied honestly, hoping that he could follow behind the rabbit, who always seemed to know just what to do.

"Oh do come on! This is a good exciting, Sir Thomas. For once, *we* get to do the interrogations!" Herr Adelstein growled, leading the way down the hall to the next compartment. Miranda had already moved up the hall, leaving Zed standing beside the compartment where the countess still sat with her legs crossed.

"My water?" Countess Vanessa asked coyly, again fluttering her eyes a little. "Sitting beside the dead woman has made me terribly dry, detective." Once more under her spell, Zed headed up to the next car, the diner. A minute later, he returned with a bottle of water for the elegant young woman.

"Here you go, Countess Vanessa." He handed her the bottle and watched as she opened it, fascinated with her long talons as she gracefully opened it.

"Thank you. Please, come sit beside me a moment. You are a most handsome young man, detective," she replied demurely, again batting her eyes slightly. Zed found himself unable to resist her suggestion and sat down beside her. Such a woman! Zed thought to himself, only vaguely aware that Miranda had returned and was now just outside the compartment.

"You will do very nicely. I can't tell you how much this means to me. It has been so long in coming," Countess Vanessa said softly, her voice carrying an unmistakable tone of some great relief. Poof! Magic flashed. Zed felt very strange. It was as though he was now in the countess' body looking over at his own body.

He heard his own voice speaking. "There, free at last! Thank you Zed. I hope that you enjoy my body as much as I have. When you get to the next station called Malbon, get off and have a taxi take you to the Graves Mansion. The ring that you are wearing will unlock the gates and doors. We were expecting pairs, but Count Henri, my husband, found a woman traveling alone several weeks ago, and he seized the moment, as one might say. I told him that we should wait, but he didn't — he deserted me, the *rat*. Wait until *I* find him. Well, no matter. Good luck solving your murder. If you cannot, there are sufficient funds in my purse to pay the conductor for your tickets. I must be off now. Again, thank you for the gift of your body. I do hope you enjoy mine. Bye." Poof! Zed disappeared from the Malbon Express, leaving a startled Miranda standing at the entrance of the compartment looking at Countess Vanessa, who stared in disbelief at the empty space where Zed had been sitting an instant before.

"What's happened to me?" Zed asked, hearing not his own voice, but that of the countess. "Oh my god! I'm in her body! Miranda! Help! It's me, Zed. What's she done to me? I can't breathe right." She stood up and nearly fell over. Miranda quickly came to her side and balanced the curvaceous woman on her precarious heels. Miranda's face paled.

"Zed? This — this is you? Not Countess Vanessa?" she inquired, fumbling for words. Never had she heard of such a magical feat.

"Of course it's me. I have my memories, my mind. I am me, but somehow I am in her body. I feel so weird," Zed attempted to explain what he felt and sensed.

Miranda's hands slipped down along the waist of the woman. "Oh, you are wearing a tight corset. I thought so when I first saw her. That's why you are having a hard time breathing. I think you ought to take shallow breaths. So the countess has somehow swapped bodies with you. I wonder how she did that trick?"

"I want my body back!" Zed exclaimed.

"Well, you are a knock-out in this one," Miranda couldn't help teasing him. "You will attract every man's eyes."

Zed flushed. He rather fancied attracting Miranda's eyes, but this was embarrassing. He was now in a woman's body, a totally foreign experience for him. Just then, Herr Adelstein and company returned, "I say, no one has heard any loud noises," he began to report before he noticed that Zed was missing. "Where has Zed gone?"

"No — no one has heard any noises," Sir Thomas added, fidgeting on his feet, though he seemed relieved that no one had heard any bangs. "Perhaps this was not one of your gunshots."

"Maybe she isn't dead," suggested Albert, adding, "though I distinctly recall seeing her sitting there motionless. Then again, perhaps what I was seeing I was not really seeing or maybe I was seeing what I was not seeing or maybe I was not seeing what I was seeing. Oh this is so confusing. Please, Herr Adelstein, ask Zed to help me sort this out. I am so tired of always being wrong."

"I will Albert, just as soon as Zed returns," the rabbit answered rather annoyed that the tortoise was interrupting their official report.

"I'm still here," the soprano voice of the countess spoke up. "She somehow stole my body. I'm still here; it's me, Zed."

"Hum, this is most interesting," Herr Adelstein proclaimed, rubbing his paw across his nose thoughtfully. "It seems that these 'umans can swap bodies as well. Most impressive."

"But, but, but," Sir Thomas tried to protest, but became so nervous that he could not get his protest enunciated.

"Oh, you can have my body if you like, though I expect that no one else would want it," Albert volunteered somewhat apathetically. "No one ever does. Say, does this happen often with you humans — body swapping, that is? Correct me if I am wrong, and as you know, that is nearly all the time, Herr Adelstein, but isn't body swapping impossible?"

The squirrel's shaking subsided, and Sir Thomas looked at the rabbit. Herr Adelstein replied, "Of course body swapping is *not* possible, Albert." He hastily amended his pronunciation, "Excepting that these 'umans have just done it. Relax, Sir Thomas, you are not about to lose your body. Body swapping must be an action among the 'umans. Isn't that right, Zed?" He looked to the Countess Vanessa for support, hoping that Zed would back him up. It would do no good to overly worry Sir Thomas in this matter.

Zed was still far too confused to properly reply. Miranda spoke up, "Well, it is impossible among us humans as well. I've never ever heard of such a thing happening, but as you can see, it has happened. Don't worry, Sir Thomas. I don't believe that anyone will be trying to steal your body or yours either, Albert. I think that there is far more to all this than we are seeing at the moment. However, I believe that we should continue to try to solve the murder. That conductor is likely to return at any time, and I have a bad feeling that we simply have to solve it before we can leave this Malbon Express train. Come on, Zed; let's examine the crime scene for more clues. Here, put your arm over my shoulders." Zed did as she asked, taking small steps and grateful for her support. He felt so strange in this foreign body and so confused.

The five gathered inside the compartment, though the three stood as close to the door and as far from the corpse as they could. Miranda began examining the compartment looking for clues. Zed, wobbling on his heels, decided to sit down next to the corpse and examine the deceased elderly woman more closely. Something was definitely wrong here, besides this wild body swapping of the countess. As Miranda chatted about her continuing observations, Zed looked at the woman's face. Tentatively, he extended his fingers and touched her forehead, trying to keep his long nails out of the way of his touch. "Plastic!" he exclaimed in his new soprano voice.

"What?" replied Miranda, slightly confused by Zed's seemingly misrelated remark. She had been confirming the woman's identity from the label on her suitcase.

"This is not a human body. She's a plastic doll. Look," Zed lifted the wig off of the doll's head. "This isn't a person at all. It is simply a toy doll that someone has dressed up to look like an elderly woman."

"Ah ha!" exclaimed Albert decisively. "I told you that I am always wrong. See, it isn't even a human."

"Right, Albert. Do you have plastic dolls that are alive and walking around on your world?" Countess Vanessa asked.

"Well, I must admit that we have seen many strange things, but we have never seen a walking plastic doll," Herr Adelstein declared decisively.

Calming down rapidly, Sir Thomas added, "Never Zed, er Countess Vanessa. Sometimes we have seen plastic dolls floating in the sky as fancy balloons, but then someone was on the ground holding onto a string attached to the balloons. Does this mean that there was no murder after all?"

"Right, no murder, no crime to solve," Zed replied.

"I think this whole thing was just a wild charade by the *real* Countess Vanessa Graves so that she could *steal* Zed's body," Miranda concluded.

"Whew! That is a relief!" Sir Thomas declared, very much relived.

"Hey, speak for yourself! I'm stuck in this woman's body! I want mine back," Zed or rather the Countess Vanessa added.

"Well, Zed — gosh, this is so confusing," Miranda spoke up, biting her lip slightly. "It feels so utterly strange calling you Zed. Boggles my mind. I think that I best call you Countess Vanessa, Zed. I hope that you don't mind too much."

"This is so confusing. No, I guess that is best, Miranda. It will look even weirder if you keep calling me Zed, though I am Zed."

"Right. Then, there is no crime. I'm going to summon the conductor. We have to get off of this train and figure out a way to go after the real Countess Vanessa, er Zed," Miranda replied. She pulled lightly on the cord.

Shortly the immaculately dressed conductor returned. "Have you solved this crime? Arrested the murderer?" he asked politely. Glancing at the countess, he added, "Ah, swapped bodies have you?"

Miranda spoke up. "Yes. First, there has been no crime, no murder. If you will examine the supposed body, you will see that this is a plastic doll, a dummy. It was never alive. This was all some kind of weird stage play, probably so that the real Countess Vanessa Graves could steal Zed's body, leaving Zed stuck in her body here."

"Yes, and I want my body back. That is the real crime. I want you to have the authorities arrest her and make her give me back my body," Countess Vanessa added sharply.

"Oh dear me. No murder has been committed here? You must forgive me. I am but a conductor, not a detective. I accept that you have solved this crime. As far as the authorities are concerned, they are you two. Since the body snatching crime occurred on the Malbon Express, you two are the authorities responsible for the apprehension of the guilty party or parties. Well, I do hope that you can solve that one soon. We will be arriving at the Malbon Station in," he paused and pulled out a golden pocket watch. He finished up, "Yes, in three minutes. I do believe that you will have to hurry up. If you will excuse me, I have my conductor duties to attend to at this time. Well done, detectives on solving the crime. If you get off here, there is no refund on the lengthier trip to Sagacity." He bowed slightly, turned, and left them still in the compartment with the dummy plastic doll.

"Now what?" asked Countess Vanessa. "How the devil are we supposed to go after Countess Vanessa now? We don't have any idea where she — I mean he — I mean me, actually went. She or he just vanished."

Miranda bit her lip. "I just don't know, Zed, er Countess Vanessa. I have to admit that this unexpected turn of events has taken me by total surprise. I never knew that such a thing could possibly happen. Are you really sure that you are Zed?"

"Of course I am sure. I'm me, still me," Zed's soprano voice replied. He or she was growing more and more worried by the minute.

"I think that you should just relax and enjoy your new body. There is nothing wrong with it, is there?" suggested

Albert, trying to calm Zed or the countess down a little. Zed shook her head and he added, "So, if there is nothing wrong with it, why not continue with your search for Miranda's mother? That would seem to be the likely thing to do to me, but then, as you know, I am always wrong. Perhaps that is not the thing to do. Oh dear me."

"We don't have much choice, Zed, er Countess Vanessa," Miranda broke in. "The train has stopped. We're here, wherever here is. After we get off of the train, let's see where we are at and how we can go after the countess or Zed. Sorry, this is so confusing, Zed er Countess Vanessa."

Soon, many other passengers made their way past the compartment on their way to the various exits. Most could not resist a glance their way in hopes of seeing the dead body which wasn't a dead body, but had given them all a scare this trip. The elderly pair of women, Mrs. Hanna and Mrs. Doubttree, paused by their compartment. Mrs. Hanna said, "Good afternoon, Countess Vanessa Graves. *So* good to see our most *beautiful* monarch again." Looking at Miranda, she added, "I am *so* glad that you *solved* this one. You know that *another* murder occurred on this *very* Malbon Express not more than two weeks ago. Mrs. Doubttree and I were returning from a shopping trip and were positively terrified, and the detective then did *not* solve the murder. Not a very good detective, I say. You and your male companion are much better detectives. Thank you so *very* much."

"I'm glad that we were able to solve it," Miranda replied, unable to think of anything better to say. After the elderly pair moved on, with her arm around the countess, she led her party out into the corridor and towards the exit. Miranda's mind was racing. What had she gotten poor Zed into? This was wholly wrong and totally unexpected. Besides, it was far beyond anything that she had ever thought remotely possible. Now it was all up to her to put things right, and she knew that she had no ideas whatsoever about just how to proceed. She knew next to nothing about the real countess and where she might have gone with Zed's body, let alone why she so greatly desired it. Why steal a body in the first place? Hers was just fine. None of what had happened made any sense to her, and yet, she now felt a huge responsibility resting on her shoulders. She had to make this right somehow.

# Chapter 5 Malbon and Explanations

"Don't let go of me!" Zed whispered as he struggled to descend the stairs to the station platform.

Miranda chuckled, "At least now you are experiencing what we women sometimes have to endure to look 'pretty' for you men. Don't worry. I have you. Wow, this is quite a train station."

The long line of passenger cars were all painted black with an orange strip running along the top of their sides above the shuttered windows. Zed wondered why all of the windows were painted over with the same black paint, but soon his attention was drawn to the hundreds of bustling people walking along the platform. Miranda stopped suddenly; her fancy dress had just vanished. She was once more wearing her tee-shirt and jeans. "Oh. I do now look so out of place," she remarked. Countess Vanessa's appearance had not changed nor had that of their three companions trailing behind them.

Many men gazed lecherously at the countess as they passed her by. However, Zed was too busy trying to grasp his new surroundings to notice this aspect. She saw other humans, men, women, and children going to and fro, but also she saw many other animal life forms. A doe with a fawn in tow was chatting with a porter over her many bags. Further off, a centaur was unloading baggage for those who had just arrived. A stately lion walking on his hind legs slowly came towards them. Countess Vanessa also smelled the distinct odor from the coal-fired engine down at the far end of the station, and she noticed the smoke was slowly drifting over everyone here on the platform.

The brown and black centaur suddenly motioned to her. "Countess Vanessa, over here. I am privileged to unload your packages now, your majesty." Zed flushed, unsure of what to do. He'd so hoped to somehow just vanish into the city and get on with their search somehow, someway. Packages? What packages? Shopping. He recalled the two elderly women mentioning having gone shopping. Evidently the countess had done some shopping on her trip as well.

Miranda whispered, "We'd best play along for now. Head towards the centaur. Incredible. I've never seen such a creature before."

"Me either. I thought that they were just someone's imagination running wild. Okay. Play along. Just don't let go of me. I might lose my balance and take a spill," Countess Vanessa whispered back.

Herr Adelstein whispered, quite unsure just why the two were whispering,
"Where do you two come from anyway? Centaurs are all over, though usually they are found in the open grasslands and not here in the big city."

"That lion is coming towards us too," exclaimed Sir Thomas, becoming rather nervous once more. The lion was three times his size.

"Ignore him. Maybe he will pass us by," suggested Albert.

Of course, Albert's pronouncement only made the squirrel all the more nervous, since Albert was always wrong. This could only mean that the lion was actually coming for them! As the lion drew closer, Miranda saw that he was wearing a butler's uniform. Curious. Sir Thomas carefully put his body behind that of the rabbit's.

As they drew close to the centaur, he spoke. "Here you go — all ten packages, Your Majesty. Shall I help you carry them?" he asked politely. His back was as high as the head of the countess. His arms were well-muscled, and he appeared quite strong to her. He could easily have picked her up.

While Zed's mind raced trying to work out what to do next, the lion spoke up, "Your Majesty. Count Henri sent me with your carriage. He figured that you would need help with your purchases. I take it that shopping went well? Able, you may carry Her Majesty's packages to the Royal Carriage," the lion indicated with a sweeping motion of his enormous paw and giant claws. He stood much taller than the countess. A wave of panic swept over Zed. Play along was the only thought that he could manage.

"Thank you. Yes, it went well. I have brought some friends back with me. They will be staying with us," Countess Vanessa said, her voice trembling from the strain.

"Of course, Your Majesty. If you and your guests will follow me," the lion said politely, as though the countess bringing new friends to her palace was an expected, ordinary event. Zed suspected such was far from the case and hoped that the butler-dressed lion would accept her pronouncement. If she were somehow separated from Miranda, all would be lost! Zed realized that until now, he'd never really been totally dependent upon another, not since childhood. He did not like the feeling, but was helpless to do anything about it just now. The five slowly followed the lion to the waiting carriage.

As they made their way through the crowd, Zed began noticing that men were gazing lustfully at him or her, and he flushed even more. Evidently, Miranda sensed his embarrassment. She whispered, "Just ignore them." Countess Vanessa tried, but simply couldn't ignore the constant stares that she received. At last the ornate, eighteenth century style carriage appeared parked on the cobblestone street. Trimmed in gold, the black carriage was spotless and rather large. Any uneasiness that they would all not fit inside vanished from her mind. The driver's box was some four feet above the street level giving the lion a good field of view. While the lion held the door open, Miranda held on to the countess, helping her negotiate the three steps up and into the carriage. She sat beside her and motioned for the three to sit opposite them. From the corner of her eyes, she saw the centaur and lion loading the packages into a rear compartment.

Soon, they were rolling through the great city of Malbon. Now Zed began to have an entirely different worry! "My god! Miranda, there is this Count Henri. That must mean that he is married to her, er to me. My god! What if he expects to kiss me and to — well, you know, take me to bed with him! I can't possibly do that!"

Now it was Miranda's turn to flush. "Oh hell! This is going from bad to worse. What have I done? I should never have brought you with me. It's all my fault, Zed, er Countess Vanessa. Maybe he won't. This is turning into a nightmare," she admitted, fighting hard to hold back tears.

"Don't you 'umans like to procreate?" asked Herr Adelstein. "We all do here. You must have strange customs in your land."

"We like to as well, only just with our married partners," Miranda tried to explain without becoming too graphical. "She's not she, but Zed, so he or she isn't really married to this Count Henri, but he will still see his wife as herself, but she won't be she, but he, Zed."

"Oh this is so confusing. He's she, and she's he. Why not just tell this count fellow that and leave it at that?" suggested Albert, rubbing his round forehead with his right front foot. "I'm going to call her Countess Vanessa from now on. It is far less confusing. What say you, Herr Adelstein? But then, I suppose that I am wrong once again."

"Oh I do agree, Albert. Somehow I can't see she as Zed," the rabbit declared. Looking at the gorgeous woman, he stated flatly, "From now on, we are going to address you as Countess Vanessa and not Zed, since you do not look like Zed anymore."

"Of course he doesn't; he's a she now," the confused Sir Thomas agreed. "I am certainly glad that we don't go around snatching other people's bodies here, Herr Adelstein. After all, life is confusing enough without not knowing if you are still my friend. You are still Herr Adelstein, aren't you?"

The rabbit glared at the squirrel, as if his eyes could bore a hole through the rodent's head. "Of course I am," he finally growled, much to the relief of Sir Thomas. Looking at Countess Vanessa, he added, "Why, we rabbits like to procreate at every opportunity. My advice is to relax and enjoy it." Countess Vanessa flushed; her cheeks felt hot. While he wanted to help Miranda find her mother, this was not what he had bargained for — he'd witnessed many strange things, but this was over the top!

Miranda deftly changed the subject. "Say, we are in the city of Malbon. Have any of you been here before? Do you know anything about the city? What should we expect here in the city?"

"No, we have never been here before," Herr Adelstein decided to speak for his friends. "Often we have heard others talk about the Great City, but until we met you two, we had no way of getting here. We should go for long walks about the city and see the sights, don't you think?"

"Yes, I like that idea, although I suppose that perhaps I ought not like that idea, then I might be right," added Albert with a sigh. Clearly, he wanted to see the sights of this Great City too.

"Do you suppose that it is safe?" asked Sir Thomas. "There are an awful lot of people in this city. I've never seen so many humans before. Are you two sure that you did not come from here? It would seem that there are many of your kind here."

"No, I assure you that we did not come from your world," Miranda grinned.

"Of course they didn't, Sir Thomas. You saw them drop in from the sky, just as we did. Don't be silly," growled Herr Adelstein.

"If we are accompanied by Countess Vanessa, we should be safe, don't you think?" Albert suggested, but then wished that he'd expressed the opposite of it. Fortunately, neither of his companions picked up on his positive statement.

"Well, I have heard that the Great City is ruled by a Count and Countess, though I don't know if Countess Vanessa here is *the* Countess," Sir Thomas replied.

"Oh crap! What if I am supposed to be the ruler of Malbon?" Countess Vanessa burst out. If so, this would only add to her misery.

"Oh surely not, Zed, er Countess Vanessa," Miranda tried her best to put her at ease once more. "There may well be many counts and countesses in these lands. There certainly were in our earth history." Just then, the carriage came to a halt. Countess Vanessa's nervousness rose.

Miranda whispered in her ear, "Just remember to play along; play the role of the countess. I'll do what I can." The door opened and the lion extended the steps. Hastily, Miranda climbed down, pivoted to lend her hand to the countess, who had quite a precarious time descending the three steps. Play the role, play the role, Zed continually reminded himself or herself, meanwhile trying to catch her breath and keep from falling out of the carriage.

As she finally stood on solid ground, she saw that the carriage had pulled up before a huge mansion. Red stone work with ornate designs of lion heads rose up three stories tall. The mansion was huge just as the stonework blocks, each of which was two feet tall and three feet long, mortared together with precision and attention to artistic details. Here was an architectural marvel. Under other circumstances, Countess Vanessa would have enjoyed merely spending the time to take in the view. At the moment, she was terrified of what was about to happen here.

Just then a strange cat woman, walking on her hind legs and wearing a French Maid's outfit, came out of the huge double entrance doors. Two enormous lion head reliefs adorned each door. She walked up to the countess, curtsied, and said, "Welcome back, madame. I trust that your shopping went well."

"Yes, it went. I have brought some new friends back with me. They will be staying with us for a time," Countess Vanessa explained, hoping that her word would carry enough weight with this cat woman.

"Wee Madame. It shall be as you wish, as always. How you say — the young woman must be more appropriately dressed. You know the Count, your husband. He will not take kindly to such apparel," the cat woman replied. Did she speak with a French accent, she wondered?

"Can you find her something the Count would find appropriate?" Countess Vanessa asked, hoping so.

"Wee Madame. I will find her something. This way. The Count awaits your return in his study. Perhaps you may wish to help you freshen up after so long a journey?"

"Yes, that would be most helpful," Countess Vanessa replied, breathing a sigh of relief. The longer she could put off facing her supposed husband, the better. Miranda put her arm around Countess Vanessa, steading her, and they followed after the cat woman. The trio followed behind the two, their heads glancing in all directions, obviously most impressed with the sights and their incredible good luck.

From behind them, the lion called out that he would be bringing in her purchases shortly.

A new wave of panic swept over Countess Vanessa. She did not know the name of this cat woman servant or the layout of the rooms inside the mansion! Hastily, she suggested, "Can you lead us to my rooms? I'd like Miranda here to stay close to me as well as my three new friends. Can they have rooms near ours?"

The maid or servant paused, half expecting to be introduced to the newcomers. Since Countess Vanessa was not doing so, she took it upon herself. "I am Mademoiselle Janice, Countess Vanessa's Personal Assistant. It is my duty to look after her every need, to dress her, and even do her makeup. You three can have Room Eight, which is right next to the Countess' Suite. And you must be Miranda?" she said in her thick accent.

"Yes, I am. This is Herr Adelstein, Sir Thomas, and Albert. Thank you for showing us the way. It has been a long trip, rather a frustrating one, Mademoiselle Janice," Miranda replied politely.

"Please, just Janice. Our rooms are on the second floor. This way please," she replied, leading the five gaping companions through the ornate hall and to the wide stairs. Two suits of armor stood in one corner. The hardwood floor shone brightly.

"Say, this place is a palace! How many live here?" asked Miranda, beginning to focus on obtaining key information that Countess Vanessa was soon going to desperately need. Could they even hope to pull off this masquerade? Perhaps they should just explain to this Count Henri what had happened and hope for the best. Many ideas flooded through Miranda's mind. Which path to choose? There were so many at the moment.

"Ah, here are your rooms, sirs," Janice pointed out.

"You three clean up. I will drop by to pick you up when we go to meet the Count," Countess Vanessa hastily ordered, feeling confident that at least this would go well. She followed after Janice into her new luxury suite. They were in a sitting room complete with three plush sofas. Even here the hardwood floor was so highly polished that she could see her reflection in it.

"Miranda, you may have that spare room there. This one here is the Madame's, and that one is mine. Our bath is just through that door. Please, get out of those rags; take a refreshing bath while I get Madame settled and find you some appropriate attire," Janice ordered.

Countess Vanessa took a hold of Janice and headed into her new room, though she cast a last look over her shoulder as Miranda headed into the bathroom. She grew more nervous now that she was alone with her Personal Assistant. "There now. Let me get you out of your dress. I am sure that you will want to put on the new dresses that you just purchased. I'll unpack them as soon as Leo brings them up." Good, his name is Leo, Vanessa thought, greatly relieved to at least know the lion's name.

Presently, Janice had her tight-fitting dress removed as well as her satin slip. Now she could see why she was having such a hard time breathing. A white cotton corset with heavy metal stays constricted her waist and supported her massive breasts. "I should allow you to breathe a little," Janice said though Vanessa had no idea what she meant. Soon, some of the impossible constriction eased as Janice removed the sturdy corset. Now she could see the enormous size of her breasts, which were at least as large as her head. However, she also saw that she wore yet another even tighter corset around her waist, but this one provided no support for her massive bosom.

Seeing her charge looking at herself, Janice chided her, "You would not have such enormous knockers if you had followed my orders so many years ago. I told you a hundred times that they would grow and grow as long as you insisted on not wearing the tight corsets. You only have yourself to blame on that account."

"Can't you loosen this one too? Maybe a little?" Countess Vanessa asked pleadingly.

"Madame has forgotten already? If I do, you will be unable to support yourself. You know that I have to help you with everything when we bathe. Now don't give me any more protests. I have to find the waif something presentable. After all, Madame does not want Miranda to also grow enormous breasts or do you?" She looked coyly at Vanessa.

"No, of course not," she replied, though she began to imagine what Miranda might look like if they did. She flushed and put that thought out of her mind. "Very good, Janice. See to Miranda's needs please. I will rest a while." After Janice left the room, she tried to bend over to at least take off the impossibly high heels. This was a struggle; she still couldn't bend much at all. "Ah, that's better," she said to herself and stood up in her stocking feet. "Oh my!" Vanessa discovered that her feet could not go flat onto the floor; her leg muscles could no longer stretch that much, not even remotely. In fact, her legs throbbed, and she quickly slipped back into her heels, rather frustrated with this whole body switch.

"Well this is the most luxurious bath that I've ever had," Miranda called out to Janice. "Are these real gold fixtures?" The bath itself was more like a small swimming pool! The floor was white tile, and the bath was well illuminated from a dozen lights.

Janice chuckled, "Yes, real gold. This is the Royal Palace of Malbon after all. When you are dried off, I have found some clothing that is most appropriate." Drying off, Miranda joined Janice in her new bedroom. She saw the corset and heels at once. Before she could protest, Janice explained, "Madame, you must wear these corsets. If you do not, your breasts will expand, just as those of the countess have. She refused to wear them and now look at her! She was so stubborn. Now she is paying the price."

"But how is this possible?" Miranda asked, becoming more and more annoyed with this entire mess. All she wanted to do was to find her mother and rescue her.

"I'm sure that I do not know that, only that Madame's breasts will grow rapidly if you do not wear them. Come, I will help you dress."

"Does it have to be so tight?"

"Wee Madame, it must be so, unless you wish your breasts to grow large."

"Two corsets?" Miranda complained as Janice cinched her tightly into the waist high corset and prepared to put on the second one which would support her breasts as well.

"Wee Madame, it must be so." Janice repeated herself. "It happens to any woman who stays here in this Royal Palace, excepting we servants though." She chatted on, relating what had happened to several other guests over the years. She added, "You must also sleep in them. I believe that the breast grow during the night when a woman is not wearing hers. I've seen it happen six times now, though Countess Vanessa's have grown far more than any others. She can be so obstinate at times, you know."

She finished dressing Miranda in a deep blue satin gown that now fit her form tightly, showing off her curves nicely. She finished up tying on matching oxford heels nearly as tall as those worn by the countess. "If you will excuse me, I must finish dressing the countess in her new dress and heels."

Having tightened the countess' outer corset, Janice helped her into her new light red satin dress. She noted that the style was pretty similar to the one that she had been wearing. "This one matches your nail polish, Madame. You have such a good eye for colors, Madame," Janice praised the countess. Her accolades fell on deaf ears, however. Zed had no idea what she was saying, only that she felt that awful tight constriction once more.

"I'm starving," she said what she felt. When had she last eaten?

"Well, there now, you look fabulous for Count Henri. Come, let's get Miranda and the others. We cannot keep him waiting forever you know," Janice replied.

"Wow, you look really hot, Miranda!" Countess Vanessa exclaimed as she entered her room and got her first look at Miranda in her new deep blue dress and matching heels.

"Thanks. I'm afraid that we are both going to need to help each other," Miranda replied gloomily. Everything had gone so terribly wrong. Holding hands, the two women followed slowly after Janice, who paused to get the trio of guests. The three had indeed washed up and did look their best, Vanessa thought. The trio fell in line behind the two women who followed after the Personal Assistant. Fortunately, Janice took the long stairs slowly, much to the relief of the two women. Then, she moved on down the hall taking the first door on their left. As she opened the door, the smell of musty books greeted them. Vanessa took as deep a breath as she could; this was the proverbial *it*! Could she maintain this masquerade longer? Was she actually supposed to be married to this man? God, what if he wanted to sleep with her? Vanessa's face reddened more and more. She felt hot and faint, to say nothing of her nerves.

Janice spoke, "Count Henri, your wife has returned from her shopping trip and has brought along some new friends who will be staying here with her for a while." The two stepped into the study. Floor to ceiling book shelves dominated this reading room. A mahogany table with six matching chairs occupied the central area. A man in his twenties wearing a dark blue tuxedo and top hat rose from the far end of the table. Quickly, he removed his hat. He had a well groomed moustache and black hair. His eyes shone with brightness, probably a reflection from the many overhead lights in the room.

"Welcome home my Countess Vanessa," he said, rather formally, she thought, for a husband. "Is that your new dress, dear?" He moved rapidly over to her.

Oh no, is he going to kiss me? wondered Vanessa, growing even more ill at ease. This was rapidly becoming a nightmare without end!

"Good god! Miranda? Is that you?" suddenly Count Henri stopped dead in his tracks, his eyes staring in utter shock or disbelief at Miranda. Countess Vanessa could not actually tell which it was. Did he somehow know Miranda? If so, why had Miranda not told her about him? Her confusion only grew larger and she glanced at Miranda.

The countess relaxed slightly. Miranda was just as surprised by the unexpected greeting from this strange man as she was. "Yes, I am afraid that you have me at a disadvantage. I am Miranda Whitney."

"Miranda! It is you! My god, it is you!" the face of Count Henri became highly animated indeed. Countess Vanessa decided that it was one of total surprise. "It's me, your mother, Rose! Oh, this is just awful! Janice, please take the other guests on a tour of the Royal Palace please. I will greet them when you get back." Janice, somewhat startled by the count's reaction, nodded and motioned for the trio to follow her. Soon she shut the door to the study.

"Please have a seat. I'm sorry, Countess Vanessa, this is my daughter," he said apologetically, becoming flushed himself. "You have to excuse me. I don't mean to upset you."

"Mom? You? How?" Miranda tried to vocalize her stream of questions, but failed completely.

"Please, have a seat. This is so messed up," he pulled out a chair for each woman, helping them get seated, then sat down himself, beside Miranda. He leaned over and ran both hands through his hair and sighed. "I screwed up big time this time, dear. You must have guessed that I went and used Montford's Portail Mystique d'Univers. I should have listened to you and not come in here alone. Now I have really gotten things screwed up."

"Mom? It really is you?"

"Yes, it's me. I got into one trouble after another, ever since I landed on the grasslands. Say, those three others — they look like the ones that I first met."

"They are. Herr Adelstein, Sir Thomas, and Albert. Zed and I befriended them, and they are tagging along with us. Mom, this is really Zed and not Countess Vanessa," Miranda explained. "The real countess stole Zed's body while we were on the Malbon Express. Well, actually, she somehow swapped bodies with him."

"Ah, so much makes sense to me now. Hindsight is so perfect you know. Yes, that's what happened to me. I was on the Malbon Express — don't ask me how I even managed that one. I got exiled — some stupid court judge wouldn't listen to reason. Then I was ordered to solve a murder, and the next thing I found myself in this body, and he stole mine and just vanished from the train's compartment! Mind you, I don't mind being thirty years younger; it's just that being a man is so terribly awkward. I've had to use all manner of pretenses to keep from sleeping with my wife there, but if you are not her, then you don't know about that."

"No, sorry, I don't know what you are talking about," Vanessa replied, greatly relieved. Surely Miranda's mother would not insist on taking her to bed with him.

"When the countess left yesterday, I had a feeling that something was afoot, but I didn't know just what. Well, this is one fine mess that I've gotten myself and you into, Miranda."

"Mom, you don't know how glad I am to have found you. Zed and I have been following you, hoping and praying that we'd find you."

"Well, you have at last. I can't say how proud I am that you have managed all this on your own. Say, who is this Zed anyway? You've not mentioned him before."

"Just met him. He's really good, mom; only now he's stuck in her body, and we don't have a clue where she, I mean he, went. What are we going to do now, mom?"

"Well, let's keep up the pretense of being Count Henri and Countess Vanessa Graves. They are the rulers of this city of Malbon. We are the power in this large city. I've been spending my days researching everything I can find in this library, hoping for a clue, you know."

"Have you discovered anything? Anyway for us to get back our bodies?" asked Vanessa.

"Well, as a matter of fact, I believe that I have discovered an exit portal here in this Royal Palace," he replied with a smug smile that quickly evaporated.

"You did? Great mom."

"Only one catch, dear. If we exit through it, we will be permanently in these new bodies. I've thought long and hard about doing just that, dear. You know, to suddenly be thirty years younger is most appealing. I can live my life a second time, only as a man this time."

"Mom! You can't do that! Can you? I mean you really aren't considering that, are you?" Miranda asked. Somehow she could not deal with her mother suddenly being barely a year or two older than she to say nothing of the sex change. "We — I can't leave Zed like this. Not unless," she turned to face the countess. "Not unless you would prefer to return to our world as you are now, Zed."

Countess Vanessa smiled, "Of course not, unless there is no other alternative. How would I possibly explain all this to my family?"

"Well, Countess Vanessa, er, I guess the other countess rather, explained quite a lot to me during these past few weeks. She caught on to the fact that I was not her Henri right away. Evidently, I do not play the part of a man at all well. Anyway, apparently those two were captured in a similar manner as we were. According to Vanessa, visitors are supposed to enter in pairs. They did so and were captured on the Malbon Express much as we were," she nodded to Vanessa. "According to her, that was over a hundred fifty years ago. They both have been waiting that long for other visitors to come and exchange places with themselves. The real Henri swapped bodies with me, much to Vanessa's dismay. She swore to get revenge on him for abandoning her two weeks ago. Apparently a gong sounds when off-world visitors arrive. That's when we are to get onto the Malbon Express. According to her, when you find the visitors, all you need to do is to think Swap Bodies and it happens. Of course, the catch, as she pointed out, is that the swap is between opposite sexes. Darn that Able Montford anyway! Diabolical swap."

"So that means the woman who swapped bodies with me was really a man?" asked Vanessa.

"I believe so, Vanessa. The old Henri had been a woman. Imagine being here a hundred and fifty years and not aging in the slightest! Pretty incredible." He added, "Oh yes, that also explains how come you have such enormous breasts.

She told me that she refused to wear the designated outfits. But when her breasts became whoppers, she had very little choice any longer. She also explained that if I don't wear these fancy tuxedos, then my body will rapidly age. She said that Henri did just that, but that he finally gave in and put them on when his body looked to be around seventy years old. Not long after that, magically his body sort of un-aged back to where it was. On the other hand, she was really annoyed that her breasts did not return to normal once she donned the corsets. This sure is a crazy place that Montford created!"

He continued, "Miranda, I wish that you hadn't come after me. Now you are trapped here as well. On the other hand, I am so thankful that you did. I've really missed you. Whatever are we going to do now? If Countess Vanessa is to be believed, we are to wait until the gong sounds, announcing another couple have entered this strange universe and then go snatch their bodies, much as ours were stolen. Yet, how do we ever get our own back? Still, there is always the emergency exit that I've found." He tried to sound hopeful.

"Oh, here come the others back. Keep up the pretense, Vanessa," Henri requested.

The trio entered with broad smiles. They had enjoyed the tour, and Miranda introduced them to Henri, who definitely recognized them now. However, her mother had mostly ignored them when she'd first floated down into this world several weeks ago. "Well, I am starving. Can we please dine?" Countess Vanessa finally asked.

Henri put an arm around each woman and led the way to the dining room. He whispered, "Be careful; you won't be able to eat as much as you are accustomed to eating. Vanessa told me that too. We often dine five times each day as a result."

"Now that is being entirely civilized!" Herr Adelstein broke in. He'd overheard the Count's words and agreed with him. "Now we take High Tea nearly all day long. Such good fun and taste, don't you think, Sir Thomas? We've found like-minded folks. High Tea, here we come."

Leo and Janice served them and then joined them for the light meal. They also met their chef, another cat woman named Leonora, who accepted Vanessa's request to join them at the table as well. Henri pointed out that these were the only servants in the mansion. Most of the rooms went unused, but still had to be cleaned regularly.

Later that evening after the trio and the servants had retired for the night, Henri, Vanessa, and Miranda met in the study once more. "So what's the plan?" asked Vanessa.

"Well, I have not been sleeping with Vanessa these past weeks, though she didn't seem to mind. Of course, Miranda, if you want to sleep with Vanessa or Zed, it is possible that you and I can swap bodies. I believe that I can do that any time you should desire it," Henri or Rose suggested.

Miranda flushed and Vanessa noticed it. "Mom! Don't you dare. We are good friends." Henri chuckled.

"Okay. The plan. Let's meet here in the study tomorrow, and I'll show you what all I have been able to discover about this universe of Montford's." They agreed. Hand in supporting hand, Miranda and Vanessa headed up the stairs to their suite. Janice was in her nightgown and quickly helped the two women out of their dresses and into their own nightgowns.

"You mean we have to sleep in these corsets too?" Miranda complained, knowing this was also what was bothering Vanessa or Zed.

"Wee Madame. If you do not, your own breasts will become larger by morning," Janice replied. Miranda sighed, while Vanessa grumbled and tiptoed into her bedroom.

The next morning Vanessa commented as she finally joined Miranda, "Boy it sure takes a long time to get dressed and all that makeup on in the morning. Oh, Janice has fixed you up as well."

"I hate all this makeup on me, Zed, er Vanessa. Still, there was no talking Janice out of it. Just look at my nails! They are as long as yours! I've never allowed my nails to get anywhere this long, not ever. So darn inconvenient," Miranda complained. "Somehow, they just grew during the night." The two headed down for breakfast and found that the trio and Henri had already dined.

Herr Adelstein announced, "If you have no objections, we three are going to explore the city a bit this morning. We'll be back for High Tea."

Vanessa cautioned them, "That's fine with us, but do try to stay out of trouble."

"Yes, but you two are the rulers. So if we do get in a pickle, you can rescue us," the rabbit declared proudly. Vanessa chuckled and the trio headed out of the dining room. She added for Henri's benefit, "They truly enjoy life and exploring new things."

A half hour later, the three headed into the library to see what all Henri or Rose had already discovered about this world, this universe. Vanessa was not much impressed with his research, however. He or she had already worked out much of what he'd discovered. Able Montford created this world or universe. His postulates ruled above all others. However, they could be twisted or altered, as he had done with the Judge, placing the trio's names onto the list of approved magic users.

Perhaps the most useful data Henri had found was that there were apparently three emergency exits from this world or dimension. One was located in the basement of this very Royal Palace, which he insisted on showing Miranda and

Vanessa. "It looks like a window," Miranda commented as she stood looking at it. She'd opened the double doors which appeared much like the one that they had entered to get here in the first place.

"Yes, dear. Now you know what we are looking for," Henri advised her.

"But do you know if it leads back to our own world, mom, er Henri?" she asked, slightly annoyed with her mother. This was key data that had to be known. If they chose to exit here, where would they wind up? In another strange world? This one was bad enough.

"Sorry dear. I don't know for sure, not having tried it. However, it is supposed to be an emergency exit. How could it not lead home and still be an emergency exit?" Henri replied.

"Say, did Vanessa or the other Henri know about this exit? If they did, why didn't they try to leave that way instead of staying here for a century and a half?" asked Countess Vanessa.

"As far as I know, neither knew of it. Neither spent much time in the library as far as Vanessa said. She was more into all the fancy clothes and such. Have you seen her wardrobe?" Henri asked.

"Yes, this morning. She's got hundreds of outfits. I picked this red one because I like red," Vanessa replied.

"She also said that Henri, the real Henri that is, was really into leading the city and spent most of his time micro-managing the city. I've gotten several compliments about leaving them to run their own affairs," Henri pointed out. Vanessa filed this fact away, thinking it might one day be useful to recall.

"We need a map of this universe or world. How many areas or sections does it have? What is the usual route that visitors travel to get to the proper exit point? We need answers to these questions," Countess Vanessa pointed out.

Henri flushed. "Well, I haven't found out everything about this world yet. Come on; let's see what else can be found in the library." At least he kept his arms around each woman supporting them as they walked.

"Look, we could always step out of the emergency portal and see where we are at and what happens to our bodies," Henri suggested. "If all didn't go well, we could always step back inside via that same portal, don't you think?"

"Mom, I know that you are trying to be helpful, but that is terribly risky. Countless things could go wrong. You and Zed could end up staying in these wrong bodies. We could end up in yet another world with no way to get back to this one. The portals might be one-way affairs."

Countess Vanessa stuck up for Miranda. "It does say exit and not entrance. I'd hate to be stuck in this body for the rest of my life."

Suddenly, Miranda looked up. "Mom! Are you trying to say that you'd like to return to our world like you are now — young again?"

Henri flushed crimson. "Well, you are not fifty years old! My hair was streaked with grey. I've no prospects for a new husband at my age. This is like a new lease on life for me. This new body is strong and robust and so very much alive. Is that so bad to want to start over again? We have enough money to support the both of us for our lives — Vanessa or Zed too for that matter. Besides, this game of his has been inactive for a century and a half now. Who knows if it is still running according to Montford's original designs? We could run around in here forever and still never get out or find our original bodies again. Lord knows where those two went with them."

"Honestly, dear, I was just about to use the exit portal when the gong sounded and Countess Vanessa left. If it hadn't, I was planning to use the exit, find you, and explain all this," Henri admitted. "I guess that is out of the question now, unless. . ." His voice dropped off.

Miranda put her hands on her hips. "Unless what?" she then asked, insisting her mother or Henri finish her statement.

"Unless Vanessa here wishes to come with us and remain a gorgeous young woman. Honestly, you are an amazingly attractive woman. You could get any man you might desire." Henri again stopped short. "Oh, you want Miranda!" Both Vanessa and Miranda flushed.

"Mom!" she gushed.

"Dear, it's only natural that Zed or Vanessa here might want to marry you," Henri stated the obvious. Henri grinned and rose. "I am going to fetch us all some tea. How do you take yours, Zed or Vanessa? Black? Good. Back in a bit." He left the two sitting facing each other across the elegant table.

"You have to forgive mom. She is sometimes way too overt in her thoughts," Miranda tried to find a way to soften what he'd said or implied.

"Look, Miranda. We've known each other only a few days, right? If these have even been real days. However, I have to say that I really do like you quite a lot. I promised to help you rescue your mother, and I still stand by that. I gave you my word and I won't break it. We've found her and I can see her point; she thinks that this will give her a whole new lifetime to live. Perhaps we should not be so insistent that she give up that dream. Maybe that was one reason she came through the portal alone."

"But you are stuck in the countess' body. Surely you don't want that. Okay, Zed, Vanessa, if you want to give mom this chance and you still want me, I will go along with you. I really do like you too, more so than anyone else that I've ever met. I suppose that we can make it work out somehow, but are you really sure that you want to sacrifice everything for mom?"

Vanessa smiled, "I've never been this happy around another person in my life than this time I've spent with you, Miranda. If your mom wants this chance, I say let's allow her the opportunity. Later on, I can always come back through the portal in your house and try to track down my body somehow."

"I could kiss you! Thank you! Yes, I promise you that once we have mom taken care of, you and I can return here and try to sort out this mess — that is, if you still want your body back. Honestly, you are a knock out — your new body, I mean." She moved over to Vanessa and the two shared her thank-you kiss. Unfortunately, at that moment, Henri entered carrying a tray with their tea. Both flushed and returned to their seats, while Henri poured out their tea.

"Mom, we've been talking. We have decided that if you want to try the exit portal now, we will go with you. If you want to have the chance to be young again, we both will back you up. Only don't you dare interfere with our relationship, however it may go. Zed or Vanessa here is the best person I've ever met since dad. You must promise us that you will not interfere with us in anyway." Later, Vanessa told Miranda that Henri's eyes seemed to radiate happiness and joy when she told her that they would allow her to use the exit portal and have a whole new lifetime to live.

"Miranda, I give you my solemn word that I will never interfere with your happiness. This is almost too good! After we drink our tea, let's return to our world!" Miranda grinned at Vanessa, who returned it. Henri hugged Miranda.

A short while later, he led the two into the basement and to the concealed portal. Henri opened the double doors.

"Okay, we just lean into the window, and we'll be transported back. I'll go first. You two follow me. Again, thank you both, thank you!" Henri leaned into the portal window, and as the two watched, his body was sucked into the window and vanished.

"Here goes nothing," Miranda said. "Thanks Zed or Vanessa. Are you ready?"

"Yes, but I seriously doubt that this is going to work out the way that your mother is expecting. This Montford guy has been both creative and a tad sadistic. I don't think that this is going to be what your mother really wishes it to be. Nevertheless, let's get going." Holding hands, the two leaned into the portal. Again, Zed felt like he was falling through empty space. Miranda began to think of stairs and they appeared. She and Vanessa then began to carefully and slowly descend them, arriving back in Miranda's home not five feet from the portal through which they had entered.

"Well, I still have a woman's body and the same clothing on," Vanessa declared, feeling her body carefully.

"Me too. I've still got the same dress on too. Come on. Let's find mom, er dad. What am I going to call her now? I can't call her dad. She's going to be only a couple years older than I am."

"How about your older brother?" Vanessa suggested as the two made their slow way into the kitchen where they heard some noise.

"Thanks again, you two! Just look at me! I'm barely over twenty-one, fit as a fiddle. Vanessa, go look at yourself in our full length mirror. You are a real knockout. You too, dear. You look positively smashing in that dress. You should dress up like this far more often. I am making tea. Oh, you must have had a pizza. Shall I order a pizza? Yes, I am famished." Henri rattled on and Miranda smiled. She led Vanessa to their fancy mirror.

"You do look ravishing," Vanessa commented. Miranda flushed.

"Yes, but look at yourself. If I am ravishing, then you are a goddess or something."

"Not with boobs as big as my head," Vanessa replied. Both chuckled.

"More of you to love," Miranda teased her. "Come on, I am dying to get out of this horrible double corset thing. I bet you are too. Too bad that you will have to continue wearing those heels. Your feet don't go flat, right?" The two headed to Miranda's bedroom.

"Well, since we are both women, I guess we can help each other undress. I've got some tee-shirts and jeans we can change into," she explained. Vanessa had a challenging time getting Miranda out of her clothing. Her long nails continually interfered. Finally, Miranda was free of both corsets. "Now that is vastly better! I can breathe again." She slipped into a tee-shirt and jeans.

Next, she began to help Vanessa out of her outfit. However, once the inner waist only corset was removed, Vanessa collapsed. "My god, I can't support myself! My stomach muscles are so incredibly weak!"

"Damn! I guess there was a reason that Vanessa was always wearing the corsets." Try as she might, Miranda couldn't quite get Vanessa back into her outfit. Her long nails interfered and she had not the strength to pull the laces tight enough. At last, she had to have Henri come and lend a hand. A half hour later, Vanessa was finally back into her outfit. "Well that was a shocker, Vanessa. Sorry about that."

"Janice mentioned something about this. Now I know what she meant by having to help me bathe. I suppose in time and with some exercises I can get stronger."

"Pizza will be here in a couple of minutes," Henri announced.

"Take Vanessa with you. I'm going to cut off these infernal long nails," Miranda suggested. She'd just finished when the pizza arrived, and she met the man at the door.

The three ate their fill, but Vanessa found that with her nails, she couldn't readily open her Coke can. Miranda grinned and opened it for her. "I can cut yours later on, if you like." The three chatted.

As the hour grew late, Vanessa asked, "Where am I going to sleep? I am so tired."

"With me. Come on; you deserve it," Miranda teased her, leading her off to her bedroom.

"No tricks this time. I don't think I can handle an upside down bedroom at the moment. Not in these heels and dress," Vanessa teased her back.

Vanessa slept poorly in her tight corsets and was aroused by a loud cry coming from what had been Miranda's mother's bedroom. Miranda rose sleepily and the two got out of bed. While Vanessa struggled to get her heels on, Miranda dashed off to see what was wrong with her mother. Just as Vanessa got her shoes on and rose, she heard Miranda's screams too. She headed after her as fast as she dared go.

Nothing could have prepared her for the sight. The young Henri had changed during the night. A heavily wrinkled old man stared up at them from his bed! He was crying. Miranda was also crying but for a different reason. "Look at them!" she pointed to her own breasts. They had doubled in size over night!

"I thought you cut your nails last night," Vanessa said, thinking the simplest thing seemed to be the path of least upset to Miranda.

"I did. Now look at them! They are even longer than yours! Look at mom! She's an old man now! We've got to get her back into that world right away!"

"No, we have to get you and her dressed first. If you wait much longer, your boobs will become as large as mine. Come on. Back to your room. I hope between us, we can get you back into your dress," Vanessa ordered. It took them nearly an hour to do it. What surprised both of them was that the bodice top magically enlarged to fit Miranda's much bigger bosom. Finally, they got Henri up and dressed. He could barely walk. The three stuffed themselves with leftover pizza and then headed to the portal on their wall.

"I'll go first with mom, er Henri. See if you can manage by yourself this time. Just remember to think steps." Miranda helped Henri lean and soon both vanished. Vanessa sighed and followed after them. Once more, she began falling in the vacuum of utter nothingness. This time, she focused on making steps. At last they appeared and she concentrated on landing on them. Smiling over her success, she began her slow descent. Before long, she stepped out into the basement that they had left the night before.

Countess Vanessa was surprised to see Janice was there talking to Miranda. "Ah there you are, countess. We wondered where you had gone. Come; let me fix you both up. Your hair needs brushing and you need a change of dress. Henri can manage on his own." Vanessa glanced at Henri. Miracles happen, she thought. His youthful body had magically returned. The old man was gone, and she saw that both Miranda and Henri looked immensely relieved. Vanessa smiled; she had had a hunch that this plan of Henri's would not work, and she'd been right. There was a whole lot more to this strange world of Able Montford. Somehow, they have to finish this game, if a game it actually was.

A couple of hours later, bathed and in a dress of her own choosing, Countess Vanessa finally joined the others in the study. She'd searched through the hundreds of dresses and chosen this cherry red, full length satin gown that hugged her curves. A small walking slit allowed her to take her usual small steps. It matched her nails and the lipstick that Janice carefully applied.

"Wow, you look hot!" Miranda teased her as she entered the study.

"You are not bad yourself, Miranda," she replied. Miranda had chosen a sky blue satin gown that exposed most of her long legs, currently covered with a black nylon hose. Miranda flushed slightly.

"I'm truly sorry, Zed or Vanessa," Henri or Rose interrupted the two women. "I have no way to justify what I just put us all through. Folly of an old woman."

"I can understand, Rose — er Henri. Gosh, this is still so confusing. Why don't we just call me Vanessa until I get my body back, and I'll call you Henri."

"Deal Vanessa. I really am sorry for my silliness. On the other hand, Vanessa, I just wanted to tell you that you have really impressed me. You were willing to give up everything to help my daughter, who you barely know, and me as well. I just want you to know that from now on, I will do everything I possibly can to get you your body back and us all safely out of this mess," Henri said, quite seriously.

"Thanks Henri. I had a feeling that it would not be so simple as just using the emergency exit. I guess one could go back to fetch something that one desperately needed, like medications or something. Where do we even begin to look next?" Countess Vanessa replied and asked.

"We'd best look through this whole library. Mom, er Henri, has found some clues. There must be more to be found. Surely something will clue us in on what our next move must be," Miranda declared, more hoping this would be true than she actually felt about it. "Henri, you are going to have to fetch the books higher up for us. We will have a devil of a time doing that in these dresses." He smiled and thus the search began. Clues, hints, ideas — somehow the three had to figure out just what and where they needed to go next.

Hours passed. Books came and went. Vanessa found herself playing with her long hair, thinking hard. "Look, Miranda. After we arrived the first time, we met the trio and one thing sort of led to the next. Then, we followed your mom's trail to the ants and hence onto the Malbon Express and here. Surely that was the route that new 'guests' to this world were meant to follow."

"I agree, but where does that get us? Are we to wait here until other 'guests' come to this universe and allow us to swap bodies with them?" she asked with a hint of rejection in her voice. "I can't imagine spending a century dressed up like this with my whole life on hold. I feel badly for the real Countess Vanessa and Count Henri, but I don't want to stick around that long. Besides, my breasts haven't shrunk yet."

Vanessa chuckled, "At least yours are not monsters like mine." Miranda cracked a smile and Vanessa continued, "I don't want to wait that long either. No, there must be other ways of proceeding. The previous Count and Countess just didn't discover those other ways. Surely Able Montford didn't plan to have his guests wait here for an eternity for other guests to arrive. Besides, how did those two know where to head off to next? I say that there must be clues here for us to find — at least the clues that they are following. We just have to be smarter, Miranda. We must be missing something vital in all this. I can't help but think that this Able fellow must have made provisions for those who got this far to discover what they needed to do next and where they needed to go. Perhaps it is only a step at a time, but there has to be a clue here. We just are not seeing it yet."

"She's right, daughter. Able must have left clues for those who got this far to know how to proceed and quite possibly a way to proceed without waiting for more guests to arrive for body snatching. It doesn't make sense that the only way that we can proceed is to wait until others enter this strange universe of his. After all, he must have known that at some point people would stop entering and thus trapping all those who had entered before and not yet exited from Malbon," Henri backed up Vanessa. Miranda smiled; her mother was finally back to battery, thinking the way that she was used to having her mother think.

Hours passed until at last, Vanessa held up a map. "Gang, look what I just found! A map! Here's where we landed; here's the train route," she traced out the rail line with her long nails. "And here is Malbon down here. Gosh, there is a whole lot more world out there to explore."

"We should make a copy of it and leave this original here for others who might come after us," Miranda suggested. "Make copy!" she declared with full intention.

Vanessa grinned. "How did you do that one?" A duplicate map suddenly appeared in Miranda's hand.

"Oh my daughter is *good*!" Henri added, very much impressed as well.

"My postulate held. You have to have confidence that your postulate will stick and it does," she replied with a smile. "Good work dear. Now we have some idea of the universe here. Let's keep at it, everyone. There has to be more. This doesn't tell us where to go next."

Though they spent the rest of the day searching, nothing more showed up. Later that evening when Miranda and Vanessa retired to their suite, Miranda moved close to Vanessa. "I want to thank you for all that you've done for me and mom. You do look really hot in red, you know. And satin feels so soft on our fingers." She pressed her body close to Vanessa's and kissed her. "Thank you, Zed." She whispered, "Come sleep with me tonight." Vanessa didn't hesitate.

Though they spent the next four days searching for more clues, none turned up. On the sixth day, Herr Adelstein began complaining, "I say, countess, are you going to spend all your time inside this mansion? We three have been all over this huge city. There is a lot to do out there."

"Okay, I can take a hint. Henri, can you ask Janice or Leo if it is permitted for us to go out for a walk with our friends here?" asked Vanessa. Shortly, Miranda and Vanessa, holding onto each other for support, followed their friends out into the city proper.

"Do you realize that we have so far counted fifty different kinds of people?" Herr Adelstein pointed out.

"Oh yes indeed. That includes the centaur, cat women, and lion," Sir Thomas added. "Gee, you move as slowly as Albert does."

"Can't be helped, Sir Thomas. These heels slow us way down and our legs won't permit us to wear sensible shoes any longer," Vanessa pointed out. "Besides, we can see more if we go slowly."

"We should go on one of those vacations," Albert spoke up.

"What are you talking about?" growled the rabbit.

"Look there. Those signs. They are everywhere," Albert pointed to a large billboard just across the bustling street. "Take a vacation today. Visit the Badlands. Perhaps that is what we should do next, only I don't know what a vacation is. Do you, Herr Adelstein?"

"Hum, everyone knows what a vacation is," the rabbit growled. "It's where you go to have fun."

"But aren't we having fun here? I mean, we did tag along with those two to see the world and have fun, didn't we?" asked Albert. He added quickly, "But then perhaps that is all wrong. You know that I am always wrong."

"No, Albert you are not always wrong. We did come along to have some fun and sort of escape from our grasslands," Herr Adelstein replied, admitting a little of their true motivations in following the two.

"That's it! Albert, you are a genius. That's the next clue, Miranda. We are to go to the Badlands! I'll bet anything that's where the real count and countess headed for after they swapped bodies with us!" Countess Vanessa declared, showing a good deal of excitement.

"Hurrump!" Herr Adelstein stuck up his nose. That Vanessa called Albert a genius annoyed him. After all, Albert was always wrong, but not always, he mused, tweaking his long nose hairs.

"By golly, you might be right! The clue has been staring us in our faces all this time. I wonder if we can actually go to the Badlands without swapping bodies first?" Miranda asked.

An hour later, they re-entered the Royal Palace and told Henri of their discovery. He too became enthused. "Okay, I am leaving it up to you to make inquires to see if we are allowed to take a little vacation," Vanessa said to him, pointing a long red nail at him for emphasis. Henri smiled and agreed.

Over dinner, he broached the topic with Leo and Janice. "My wife and I want to take a little vacation to the Badlands. You know, the advertisements are all over the city on the billboards. I've got the city managers handling the affairs of Malbon very well now. Is it permitted for us to take a little vacation?"

"Well, I suppose so, though you will need to go by carriage. It is far too distant for the women folk to walk," Leo said slowly, pawing at his mane.

"But the Madames will need me to come with them to help them with their needs," Janice pointed out. Vanessa did not doubt her sincerity. Janice had a nightly and morning ritual that she followed without fail. Besides, she knew that she had no idea how to put on makeup, and constricted as she was, getting dressed was awkward without Janice. Then there was her long hair that had to be constantly brushed out, several times a day.

"Perhaps you can drive us. Leo and Janice can come along with us. You two also need a vacation," Countess Vanessa suggested.

Janice looked at Leo and he, her. "When was the last time you both had a vacation?" Vanessa asked, knowing well that they probably had never had one before. "After all, the city signs say that we ought to all take a vacation to the Badlands."

"Well, as long as you women stay properly attired," Janice gave in.

"Of course, we must look our best," Countess Vanessa declared, much to the relief of Janice. "We *so* do depend upon you, Janice — to look our best. Without you, we would look just awful." The cat woman smiled, and Vanessa thought that she even heard a faint purring sound!

Henri spoke up, "Then that's settled. We all shall go on a vacation as soon as we can get ready. Tomorrow, Leo and I will make inquiries — you know, how to get there, how long the travel time will be, and such. You ladies, pack your finest dresses. You too, Janice. Prepare for a fun vacation." Leo and Janice smiled.

The next day, Janice complained, "But Madame, you are packing only red dresses."

"Of course, Janice. I am now in my red dress phase." The cat woman smiled and accepted this explanation and continued to pack a dozen cherry red dresses and matching heels. Miranda packed a dozen blue dresses, but not all the same shade of blue.

The night before their planned departure, Miranda, who now slept in Vanessa's bed with her, asked, "What can happen to our bodies if we leave here? I'm worried about mom, er Henri."

"I know, dear. What if he suddenly ages again? If so, we can order Leo to return us here at once, and he should be all right. I don't think that is going to happen. The signs must be the clue. We are meant to go to the Badlands, perhaps not with these bodies though. I do hope our breasts don't grow more or our nails, for that matter."

"Me either. It is tough managing to get around in the heels we are forced to wear. I hope they don't get any higher or we will be walking on our toes like ballerinas," Miranda replied and snuggled up close to Vanessa.

# Chapter 6 The Badlands

"Why don't you ride topside with Leo, Janice? That way, you can see the scenery as well. I'll sit with the countess and her new friends," Count Henri suggested. He'd just helped the two women aboard. He and Leo had previously stowed numerous suitcases of clothing and incidentals onto the back of the Royal Carriage. It was now time to depart.

"Are you sure?" Janice asked timidly. Henri sensed her eagerness to really see the countryside, and he helped her up and watched her broad smile as she joined Leo in the driver's box. He hopped inside, latched the door, knocked once, and the group was off on their vacation to the Badlands.

Miranda squeezed Vanessa's hand and gave her an appreciative smile. Zed or rather Vanessa had worked out their next move, and she wanted to validate him or her for that. Vanessa returned her smile. Together, although still uncomfortable, the two watched as the city passed them by. "I wonder if they had any theaters, movies, or dances in the city?" Vanessa inquired.

The trio sat across from the humans. Herr Adelstein answered first, "Dances — yes. We visited several, but they only allow certain individuals into them. We snuck into one, though. Rather boring, no tea."

"Oh yes, yes we did. I was petrified that we would get caught," Sir Thomas quickly added. "Such body gyrations. Oh my."

"Well, they did seem to be having fun, but I might be misinterpreting that," Albert said in his sad monotone.

"Well, I would have liked to have visited some. Just curious, you know," Vanessa replied.

"Say, this is more like it!" Sir Thomas exclaimed. The city had dropped behind them. Rolling grasslands dotted with huge oak trees replaced the throngs and stone buildings of Malbon. "Just look at the nut trees. Do you suppose that we could stop and take High Tea among these trees?"

Now in great spirits, Henri knocked and called out, "Let's take a break among these trees and have High Tea." Leo promptly obeyed, pulling the Royal Carriage over. The trio bounded playfully out first. By the time that Henri had helped the two women down, Herr Adelstein was busy conjuring their table and chairs, while Sir Thomas conjured their table cloth and dishes. Albert was busily conjuring up the tea. Hence, all that Henri had to do was escort the women to their chairs, returning to the carriage to assist Janice down.

"Mighty fine day for a High Tea!" Sir Thomas declared as everyone finally got seated properly and Albert passed the tea pot around. "I don't suppose that you 'umans will want acorns with your tea. Herr Adelstein and Albert certainly do not." He already had a huge pile sitting beside his tea cup. Instead butter cakes appeared before the others.

"Why thank you three gentlemen for setting us a fine High Tea," Countess Vanessa praised the trio, who puffed up, looking very pleased with their contribution.

"I've never seen the countryside," Janice spoke up. "It is really so pretty out here. Thank you ever so much for inviting me along with you!"

"It is the very least that we can do to thank you for caring for our needs all these years," Countess Vanessa replied diplomatically. Miranda gave her a big smile and thought, *Zed really is something.*

That night they stayed at a quaint inn in a small town that was about halfway to the Badlands. Late afternoon of the next day they paused at the rim of the Badlands. A tourist inn sat perched on the very edge overlooking the spectacular view. Stretching out for miles lay the Badlands. Deep canyons cut through the landscape, revealing seven different colored layers of sedimentary soils. The topmost one was reddish. The deepest one was indigo. "I say, this is the pattern of a rainbow!" Countess Vanessa declared, very much surprised.

"Why, I have never seen anything so beautiful before!" Janice gushed, thoroughly enthralled with the view.

"Neither have I," Leo added his enthusiasm to hers. All eight stood beside their carriage gazing out over the Badlands. To their right lay the tourist inn.

"Where are all the trees?" asked Sir Thomas. "I fear that we will be in trouble since there are no trees down there." He began to grow a bit nervous once more.

"No grasslands either," Herr Adelstein added.

"That can't be a good sign, can it? I never know which way to say it though," Albert added his opinion to the mix.

"Well it is beautiful to see," Countess Vanessa pointed out.

A nearby voice interrupted them. "Yes, it is beautiful to see, but dangerous to visit. That's why we have placed the tourist inn here on the rim where it is safe. Homer Watson, at your service," the giant rat wearing a tuxedo bowed to them. He'd already removed his top hat. "I assume that you will be staying at our fine inn? If not, the trail head is clearly marked over yonder. If you chose to go down into the Badlands for a closer look, please do not stray from the path."

"Yes, we will be staying at your inn," Count Henri announced. "However, let's go take a closer look at the path first. Leo, you and Janice may carry our things inside and arrange for our rooms. Nothing but the finest for all of us, including you two, mind you."

"Yes sir!" Leo exclaimed, very much pleased with this offer of elegance. The rat also seemed very pleased with Henri's proclamation, though it most likely meant more money coming in, Vanessa thought.

As the six ambled over to the path with Henri supporting both women who found walking on the uneven ground in their heels immensely challenging, a strange thing happened. As they approached the start of the path, suddenly Zed's male body began moving out of his female body. Likewise, Rose's female body moved out of Henri's body. Even Miranda found her body moving out of the one that she currently had, though her big change was that her bosom returned to normal along with her fingernails.

"What the devil?" exclaimed Zed in his own voice. He stopped and looked back at his Countess Vanessa body, which had stopped dead in her tracks, along with Henri and Miranda's Malbon bodies. He saw Rose standing three feet from Henri's body; her mouth was open, but no words came out. "This is really weird!"

"Wow, look at the 'umans!" Herr Adelstein exclaimed. "Now there is two of each of them. Fascinating."

"Hey, Zed. There's your Zed body," Sir Thomas pointed out the obvious.

"Oh dear me. Now they have two bodies each. Can you teach me how to do that trick?" asked an impressed Albert.

"Hey, this is really me!" Zed exclaimed, feeling his arms, legs, and head.

"Mom! It's you again," Miranda called out. "Are you all right?"

The fifty year old woman felt her body much as Zed was doing. Apparently satisfied, she grinned, "You bet! This is incredible."

"Hey, I wonder what happens if I walk back," Zed broke in. He slowly walked back and while the others watched, his

Zed body seemed to vanish into his Countess Vanessa body, leaving only the elegantly dressed woman in red standing there looking towards the rim and path down into the Badlands. Zed walked back towards the path and out his body came once more.

"Hey, I get it. If we head down the path, we get our real bodies back. If we do not, we get to keep our other bodies. This is pretty darn cool. Try it Rose. You too, Miranda. What a weird sensation it is to walk out of your body like this!" Zed proclaimed. For a minute, the trio moved in and out of their Malbon bodies, and then all three broke into a hearty laugh.

"Well, tomorrow when we set out down into the Badlands, we will be back to our normal selves!" Henri declared. "Zed, Vanessa, thank you! Thank you!" Vanessa smiled as the six headed slowly back to the inn for dinner and a good night's sleep.

Over a delicious meal, Miranda suggested that they make inquiries about what to expect down in the Badlands and what provisions they ought to take. Henri took charge and did just that. Later in their rooms, he explained what little he had learned.

"Well, Homer was not too helpful. Apparently it is dangerous to stray from the path. He suggested that we take along a lot of water, since he is unaware of any fresh water down in the canyons. Other than that, he provided little useful information, save that it can be dangerous down there. Pretty yes, safe, no."

"Well, it *is* called the Badlands," Vanessa teased them. All chuckled.

The next day, Henri purchased six small backpacks and stuffed them full of water. He had Homer's staff carry them to the trail head for them. Around nine, the six headed out of the inn for the next leg of their adventure. Leo and Janice waved good bye to them and waited for their two charges to return. Once more as the three drew close to the path down into the canyon land, their real bodies magically slipped out of their Malbon ones.

Zed announced, "Okay, Countess Vanessa, you may return to the inn now and enjoy the rest of your vacation." Miranda gave him a queer look as did Rose. To their amazement, Countess Vanessa waved goodbye and turned to make her way back to Janice and Leo. Hastily, Miranda and Rose said similar words to their other bodies and they too headed back towards the inn. Interestingly enough, Miranda's Malbon body promptly vanished from sight when it reached Leo and Janice. "Curious!" Zed exclaimed.

"No kidding. It is like I didn't exist in Malbon, yet I did," Miranda replied.

"Well, Mrs. Whitney, you look just like Miranda's photograph of you. Glad that we've got you sort of rescued," Zed said encouragingly.

"If I must speak the truth, I am rather glad to be back in my own body, old as it is. Still, it is mine and I am comfortable with it, though I was having fun with that young man's body. What an interesting experience this has been," Rose admitted.

"We still have to find our way out of this universe, mom. Come on; we have to head down into the canyons of the Badlands. Remember that we are not to stray from the path. I do hope it stays as clearly marked as it is here at the start," Miranda declared.

"What can possibly go wrong?" Herr Adelstein asked rhetorically. No one dared answer him. All donned their water packs, and with Zed taking the lead, they headed down the steep path into the rainbow landscape.

"It is incredibly pretty from a distance, but it's awfully dry when up close," Zed announced, raising a small reddish dust cloud as his feet slipped a little. Down the six went into the heart of the Badlands.

It was hot. It was dry. It was sweaty, but it was beautiful. "These colored layers are incredible!" Miranda exclaimed as they took a rest break to drink and wipe the perspiration from their faces and necks. Already Zed and Miranda's tee-shirts were soaked with sweat. The others faired equally poorly. "I wonder where we are to go?"

"I don't know, but we are certainly on the right path," Zed replied. Still, he had a bad feeling if only from the name of this place, Badlands. The distinct lack of water could possibly be why he felt uneasy about their trip, but Zed just didn't think it would be this simple. However, he wisely chose to keep his misgivings to himself.

"True. I am so glad that we have our own bodies back again. Could you imagine us trying to walk this in those high heels?" Miranda teased him. Both laughed and the group set out again. They reached the canyon floor and now found the going much easier, following a dry stream bed.

"You don't suppose that there will be an inn ahead of us?" Rose asked. Already her thoughts began to focus on mealtimes. They had skipped lunch and would certainly need to come up with something at suppertime. Thus far, they'd seen no one at all and no plant or animal life either. Rather discouraging, Rose thought. Surely something must be down here.

"I am glad that I brought my house with me. Come nightfall, I will have a place to sleep," Albert commented from the rear of the line.

Zed grinned and called back, "You might well be the smartest of us all. I could use a nice bed pretty soon. This is tiring. Still, it is very pretty. I wonder what makes the soil here indigo?" No one had an answer for that one.

By suppertime, all six were dragging! They were soaked with sweat, exhausted, and hungry, though they still had some water reserves fortunately. "What I wouldn't give for a nice bath and meal about now!" Rose declared. "I am too out of shape for such grueling hiking." Miranda smiled, her mother was right about that point. She often had tried to get her mother to take up some form of exercise at the YMCA but she hadn't. Always too busy was her excuse, and now she was paying the piper.

"I don't suppose that is really an inn ahead of us," Albert called out from the rear. Everyone else was staring at the ground beneath their feet, dragging their bodies along step by step.

"Albert! You are right, old fellow. That is an inn of sorts," Zed called back. Ahead of them was a single story wooden building. It looked a bit rundown and weatherbeaten, but a faded sign read: Badlands Inn. "Hope they have a bath or we will need six different rooms!" Everyone chuckled, but that was the truth. The six marched on up to the main doors and Zed opened them. Peering inside, he saw what appeared to be an old western style dining room, lit by a number of oil lanterns hanging from a giant wagon wheel suspended from the ceiling. An old man was asleep behind the bar counter.

"Excuse me, sir. Can we get rooms for the night?" Zed asked, while the others crowded around him trying to peek inside.

He stirred, "What's that you say? Speak louder, kind of hard of hearing," the man said. Zed repeated his question. "Sure enough! Don't have many visitors here. Come on in out of the hot sun." He got to his feet and straightened out his shirt which was so heavily patched that Zed could not tell for sure what its original color might have been. "Howdy partners. Jest call me Pecos. How many are ya? Come on in all of ya."

As they filed in, a registration book suddenly appeared before Pecos. "Come on in and sign the guest log. Got a room fer each of ya. Bath too. You be a want'n some supper I expect. Well, ya get ya-selves signed in and bathed while I rustles up some grub. Mighty hungry, I expect." Pecos seemed friendly enough, Zed thought, though he was still a bit uneasy about finding this inn precisely where they most assuredly needed it. Then again, perhaps that was by design, placed where adventurers on foot would likely need it at the end of a day's travel.

The old man moved slowly, taking them down a dimly lit hall whose side lanterns had not been cleaned in ages. Lamp black was so thick that barely any light came out. Each room had a wash barrel, clean bedding, and towels. "Jest say 'fill'er up' and the barrels fill up. Say 'Empty barrel' and the barrels empty out the dirty waters. Bit'o magic here. Supper's in an hour, thereabouts." After showing each of the six to their own room, he left them to bathe while he ambled off to fix supper.

Pecos was the only person working at the inn. That much Zed managed to get out of him. Curious, he thought, only one old man. Then again, there probably were not many visitors here, he justified. Zed enjoyed the bath immensely and took time to wash out his sweaty clothes, having discovered some clean clothes laid out on the western style bed. He liked the new shirt; it had snaps instead of buttons. The jeans fit well and he wondered how Pecos could possibly have known his size. Again, he chalked this up to "magic."

When he headed out to the dining area, he saw that the others had also washed out their clothes and were wearing the provided western garb. While the plaid western shirts varied slightly in color, all of the jeans were identical, except for size of course. Albert did not need the clothes, however, but he donned his top hat. Not to be outdone, Herr Adelstein conjured his top hat as well, followed at once by Sir Thomas procuring his. "Must appear civilized. These spare clothes are pretty crude," Herr Adelstein declared gruffly.

They found that they were the only guests in the dining room, though Pecos joined them. "Serve ya-selves 'round here," he explained and they all did just that. The meal was a hearty stew, one course only. However, Pecos provided a pot of strong tea and lemonade which hit the spot. Pecos was not big on table talk they soon found out. In fact, he fell asleep twice during the meal, and Zed carefully wakened him each time. "Jest leave the dishes. I'll get'em in the mornin. Spect you be most tired. Have a good sleep."

Indeed they were all quite tired and once they finished eating, they headed to their rooms. Zed collapsed onto his bed. He found it quite comfortable and soon fell asleep, wearing his clothes and with his room's lantern still on. At first, he slept soundly. Then he began to have nightmares. In fact, it was the same nightmare that he often had as a small child. He was on a battlefield somewhere. Boom! An artillery shell landed near him and he felt a hideous pain in both of his arms before passing out. A bit later he awoke in a hospital somewhere. The smell caused him to gag involuntarily at which point he felt utter panic! His arms were gone, replaced by thick bandages. Well, that was a slight exaggeration on his part. He still had about four inches of his upper arms remaining. He passed out again and woke later on. Zed was in a small private room now. He looked at his pink stumps which had healed and was overwhelmed by his utter and complete helplessness. He screamed. Somewhere in the back of his mind, Zed realized that he had not had this childhood dream for over fifteen years now. Yet it had come back again to haunt him.

Screams! Zed heard more screams. Was he still dreaming? Suddenly, he realized that in his nightmares, it was only his own screams that he heard. Now he was actually hearing many others screaming. Was that Miranda's voice? With a supreme effort, Zed forced himself fully awake. Then, he too screamed again. Sitting up in his bed, he looked at his two short arms. Each was barely four inches long! He was utterly and totally helpless now. "This can't be real!" he screamed and struggled to get out of bed. Purposely, he kicked the bed with his foot. "Ouch! Damn, damn, that hurts! What is happening to me? I'm living my worst fear! Help me, someone help me!" he cried out. In return, he heard the terrified screams from his other companions. His stomach knotted tightly. No help would be coming. What had Pecos done to him while he slept? How long had he been "asleep?" It had to be months for his arms to have healed so completely!

That was definitely Miranda's high pitched screams. "She's in trouble too! I have to help her somehow, but how? I am so utterly helpless like this!" He moaned and began crying. Still Miranda continued to scream for help; she sounded desperate. Finally, Zed forgot about his own predicament and walked to his door. It had a latch. Using his foot, he struggled with it and at last got it opened. Stepping into the hallway, he heard screaming coming from all of the rooms where his companions were sleeping. "Damn! Damn! Damn! Coming," he called out and walked to the room in which Miranda was staying. Again, he cursed his helplessness and used his foot to attempt to open her door. After a long struggle, he finally got the latch moved and pushed his way inside.

She had fallen asleep with her lantern on as well. Zed thought that was fortuitous, since he no longer could light it. He moved to her bedside. Miranda was sitting up, holding her enlarged belly, and screaming wildly. "I'm here, Miranda. Calm down. What's wrong, dear? It's me, Zed."

She stopped screaming and sort of turned her head towards him. "I can't see! My eyes! I'm totally blind. I'm in labor. The baby is coming and it hurts so. I can feel it! I am going to die giving birth! Help me, help me, please Zed!"

His stomach knotted again. He moved closer and saw that her eyes were now mere grey balls; something had totally ruined her eyes. "My god, Miranda! What's happened to your eyes? They are gone, just grey balls!"

"I don't know! I can't see. Oh, it hurts so! Something is wrong with the baby. Please help me, Zed."

"Miranda, you can't be pregnant. We've not had sex."

"Yes, I am. I can feel it. Can't you see how big I am?" she wailed.

"Er, Miranda, I can't feel it. I don't have any arms anymore. I'm totally helpless."

"Huh? Where are you?" Her arms groped about and he moved so she could reach him. She fumbled about, feeling what was left of his arms. "Oh my god! You don't have any arms! Oh god! The pain. Look and tell me what is wrong." She pulled the covers off and slid her pants down.

"Well, Miranda, you are right! You look like you are nine months along! How is this possible? Damn, I can't do a thing to help you, dear. Hang on a bit longer. I will see if I can get your mother in here. Maybe she knows a thing or two about child birthing."

"Okay, please hurry! It hurts so bad! I must be dying!"

"I will; take deep breaths and try to relax a little. I'll be back as soon as I can." He headed back out of the door into the hall. Which room was Rose in? He heard her screaming and moved to her door. Once more, he struggled with his foot to get her door opened and stepped inside.

"Rose! Rose! It's me, Zed. Are you all right?" He saw that she too had fallen asleep leaving her lantern on. He made a mental note of this anomaly and moved to her bedside wondering why she was so upset and crying. Zed soon found out!

Rose sat on the edge of her bed. Her body appeared to be in its late eighties! Her hair had turned grey; her face was full of heavy wrinkles. Her hands were curled; arthritis had taken a horrible toll on her. She moaned, "I am so alone. I am dying and there is no one to be with me. My life is a total failure. I can't even remember my own name anymore. I can't use my hands. I can hardly walk. I can't even care for my own needs any longer. Here I am dying as an unwanted old maid who doesn't even know her own name. I am beyond pathetic!" She broke into another sobbing fit.

"Damn!" he said and then sat down beside the aged woman. "Rose. Your name is Rose. You have a beautiful daughter in the next room. She really needs you now, Rose."

"Who are you? Am I Rose? I don't know that name. Have I ever heard it before? Who are you?"

"I am Zed, a good friend of Miranda. She's your daughter. Miranda really needs you right now. Please, you must come and help her, Rose."

"I don't have a daughter. I am an old spinster maid, forsaken by the whole wide world. I don't know any Zed. What kind of a name is that?"

"I think it may be German. Anyway, let's just call you Rose, since you don't know your name. How do you like Rose?"

"Well, I don't know. I suppose that it is better than no name at all. I don't have any children."

"Good, I'll call you Rose then. Let's pretend that you have a daughter called Miranda. Can you do that? This young woman needs your help. She is blind and is giving birth and is in great pain. Can you at least come and take a look at her? Maybe you can talk with her and give her womanly support in her time of need. What say you, Rose? Can you do that?

You can lean on me. I don't have any arms, but I can walk and support you."

"I suppose that I can talk to her. I don't know anything about child birthing. It seems the only thing I can do is talk a bit. Okay, I can pretend. My hands are useless now, but I can use you to steady me. Walking is to painful and treacherous, you know. Arthritis." With a great effort, Rose managed to get to her feet, pulling heavily on Zed in the process. She took tiny, shuffling steps but the two made progress. A few minutes later, she sat down on the bed beside Miranda.

"I've brought Rose to you, Miranda. You can feel her. She is about eighty plus years old, crippled with arthritis, and her memory is not so good, but she is willing to help you through this," Zed explained. He watched her blindly feeling for Rose and then using her hands, getting the shape of the woman.

"Oh dear me, child. You are so very pregnant aren't you?" Rose said sympathetically.

"Yes, it is time for the baby to come, but something is horribly wrong. It hurts so bad, and I can't see what's wrong. Can you see for me? Can you help me?" Miranda pleaded with every fiber of her being. Zed fought hard to keep from crying himself. The screams and shouts from the other rooms tore his attention off of her plight.

"I have to see what is wrong with the others, Miranda. Back soon." He left and headed to find out why Albert was screaming. He sounded as if he were in intense pain. Again using his foot, he managed to eventually get Albert's door open, and the tortoise's screams were now almost deafening. He saw Albert sitting on his bed, eyes closed, screaming wildly.

"Albert! Albert! What's wrong? It's Zed."

"Are you blind? They are boiling me alive! They are making soup out of me! God the pain! I can't take much more of this! Help me, help me!"

Zed looked around the room and saw nothing at all out of place. There was no pot and no fires. No one was cooking him alive. In a flash of insight, Zed saw a way out of the mess. "Albert. You trust me, don't you?"

"Yes! The pain! I am burning up! I don't want to be soup!"

"Good. Albert. You know that you are always wrong, don't you. You remember telling me that many times. Right?"

"Yes, I am. But the pain, Zed, I can't take it any longer. I am going to become their soup soon!"

"Good. So Albert. You say they are boiling you alive in a pot, right?"

"Yes, can't you see me floating in the steaming pot? It's right here."

"Ah, Albert. Once again, you are completely wrong! You are not in a pot. No one is boiling you alive. No one is making soup out of you. In fact, there is no one in your room but you and me. Open your eyes. See how wrong you are, as usual."

"Huh?" Albert blinked ten times. "I am always wrong. I know that. Oh, I am wrong again! I am not being boiled alive and being turned into soup, am I?"

"No, I am sorry, but you are once more wrong again. You are sitting on your bed talking to me at this time."

"Well, so I am! So I am. Now that was very strange. I must have been having a really bad dream, Zed. I am not even hot! Strange. Well, I have to admit being boiled alive and turned into soup is my worst fear. I used to have nightmares about that when I was younger. Say, isn't that Sir Thomas screaming? We'd better go help him, Zed. Say, what's happened to your arms? They have disappeared."

"I know. I am totally helpless now. Come on. I'll let you open Sir Thomas' door. We have to help him right away. He sounds terrified," Zed urged. Albert got to his feet and headed rapidly next door. He opened it, and the squirrel's shrill screamed nearly deafened both of them.

Sir Thomas was writhing around on his bed, screaming all the while. "Stop eating me! I am not yet dead! I taste terrible. Please don't eat me anymore. Ieee! That hurts really badly. Please kill me first. Ieee. No kill me. I am not dead yet! I feel your teeth chewing up my leg. Stop! Stop! Stop! Please stop!" He writhed and had totally trashed his bedding. Straw and torn cloth bits covered the floor beside his bed.

"Sir Thomas! It's Zed and Albert. Stop wiggling around so. No one is eating you! You've gotten your legs twisted and stuck in the bed boards. Hold still and we'll get you free. Stop writhing this very instant, Sir Thomas!" Zed finally resorted to a direct command. He keenly felt his own utter helplessness to free his friend from the tangled mess he was in. "Albert, can you possibly get his feet untangled? I am totally useless now."

Albert worked hard, fighting against the squirrel, who continued to wiggle in great pain, though not as much as before. Albert nearly gave up, but Zed continued to encourage him softly. "Yes, that way, gently, gently. Yes, bring it up." Finally, Albert had disentangled both of the squirrel's legs from the remains of his bed and the intense pain subsided.

"Ah that is better. You got them to stop chewing up my legs. If they are going to eat me, please have them kill me first. I can't take much more of this," Sir Thomas wailed, tears flowing down his cheeks, soaking his fur.

"Open your eyes, Sir Thomas. No one is here biting you or eating you. It is just Albert here and me. You got your legs all tangled up in what's left of your bed. Come on, open your eyes, Sir Thomas.

Fearfully, the squirrel opened one eye a tiny crack. Then the other eye flicked open and then shut very fast. Then he blinked. Finally satisfied, he opened both eyes and looked around. He let out a sheepish noise, reminiscent of a foolish giggle, Zed thought. "Oops. What a mess I've made. Oh dear me, what will Pecos do to me when he finds that I've destroyed the entire bed? Oh my, oh my!"

"We'd better put it all back right," Albert suggested. Poof! Poof! The total mess and destroyed bed suddenly looked pristine once more.

"There that's better. You know, being eaten alive is my worst fear. I often have nightmares about it. Oh my goodness! Zed! Someone has actually eaten both of your arms!" Sir Thomas declared. "How awful! Did you see who ate them? Are they coming after me next?" Fear flooded into the squirrel once more.

"No one ate them. It is my nightmare come true. Come on. We need to help out Herr Adelstein," Zed kept his explanation short. If he said more, he was sure that he would break down into a bawling baby.

"Okay Zed. We can open the doors for you. We need to see what's wrong with Herr Adelstein. He's gotten awfully quiet," Sir Thomas declared, becoming a trifle braver. Soon, they opened and entered the rabbit's bedroom. At least he wasn't screaming, Zed thought. He'd had all the terror screams he could handle for one night.

Quite the opposite. Herr Adelstein was sitting on his bed bent over, his head buried in his hands, moaning softly to himself. "I'm completely, utterly wrong, wrong, wrong, wrong. Worse than old Albert. There is no hope left for me. I'm wrong, wrong, wrong, wrong. I can never, ever be right again. Woe is me. This is worse than death. I wish they'd just hurry up and kill me and be done with it. I can't live like this anymore. So wrong, so utterly wrong." Zed realized that Herr Adelstein had dropped down into an utter apathy. The why eluded him completely. He could see nothing else in the room save the rabbit and themselves. How was he wrong? About what?

Sir Thomas and Albert tried to reason with their leader, but had no luck at all getting through to the rabbit. He sat there moaning rather apathetically, continually running his hands over his face, ruffling up his fur until he looked positively awful. Worse, he started rocking back and forth as he moaned. Finally, Zed decided to take a chance, nothing else was working.

In as loud and commanding a voice tone as he could muster, Zed barked, "Herr Adelstein! Attention! You will stand up when facing your superior officers!" Almost as if the rabbit had no control over his body whatsoever, the rabbit suddenly jumped up and stood rigidly at attention, quite startling Sir Thomas, who fell over on the floor as he tried to fearfully back up and tripped over Albert's big shell.

"That's better Herr Adelstein. Now you will look your superior officers in their eyes right now and salute them." Under other circumstances, Zed probably would have burst out laughing at the sight of the wild arm motion salute done so frantically by the rabbit. He managed to keep a straight, serious face however. "Excellent, Herr Adelstein. Now then, report! Why and how are you so completely and totally wrong? Report, Herr Adelstein!"

"Yes sir!" the rabbit barked. "I led my friends here to the Badlands and told them that it was completely safe and that we would have a fine time of it, seeing new lands and all. I am completely and totally wrong on all accounts, sir! Albert has been boiled alive in a soup pot. Sir Thomas has been eaten by hungry mouths. Sir, they could not even wait until he died before dining on his legs! One of my 'uman friends — she's been blinded and has now died during child birth. My other one has lost his arms and is completely helpless. All is lost. I am so very, very wrong. I should be shot, sir! Execute me immediately! I demand to be put out of my misery like some wretched beast. I don't deserve to command any longer. I admit it. I am a total failure, sir."

"Thank you, Herr Adelstein for your report! Now then, are your eyes open?" Zed commanded.

"Yes sir!" the rabbit barked back, military style.

"Good. Look there at Albert. Is he stewing a soup pot?"

The rabbit turned his head and looked at the tortoise. A confused look appeared on his face. "Er, no sir. I don't understand."

"Good. Look there at Sir Thomas, are his legs gone? Can you see them eating him alive?" Zed barked commandingly.

"Er, no sir. He seems fine." Sir Thomas was brushing himself off and straightening his ill-fitting western clothes that Pecos had left for him. "Sir, I swore he was being chewed alive. I — I don't understand." The rabbit yawned heavily. "Sir, what's going on here? Oh, wait! I am wrong after all! You've lost your arms. So I am wrong after all, but no. Sir Thomas, Albert — they are unharmed. I don't understand." Herr Adelstein slumped slightly. Rubbing his eyes, he looked from person to person. "Two out of three?"

"At ease, Herr Adelstein. We have been under some kind of spell in which our worst fears have come true," Zed theorized. Well, he really didn't know what everyone's worst fears actually were. This was certainly his and likely so for Albert and Sir Thomas.

Herr Adelstein broke down. Sobbing, he admitted, "Yes, I am terrified of being wrong, totally wrong. I guess that's why I always have to be in charge. You know, to make sure that everything goes right. I just cannot be wrong. I have to be right or I will be destroyed utterly and completely and totally." He yawned heavily once more. "I'm sorry Albert, Sir Thomas, if I have been too bossy, but I have had to fight this all my life you see."

"That's — that's all right, Herr Adelstein. I need someone who is strong. I am always so fearful you know. I get my strength from you," Sir Thomas admitted.

"Yes, me too, buddy. It is no fun always being wrong. I ought to know. We need you, Herr Adelstein. Without you, we'd be lost, but then, am I wrong yet again?" Albert suddenly looked confused. He was trying to support his dear friend, but realized that this could be completely wrong!

Zed jumped in. "No, Albert. You are not always wrong. This time, you are exactly right, my friend." The tortoise smiled, greatly relieved. Herr Adelstein hugged his two close friends, and they, he.

"Wait, Zed, you have lost your arms!" Herr Adelstein again noticed Zed.

"My greatest fear, I am afraid. Come on, we three have to rescue the others from their fears," Zed suggested hoping to keep the rabbit from relapsing. The four headed back to Miranda's room. They found the aged Rose still comforting the very pregnant Miranda, who was still grimacing from the awful pain. Herr Adelstein very nearly relapsed on the spot, but his two friends held his hands which kept him from doing so.

"How is she?" Zed asked.

"Not good. I think she might be dying," Rose replied.

"I know I am. It hurts so bad. I am dying, but maybe you can save my baby. Please, save my baby at least," Miranda wailed and pleaded.

Zed took command once more. He barked, "Miranda. Think. You know that you must have had sex with someone in order to have become pregnant, right?"

She looked startled. "Well, yes. Oh, I see, you want to know who the father is. That way, he can raise our child when you save her and I am dead."

"Yes, something like that. So when did you and with whom?" Zed asked, his voice so full of intention that she dare not refuse to answer.

A strange look came over her face. "I, ah, er, well, I — I can't seem to remember that. Surely I must have." A slight doubt entered her voice.

Zed picked up on that. "Yes, I am sure that a woman can remember such a thing. I want you to remember when you had sex and conceived your child. Think, Miranda, think."

"I, well it was when, no, it was, no. I — no, I. Say, I've never done that! How can I possibly be pregnant?" Poof! Magic flashed. Her enlarged womb vanished as well as that terribly pain that she had been enduring. Her hands moved over her lower abdomen and a great relief crept over her face. "I'm not pregnant after all! I feel so much better!"

"Well done, Miranda. Now Rose, how old are you?" With the worst handled with Miranda, he had to do something for Rose.

"Are you talking to me? Am I still pretending to be this Rose person?" the aged woman answered.

"Yes. How old are you?" Zed asked.

"Mom? What's wrong with you? I can't see you," Miranda exclaimed, realizing for the first time that something was terribly wrong with her mother. Her hands felt the woman's body.

"How old are you, Rose? Think." Zed focused his full attention on the decrepit woman.

"I — I — I don't remember," she fumbled about, very confused.

An idea entered his mind. "When I snap my fingers," he said without thinking and then stopped abruptly! He now had no fingers, no arms to speak of. Zed fought to control the overwhelming urge to break down and cry. Tears swelled, but he fought them back valiantly. He began again, "Rose, when Miranda snaps her fingers, your age will appear in your mind. Miranda, now." Though Miranda could not see anything, she did snap her fingers for Zed.

"What did you get, Rose?" Zed asked.

"Fifty-one, but that's wrong. Just look at me! I am at least eighty-eight, decrepit, crippled with arthritis, and forsaken by everyone. I am an old maid, all alone in the world, and I must have dementia, since I cannot even remember my own name anymore."

"Yes, Rose, that's right. You are fifty-one. So please tell me how you can look like you are eighty-eight if you are only fifty-one?" Zed probed.

"Mom! You can't be eighty-eight!" Miranda now fully realized what must be happening to her mother. "I am your daughter. I'm only twenty-one. You can't be eighty-eight. Think, mom. Think."

"Is that right? I do seem to remember having a daughter, now that you mention it. Am I really only fifty-one? You know I have always been terrified of growing old and crippled up with no one to look after me, becoming a helpless old maid. I so wish your father had not died, Miranda." Suddenly, Rose began to remember the tragic loss in her life. Poof! The aged, decrepit body vanished. Rose appeared her normal self once more, much to her relief and Zed's as well.

"Oh! I was living my worst nightmare!" Rose exclaimed. "Miranda! Are you all right?"

"No, I am blind! I can't see anything, mom. Help me, please?" Miranda begged.

Just then, they heard other screams and crying coming from another room. The sounds came through the open door from the hall, jarring them all. "Who — who is that?" asked a suddenly fearful Sir Thomas, counting the people in this room on his fingers. "There are only six of us. Who?" He dare not finish his thought. The cries could only mean that there were others in trouble, but what others? That was what so frightened the squirrel and caught the instant attention of his companions.

"There must be others trapped in here besides us," Zed concluded what most were now thinking. "Come on gang. Let's see if we can help them."

"But I can't see, Zed."

"Here, grab on to me. I can lead you. You all go ahead of us and open the doors, please," Zed ordered. Rose led them out of the room and down the hall, trying to locate the rooms from which the yelling had come.

Rose focused on the woman who was screaming loudly, ignoring the yelling of the man's voice, naturally. She burst into the woman's room and stopped abruptly. The rabbit bumped into her and the squirrel and tortoise fell into him, nearly losing their balance. "What's happening?" whispered Miranda, holding tightly onto Zed, as they finally reached the doorway.

Rose recovered and went to the bedside of the young woman, while Zed whispered what he was seeing to Miranda. "There is a young woman lying on the bed. I make her to be about your age, dear. She's wearing funny clothes though, like something out of history, maybe the eighteen hundreds or so. She has black hair tied in a bun. Kind of pretty. She's not moving at all."

"Hello dear. I am Rose. It will be all right. Please, who are you and why are you screaming so? Can we help you?"

The woman's eyes were bloodshot from crying. Her cheeks were quite wet as were the sheets on either side of her head. In a sobbing voice, she said, "Trina. I am Trina Noxwood. I was a dressmaker before I got trapped in here. I got that awful disease, polio. I am now paralyzed! I can't move my arms or legs at all! I have to go to the bathroom and I am starving. I can't rouse my husband. He's here somewhere too. Please help me, please, I beg you!"

"Oh dear me! How awful! Trina, we'll help you, that's for sure. Rest your pretty eyes. Here, let me wipe them for you. Rabbit, see if you can find a chamber pot will you, dear fellow? Squirrel, see if you can fetch Trina a glass of water. Albert, see if you can rouse Pecos and have him rustle up some breakfast. Trina here is quite hungry. Ah, Miranda, dear. Come here, Zed, bring her to me. She and I will help Trina use the pot. You men, please leave us alone. We women need a little privacy," Rose barked her orders. The others scampered about to carry out her orders. Zed brought Miranda across the room to her mother and then left himself.

A while later, Rose announced that they could enter again. Somehow the two had managed to help Trina go to the bathroom. Rose explained, "Zed, this is just awful. Trina is completely paralyzed. She cannot move her arms or legs, but at least she can breathe on her own. She is greatly relieved to not have to be put in one of those iron lung things for the rest of her life."

Zed began to doubt that Trina had polio. None of this could be real. "Hi Trina. I am Zed. Can you tell me when you contracted polio?"

"I've always feared that I would get it, you know. Ever since I was a child and my best friend got it. She died, you know," Trina tried to remember.

"Yes, I understand," Zed said sympathetically. "But when did you come down with polio? Can you remember when that was?"

"Well, I don't rightly know, sir," she replied, a frown lined her pretty face.

Inspiration flashed. Zed said, "Well, when were you born, Trina?"

"Eighteen twenty-nine, sir."

"Ah, that explains it, Trina. We come from the twenty-first century. Call us time travelers, if you will. In our century, we have wiped out polio. No one gets it anymore. If they do, we have a vaccine which we can give that totally undoes all of the paralysis that a victim has from the disease. In fact, we have some with us. Would you like us to give you the cure, Trina?"

"Oh yes, sir! Please! My life is ruined utterly. Please, please, I will do anything you ask of me." Hope sprang over the young crippled woman.

Zed whispered to Herr Adelstein, "Can you conjure a syringe?" Poof! Herr Adelstein obliged, but shuffled from foot to foot, wondering how he could give it to the armless Zed. "Thanks. Give it to Miranda. Dear, Herr Adelstein has the syringe with our vaccine in it. Will you please inject the cure into Trina's arm for her?"

A smile creased Miranda's lips. She did not need eyes to know what Zed had in mind. A fake shot would more than likely "cure" this illusory polio. She nearly broke into tears, though, as she blindly had to feel for the woman's arm. All this would have been child's play if she could see. Still, Miranda desperately wanted to be somehow helpful. After several fumbling attempts, she finally injected the syringe into Trina's arm.

"There, now it is relatively fast acting, Trina," Zed continued. "By now, you should start to have a little feeling in your fingers and toes. Can you wiggle them a little bit? Go on, give it a try."

Everyone watched her fingers, save Miranda, who fought hard from crying again. She couldn't see what was happening, but dare not ask and possibly "spoil" the cure.

"Yes, that's it. See, your fingers are moving a little. Now you should get back full sensation in your hands and feet.

Can you bend your wrists? Yes, very good, Trina. See it is working already." Before long, she was moving her arms and finally her legs. A couple of minutes later, she sat up on her own.

"Thank you kind sir! It is a miracle! I am cured! I feared that I would be a helpless cripple the rest of my life and never be able to make another dress. Oh thank you sir," Trina gushed her heartfelt appreciation towards Zed.

Just when everyone was smiling over this miraculous cure, Trina gasped. "Oh my goodness! I know you, sir! I — I — I stole your body on the Malbon Express! Please, please, please forgive me. I had no choice, please. I am so sorry that I had to do that —."

"I understand fully, Trina Noxwood. All is forgiven. I would have done the same if I were in your shoes," Zed raced to defuse what could be a disastrous situation.

"Then — then you know how we were trapped in here?" Trina tried to calm her guilty conscience. This man had said that he understood her action. "I've never stolen a thing in my life before then, sir."

"I know. You really had no choice, Trina. I do understand. It is all right. Why don't you tell us your whole story? Perhaps we can help you further," Zed suggested, quite curious to hear what had happened to her. It might give me more clues, he thought.

"It was eighteen-fifty. We were invited to an elegant party at Mr. Able Montford's mansion. He had a special treat for us, an exciting game, he called it. If we had only known, we'd never gone along with him. He took us aside and had us look at a strange window that he had mounted on his wall. While looking into it, we got sucked into this world! It was awful, but somehow Regi, that's my husband, somehow Regi got us onto a train. He said that it might take us back to Peoria. The next thing we knew, a man and woman somehow stole our bodies and we found ourselves in theirs! It was so confusing. I was now this Countess Vanessa woman. We tried and tried to escape, but nothing worked. Regi kept track of the years. We waited one hundred fifty years. He and I tried to kill ourselves twice, but that failed as well. Then a gong sounded and Regi knew that he had to go to the train. That was the last I saw of him for a long time. Someone else was then in Regi's body when he came back — a total stranger! I kept my distance from him after that. I was lost, but then the gong sounded again, and I found myself being summoned to the train! Honestly, I had so little choice, sir, when I saw you there. As we were sitting there, somehow I was freed and back into my own body, which you see here before you, sir. And I was standing at the edge of this beautiful rainbow canyon land. There was an inn close by, and I learned this was called the Badlands. I made some inquiries and learned that Regi had been here a few weeks before I arrived and that he had gone on down into the canyon. So I did too. I nearly died from thirst, sir, before I stumbled into this inn. I was well treated, but when I awoke, my worst childhood fears had somehow materialized. I had gotten polio, probably as a result of very nearly dying in the canyons, I expect. Then, you came into my room and cured me. How can I ever thank you enough?" Trina finished up her tale.

"That you are safe now is thanks enough," Zed said diplomatically. "Have you found Regi yet?"

"Well, no I haven't. I got polio and have been confined to my bed all this time. It must have been weeks. Pecos has helped me some, though. He is quite understanding, but a bit old."

"Excellent, say, there was one more room that we need to check out. I heard noise coming from there too," Zed remembered. Perhaps it was her husband, Reginald

Noxwood. "Come on everyone; let's check it out." Again, he had Miranda hold onto his body and followed after the others. Herr Adelstein led the way to the last unopened door. They heard the sounds of a man suffering horribly inside, and the rabbit opened it for the others, but allowed Rose to enter first. After all, it did sound like a 'uman's voice, he thought.

As they gazed inside, they saw a man wearing an eighteen hundred's style suit sitting on his bed. He was moaning and groaning. Perspiration dripped from his face. His shirt was totally soaked. His eyes were shut. Trina gasped, "That's him, my husband, Reginald! We have to help him." She rushed to his side, but he did not even sense their presence in the room. His full attention was entrapped in his own mental nightmare.

They tried all manner of actions to somehow get Regi's attention, to get him to open his eyes at least. Nothing worked and Trina became more and more alarmed and worried. Finally, in desperation, Zed suggested, "Trina. Slap him hard on his face. Make it really sting. Tell him you are mad at him for deserting you, leaving you behind, trapped. Go ahead. It might work."

Trina was very hesitant to do it, and he had to prod her some before she finally did it. Smack! She slapped him hard and railed against him. "How dare you go off and leave me! You brute!"

"Honey, I had to, I had to. I have to find a way to get us out of here," he wailed, though he did not open his eyes. "I am being eternally tortured now for having deserted you. I deserve all this punishment that they are giving me. I am nothing but their slave now, breaking rocks up for gravel until I die. You must forgive me, honey. I deserve nothing more than to be their tortured slave until I perish from this earth." He moaned some more, as if he were being whipped.

"Yes, whip me more. I deserve it!" He yelled and grimaced from some imaginary blow that seemed terribly real to the man.

That gave Zed the opening that he was looking for, and he took advantage of it. He had her slap him again and order Regi to open his eyes and confront her. With a bit more encouragement, coaxing, and convincing, Regi finally pulled out of his own personal nightmare. Zed learned that Reginald's worst fear was becoming a pauper and forced into hard labor. Well, it had come true for him after he had deserted his wife in Malbon, though in fact, he had had no choice in the matter. The body exchange had happened automatically, and he found himself in Rose's body standing at the rim of the Badlands. He'd been trapped in his eternal torment for weeks now, and his body was physically drained and exhausted.

"Where's Albert? He was supposed to find Pecos and get us all some breakfast," Zed asked. Everyone shook their heads. "Okay, let's go find Albert." Again, Herr Adelstein led the way with Zed leading Miranda along brought up the rear.

"We are so hopeless, Zed. I am blind and you've lost your arms. How come we can't get fixed up like the others have?" she asked him.

"Don't know; it is my greatest fear, you know."

"Mine too," she admitted.

Just then, both saw the bodies of Count Henri and Countess Vanessa appearing before them. As they tried to walk on down the hall after their friends, the two bodies were squarely in their path. Suddenly, they merged once more. Poof! Zed found that he was in Vanessa's body and Miranda was in Henri's body. Both found themselves back in the Royal Palace in Malbon, shocked and standing in the study! Her vision was perfect and his arms were whole once more.

"Oh my!" Henri exclaimed.

"Not again!" Vanessa added.

# Chapter 7 Repeat

"Well, I can't breathe again and can barely walk, dear. Hold on to me please," Zed or rather the soprano voice of Vanessa declared, somewhat annoyed.

"Coming. There, got you. Well, isn't this a fine howdy do," Miranda or Henri replied, taking a secure grip on Vanessa, steading her.

"Well, at least you can see again, and I have my arms back," Vanessa stated the rather obvious.

"What the devil do we do now? The others are all right and pulled out of their nightmares, but we didn't. Why? How come we were not fixed up? How come we are back here?" Henri asked, very confused.

"Those are the million dollar questions, dear," Vanessa replied. Just then the door opened and Janice entered.

"Oh, here you two are. Come, I have your breakfast tea prepared. Countess Vanessa, we must get you out of your nightgown and make you presentable to Henri. She will join you shortly, Henri," Janice ordered. Zed noticed a subtle change in Janice. As Vanessa slowly followed her to her suite, she realized that Janice was more in control, even to the point of giving Henri orders. Somehow, she thought that was a good thing for the cat woman, but she wasn't certain why she thought that.

"Please, I am into red again. Yes, that one, it matches my nails," Vanessa suggested as Janice began dressing her. A while later, her makeup perfect, Vanessa and Janice headed to the dining room.

"Wow, Vanessa, you do look really hot in red!" Henri exclaimed as they entered. Leo was also taking tea with Henri.

Leo added, "Yes, Countess, you do look smashing in red. Well done, Janice." The cat woman looked rather pleased with herself. While Henri rose and helped Vanessa get seated, Leo did the same for Janice, something neither had seen the two servants do before. Something was very different this time, Vanessa noted.

Later, when the two were finally alone, Vanessa began, "Dear, have you noticed that Janice and Leo are somehow acting a bit different this time?"

"Yes, love, they seem to be more in control of things. It is almost as if they now consider us their equals, if that is possible. I can't get over how gorgeous you look, Vanessa," Henri added. "By the way, I want to thank you for rescuing me from my awful nightmare and my mom too and all of the others. Zed or Vanessa, you were brilliant back there, and I was a dismal failure. I've never been so out of control in my life before. I always prided myself on being in total control, even over my father. My illusions always won. This time, I totally lost it. I would have been trapped like that forever, just as Trina was. Thank you," she added. Henri put his arms around Vanessa's slim waist, pulled her close, and kissed her passionately. Vanessa returned his passion.

When they separated, Vanessa admitted, "Dear, I was not wholly successful. I couldn't get rid of your blindness or get my own arms back, if you will recall. Still, the others ought to be in good shape now. Oh! What will happen to them now that we are gone, er back here?"

"Gosh! You are right! Well, mom's with them. If she has any brains, she'll try to lead them out of the Badlands and not gamble on having repeat nightmares. Somehow, Vanessa, we have to catch back up to them."

"Right. We have to redo everything and get back to them. Maybe it is time for another vacation," she teased him.

A bit later, Vanessa added, "You know, perhaps we should think about this a bit. So far, I have seen that there has been some form of logic in Able Montford's universe here. Everything that has happened has had a reason, a purpose behind it. Usually, though, we can't see it until afterwards. Why were we the only ones not 'cured?' Why were we brought back into these bodies? This time, it is probably the way that Montford intended. I mean you and I entered as a pair and here we are as a pair at last, not like before."

"Good point, Vanessa. You are on to something, I believe. I am not sure what, though. One thing is for sure, dear, I just can't get over how fabulous you look! Goodness, what's happening with this body?" Henri began squirming, adjusting his pants. Vanessa flushed, she recognized what was happening to Henri.

She replied, "It's a guy thing, dear. We often get — shall I be polite?" he teased her. "We get excited around pretty women."

"But it is getting so —," she stopped, too embarrassed to say the words.

"Maybe we are supposed to learn how the opposite sex operates," Vanessa suddenly vocalized her realization. "My god! I bet that is what Montford had in mind for Malbon all along! We are to experience what life is like for the opposite sex!"

"This is *so* embarrassing, Vanessa," Henri flushed crimson. "It began right after I kissed you, Vanessa," he admitted. "Does it go away soon?" he whispered to her. "This is so unreal."

Vanessa chuckled, "No, it is quite real, dear. Come on. Let's operate on the assumption that Montford wanted us to experience this and see if we get additional clues from it."

"I'd love too, Vanessa, but I wanted our first time to be special, not in these strange bodies, Zed."

"Same here. But if we are ever to get out of here, we probably have to play Montford's little game," Vanessa found herself justifying. That kiss stirred something in her body, a thirst. She wanted more.

"Okay. Come to our bedroom," Henri replied, putting his arm around Vanessa, helping her up the stairs to their bedroom. After shutting their bedroom door, Henri had to help Vanessa out of her enticing red satin dress. An hour later, the two lay beside each other, highly contented.

"Well, if nothing else, we two have had the unique opportunity to experience how our opposites experience this," Vanessa pointed out. "I had no idea of a woman's point of view."

"Same here. Besides venting our passions for each other, we also got an education," Henri teased her a little bit and then gave Vanessa another loving kiss.

Just then, Zed found himself slightly separated from his Vanessa body and Miranda was likewise a foot from her Henri body. All four could see each other's bodies. Vanessa's thoughts arrived in the other three's minds, just as Henri's thoughts did a moment later.

*Thank you both. Please, can you rescue us? We have been trapped here for two centuries. We stole you back hoping that you could rescue us,* Vanessa's thoughts impinged upon the others.

Henri added, *We know that we are not real people, but we are so tired of Montford's game here. Please, find a way to take our bodies with you. Vanessa is right. We both thought that you two were awfully powerful, and we defied*

*Montford's orders and kept an eye on you when you entered the Badlands. I am sorry that we worked so hard to prevent you both from recovering from your nightmares. We felt that this was our only avenue to escape from here. We brought you back into our bodies, using Montford's own postulates to our advantage. Yes, you are right. His goal was to have you experience sex from the opposite point of view. That's why you were brought back to us when you didn't fully recover from your nightmares. We knew that would happen and prevented your complete recovery so that this would happen. We are sorry if you hate us for doing that to you.*

The real Vanessa added, *Please, will you help us to escape from here? We beg you. The only time that it is safe for us to separate like this is right after you have been intimate with each other.*

*How can we refuse to help you both?* Zed replied. *Yes, we will do our best to bring you with us this time.*

A knock on their bedroom door interrupted the strange experience. Instantly, Zed found himself back in Vanessa's body. Miranda, likewise. Gone was the separation between the four. "How utterly strange!" Henri remarked.

Janice helped Vanessa get dressed again and freshened up her makeup. Vanessa took this opportunity to chat with the cat woman. "I can't help but notice that you are feeling more in charge around here. Good for you, Janice," she said, placing the emphasis on the idea that she highly approved of this change.

The cat woman smiled. "I hoped that it would not be so obvious, Madame."

"Well, it is about time that you get what is owed you. After all, you have cared for Vanessa for ages."

"I am so glad that you approve. Leo thought that perhaps you and Henri would be most angry with us for being so forward," Janice admitted.

"On the contrary, Janice. I think that it is high time that you two are heavily rewarded for your tireless service here," Vanessa declared, adding, "and I think that I know a way to do just that!"

"Oh please do so. Thank you, Countess Vanessa, thank you." She finished up adjusting Vanessa's makeup and the two headed out of her bedroom.

Alone in the study once more, Vanessa outlined her brief conversation with Janice to Henri. "So what is your grand plan?" Henri asked. "No, let me guess. No, I can't. Go ahead, my love."

"I like the sound of that, Miranda, er Henri. I think that we ought to get Leo and Janice appointed as the official Count and Countess of Malbon. It is time that we retired from public service. We can pack all our clothes and stuff, buy us a carriage, and ride out of Malbon by ourselves. Back to the Badlands for a second go around with our nightmares."

"Love it! It's better than anything that I had thought of. You are brilliant, dear," Henri exuded. Just then, Leo entered bearing an official document. He handed it solemnly to Henri.

"Ah, we are to attend the Spring Royal Ball in two days. This is our invitation," he explained, showing the fancy document with its highly ornamental writing to Vanessa.

Leo commented, "The Royal Ball, sir? Excellent. Countess, you best let Janice know. It is a very formal affair and she will need time to do your hair and get you fully prepared. Count, you will need to get your best tuxedo out of storage for this ball. Come, I know where it is kept."

Vanessa, holding the document, headed off to find Janice. "Oh dear, only two days to prepare Madame. Well, we must hurry then. Come on. Let us pick out your gown first. So much to do and so little time. You must look your very best. This is Malbon's fanciest dance. Everyone will be looking at our Royal Couple." Janice chatted on as she led Vanessa to a locked wardrobe which opened into a huge walk in closet, filled with extremely elegant ball gowns.

"Red, I presume, Madame?"

"Right. Cherry red. I do look so hot in red, don't you think?"

"Wee, Madame, wee."

Late the afternoon of the Royal Ball, Janice finally finished getting Countess Vanessa properly dressed. She brought Henri into the bedroom to both show off her handiwork and to get his okay on how her charge looked. Vanessa wore a cherry red, satin ball gown. Her underlying hoop skirt flared out nearly twelve feet; her outer skirt was layered in yards of the satin, forming six tiers of satin bands. Red rubies embedded in large golden bands hung from her ears with a matching ruby studded broach necklace hung around her neck, resting on her pronounced bosom, bared considerably by the style of the dress, though it did cover her shoulders slightly. Her hair was as wavy and long as usual, nicely brushed out. Her long nails and lips matched her dress.

"Holy cow! Wow, Vanessa, you look positively stunning!" Henri remarked. Vanessa noticed the growing bulge in Henri's pants and smiled, glad that their roles were reverse at the moment. That didn't last long, though.

"Dear, I can't see my feet at all. You are going to have to hold on to me at all times," Vanessa explained. Wearing such a dress gave her a bit of a scare.

Henri laughed. "Oh you will get used to it. We women always do, though a helping hand is most welcome. Come on; don't panic. I've got you. Let's head downstairs for a quick bite before we go." He took her arm and led her out of her bedroom, giving an appreciative nod to Janice, who smiled. Things were going far better than the Personal Assistant had ever imagined they would.

An hour later, accompanied by a loud fanfare of trumpets, the Count and Countess entered the huge dance floor while nearly a thousand well-wishers applauded their arrival. Vanessa noticed at once that all of the women, whether human or not, wore gowns similar to hers, just as the males wore expensive tuxedos. As they mixed with their subjects and the musicians played, the two found themselves separated from each other. Many men requested a dance with her, and Henri found himself having to dance with other females, including cat women and other life forms.

Vanessa was terribly embarrassed from all of the male attention bestowed on her. However, by the end of the evening, she had grown a bit more comfortable with it. Both were more than ready to head home when the dance finally ended near midnight. "My feet positively ache, dear," Vanessa whispered, once they were in their carriage.

"I'll massage them when we get home, my love," Henri whispered back. "I'll massage more than your feet thought," he teased her.

"You'd better!" Vanessa teased him back.

Two very satisfied people woke the next morning. As always, Janice insisted on dressing Vanessa before allowing her to head downstairs for breakfast. When they were finally alone once more, Henri said, "I'm going out today and see about making the arrangements you had planned. Want to come with me and do some shopping?"

"No, I am going to sort through the clothes here. Honestly, there are enough dresses here to last several lifetimes."

"Well, pick out the red ones. You look incredible in red, dear." Vanessa flushed and flashed Henri a big smile.

When Henri returned that afternoon, he found Vanessa patiently waiting for him. "Well?" she asked the second he took off his top hat.

Henri smiled, "Perfect! I explained that it was time for us to retire. They didn't buy that until I asked them how many years we had been reigning over Malbon. Can you believe two centuries? Well, that convinced them. I have them convinced to allow us to appoint our successors. Shall we?"

Vanessa grinned and kissed him. "Let's!" Henri summoned Leo and Janice, who came quickly to see what the Count and Countess desired.

"Leo, Janice, Vanessa and I have an announcement to make. She and I are retiring from the leadership of Malbon, effective next Monday. Further, we have been requested to name our successors, the new Count and Countess," Henri explained.

"Oh no, Madame is not going to be our Countess any longer?" a disappointed look flooded over the cat woman.

"No, it is long past the time that Henri and I moved on and gave others the chance to be the official rulers. Henri, I give you Malbon's new Countess Janice. Leo, you are to be our new Count."

"What? Me?" shrieked Janice taken wholly by surprise. She looked delighted.

"Why, I would be most honored indeed, sir," the reserved Leo replied, trying to hold back his excitement.

"Congratulations to the both of you," Henri declared. "You have more than earned the opportunity to serve as Malbon's rulers, Count and Countess. Well done, both of you. I've already submitted your names to the city councilors. On Monday, they will come to meet with you both. There will be a formal swearing in ceremony after that. Congratulations!"

Henri and Vanessa, arm in arm, left the two behind, heading for the kitchen to find some tea. As they left, they overheard Leo. "I told you that these two were very special! I can't believe it. After all these years, Janice, we are now the Count and Countess!"

"I know! My fondest desire has finally come true, Leo. Now we can be married!"

When they were out of earshot, Vanessa whispered, "I had no idea about that!"

"Cause you didn't look, dear. A woman senses these things," Henri whispered back.

The next day was spent in packing their new carriage with the clothes they wanted to bring along with them. Henri had one large suitcase and two hat boxes for his top hats. However, Vanessa brought along ten dress crates. "A woman's clothing takes more space, silly," Vanessa teased Henri, who had to pack all these onto their carriage. "Make sure that we have a whole lot of water with us."

"And food too, easy to prepare food, I think," Henri added. "If we keep these bodies, you are not going to be able to fix our meals. I will have to do that." Vanessa smiled and thanked him for that offer.

Sunday morning, Janice dressed Vanessa for the last time, adjusting her fancy red satin dress and doing her makeup. She and Leo joined Vanessa and Henri for their last breakfast. "We are so happy for you and for us," Janice said sipping her tea.

"Are you two going to get married?" Vanessa asked demurely.

Both flushed. Janice grinned, "Yes, we are. I had so wanted you to be my bridesmaid, but that isn't going to work out, is it?"

"No, we must be going this morning," Henri replied. "You both have our best wishes and blessings for a long, happy, and prosperous marriage and life. You have been the best assistants anyone could ever hope to have. Thank you both from the bottoms of our hearts." Both seemed very pleased with that, and at last Henri and Vanessa rose, shook their hands, and headed out to their waiting carriage.

"That was very nice, dear," Vanessa complimented Henri. "Well, we certainly are ending cycle on this Malbon thing. I hope our plan works. Can I ride topside with you for a while? Of course, you are going to have to lift me up there. I can't possibly make it in this dress. It's way too tight."

"My pleasure, my dream woman," Henri teased her.

Both held their breaths as they began moving down the city cobblestone streets. Would they be allowed to leave or would some other of Montford's magic interfere with their great escape? When the open countryside appeared and nothing had yet happened, both began to relax a bit. "So far so good," whispered Vanessa. She finally uncrossed her fingers; she'd had them crossed all the way through the city.

That evening, they stopped at the same village inn that they had stayed on their previous journey to the Badlands. Still nothing had happened, and Henri had to assist Vanessa down and into the inn. Further, he had to help her undress for the night. In the morning, the satisfied couple rose and still nothing had happened. Henri had to help dress her though. "Shall we forgo all the makeup dear?" he asked hopefully. Miranda hated to wear much makeup and hoped that Vanessa would agree. She did and Henri breathed a sigh of relief.

"Dear, I had no idea how long it takes for a woman to get herself ready. Incredible. Please, let's forgo that makeup. I don't like it either," Vanessa replied.

Henri chuckled. "Tell me about it. I know. I know how long it takes us." Both laughed and set out on their way once more.

They halted at the rim of the Badlands once again. The view was just as spectacular as before and they spent a moment taking it in. How could something be so beautiful and yet hold such nightmares for those who entered, Vanessa wondered. Montford had a diabolical mind, she thought.

"Well, so far so good, but dear, what do we do now?" asked Henri. "In your outfit, you can't possibly walk down that steep trail. There isn't enough ease in your dress and those heels will make it impossible for you. Besides, with all your clothing, you are going to positively melt in the heat down there. Remember how soaked our thin tee-shirts got."

Vanessa bit her lip. "I don't know. I can't take the infernal corsets off and I can't take the heels off either and tip toe down there. Can we possibly drive the carriage down?"

"Not a chance. It is way too steep for the horses," Henri concluded.

"Well, dear. It seems that we have only one choice left to us."

Henri looked at Vanessa and then smiled. "You are right, love. You know that I have really fallen for you, don't you?"

"Same here, Miranda, er Henri. Okay, let's do this together. Perhaps together our postulates will stick here. Ready?"

"We'd best get our wording right, love." A few minutes later, both were satisfied and together they decided firmly, "We and the carriage and the horses are now at the bottom of the canyon on the path that leads to the inn." Poof! Two surprised horses looked around in all directions wondering just how they got here. Henri looked at Vanessa, both nodded to each other. "Giddy up," Henri said and the horses obeyed, heading along the trail. Miles ahead lay the inn and the keeper, Pecos.

As they rode along in the heat, which was taking its toll on Vanessa in particular, they chatted about what would likely happen tonight when they went to sleep. That is, the nightmares — would they recur? Both concluded that in all likelihood they would be forced once more to endure their worst fears in life.

"Wait a minute. We are in different bodies this time. Maybe the worst fears that we will experience this time will be theirs, I mean Vanessa's and Henri's," Henri pointed out.

"If we don't change back into our own bodies, I think you may well be right. I wonder what her worst fears are?" Vanessa asked rhetorically.

They discussed this for some time. "You know, I think that we may already know what their worst fears are," Henri suggested. "They are terrified of never ever being able to leave Malbon, being forced to be the Count and Countess forever. That would terrify anyone."

"By golly, I think you are right. All else or rather what little we know of their lives — all else has been good to them. Their bodies are healthy; they've plenty of food, clothing, and shelter, far more than most people ever have in their whole lives," Vanessa concurred.

"If that is so, I have an idea of how we can overcome their fears, love," Henri stated. He then explained his idea. Vanessa grinned and agreed with it for more than one reason.

They arrived at the inn. Although drenched in sweat, they were nowhere near as exhausted as they had been the first time. Not so for their horses. Fortunately, Pecos knew well how to handle their two mares, and Henri was more than thankful for that. He or Miranda had no experiences with horses in her life. Inside, they took only one room, not two, claiming that they were married, which they were. Pecos didn't seem to mind, which Henri found curious. Perhaps other couples had come in the past, he thought. Well, he was determined to thwart the nightmares this time.

After a pleasant supper with Pecos who did not seem to recognize them at all, the two headed down the familiar hall to their room. Once inside, they both sketched two large signs which read, Henri and Vanessa will be leaving the Badlands in the morning. They placed the signs where they could see them from their bed. Then, though yawning heavily, Henri helped Vanessa out of her dress and slip and into her nightgown. He also turned up the lanterns and checked a third time for the signs' visibility from their bed. So far so good, he thought.

Vanessa was already in their bed; she was yawning too, and Henri knew that he had to act soon or they would both be asleep. He crawled in beside her and began passionately kissing her, and Vanessa responded in kind. Soon, their passions took hold, and all sleepiness dissolved. Four more times that night, Henri fired up their mutual passions both for their own pleasure and more importantly to keep them both awake.

At long last, the sunlight began illuminating their room. "We did it. Time to rise and shine my gorgeous babe," Henri teased Vanessa.

"Yes, my handsome young man," she replied, offering him her hand. "But you have to dress me and brush out my hair, dear. I have no idea how to do that, and I can't bend enough to dress myself."

"Women!" Henri said in a fake annoyed tone. Both laughed. Later, they headed out to find breakfast.

"Sleep well?" asked a curious Pecos.

"We did, sir. Thanks for asking. I would be very much obliged if you could possible hitch up our team to our carriage after we eat your hearty breakfast," Henri replied, hoping the Pecos would do so. If not, he knew that he would have an awful time of it. He knew nothing about such things.

"Certainly sir. I love horses. Though seldom do I get the chance to work with them anymore. Not many riders out here in the Badlands."

"Thanks. Say, do you get other visitors or vacationers passing through here?" Vanessa asked, batting her eyes as she recalled Vanessa had done to him while on the Malbon Express before she'd taken his body. Flirt with him, she thought to herself.

The old man grinned, responding much as any man might. "Not often, but some. Why only last week a party of six passed through here."

"Well, that's good to hear. We traveled all day yesterday and didn't see a soul. I suppose that those six are now long gone. It would be *so* good to have some company to visit with on our vacation," Vanessa pumped him while continuing to emulate the subtle flirting gestures that Zed had seen her do to him while on the train. Henri smiled, realizing just what Zed was doing and marveling at how naturally she was doing it.

"Oh yes. Like you, they only stayed one night, but they did take two others with them that next day. I had a young couple that wanted to stay here for several weeks. You know how beautiful these canyons are. Can't say that I blame them for wanting to spend weeks here. Yes, they all left together. I guess that you might catch up to them."

"How so?" she asked, not grasping his meaning.

"Oh, they were on foot you see, and you are going by carriage. My guess is that you might catch them in a couple of days," Pecos answered. "I'd best go get your horses hitched."

An hour later, the two set out once more. Vanessa insisted in sitting in the driver's box with Henri. As they left the inn behind them, Henri admitted, "Vanessa, I am so exhausted and tired I can barely keep my eyes open."

"Same here. Let me spell you. You can doze while I drive and vice versa. Probably nothing will happen in broad daylight," she suggested. During the long day, they took turns dozing while the other drove the team. The path was clearly marked and though constricted as she was, Vanessa had no real trouble with the horses.

Near sunset, they rode up a hill and discovered that they were now out of the Badlands. A wooded forest beckoned to them, bringing a distinct coolness from the intense heat of the dry lands behind them. "We made it dear!" Henri exclaimed.

"Look. There is a road sign — the first that we've seen," Vanessa pointed out. She halted their carriage so they could get a good look at it. "Now entering Worthy Forest. Wonder what that means? Badlands were bad. Worthy sounds more benign. Don't you think?"

"Everything about this universe or world isn't quite what it seems, dear. We should be on our guard, just in case. I wonder if there are inns along the way and how far ahead our companions are?" Henri asked.

"Worse, it is going to be dark soon. Keep on going?"

"Hey, you are the pants in our relationship," Henri teased her.

"True, but at the moment, you are wearing them," Vanessa teased him back. Both laughed. She slapped the reins and they continued on their way. They had only gone another mile when they came upon a small village. A few dozen wooden homes lined the rutted road and one was definitely an inn. "Wow, I bet Sir Thomas enjoyed this village." A number of squirrels wearing various apparel moved about their business along the single street. A few smaller children were playing ball and grew excited as the carriage approached them. Squirrelton read a small sign at the edge of the village. Henri grinned; indeed, he thought, Sir Thomas probably enjoyed his visit here, assuming their friends had made it this far. Vanessa pulled up at the inn.

After Henri lifted her down, the two entered the inn in search of lodging and supper. "Hallo, welcome to Squirrelton. Amos Padfoot here. How can I help you?" the innkeeper asked, wiping his hands on his white apron and then untying it, revealing a rather worn business suit beneath.

"A room for the night, a hot meal, and someone to care for our horses, kind sir," Henri took charge.

"Excellent, excellent. Yes, all rooms are vacant. Such elegantly dressed visitors. Impressive. All the way from Malbon, I expect?"

"Yes, as a matter of fact we are. Taking a vacation. How did you know that?" Henri answered, curious about that detail.

Amos smiled, "Your fine suit and your misses' elegant dress. Could only come from Malbon. We don't get many visitors here in Squirrelton. I'll send Fred to take care of your team. If you will follow me, I'll show you to your room. My misses will have supper in about an hour. We are pretty informal around here. I hope that you don't mind dining with my family."

"Of course not." The two followed the squirrel who led them to a cozy, but small bedroom just off of the main dining room. "Excellent, Amos, this will do quite nicely," Henri replied and Amos left them alone.

The room held a bed that would sleep both of them, but not by much. There were two small chairs, a small dresser, and a mirror. A pitcher held water and there was a wash basin and chamber pot lying on the floor. The towels were embroidered with a forest scene, and Henri guessed that his wife had done the needlework. Quaint, but homey, he thought. The two washed up and stretched until Amos called them for supper.

In the dining room, they met his wife, Betsy, who wore a simple cotton dress filled with more of her fine needlepoint. They had two children who stared constantly at the two guests. She served them a filling stew with homemade biscuits. Later over tea, they chatted. Slowly, Vanessa turned the topic to recent guests, hoping to obtain word that their friends had passed this way.

"Why yes, we did have a party of six pass through here not two days ago," Amos pointed out. "We really did enjoy the company of Sir Thomas. He is one of us, you see, a squirrel. They stayed for two days. They said that they were waiting on two of their friends to join them. Left two days ago."

"Terrific. We are their two friends and are trying to catch up with them," Vanessa replied, greatly encouraged with this news. Their friends had made it out of the Badlands and were going slowly hoping that they would catch up with them.

"Dear, don't forget the note that they left for their friends," Betsy broke in. She retrieved it, handing it to Henri.

"Thanks, this is perfect," he said after reading it. "Says that they are keeping to the main road. We ought to be able to catch up with them by tomorrow night, love," Henri suggested, greatly relieved. Rose was safe and had her wits about her. She'd left the note, and Miranda was pleased at her thoughtfulness.

Later when they were in their room and Henri had helped Vanessa out of her dress, he whispered, "Love, we should make use of this last private night. We'll likely have company tomorrow night." She responded with a passionate kiss. Later, both slept soundly making up for the previous night.

Over breakfast, Amos told them that the next inn was in Broadleaf, three days journey on foot. Once on the road, both became worried about their companions again. "No inns or food for three days. This does not sound too good. Let's hurry as much as possible today. Maybe we can catch up with them by nightfall," Henri suggested. All day long, they pushed the horses as much as they dared, though neither knew whether or not they were over doing it with the horses.

Towards dusk, which came early among the dense forest canopy of oak trees, fifty men holding longbows with swords at their sides suddenly stepped out in front and at the sides of their slow moving carriage. A tall man with a black beard and fierce looking eyes barked out loudly, "Halt! Or we will turn you both into pincushions!"

"What the. . ." exclaimed Henri. Vanessa, who currently held the reins, decided not to chance it and reined in the horses. In her mind, she estimated how fast they could go to get past these men versus how fast they could shoot and realized the man was right. Even though they could probably drive the carriage right on through these bandits, they'd likely be struck by numerous arrows.

"Now you are being sensible. You will come with us," he barked. Most of the men kept their arrows at the ready, but three lowered theirs and grabbed the horses, leading them off the path and deeper into the forest.

"What's going on? Why are you stopping us?" Henri attempted to get the man to talk further, but he said nothing, merely waving his men onwards into the dark forest. Both began to have a bad feeling about this. Where were their friends? Had they run into these bandits as well?

# Chapter 8 The Worthy Forest

The Worthy Forest grew quite dark as they rolled slowly along, escorted by the band of bandits, for surely that is what they were, Vanessa thought. Images of Robin Hood came into her mind. She fully expected that they would be robbed, but frowned. They had not brought along any substantial funds, just a few coins for the inns. Well, these bandits would be in for a big surprise, she thought.

Henri, or Miranda rather, was used to being in control of her life. While she didn't particularly like being stuck in the Henri body, she realized that it would be her role to take care of Vanessa, since her body was the male. Yet, what could she do? There were way too many of these bandits. If there had been only a few, she might have urged their horses on, gambling that they'd not be hurt by too many arrows. Fifty men were too many. What to do? What to do?

She tried postulating that they were back on the road, free from the bandits. However, she felt a huge counter-postulate negating hers. Interesting, she thought. Something powerful is at work here, but what? Does Worthy Forest have anything to do with it? Surely the name implies good things, not being waylaid by bandits!

Just when it was nearly too dark to even see the path that the bandits were following, a large encampment appeared. Dozens of bonfires dotted the dense forest, and the two saw a huge wooden fortress, complete with a wooden outer wall made from eight inch diameter logs whose tops were pointed. Henri smiled; it looked like something out of the Middle Ages. Well, this was a dense forest, and wood was plentiful, he thought. The bandits led them in through the wide gates which were promptly shut behind them. Vanessa got a feeling of being trapped inside this place, whatever it was. She felt a bit unnerved.

Ahead, they saw a large wooden, single story manor house, and the men led the carriage to its door. A wagon was also parked just outside the door as well. They could not help but notice that many gold coins lay in its bed. "Bring them inside," the dark man ordered, quickly heading inside. Henri dismounted and helped Vanessa get down. He made sure that his arm was around her, just as the men gave them both a little push to the doors ahead of them.

"Easy does it," Henri complained as Vanessa nearly lost her balance from the push. He steadied her and they entered. Vanessa was grateful to find that there was a solid wooden floor inside. She could now walk more easily and breathed a little sigh of relief. They were escorted down a smoky hallway to what appeared to be a crude representation of a throne room. The bandit leader was now sitting on his large wooden throne. A dozen crackling torches illuminated the room.

To the far right of the man, their eyes spotted a huge pile of gold coins and gemstones. A few ornate pieces of jewelry were intermixed in the hoard. The dark man's eyes spotted their eyes observing the treasure trove. However, neither of the two was interested in such, and their eyes returned to gaze upon their captor. This too he noted. At last he spoke.

A deep bass voice barked out, "Welcome to the Worthy Forest. I am Finigan Flake, Master of the Woods. I see you are a pair; that is good and as it should be. Are you not interested in my magnificent treasure?"

Henri spoke, "Nice pile. How many travelers have you had to rob to build that pile up, eh?"

Finigan laughed, "Far too many. So you are not interested in my gold?"

"Of course not. If you think that you will be adding to that pile by stealing more from us, you have a surprise coming. We only have a bit of traveling coins. Nothing more," Henri replied honestly. Best to be up front here at the get go than to raise his ire when he looted their carriage and persons.

"No, I can see that neither of you are interested in gold. For now, you are my guests. Come, it is suppertime. You must be hungry." He clapped his hands and a number of scantily clad young women came rushing in carrying trays of food and dishes. Finigan led the two over to his crude oak table and bad them sit and dine with him. The women sat places for Vanessa and Henri and served them ample portions. Another brought in a tray of various wines.

"I am known to have the finest wines in all the lands. Come, would you like to sample them and chose the best wine for your fine dinner?" Finigan asked.

"Not really. Water will do fine," Henri replied. He guessed that the wine might be drugged or worse. It would be more difficult to hide poison or drugs in plain water.

"Ah, not interested in fine wines, eh? So be it. Water it is." He clapped and another pretty young woman came rushing over with a pitcher of water, serving the two. Henri sampled it and nodded subtly to Vanessa that it seemed okay to drink. "Eat and enjoy. I have the finest chef in the entire world here. Eat, my guests." Although the accommodations seemed on the crude side, Finigan ate with an elegance that suggested he may have once been a king at a fancy court, Henri concluded.

As they ate, hesitantly at first, they discovered that the food was delicious. Finigan had not lied when he claimed to have an excellent chef. Both were hungry and at last they began eating as well. "Is it not the best ever?" Finigan asked them.

"It is good, yes, but it is just food. Why have you waylaid us?" Henri attempted to steer the conversation back to the main point.

"Ah, food does not prick your interest. No matter. I am not insulted. Perhaps we should have some entertainment while we dine." He clapped again and some musicians entered along with four dancers. The two male dancers were not only young but extremely handsome, perhaps the most attractive men that either had seen — perfect in all ways. The women were equally pretty and scantily clothed, much like Egyptian belly dancers that Vanessa had seen in movies and on TV shows. The haunting sounds of the nasal oboe-like instrument and the pulsing drum beats were delightful, but the four dancers' erotic gyrations created an aura of excitement and enticement.

Both Henri and Vanessa observed the dancers a bit, but mostly continued to eat their fill of the roast pheasant. "Do not my dancers incite strong feelings within you? They certainly do me," Finigan asked.

"Yes, they know their craft well and the music is really quite good, Finigan," Vanessa answered him. "You do have excellent dancers and musicians here. I would not have predicted such. So why have you brought us here? Surely not to give us a show."

"I am glad that you recognize how superb my dancers and musicians are." Finigan replied. When they had finished dining, he then sat back and stared at the two. "Well, you two are an interesting pair. Neither gold, gems, fine food, drink, nor do exquisite bodies seem to interest you two. Yet, you seem close to each other. The final question I have for you is just how far are you willing to go for each other? Yes, I believe *that* is the question that you both must answer. Yes that is it."

"Whatever are you talking about? I ask politely again, why have you abducted us?" Henri persisted.

Finigan didn't answer him. "You have both just come from the Badlands. Did you not both experience your worst fears, your worst nightmares there?" Both involuntarily reacted. Vanessa squirmed in her chair slightly. Henri blinked his eyes rapidly, but stopped his hands from moving up to his eyes. "Yes, I see that you both have. You cannot lie to me. You see, Pecos has already relayed to me just what your fears were, though in your case, it seems a bit strange. Nevertheless, I know your innermost terror. You thought by escaping or fleeing the Badlands that you would be free from the torture of your nightmares. Alas, that is not so. In a minute, my servants will escort you to one of my guest bedrooms. There you will find that your nightmare will return. You cannot escape it, for there is no escaping from one's worst fears and terrors, is there? No, they haunt us all our lives. While yours will be returning to you both shortly, the question to be asked at this time is just how far are you willing to go for each other?"

"What do you mean?" asked Henri, growing very concerned. This was not at all what he was expecting from the Worthy Forest. Perhaps there was nothing in these names after all. He glanced at Vanessa. In her restrictive clothing and heels, she would have a terrible time if her nightmare returned. At least with his Henri body, this time he could not become pregnant, he thought.

"Well, you both know each other's greatest fears. How far are you willing to go for each other?" he repeated.

"I'll do what it takes to keep Vanessa from her greatest fear, if that's what you mean," Henri replied.

"How about you, Vanessa? How far would you go for Henri here?"

"Of course I'll do whatever it takes to prevent Henri from having his nightmare returning. Don't be silly," she replied. "We all would help each other."

"Fine. So be it. We will see. And now, allow them to show you to your bedroom. I trust that you will find the accommodations to your satisfaction. Besides, you must be tired from your long journey," Finigan stated with a note of finality in his voice.

One of the costumed dancers led the two out of the dining room and into the smoke halls. It was a different hall, Henri noted, paying close attention to their route. Somehow, they had to escape and find their companions. Still he wondered if they had met up with these bandits? If so, were they imprisoned here as well? He decided to pump their escort. "Ma'am, can you tell me if Finigan captured six others, perhaps a few days ago? One was a rabbit, one was a squirrel, one was a tortoise, and three were humans like us."

"I'm Felicia, by the way. I am not supposed to tell you anything," she replied demurely. "Did you like my dancing?"

Vanessa grinned and decided to take an indirect approach. "Yes, it was marvelous. I bet you have had to practice quite a lot to be as good at it as you are."

Felicia smiled, very pleased with her compliment. "Why yes. So few ever realize that we have to work so very hard to get our dances perfect. It really is very hard work. Keeps me in good physical shape too. I guess it won't hurt to nod my head, will it?" she grinned mischievously and nodded yes.

Vanessa returned her smile, adding a flirtatious wink. "They are still here somewhere, aren't they?" Again, Felicia grinned and nodded affirmative.

"Ah, here we are. I know that you will find this room to your liking. I slept in here once while renovations were going on in the other wing. The bed is very comfortable. Finigan does place a high value on our guest's comfort while they are staying here with us, you know. Oh, breakfast is at eight. When you hear a bell chiming, that's the signal. Just followed this hall back the way that we came and you'll find the dining room again. You can't miss it. Have a nice stay. Bye." She nodded and left the two standing just inside their bedroom.

Their room was square, fifteen by fifteen. The bed was inviting, queen sized with an ornate headboard. Certainly, it was not a cheap bed. A dresser with a mirror, a table and two chairs occupied the left wall. A table holding a wash basin, towels, and wash rags lay to their right along with a tall wardrobe, currently empty. The two checked over the contents of their room, finding nothing in the drawers either. Shortly, someone knocked on their door and Henri answered.

"Your day bag," a man announced, handing him the bag retrieved from their carriage. It held Vanessa's hair brush, nightgown, and a change of clothing for each of them. Henri also checked their small money pouch. Their few coins were still there and they relaxed; they had not been robbed yet.

"What do you make of all this?" he asked. "Our friends are still here. Tomorrow, we are going to have to see if we can find them somehow and them get out of here."

"At first, I thought Finigan and his band were just bandits. Now I am not so sure of that. I think that there is more to them than they've told us. I have a bad feeling about this. Still, I agree, we're too tired to do more tonight. Tomorrow we have to try to find your mother and the others. If they are being kept here, we'll find them, Henri. Come on; lend me a hand getting ready for bed."

A short while later, Henri complained, "Vanessa, you are so hot! Look what this male body is doing again!" He had just helped her into her nightgown.

Vanessa grinned. "Women do have that effect on me, I mean when I am Zed," she teased and kissed him. Soon they were in bed, allowing their passions free rein. Later on, both drifted into a deep sleep. Purposely, they left their three lanterns burning.

Sometime after midnight, Henri began having an awful nightmare. He was on some kind of battlefield, explosions detonated all around him. Suddenly, he felt enormous pains in both his arms and saw that they'd taken a shrapnel hit. He passed out only to waken and find himself in a hospital of some kind. A bit of each arm throbbed and he tried to raise his hands to see what was hurting. Nothing was there. Panic set in as he realized that he had no arms any longer. After the initial wave of panic died down a little, he saw that was not entirely true. His arms were barely four inches long now, long pointed little cones. Henri panicked again and woke up.

He tried to wipe the sweat from his face and nothing happened. Real panic swept over him now and he sat up, but only with effort. He cried out as he saw that his arms really were just like he'd seen in his nightmare — short, stubs, barely four inches from his shoulders and cone shaped, barely an inch across at the tips. His shocked cries woke Vanessa from her deep sleep. She sat up.

"What's wrong? Who turned out the lights? Are you okay, Henri?" she asked, concern flooded over her. Had someone entered while they were sleeping and harmed him.

"My arms! They are gone, just like yours were in the Badlands! God, your eyes, Vanessa! They are grey. Can you see anything? The lanterns are just like we left them," Henri answered, his voice shaking, fighting the growing terror in his stomach.

"Oh no! I can't see a thing. Well, at least I still have my arms this time. Let me feel you, dear." She began fumbling around and found what was left of Henri's arms "God, they are just like mine were in the Badlands! You got what I had and I got what you had!"

Henri cried a bit. "I am so helpless like this."

"I know. But use your feet. I can help you with my hands as long as you are my eyes, love. We can survive this. Trust me, we can, somehow. You know I think we got what we asked for. He did ask us how far we'd go for each other. I'd rather be blind so you aren't, love. I know how that terrified you."

Henri signed and calmed down. "I am always in control, you know. Like this, I am going to have to depend on you now. It makes me feel really funny though. Still, I know how badly it impacted you, love, so I'll get by somehow. Better me than you, right?"

"Hey, now you got it. I agree. I'd rather have your nightmare than force you to endure it again. Thanks for taking mine. I wonder what happened to the others?" Vanessa questioned, not wanting to think about the ramifications of her blindness at the moment. She put her arms around Henri, pulling him close to her.

Henri kissed her and said, "Thanks for taking mine. I am so terrified of being blinded. Thanks. I'll be your eyes this time and you'll be my arms. We did it before, we can do it again."

"Right, that's the spirit, love." The two laid back down and soon fell back into an ill sleep, though sleep they did.

When Zed and Miranda suddenly vanished at the inn in the Badlands, the others didn't notice for several minutes, primarily because the two always brought up the rear. "Where did they go?" Rose exclaimed. All shook their heads; none had seen them depart. Quickly, the six launched into a thorough search of the inn, including accosting Pecos. However, he shook his head; he'd not seen anyone except Albert, who had roused him requesting that he make breakfast for them.

After the group dined, Pecos suggested that they resume their journey. However, Rose could not be dissuaded from leaving her daughter behind. The party stayed at the inn another day but no trace of the two could be found and they did not reappear.

"We can't stay here forever. We need to get out of the Badlands before we encounter more nightmares," Reginald insisted. At last, Rose agreed and the band of six, carrying packs of water, left the inn.

That evening, they took refuge in Squirrelton, much to the pleasure of Sir Thomas. "Now we will see what real comfort is all about! These are my people," he exclaimed cheerfully for the first time. Indeed, they spent a pleasureful couple of days here, waiting on Zed and Miranda to reappear. Finally, Rose was convinced that they were not rejoining them soon, and she left a note at the inn, figuring that if and when Miranda and Zed returned, they'd very likely stay at this inn.

They walked happily on their way through the Worthy Forest. Sir Tomas was in excellent spirits. The numerous oak trees delighted him, as one might expect. Only Rose's spirits were low. Where was Miranda? Was she in trouble? Ought she do more? If so, what could she do? She had no idea where in this universe the two had gone, let alone why. Reginald was not helping; he kept saying that they would show up sooner or later. Rose doubted that very much. She began to dislike the man even more.

That first night in the forest, they found no inns and had to camp out under the trees. Sir Thomas climbed into an oak tree and was in heaven. Albert merely curled up on the ground, while Herr Adelstein conjured his home and slept in his own bed. The three humans made do, leaning against oak trees. Rose grumbled all the more. This was not to her liking in the slightest! By morning they were more than hungry, though they still had their water packs.

"We won't die of thirst, gang," Reginald chastised them. "Come on. Let's get walking and find us an inn soon." Once more they headed down the well-marked trail in the Worthy Forest. Around noon, they paused; hunger was getting the best of them. "Drink up, drink up, surely the inn is not too far now," he continued to urge them onwards.

Just then, he heard the rustling of leaves and, nearly silently, fifty men armed with longbows stepped out from their concealed locations. Reginald rose to flee, but saw that they were entirely surrounded. A tall man with a black beard stepped forward. "You all will come with us now. I see that you are starving. You can take lunch with us," he barked and then chuckled. Rose didn't see anything that was funny, but the lure of food out weighted all else.

Interesting enough, when the first leaves rustled, Sir Thomas, ever the skittish one, immediately vanished, poof! Upon seeing his friend vanish, Albert shrunk himself down in size and pretended to be a rock as he so often had done in the past. Likewise, Herr Adelstein took his cue from Sir Thomas, who he trusted to sense when danger was near. That Sir Thomas often found situations that he thought were dangerous initially and later turned out to be a false alarm didn't prevent the rabbit from reacting. Best be safe was his motto. Poof. He vanished, hiding in his house for the time being. Thus, the bandits found three humans as they approached their prey.

"Come on; it's not far," one man urged them on, prodding Rose with his arrow tip. She glared at him, but continued walking. Soon they saw the wooden stockade and followed the men into the huge wooden manor house. As they entered the dimly illuminated hallway, the delicious odors of a hot meal triggered their olfactory senses and stomachs begged for food.

This was the same dining room that Henri and Vanessa would later enter. Food was brought in by the scantily clad women, though only Reginald paid them much attention. Rose merely focused her attention on the meal and satisfying her craven hunger. Likewise, Trina.

"Now then, I am your host, Finigan Flake, Master of the Woods," he deep bass voice echoed a little in the room. "I do have the finest chef in the world preparing our meals. Do you not find it so?"

"It was good, yes. We were in dire need of food, that's all. Now can we please be on our way?" Rose replied.

"Not so fast. Try the wine. I have nothing but the very best vintages here," Finigan again tempted the trio. Trina refused, saying that she did not partake of the spirits. Rose wisely said that she didn't either, all the while trying to see what Finigan was really after. Reginald did sample the wines and agreed that they were good, but that was his only reaction.

"Excellent. If you will come with me, I want to show you my throne room." He led them into his treasury room where the huge pile of gold coins, gems, and jewelry lay.

Reginald was taken aback by such wealth and asked if he could examine the pile. "You, sir, have amassed a fortune here. Why, there is more here than one could spend in a lifetime. No make that ten lifetimes." He went on about it, lovingly holding the precious metal, and he did not see his wife and Rose being escorted from the room.

"I say, you are obviously a man who knows the true value of my treasure," Finigan suggested.

"Yes, I am highly impressed. I have dreamed of amassing my own fortune, sir."

"How far are you willing to go to obtain such wealth?"

"As far as necessary, sir," Reginald replied without the slightest hesitation. With even a portion of this treasure, he and Trina would never want for the slightest thing.

"I'll make you a deal, Reginald. Except for sleeping and mealtimes, I will give you all the gold that you can carry out to a waiting wagon. Of course, there is one slight stipulation. Your charming wife will have to make each trip from the treasury room to the wagon at your side. You cannot help her in any way, and she must carry this small bag filled with gold coins each trip and place it in your wagon by herself. The offer will be null and void if you help her in anyway, but she seems to be a strong woman. I'm sure that she can carry this tiny bag alongside of you each trip. You may use these saddlebags to carry as much out to the wagon as you can in three days. Will you accept my generous offer, Reginald?"

"You bet I will! Thank you, Finigan, thank you!" he replied, ecstatic over his sudden good fortune.

Meanwhile, from another side room, Trina witnessed what was happening with Reginald and Finigan. "I am called Felicia, Finigan's wife. As you can see, Reginald is after all the gold he can take with him in three days. Is it your wish to also take away a large pile of gold?"

"No, of course not, Felicia. We have always gotten by nicely on our own. I used to sew dresses and that helped us meet our expenses," Trina replied honestly.

Felicia smiled, "I know what you mean. I am not interested either in all of Finigan's gold. You can't eat it, I keep telling him." Both women chuckled. "You are not tempted by food or wines either, or our fabulous dancing?"

Aghast, Trina exclaimed, "Oh no. I admit your dancing was good, but where we come from, it is far too, well, shall we say risqué? Honest women in my country would never show so much, well you know, show so much of their bodies to men."

Felicia chuckled. "I've not heard it put quite that way. Fair enough, Trina. I take it that you value your husband above all else then?"

"Yes, he is the center of my life. Why do you ask?"

"How far would you go to protect him and to help him?"

"I would do anything to help him and keep him from harm."

"Good. We will see if this is in fact true." Felicia outlined what she must then do.

"You mean all I have to do is walk along side of him each trip to the wagon and carry that little bag of coins with me?"

"Yes, and place it in the wagon along with the pile that Reginald is making. Do you agree to help him so, no matter what?"

"Yes, I do," Trina replied.

"So be it. Come with me. I'll lead you to your guest bedroom. When the chimes sound, it is meal time. Simply come down this hall here; it leads directly to the dining room. You can't miss it." She chatted with Trina as she led her to their room. Reginald was already there waiting on her.

As she entered, he rushed to her side and began explaining their great fortune. Felicia quietly left them alone. Later that afternoon, Finigan came and led the pair to the treasury room and handed Trina a small bag. "You two have time to make a couple of trips before the evening meal. I assume that you want to get started on this right away?"

"You bet!" Reginald exclaimed, highly motivated.

While Reginald was examining the treasure pile, Felicia led Trina to a side room and then took Rose to another room. "Rose, please wait here for Finigan. He wants a private word with you."

"Well, I want some words with him," Rose replied a bit testily.

Later on, Finigan entered. "My apologies, Rose. I was detained a bit helping Reginald and Trina. Now then, let's get down to business, shall we?"

"Yes, why have you kidnaped us? Am I free to leave now?" Rose asked, suspecting that she was actually a prisoner.

"This is the Worthy Forest, Rose, and I am its master. Now then, you are not free to leave. What do you say to that?"

"You'd better let us go. My daughter and her boyfriend will be coming soon to rescue me, if my other friends don't beat them to it," Rose said defiantly.

Finigan seemed to ignore her outburst. "How come you entered alone? Did not your daughter enter with her boyfriend and Reginald with Trina? Why did you enter alone?"

Rose flushed. How could he possibly know that? Then, she realized that she was alone. She had just told him about her daughter and her boyfriend and Trina and Reginald were married. "None of your business," Rose replied. "They will rescue me soon, if you do not let me go."

"Agreed. Just how willing are you to stake all on the fact that your friends or your daughter will rescue you, Rose? How far are you willing to go? How strong is your faith in them? Are you willing to display your faith in them?" Finigan asked.

Rose would not be blunted. "Sir, if you do not release me, they will come and rescue me. That is a certainty."

"Yes, I believe that you are right, but I ask again, how far are you willing to go?"

"All the way," Rose retorted.

"So be it. If you will come with me, I will show you to a guest room where you may wait your rescue. When the chimes sound, it is meal time. Simply follow this hall and it will lead to the dining room. You can't miss it. I am sure that you will find the accommodations to your liking, ma'am."

"We'll see about that," she replied testily. Keep up a brave front, she told herself. There is hope, she thought. The rabbit, squirrel, and tortoise had eluded his dragnet. They might rescue her or if nothing else let Miranda know where she was being held captive. She relaxed, for the room was elegant and, if the truth be told, up to her standards of cleanliness and comfort.

As the bandits began leading the trio away with them, Albert opened one eye a very tiny crack. Seeing only the backs of the departing men, he hazarded a bigger view and stuck his head out and opened both eyes. Then, he sent word to his friend. Poof! Poof! Sir Thomas and Herr Adelstein appeared. "Are they gone? Is it safe now?" Sir Thomas asked, nervously.

"Yes, it would appear so, but then you had better not trust my judgment, you know," Albert replied sadly.

"I say, Sir Thomas, well done! Once again, your advanced warning saved us from getting captured or worse," Herr Adelstein complimented his friend. Sir Thomas puffed up to his full height. His fur swelled slightly. "I wonder where they are taking them?"

"I don't know," Albert answered, even though the question was not entirely directed at him. "I don't expect that it is any place that is good for them. Yet, it would seem to me that if we are to answer your question, Herr Adelstein, then we are going to have to follow them."

"But that will be dangerous," Sir Thomas quickly interjected, twitching quite visibly.

"Albert, you are right. We are going to have to follow them. I wonder where they are going? Come on; let's see for ourselves," the rabbit insisted. Slowly and cautiously, the trio followed the clear path left by so many boots on the forest floor. Before long, they halted and stared at the wooden fortress. They were in time to see the three humans bring marched inside the wooden gates.

"Oh dear me!" exclaimed Sir Thomas.

"Well, now we know Herr Adelstein's answer," Albert said in his monotone.

"What — what do we do-do now?" asked Sir Thomas, afraid of what the rabbit would say.

"Hum. I say that we wait a while. Perhaps they are merely going to feed them and then let them go. Let's see if Rose comes back out later on," Herr Adelstein suggested. The trio took up hiding places and watched and waited. At last it grew dark and he concluded that they must be spending the night there. Well, that made sense, since Rose could not conjure her house as he could. The three spent the night. In the morning, surely Rose would come walking out of the human fortress.

The next morning, some of the bandits came out, but no Rose and no Trina. "Well, now what do we do?" asked Sir Thomas. "Ought we to take a peek inside? Perhaps we can see them and find out if they are going to continue our lovely stroll through these fine woods."

"Yes, let's. Albert, you will be our rear guard. You stay here. Let us know if Rose should come out or if they are sneaking up behind our backs. Sir Thomas, let's appear in that big oak tree there. It overhangs the walls and we can see what's inside." A bit later the two friends appeared, sitting on a huge branch and saw the large manor house. No one seemed to notice them, fortunately for the nerves of Sir Thomas. "Now we watch and wait," the rabbit advised.

Rose awoke when the breakfast chimes sounded. Instantly, she knew that her worst nightmare had returned. Her hands were curled with arthritis and her joints ached. "I can beat this," she declared and got to her feet. Wobbling unsteadily, she slowly made her way to the dining room. She was so slow that most everyone else was done by the time that she arrived.

"Rise and shine, Trina! Today, we will amass our fortune!" Reginald declared, hopping enthusiastically out of bed and hastily dressing.

"Oh dear god! What's happened to me?" cried Trina. As she pulled back the covers, she noticed that her left leg was gone! No trace of it remained! Reginald rushed to her side and together they examined her pelvis.

"It is really gone, all of it. I don't know how this is possible. Come on; we have gold to get. Put your arm around me. I'll support you, Trina," he suggested. With his aid, she was able to manage to walk down the hall to the dining room. She was extremely glad to finally sit down, though. The food was filling and of excellent quality. However, Reginald kept hurrying her up. "Come on; time is flying. We get all the gold we can carry to the wagon."

As they finally entered the treasury room, Finigan was there. "Ah, no cheating, Reginald. The deal was that Trina must follow along side of you on each trip making her way on her own. No fair leaning on you. Plus, she must carry that small bag of coins with her and put them into the wagon herself," Finigan reminded the pair of their deal.

"How can I walk?" she asked.

"I guess that you can hop along on one foot. I will go slowly, dear. Come on; let's show this Finigan what we are made of! Think of all that we can buy with all this gold, dear," Reginald added. Poor Trina did her best to hop along beside him, flailing her arms about to keep her balance. After one exhausting trip, she became more skilled at it, much to the relief of Reginald.

Because she was so slow, they only made two round trips by lunch time. Yet, twice the duo sitting in the oak tree spotted them. The condition of Trina shocked both friends. "Oh dear me! They've pulled off one of her legs!" a terrified Sir Thomas whispered.

"Yes, they have. Likely ate it too! This place is worse than the Badlands! I wonder what they have pulled off of Rose? Let's see if she comes outside too," Herr Adelstein suggested.

Trina found the long walk to and from the wagon exceedingly tiring. Unused to hopping along on one leg, by supper the poor woman was totally fatigued, and Reginald had to carry her to the dinner table and then back to their bedroom. "Well, done, my dear. Look at what we have accomplished today! Why we have hundreds of gold coins in our wagon now! We have two more days to go. I think that we will have a fortune by then."

"I know, dear. I am so tired. I think I best get some sleep if I am to keep up with you. I am sorry that I can't go any faster dear. I know how much faster you could go without me."

"Well, it can't be helped, I suppose. That was his bargain. We have to earn our gold, it seems. Night dear. Tomorrow will be better. I'll pack even more coins into the saddle bags for each trip. You'll see."

Rose dosed most of the day, but refused to give in to her decrepit state. No way would she give Finigan the pleasure of seeing her protest or that she was in tremendous pain.

The next day, Trina rose to find that her left arm was completely missing! Shocked horribly, she cried for quite some time. At last, unwilling to give up, Reginald carried her to breakfast.

"Oh my goodness! What's happened to Trina?" asked Rose, who arrived as they did this morning.

"It's nothing. Part of the game that we are playing," Reginald pretended as though there was nothing at all wrong with his wife. Trina said nothing, but sobbed and tried to eat her nourishing food, bacon, eggs, and pancakes. As soon as she took her last bite, Reginald picked her up and headed as rapidly as he could to the treasury room. Rose sighed, what was happening here? She hoped that the trio would have the sense to try to rescue her or that somehow Miranda and Zed would find her soon. She had to believe in her daughter; she knew that she'd made her bargain with Finigan.

"Oh my! Look! They've pulled off one of her arms today!" declared a shocked Sir Thomas. The two watched the poor young woman valiantly trying to keep her balance while hopping along beside her ever-impatient husband. Once she fell, but Reginald was not allowed to help her get back up. All the while, Trina was sobbing or crying to herself, the two noted.

They barely got two trips made before lunch and then another two before suppertime came. Each trip, Trina moved more and more slowly, she was tiring rapidly today. It was exhausting work for her, and she fell six times, four during the last trip and had to be carried to the supper table.

Rose tried to make conversation with her, "How did it go today, Trina?" she asked as she grimaced from the pain of trying to get her gnarled fingers somehow around a spoon so that she could possibly eat her supper. Trina only sobbed and didn't reply. She was too exhausted to even attempt to talk with Rose. All she wanted to do was to lie down; her leg was throbbing in pain from all of the hopping she'd done these last two days.

Back in their bedroom, Reginald explained, "Only one more day, dear and we will be richer than we could ever hope to be. You are doing great; keep up the good work!"

Trina, her face soaked from tears, looked up at him from her bed. Slowly she sank back down and buried her head in her pillow, sobbing quietly to herself. She'd seen nothing but avarice in his eyes. He wasn't even being sympathetic to her awful, tragic plight and the cost all this was having upon her. Well, she thought, he did abandon me back in Malbon. She finally fell into a deep sleep.

When she awoke, she was not surprise to discover that her other leg had vanished during the night. In fact, she felt a surge of relief. No more of that awful hopping would she have to endure just so Reginald could obtain more gold. She felt certain that he would now give up this futile attempt. Yet, he seemed in good spirits when he rose, completely ignoring her latest loss.

"Today is our last day, dear. We need to make more trips than before. Oh, well, no more hopping for you. That's good isn't it? You were taking too many falls yesterday."

"But Regi, how can I even follow you like this? I've only got my right arm left?"

"We'll find a way. Come, I'll carry you down to breakfast now. We have to get an early start. Remember, this is our last day at it. Tomorrow we will be fabulously wealthy!" She saw now that all Regi really cared about was his gold. She was only a means to its acquiring. Trina sighed heavily.

This day, Rose met them in the hallway as she made her own pitiful way to breakfast. "Off to an early start I see. Oh dear god! Trina?" she exclaimed, spotting the young woman's new physical condition.

"Think nothing of it, Rose," Reginald hastily spoke up. "A few more trips today and we will be wealthy! Catch you later. We have to hurry up!" Rose shook her head and continued on her slow, wobbling way to the dining room. That poor girl, she thought. I hope we get rescued soon, before it's too late.

Reginald forced Trina to somehow manage to drag what was left of her body along the long hallway. She had to carry the small bag between her teeth this time. Her rate of progress was pitifully slow, and Reginald continued to bark his relentless requests for her to speed up. "Come on, Trina.

Don't give up now. We have to make many trips today. It is the last day of the bargain. Get with it!"

"I can't! I just can't!" she cried out.

Instead of compassion or even sympathy, he continued to badger her and finally got her to continue to use her arm to pull what was left of her body along the hallway. To his dismay, they were only able to make one trip during the entire morning. Over lunch, he chastised her for being so slow. "Come on; we only have this afternoon left!" Rose, watching the pair at lunch, merely shook her head. Her heart went out to Trina, but she was helpless to do anything about it.

Later she retired to her room. She found herself napping through most of the mornings and afternoons now. Thus, she missed seeing Henri and Vanessa arrive sometime after lunch.

"Oh dear me, now they have pulled off her other leg!" Sir Thomas exclaimed when Trina made her first appearance outside the manor house, carrying a bag between her teeth. As they watched, she tried to throw it onto the wagon, but missed. Reginald chastised her yet again and had to stand impatiently while she dragged her body over to the bag only to try again. It took her four attempts to finally get that bag into the wagon's bed.

Later on, the duo received a message from Albert. "Hey, they just captured Henri and Vanessa. I think this must be Miranda and Zed, but maybe I am wrong again. What shall we do?"

The two watched and saw the two being led inside the manor house. Then, they disappeared from their oak tree perch and appeared beside the hidden tortoise. "We must do something," Herr Adelstein declared gruffly. "If we don't do something, they are going to pull off Vanessa's arms and legs too, I'll wager."

"Oh dear me. You really think so? I suppose so, look at poor Trina. How are we going to rescue them?" Sir Thomas asked, forgetting for now his fear of these men. Having one's appendages pulled off was far more serious than just about anything else the squirrel could imagine, short of being eaten alive, which these bandits showed no signs of doing to Trina. Then, he had the awful thought that the rabbit had. "Say, what if they are pulling off her appendages and eating them?"

"How awful!" Albert spoke up.

"We must do something to help the 'umans," Herr Adelstein declared. "Let's put our heads together and see what we can think of."

At supper, Reginald pleaded with Finigan. "Look, can't you just give us one more day? As hobbled as Trina is today, we only were able to make two trips. Please, give us a break. One more day is all that I ask." He continued in this vein for some time. Trina said nothing, for she was beyond crying or even caring anymore.

"You want one more day? Are you sure that you want it?" Finigan asked him.

Seeing a faint glimmer that the dark man might agree, Reginald answered, "Yes, oh yes, yes! One more day would be fantastic, sir! Please."

"So be it," Finigan replied.

During the night, no one observed the trio appearing on the oak tree once more. "Over there. That one is close to the front door," Herr Adelstein whispered. "Okay, Albert. I know that you dislike being in a tree, but we need you to man the rope." He'd conjured a sturdy rope which was now affixed to the branch. "We will go down and see if we can find a way inside. You watch our backs and pull us up later on, okay?"

"Yes sir, commander sir," Albert saluted. Herr Adelstein had appointed himself their general; Sir Thomas, their captain, and Albert, their private. Slowly the two descended the rope and moved quietly to the wagon. Both looked in it and saw a large pile of gold. Then they crept to the main doors only to find them locked. The two crept cautiously around the manor house, looking for a way to get inside. They found none, unfortunately. Still they refused to give up their attempts but had to wait until daylight, hoping then to find another way to rescue them all.

Trina slept ill that night. She fully expected to wake without even her right arm left. Such was the pattern. Just how she could do anything at all without any arms or legs eluded her entirely. Reginald had made a bargain that she could not hope to help him win. She'd given him all that she had to give and still it was not enough.

Thus, she was a little surprise to find that she still had her right arm when morning came. "See, you still have your arm, dear. We can do it. He's given us one more day. Let's make the most of it!" Reginald declared enthusiastically as he woke her up. By the time that they reached the dining room, Rose was there, and the three were very much surprised to see Henri leading Vanessa into the dining room just after they had gotten to their seats.

"Mom!" Henri exclaimed. "Vanessa, it's mom, only she's back to being really old again. Oh dear god, Trina! What's happened to you?" Henri now saw what was left of the young woman. Trina didn't reply at all, just stared at the food that Reginald placed before her. "This time, she's blinded," Henri added for Rose's benefit, as he led her over to the table. Vanessa valiantly felt for the table and her chair and then was able to sit down.

"You don't know how glad that we are to have caught up with you," Vanessa said, talking in the direction that she thought Rose must be. Unfortunately, she was facing Trina instead.

"Over here, dear. Yes, I am glad too. I knew that you would come back for us in time. I am sorry that I am again in such a pitiful state. Still, it is wonderful to see you both again. Somehow we will make it out of here," Rose said with a bit of hope in her aged voice. Trina said nothing. Neither did Reginald, who was worried that these two would somehow wreck his bargain to become fabulously wealthy. He hastily picked up his wife and carried her out of the room.

While Vanessa followed carefully directions given by Henri and her constant feeling about with her hands, she managed to fill a plate with their breakfast. While it was challenging trying to feed herself, she had great difficulty feeding Henri, who now depended totally on her. She steeled herself, determine not to let him down. After all, she had taken her nightmare so that she didn't have to re-experience her worst fears again. Her long nails kept interfering, and she hoped that she was not poking him in his eyes. Henri was patient and continually talked her through the ordeal.

Once they had eaten, Henri asked Rose to tell them what had happened to the three and where their animal friends were at. "What in heaven's name happened to Trina?" he asked.

"Long story," Rose began. With little else that she could contribute, she could do this. Carefully, she outlined all that had happened to them, including the many bargains that had been made. "Each day now, poor Trina has come down to breakfast with fewer and fewer appendages. Honestly, I expected her remaining arm to have vanished this morning, though apparently it hasn't. Somehow, we have to get out of here and soon before Trina loses her remaining arm, poor thing. Ideas?"

"Let's see if we can take a walk outside of this manor house," Henri suggested. "We can reconnoiter and see what's what perhaps. Does Finigan allow that?"

"Don't know. I'm just barely able to walk from my room to the dining room and not much more. But I'll give it a try. We have to do something, Miranda, I mean Henri."

"Good mom. Hang on to me too. Vanessa, I am going to get mom first and then come back to get you. I'll have mom on my right and you on my left. We'll see if we can make it outside." Henri was optimistic still. He could see and was perfectly fit, save for his lack of useful arms. His mother could barely walk and Vanessa couldn't see at all. He had to do something and fast.

Their ambling down the hallway went very slowly. Rose took faltering steps and had to stop to catch her breath many times. On the other side, Vanessa was challenged to walk in her heels without being able to see and was more than willing to go so slowly. "This is so scary, Henri. I feel like I can fall down with nearly every step. It helps if I sort of slide along and not try to take big steps."

At long last, Vanessa felt the warmth of the sun striking her face and knew that somehow they had gotten outside. Henri whispered, "Dear, our carriage is still here, right where we left it. However, the gates are shut and barred. No one is standing guard, though. No wait. There are some men way over there. Darn, there goes that idea. How the devil can I possibly open the gate so we can drive the carriage out of here?"

Just then, he heard a "Psst" sound in his ear. Henri turned his head and saw a partially materialized head of Herr Adelstein appearing upside down. He was hanging from the rope. Quickly, he vanished again, but Henri, Vanessa, and Rose heard him clearly.

"We've come to rescue you. General Adelstein here. Captain Sir Thomas and private Albert are holding me up. What's the plan? Can't she see?"

"No, Vanessa is blind and mom is all crippled up with age," Henri whispered back. "Good to see you again, old friend."

"Well they are a-okay then. First we've seen of Rose. Poor Trina. They've pulled off her legs and arm! Did they pull off her other arm today? Sir Thomas wants to know and are they eating her appendages?"

Rose answered, "No, she still has her remaining arm, and I don't believe that they are dining on her appendages."

While they chatted, Henri knew that if they were to escape, he would have to come up with the plan. Vanessa couldn't see and Rose could barely move. While he had no arms, he could see and had to take charge. If they could get into the carriage, Vanessa could drive the team as long as he was beside her giving her directions. Rose could ride inside. For that matter, so could the trio. Yet how could they get the gate open? Everything hinged upon the gate being open.

"Say, I have a plan. Do you suppose that you and your army could manage to lift that wooden bar and open the gates? If so, Vanessa and I could drive the carriage out of here, stopping at the gate to let you three climb on board."

"Sounds like a plan to me. When do we do it?" General Adelstein asked.

Vanessa spoke up, "We should rescue poor Trina too, Henri. I don't know how, but we must. We can't leave her here, not like she is."

"Right, love. We can't."

Rose whispered, "If they do the same as yesterday, Reginald and Trina will be coming out to the wagon with another load of gold sometime this morning. We can go then."

"Right. If she still has her arm, she ought to be coming out midmorning. Leastwise, that's when she came yesterday. We've been spying and looking for a way to rescue you,"

General Adelstein announced, proud that their work had not been in vain.

"How will we get her to the carriage?" asked Vanessa. "You can't pick her up, nor can your mom for that matter. It's going to have to be me, but you are going to have to guide me all the way."

Henri sighed; he could see no other way to do it. Trina had to be carried to the carriage and helped inside. Worse, they had to move quickly when the time came and none of them were able to do that. "I know. Let's walk mom over to the carriage now. We can pretend that she is exhausted and needs to sit down. We can open the carriage door and let the steps down and let her sit on the steps. Then, we can move close to the wagon. It won't look at all suspicious that way. General Adelstein and his army can move over to the gates. When Trina comes out, dear, I'll direct you to her and you pick her up. When we do, mom, you do your best to get yourself inside the carriage anyway that you can. Once we get Trina inside, Vanessa and I will get into the driver's seat. As we are getting up there, that will be the signal for you to get the gates open. We'll stop at the gates and you three hop aboard and we'll race out of here. If they don't have any horses, we should be able to get away," Henri finished up his plan. They agreed and he, Vanessa, and Rose moved slowly over to the carriage.

After quite a lot of fumbling around, Vanessa finally got the door open and the steps lowered. Rose was honestly grateful to at last sit down. She was completely exhausted from all this exertion. Careful not to rouse suspicions, Henri and Vanessa moved back to the wagon and got into position to wait on Trina and Reginald to finally appear.

When at long last they came out of the front doors, Henri was thankful that Vanessa was unable to see just how terrible it was for poor Trina! His heart went out to her, as did

Rose's. Trina had to pivot her body along using her arm to do it. How she had managed to move at all impressed Henri. Rose took a deep breath and struggled to her feet. She was determined to somehow get herself into the carriage. After all, if Trina could manage to travel all that long way with only her arm to help her, surely she could get this arthritis-ridden body of hers into the carriage. She endured the sharp, shooting pains and finally made it.

When Trina finally neared the wagon, she saw the blinded Vanessa and the armless Henri standing there in her way. At last she found tears again and began crying. "Oh stop your blubbering, Trina. Come on. Throw your bag into the wagon. We have to get all the gold that we can today! He's generously given us this extra day. Let's make full use of it!"

Henri quietly talked Vanessa over to Trina and she felt for the woman. "I'm picking you up, Trina," she whispered. As constricted as she was, that was no small feat. At last, she had the woman in her arms. Henri moved close and put his short arm on her shoulder and began talking her over to the carriage. "You are sure light, Trina. We are escaping and taking you with us."

"Thank you," Trina managed to say, helping to hold on with her arm. Vanessa mostly dropped her into the carriage, though. Rose helped pull her inside. Henri left the two to somehow manage while he guided Vanessa to the steps that led up into the driver's seat. As he talked her up and into the box, he saw the flaw in his grand plan. How the devil was he going to get up there?

"Oh hell, if Trina can manage, somehow I can too," Henri steeled himself and used his teeth to help him keep his balance as he climbed up, biting down hard on parts of the carriage. At last in the box, he found that Vanessa had not been idle. She'd felt around for the reins and had them ready to go. "Okay. Let's get the horses moving. Pull hard to the left. Right. Harder. Good." Slowly the team headed to the gates. Suddenly, the rabbit, squirrel, and tortoise appeared at the gates. Between the three of them, they lifted the heavy log barring them shut and swung the gates open wide. Vanessa encouraged the team and the carriage rolled up to the gates. "Stop now. Okay, they are aboard. Let's get out of here. Fast! The guards are running our way! Faster, faster, pull right. More. Straighten them out. Okay. We're clear of them. They are firing arrows at us, but they can't do more than hit the rear of the carriage. Everyone, I think that we made it! Way to go, everyone! Well done!" Henri was elated, looking back over his shoulder and then quickly back at the road ahead, giving Vanessa the guidance that she depended upon.

Just then, Henri heard a voice inside his head. It was Finigan's. "You have proved your worth." Poof. Henri's arms reappeared. Simultaneously, Vanessa heard the same thing and suddenly she could see once more, much to her great relief! Inside the carriage, the five finally got themselves positioned properly, with the rabbit and squirrel helping the two women get onto the seats.

Rose heard Finigan's voice in her mind. "You faith has been well founded." Poof. She was her old self once more!

Rose called out, "I'm back to my normal self!"

"So are we, mom!" Henri called back from the driver's box.

Finigan's voice spoke much longer to Trina, however. "You have shown your worth many times over, Trina. Do you agree that it was wasted on Reginald?"

She thought what she had dared not express as yet. "Yes, I can see it now. He is only interested in the gold, not in me."

"Go now, worthy Trina. May you find a man more worthy of a woman such as yourself." Poof. Trina's body was back to her old self once more, much to her great relief. She found the others staring at her. That she had taken far longer to return to normal had begun to worry Rose. "What happened, dear?" she asked motherly.

"He was never interested in me at all! He only wanted more gold," she began sobbing, and Rose put her arms around her, content to be her mother for the time being.

"There, there, Trina. At least you know the man's true feelings now," Rose hinted.

Much later, Henri and Vanessa discovered that their day pack of things had also reappeared in the carriage. She had her nightgown and hair brush back. However, she and Henri argued over who got to drive the carriage for the rest of the day. Vanessa won.

Late that afternoon, they entered another squirrel village, East Oak. Vanessa pulled up before the inn. After Henri helped her down, she helped the others out of the carriage. "I sure am glad to see that you are all right, Trina. Although I couldn't see you, Henri described you. I can't imagine how awful that was for you."

"I think I now have a worse nightmare than before, but please, please, Vanessa, don't make me go back into your body. I endured your corsets and heels for a century and a half. I just can't do that anymore, please," Trina begged.

"Oh no! Trina, Miranda and I are rescuing these two from their Malbon servitude bondage. No way are you supposed to take over this body again," Vanessa hastily attempted to put the young woman at ease. "Honestly, you have been through quite enough for any person."

Later at the dinner table, Trina finally spoke more openly. "I do hope that Regi will somehow come to his senses. A woman has to find the best man that she can to support her and later on their children, of course. I thought that Regi would be a good provider when I met him in Peoria. I should have seen the signs though. I mean we got a modest home, and I took care of it for us, as a woman is supposed to do — cleaning, scrubbing, and preparing our meals. Mondays were laundry days, though Tuesday was ironing day. One day he came home very tired, and he complained that I was loafing and that I had lots of free time during the day. Well, I had to admit that I did; that's when I began making dresses in the hours that I was not doing my wifely duties, you see. I am sure that he appreciated the extra money that I brought in. So honestly, I should have seen this in him back then. It is my partly fault, don't you think? I should have worked even harder to bring in more money."

Vanessa wasn't about to let Trina deprecate herself. "Oh don't be silly, Trina. Yes, a marriage is a team, but what he put you through back there is beyond all decency, all common sense. Let's face it Trina; he was just plain greedy. No matter how much gold you helped him get into the wagon, he wanted more. Am I not right?"

"Well, now that you put it that way, he did. He kept saying just a bit more, but it never stopped. He even begged Finigan to give us an extra day at it. I was certain that I'd wake up this morning without any arms or legs at all! Still, he is my husband until death do us part. Maybe I should have stayed with him. Maybe I could have helped him get better somehow."

Herr Adelstein spoke up, "Gold. How silly. You can't eat metal."

She grinned slightly. Rose took this opportunity to suggest, "Look, Trina. As long as he had you there, he had someone to blame for not acquiring more wealth. You said that he constantly complained that you were holding him back from getting more gold. As long as you stay with him, he's going to continue to put the blame for his own mess onto you. As I see it, Trina, you are doing the very best that you possibly can do for him by totally abandoning him —

leaving him to his own ways and means. Now he has no one to shunt the blame off onto, no one but himself. I think in time he may come to realized just how much he has lost. It's been my experience that men often get their priorities all mixed up, and it takes a woman to help get them straightened back out. By leaving him now, you are giving him the chance to experience what he has abandoned in his vain quest for riches. He may well recover as a result. Then, again, he may not, and at least he will not be taking you down along with himself. Greed does that to a man."

"You think he might come to his senses? Really? But how will he ever find me again?" Trina began to worry again.

"Hey, where there is a will, there is a way. Look at us," Henri pointed out the obvious.

"I say, what happened to Zed and Miranda?" asked Herr Adelstein. "One minute there were there and then poof, they were gone. You know that we searched for them for days, don't you?"

Henri spent several minutes outlining what had happened to them. "You see, we are now also rescuing Vanessa and Henri from their long servitude as the Count and Countess of Malbon," he explained.

"Did they get trapped in here like Regi and I did?" Trina asked.

Vanessa answered, "I don't believe so, but as yet, we are not sure. However, we are going to take them as far from Malbon as we can."

# Chapter 9 The Redemption of Reginald Noxwood

When the blind Vanessa valiantly picked up what was left of his wife, Trina, Regi knew that they were going to escape and that his bargain with Finigan was doomed. He also knew that he could stop them and prevent the loss of his bargain. Rose could barely walk in her aged body. Henri was helpless to stop him and Vanessa was as blind as a bat. Even if she had her sight, she couldn't do anything to stop him. However, deep inside his mind something prevented him from taking any action but watching them make their daring escape.

He saw the animals risking all to get the gate unlocked and opened. He saw the bandit guards spotting them and watched as they sounded the alarm and ran to intercept the fleeing carriage. Something long buried inside him cheered when the carriage rolled out of the fortress to freedom. Finigan appeared beside him, and all such feelings left him immediately.

"Well, you kept your side of our bargain, Mr. Noxwood. It is time that you enjoyed your accumulated wealth," Finigan said dryly.

"You mean I get to keep this wagon full of gold?" Regi asked, scarcely believing his luck. Perhaps he would be a wealthy man after all!

"Of course, it is all yours." Finigan grinned mischievously. He clapped his hands. Poof! Reginald found himself in a luxurious room in Malbon, though not at the Royal Palace, where he'd been captive in Henri's body for so many years. No, this was another room somewhere else within the city. Regi was lying on a bed of gold coins, all of the coins that he and Trina had managed to carry to the wagon. No sheets, no pillows, no covers, no mattress, just the cold, hard gold coins.

That barely got his attention. No, what stole his whole attention was his own body! He lay there naked on his bed of gold. He had no legs at all and his left arm was completely missing. He was as his wife had been! "This is not fair! I earned this gold!" he screamed to the empty air. Regi finally realized that now he was going to have to live life as his wife had these past few days. The stark reality of her sacrifice for him slammed him in his face.

"What have I done?" he screamed. "I didn't mean it, Trina. I didn't mean it. I'm sorry." However, he realized that it was far, far too late for an apology. Worse, he knew that he was fibbing. He had meant it; he had meant to gather all of the gold that he could. He just had not bargain to be a total invalid, so helpless. "This is not fair, Finigan," he cursed.

A knock on his door brought him to the present. A woman's voice said, "You all right in there Mr. Noxwood? I just came to say that lunch is ready. If you are not at the table soon, you'll have to wait until suppertime."

Reginald struggled to get himself out of his bed. Now he got to fully experience what he had been forcing Trina to endure. It took him all afternoon to get his pants, or rather what was left of them on, and his shirt and jacket. At last, he dragged himself slowly to the door. After a tedious balancing act, he was able to prop himself up enough so that his hand could reach the door knob and open it. He peered out into the hallway. Where was he anyway?

He heard noises coming from one end of the hall and decided to head in that direction. Pathetically, he dragged what was left of his body along the hall. After an eternity, he entered the dining room, just as a plump cat woman was setting the table. "Oh there you are Mr. Noxwood. Just in time for supper. Come on; get to your place over there," she pointed to a low bench and foot stool on which she had placed a place setting for him. Evidently, she knew all about his handicap, but how? He glanced about the room and saw an embroidered plaque that read Mrs. Bench's Boarding House.

So confusing. He continued to make his pitiful way across the floor to the low bench. Just then several other boarders, mostly cat people, came filing in for dinner. Several nodded to him as if they knew him. He nodded back. One cat man did say, "We missed you at lunch. Bit busy, eh?" Before he could reply, the man turned and sat down beside a pretty cat woman and began discussing the events of the day. "Say, what do you make of our new Countess? Finally we cat people have gotten the respect that we are due."

"Yes, I think that is just fabulous," she replied demurely.

No one offered to help Regi, and by the time that he got into position to actually dine, the others were taking their tea. Soon, he was alone watching Mrs. Bench clear the table. "You are going to have to speed up, Mr. Noxwood. I can't wait all day on you, you know," she chastised him. Regi made an effort to finish eating as rapidly as possible. He had just finished and gotten off his low bench when she came and picked up his dirty dishes. "Now that's more like it, Mr. Noxwood. It's your own fault for having lost your arm and legs. In the war was it? Well, I ought to have my head examined for allowing you to stay at my boarding house. Nevertheless, you are paid up for a year so I guess there is no harm in that. Just do try to be on time for your meals, Mr. Noxwood. It takes a lot of work to run a successful boardinghouse." She bustled off with his dishes, not giving him a chance to reply.

Hours later, he finally made it back to his own room, totally exhausted from his ordeal. He crawled up to a sofa and looked longingly at it, wondering how he could possibly get his body up into it. He looked at his bed of gold coins and then spent an arduous hour getting himself up and into the sofa. "I'm sleeping here for sure!" he exclaimed, looking at the cold, hard bed of gold across the room. "What have I done?"

Days passed slowly for Reginald. He was wealthy, but. Often at night, he wailed to the walls, "Finigan, take back all of your gold, only give me back my legs and arm, please." His protests, his begging, his curses fell on the deaf walls of his boardinghouse room.

Each day, he simply could not get to the dining room in time for breakfasts and thus was only able to have lunch and supper. It took him over an hour to get from his room to the dining room, and Mrs. Bench refused to hold breakfast that long for him alone. Reginald was miserable, his life ruined, though he continued to blame Finigan for several days.

After his first week of living this new life, Reginald finally hit bottom, wallowing in self-pity and not even bothering to crawl down the hall for lunch. Sobbing to himself and continuing to blame Finigan for his pitiful new existence, he reached his mental precipice. One slight nudge and he would go over the edge, becoming a miserable, sorrowful, nasty person for the rest of his lifetime. As he was about to take that plunge into the depths of despair, he saw a memory of Trina, his loving wife. There she was valiantly trying to move what was left of her body down the impossibly long hallway, a bag of gold coins held tightly between her teeth. She was doing it only for him with no thoughts of herself.

Suddenly, Reginald fully realized what he had lost, something far more precious than all of Finigan's gold! He sobbed and sobbed, "What have I done, Trina? What have I done? It is all my fault, not yours. You did everything you could to help me. I did this to myself and to us. I have destroyed both you and me. Curse this damnable gold anyway. We always got by and were happy. I know that you were happy and I was too. It is all my own doing, Trina."

Still the image of his one armed wife doing her best to move alongside of him hung there in his mind, now rather as a beacon, a shining light showing him the path that he must take. "I have to get back to you, Trina. Somehow I must find you and make this right between us. Trina, I promise you that I will do whatever it takes to win you back!"

It dawned on him that Zed and Miranda had disappeared from the inn in the Badlands, and they had returned, obviously from Malbon, since they were occupying Henri and Vanessa's bodies. If they could retrace their path, so could he! Hope returned to him, though ever he kept the image of the one armed Trina crawling at his side before him in his mind. "My guiding light!" he proclaimed.

He struggled out of his sofa and to his door. A half hour later, he called out for Mrs. Bench. After some time, she finally came. Annoyed with him, she said, "I hope this is worth it, Mr. Noxwood! I was right in the middle of fixing supper. Now be quick about it or our meat will burn."

"Please step inside my room for a minute. I have a deal for you. See all my gold there?"

"Goodness! Mr. Noxwood! You have a fortune there," the cat woman exclaimed.

"Yes, and it is all yours if you will do a simple thing for me. I want you to purchase a small wagon and team for me. Load the wagon with some blankets, food, and water, and then help me get into the driver's seat. I want to leave, and I need some help getting started. If you will do this for me, all that is yours to keep, and you'll never see me again. Please, Mrs. Bench, please help me."

"All that? Mine? Very good, sir!" Mrs. Bench exclaimed. "I'll get right on it after lunch!"

Late that afternoon, Mrs. Bench lifted him up and into the wagon that she'd just bought. "My, but you are lighter than I expected."

"Not much of me left. Thank you, Mrs. Bench. You are helping to save my life."

"Are you sure that you can manage this all by yourself?"

"No, but I have no choice by to try. I will do this or die trying; there is no other path for me, Mrs. Bench. All this is my own doing, and I alone must undo it. Thank you again." He spent another half hour maneuvering his body into a position from which he could handle the reins with his right hand and not fall over. At last, he got the horses moving slowly and finally he sensed that he was on the right path. "Trina, I am coming to find you," he said to the world around him.

He found driving the wagon an incredible challenge. Obstacles never seemed to end, barriers lay everywhere. Even getting himself a drink of water took him a half hour of careful maneuvering. Always, though, he kept the image of his one armed Trina bravely crawling alongside of him in the hallway acutely in his mind. When the challenges grew too great, he called out, "Trina, I am coming. If you could manage, so must I." Somehow he overcame each barrier.

Several days later, he halted at the rim of the Badlands. The path down was terribly steep. Could the horses make it? If not, he would have to crawl through this land. If that happened, to prevent himself from dying of thirst, he decided that he could tie packs of water to his waist and somehow drag them along with himself. Then he noticed the wagon ruts left by the carriage. "Hey, Henri and Vanessa came to Finigan's in their carriage. If they could get down this steep canyon, so can I."

As he urged the skittish horses onwards, he quickly realized that he could not maintain his precarious balance.

To keep from falling off, he lowered his body into the bottom of the driver's box, where one's feet usually were. In doing so, he left the horses to fend for themselves, trusting that they could find their way down the steep canyon. Later, the horses stopped when they reached the level canyon floor. An hour passed before Reginald was able to regain his position in the driver's seat. "We made it. Good going horses! Onward. Trina, I am coming."

Late that night, he came to the inn. To his surprise, Pecos heard the horses and stepped out to see them. "Well, I see that you are back, Mr. Noxwood. My, looks like you are a war victim!"

"Yes, I am trying to catch back up to my dearest, loving wife, if I possibly can. What do you mean war victim?" he asked, confused with Pecos' assumption.

"Wars are bad; leaves men without their limbs. You must have been in some battle!"

"Yes, it is my own fault."

"Going to stay the night here?"

"I can't get down from here on my own or back up. I reckon that I'll just sleep in my wagon as I have for the last few days. Is that all right with you?"

"Sure. Mind if I bring you some supper and share a cup of tea with you? Gets mighty lonely out here. So few travelers these days. Why years ago, I'd get lots of travelers. Nowadays, so few of you," Pecos admitted.

"Fine with me. I could use a hot meal. Mind you, I am living my worst nightmare, so don't expect me to have those awful nightmares like I had last time I was here." Pecos chuckled, he could see that Reginald was speaking truthfully.

Next morning, after fixing him a hot, filling breakfast, Pecos watched the wagon slowly moving on down the trail. He sighed and wondered how long it would be before he saw another living person.

Two long days later, Finigan and his band of bandits stopped the wagon that was passing through the Worthy Forest. "Ah, so we meet again, Reginald Noxwood," Finigan grinned, recognizing the man sitting precariously in the driver's box. "Back for more gold are you? Spent all of it already?"

"I am only passing through, Finigan. I have only myself to blame for the mess that I am in. I know that it was none of your doing. I don't want your gold. I gave it all to a wonderful boardinghouse woman. Do I have to make another deal with you to get my arm and legs back?" he asked, hoping against all odds that somehow Finigan could make this right.

"I am truly sorry, Reginald. I only have the power to take away, not to give back. There is only one person who can give you back what you have lost, and you know who that is. Sorry. You may continue your journey, Mr. Noxwood," Finigan replied. He turned and he and his band slipped back into the forest trees. Reginald clucked to his horses and moved on down the trail.

"So it is going to be heuristic, eh?" Reginald called out after the receding Finigan. "I have to find it out myself?" He got no reply. "Well, I didn't really expect him to help me out. Trina, I am still coming! I hope that I am not too late."

# Chapter 10 The Encounter Hills

"Well everyone, we are officially leaving the Worthy Forest and entering a land of rolling hills with some scattered trees. I see a large sign that reads Entering the Encounter Hills," Henri called down to the passengers in the carriage. This day, Vanessa had finally gotten Rose and Trina to help her change her dress. Of necessity, she'd worn the other one for days, since Henri was unable to help her much. Now it was torn and dirty. She also tossed away the ripped nylons as well. Today, she chose to sit in the carriage with the others and allow Henri to drive them. Herr Adelstein sat proudly in the driver's box with him.

Rose was in good spirits, far better than she had been since her ill-fated entering of this world some weeks ago. She had a new purpose: to help Trina adjust to her most unfortunate circumstance. "Look, I lost my husband too. Been over eight years now. At first, I just didn't know what to do without him around," she told Trina. Henri, hearing this, insisted on driving. She didn't want to have these painful memories brought back just now. Vanessa understood and volunteered to sit in the carriage and monitor the women.

At last, Vanessa gained a key insight into Rose and her behavior. She took the loss of her husband very badly and had been merely floating along in life, unable to latch on to any real new purposes for herself. Now she had one, looking after the upset Trina Noxwood.

"Encounter Hills?" Vanessa called out, "I wonder what that implies?"

"I say, encounter? Might not be so good, do you think?" Sir Thomas asked, once more growing slightly nervous at his own pronouncement.

"Oh encounters can be good, can't they, Vanessa?" Albert attempted to help out his dear friend. "But then I could well be wrong. You know me," he added defensively. This only heightened the squirrel's nervousness.

"Well, each place that we go, it seems that we are being tested," Vanessa pointed out. "Perhaps in these hills, which are rather picturesque — see," she pointed a long red nail out of the window, "perhaps we will be tested further."

"But haven't we had encounters everywhere we've gone?" Rose protested slightly.

"You have a point," Vanessa admitted, biting her lip. "Well, let's watch the beautiful countryside for a while."

Late that afternoon, they heard a loud thundering noise coming their way. "The Enforcers are coming!" screamed Sir Thomas. Poof! He vanished into his secret place.

"Oh dear, not again!" Albert added, shrinking himself down to the size of a fly and then landing on Vanessa's wavy hair, burrowing deep into it.

"Stay alert everyone; horsemen are coming our way. Looks official like," Henri called out.

Herr Adelstein barked, "They are not Enforcers, just 'umans wearing pretty red uniforms." The head of Sir Thomas appeared upside down in mid-air. He looked out the window and saw human men in red uniforms and promptly reappeared on his seat, acting as if nothing had happened. Albert stayed hidden in Vanessa's hair as fifty soldiers came riding up to the carriage. One ordered Henri to halt and he obeyed.

"Perhaps this is the 'encounter,'" Rose theorized.

"Climb down sir; the general will want a word with you and your party. Passengers, please step out of the carriage," one soldier ordered.

Henri hopped down, as did Herr Adelstein. The men had guns, he noted, though the rabbit did not know what they were, having never seen one before. "We have women inside; permit me to assist them out," Henri said politely. He held his hand out and Rose took it, stepping down; Trina followed her. Henri had to lift Vanessa down, since her apparel and heels didn't permit her to easily navigate the three steps. Finally, Sir Thomas stepped out, followed by Albert, who had finally decided that he didn't need to hide any longer.

As Vanessa stepped out and the mounted men got their first look at this overly endowed woman in her red satin, form-fitting dress, black nylons and tall heels, they catcalled and whistled at her. Vanessa flushed. This was so embarrassing. Henri grinned; Zed was getting quite an education, she mused.

Just then, several moved off to one side as their leader rode slowly up to them and dismounted. He was quite tall, towering over Henri. "What have we here?" he spoke in a surprisingly deep bass voice, rather unexpected, Henri thought. "Well, aren't you quite the babe!" he said to Vanessa. He judged the man to be perhaps fifty; a twinge of grey marked his otherwise black hair and moustache.

"My wife, sir. Vanessa," Henri hastily moved to her side.

"Luck man, such knockers. Bet she is really something in bed. Ah, I see that we have some spies with you. No matter. We know how to deal with spies. Let me welcome you new recruits to my army, the Human Army, that is. We are about to launch a major offensive against our enemies, so you new recruits are most welcome. Take the evil rabbit and wicked squirrel into custody boys. Don't make a move, you two traitors. We have guns. One false move and my men will put a bullet hole through your heads. Sir Thomas and Herr Adelstein recalled the dead plastic woman on the Malbon Express and suddenly knew what a gun could do. Several soldiers tied their hands behind their backs and began marching the pair off over the hills.

"What are you doing to our friends?" Henri protested.

"Friends? Hah, you have been deceived. They are enemy spies. Now get back in your carriage and follow us to our magnificent encampment. There, I'll issue you your new duties, privates. We need new recruits. Time is moving so fast. The Great Battle is nearly upon us." He mounted up and followed after the men who were leading the squirrel and rabbit away. Henri hastily helped the women back into the carriage and soon drove their carriage after the general.

"Men! Always thinking of battles!" Rose declared angrily. Vanessa gave her a strange look. "Well, you don't see women playing general do you or starting wars?" Vanessa had to agree with that point.

The encampment consisted of a hundred colorful tents pitched on a hilltop overlooking a wide valley. They were taken to the general's tent and again asked to leave their carriage. As they did, hundreds of men whistled and catcalled when Vanessa stepped awkwardly onto the soft ground, wobbling a bit to keep her balance. High heels and soft ground do not mix too well, but the soldiers were delighted with the general's new recruits.

Soon, they were seated around the field table beside the general's colorful red tent. "I am General Wilhelm Frank, Supreme Commander of the Human Army. As you can see on that distant hill to your right lies the Wicked Squirrel Army, while on that hill to your left lies the Evil Rabbit Army, our bitter enemies. Soon, we shall engage them in a massive battle, eliminating them from the face of these Encounter Hills forever! Now then, new recruits, you are appointed to be Private Henri. Someone will give you your gun, which you will treat with tender loving care. Your gun is your life out here on the battlefield, son. You'll be assigned a tent as well. More orders will be forthcoming. Sergeant, take Private Henri here and get him equipped pronto. No telling how soon our enemies may attack us. Be prepared at all time, Private Henri." Henri tried to protest, but was dragged away by the heavyset man who was twice his weight.

"Now then ladies, how best to use you?" the general pulled on his moustache thoughtfully. "It will not do to put you into uniforms. That will spoil the morale of the men. No, you three will become our nurses. Yes, take them to Surgeon Milan; they can stay with him and assist him with our casualties. Now for the traitors, that rabbit and squirrel. What have you two to say for yourselves? Spying on our positions, eh? Well, off with their arms and legs! Draw and quarter them, I say. Take them to Surgeon Milan and have him draw and quarter them at once." He completely ignored the tortoise, who chose to amble along after the women.

Herr Adelstein glared at the general, but wisely kept quiet. Sir Thomas merely fainted, and the soldiers had to carry him to the surgeon. Meanwhile, General Wilhelm added, ladies, please continue wearing your dresses. It will raise the men's morale. If you will, please dine with me here at my tent each day. Now take them to Surgeon Milan and let them get prepared. Casualties will be forthcoming any day now. Be prepared. Remember that always, nurses. Be prepared!"

"I can't walk by myself on this ground," Vanessa whispered. Rose and Trina moved to either side of her and supported her. "This is ludicrous. We have to save our friends."

"They ignored me. I must not be important at all," Albert muttered to no one in particular.

"That's not true, Albert!" Vanessa declared. "You'll see." She didn't know quite why she said that, but it appeased the tortoise.

They arrived at a tent with a stripped red and white pole out front, the Surgeon's Tent a small sign announced. "Surgeon Milan, front and center," the soldiers called out. Presently a thin man, who was also about fifty Vanessa guessed, stepped out. He wore a white apron over his red uniform. He had spectacles on and was quite blonde. "Got two spies here to be drawn and quartered. You know, remove their arms and legs at once."

"Oh my, more spies, eh? Well, you've brought them to the right place, soldier. Usher them inside my tent. My, what do we have here?" he said, noticing the three women, especially Vanessa and then Rose.

"Your new recruits. They are to become your nurses. See that they are well trained — general's orders." The soldiers pushed the two prisoners inside the tent and then left.

"Milan Ward. And you are?" he said politely, extending his hand to Vanessa.

"Vanessa Graves. My husband, Henri, has been forced to become a private. We have been waylaid by these soldiers. We just wanted to cross the Encounter Hills, not take part in some silly battles."

"Well, you look smashing, my dear, positively smashing," Milan replied, shaking her hand. He had a distinctive English accent the three women noted. Strange. He held his hand out before Rose.

"Rose Whitney," she replied politely. "Those two are our friends. Surely you are not going to murder them. They have done nothing wrong!"

He ignored her slight outburst and offered his hand to Trina, who introduced herself. "Come, dear ladies. Inside please; we have urgent business with the two so-called spies." He ignored the tortoise, and Albert merely followed the women inside the tent, which did look much bigger on the inside than he thought from the outside.

"Around here, I am the doctor. Now then, rabbit, squirrel, I know that I am supposed to detach your arms and legs and put you onto the general's trophy display, but I hate to disappoint you, that is not going to happen in my tent. The general be damned. The safest place for the both of you is over yonder on those hills. Rabbits are there, squirrels, there," he pointed out the two directions. "Of course, you are both welcome to simply vanish if you prefer. Only I cannot caution you both too strongly, do not get caught by the general's soldiers a second time."

"Why thank you doctor for not harming our dear friends," Rose complimented him. She liked the way that he was handling this. "I think that it might be wise of you to join your brethren for the moment. What about Albert here?" she asked.

Doctor Milan looked at the tortoise as if only now noticing him for the first time. "Oh, no one pays the slightest attention to turtles. He can come and go as he pleases. He is large enough to avoid being stepped on by accident."

Vanessa suddenly got a bright idea. "Fellows, you go join your kind. Albert here will act as our messenger, delivering messages between us all. Okay with you Albert?"

"Oh sure. No one notices me anyway. Glad to do it," he replied. Poof! Poof! The two vanished from the tent. No one spotted their footsteps in the grasses of the hills as the two headed off to see the other two armies.

"Ladies, if you will follow me, I'll show you around my field tent here. Have you any medical training?" All three said no. "Pity. If the general actually does finally launch his attack, so many men will need our services. It would have been most helpful if I really did have some honest nurses.

Silly general keeps recruiting men and women who have no training whatsoever, and then he thinks that by merely appointing them to a post that they are then competent at it. Stupid man, bloody stupid if you ask me."

"So why are you still here? Can't you leave?" asked Rose.

"I probably could, but you see sooner or later, they are going to battle it out, and the men will be grievously wounded. Think what will happen if they only had a doctor who was 'appointed' by the general to care for their wounds. I've seen enough of that in the field hospital of Wellington. That was in my youth, mind you, 1812 to be precise. Men lost limbs right and left. Afterwards, most men wished that they'd just died though. Still, I am sticking around to help them here. Care to dine with me tonight?"

"We've prefer it, but the general has asked us to dine with him," Rose replied.

Doctor Milan chuckled. "He mostly wants the company of Vanessa here. Perhaps she could dine with him and you with me?" he suggested.

"But in her heels, she needs one of us to help her navigate the grassland," Rose pointed out.

"I'll go with her, you can dine with Doctor Milan," Trina offered.

"There, that's settled. Now then, I suppose that I should show you what I keep where. If we have an emergency, I cannot expect more of you than to fetch the things that I will need. But first, I need to add two more stuffed animals to the general's trophy case, just in case he comes by. Follow me."

The neighboring tent held a huge wall filled with stuffed squirrels and rabbits, all minus their appendages. Milan conjured another pair and added them to the shelves. Rose chuckled at his deception. She began to take a fancy to the doctor.

"So glad that you could join me for supper," General Wilhelm declared, his mischievous eyes focused on Vanessa's enormous breasts, though he alternated between them and her well-shaped legs. He mostly ignored Trina for which she was thankful. Vanessa picked that up and endured the lecherous man for Trina's sake.

"Tomorrow is our big day. We are going to test the Ultimate Weapon that my soldiers have just perfected. We are calling it a Canon. If the tests go well, then I will launch my major offensive against our enemies, assured of total victory," he boasted. Vanessa didn't like the sound of this or the direction that it was going.

"Whatever have the squirrels and rabbits done to humans? You must forgive me, general, I am not from around here, rather from the city of Malbon," Vanessa asked, remembering to bat her eyes at the general and re-cross her legs so that he could see them better, which he greedily did.

"Well, everyone knows that the squirrels and rabbits are man's fiendish enemies," he replied.

"Yes, but who is everyone? We have squirrels and rabbits in Malbon, but we are all at peace with one another," Vanessa persisted.

"Well, they just are. You cannot expect mere women to know these things," General Wilhelm replied condescendingly, which only raised her ire all the more.

Later when they rejoined Rose for the evening and having told her of their conversation, Vanessa vented, "Well, this is just what you get when you have ignorant, pompous buffoons in charge of governments and armies. This whole thing is completely idiotic, to say the very least. I hope their canon blows up tomorrow."

"Oh don't say that! We would have a bloody mess to deal with in the surgery tent," Rose pointed out.

At noon on the following day, hundreds of soldiers gathered around the hilltop to watch the final testing of their Ultimate Weapon. The three women stood beside the doctor some distance from the general, who walked around with his chest pushed out. "I hope it doesn't malfunction! Look, Henri is part of the firing crew!" Vanessa pointed out. She kept her fingers crossed.

Boom! A huge explosion rocked the hilltop. A giant puff of black smoke came out of the cannon. Vanessa blinked, but Henri was all right. After several seconds, the shell landed short of the rabbit's hilltop. A fainter boom echoed across the valley. A huge plume of smoke, grass, and ground rose into the air, and then descended. The general led the cheering, and many soldiers jumped for joy, patting fellow soldiers on their backs. After a short repositioning, the cannon fired again, lobbing a second shell just short of the squirrel's hilltop.

Over the celebration din, Vanessa heard the general, "Now if we could just get them to have a bit more range, why, we could wipe them all out from here and not even have to charge over there. Soldiers, get to work on increasing the range, will you?"

Before they could reply, a pair of faint booms came from the enemy hilltops. All eyes turned to the hills where puffs of black smoke could be seen. "What treachery is this?" yelled the general. Boom! Boom! Huge piles of dirt, grass, and shrapnel came flying up over their cannon crew as the two enemy shells landed just short of the human-held hilltop.

"Casualties!" someone called out.

"With me, nurses," Doctor Milan requested. The three followed after him to his tent, but because of Vanessa, they were slow to arrive. Soldiers carrying the wounded men beat them to the tent. While they feared the worst, none were badly injured. Henri was there; he'd taken a bit of a scratch and was using this opportunity to visit with everyone, trying to find a way out of this escalating mess.

"Well, I am greatly relieved that Herr Adelstein and Sir Thomas are okay. I was a bit worried about them. You know the soldiers are now getting worried about the effects of the enemy cannons. These blasts today were darn close," Henri pointed out.

"Enough that they might mutiny?" asked Vanessa.

"Probably not that much. Still maybe we can find a way to use it to our advantage. I guess I had better be getting back. If you need something, send Albert to me. It's amazing how they completely ignore him," Henri added. "Perhaps Albert should check on Sir Thomas and Herr Adelstein this evening and make sure that they are okay."

"I like being invisible around here," Albert declared and headed off to find his friends.

Later, Rose made them tea, and the four sat around the doctor's table chatting. "Doctor Milan, I take it that you are not from around here. You mentioned Wellington and 1812," Rose inquired, curious to know more about this unusual doctor.

"Oh no. Not from around here at all. I came from another place entirely, but you probably have never heard of it."

"Do tell us, doctor," Rose insisted.

"My wife and I came from London, England. See, I told you that you have never heard of it."

"Of course we have. I admit that I've never been to London. Four of us are from Peoria, Illinois, USA," Rose admitted.

"What? From the colonies? My word, this is amazing!" His eyes brightened as though a long extinguished candle had suddenly been relighted.

"So where is your wife? I'd like to meet her," Rose said somewhat less enthusiastically than she had been. Perhaps Vanessa was mistaken about this point.

"Oh, she passed away many years ago. Took a bad fall and broke her neck, I am afraid. We both came here in the Year of Our Lord 1849. We met a visitor from the colonies, Montford was his name. He said he had something that would interest and intrigue us. He showed us this window-like affair, and the next thing we knew, we were both in this world. The Badlands were particularly bad for us. Mind you, I'd seen terrible things which all came back to me during the night there in the inn. But that was where she took her terrible fall, down a canyon precipice. We sort of got off of the trail and she slipped. My fault really. I wanted to see more of the canyon. I continued in sorrow but when I got here, I found my services were in great demand."

"You realize that at first, they were merely hacking at each other with swords. Later on, someone convinced them to use arrows too. My, I had my hands full with the wounded then. More recently, they invented these guns and now it is cannons. Where will it all end? I've been sticking around to patch the men up as best I can under these primitive field conditions. Besides, how can I go on without my wife? It's been a very long time now, and I haven't aged at all. Isn't that strange? In my spare time, I have been trying to figure that one out, but as yet, I have no clue to my longevity. Perhaps it is so I can be here to help the wounded men. Jolly good, if that's so, I say."

Rose thanked him and explained that she lost her husband eight years ago. Vanessa wondered why she mentioned that detail. It seemed awfully personal and she vowed to ask Henri about it the next time she could meet with him. Meanwhile, the war had to be stopped. Henri was not in a position to do anything about it, not as a mere private. Perhaps she could somehow use her "feminine charms" on the general, but wished that she knew more about such things. She chided herself for not having paid more attention to Vanessa when she was with him on the Malbon Express.

The next evening, she got a chance to make an attempt. General Wilhelm Frank again insisted that she dine with him. After the general's fine meal was finished and he had drooled over her a bit, she coyly said, "You know, general, I can't help but worry for you and your men. You didn't tell me that the enemy armies also have their own cannons. They almost hit ours the other day."

"Well, that's not really important if we can get our perfected first, you see," he justified.

"That may be, but have you given any thought to what might happen if the squirrels and rabbits get their cannon perfected before you get yours? Why I dread the terrible loss of life should their shells explode right in the middle of all these tents! Oh dear me, what if you, sir, get hit and are brought to us to doctor? You know, your legs mutilated by the shrapnel or perhaps your arms — it would be so awful for me to have to watch Surgeon Milan removing what was left of your legs or arms. Terrible, terrible." She feigned an imagined tragic loss.

The general's countenance grimaced. For the first time, she felt that she might actually be reaching the buffoon's mind clearly. He rubbed his forehead, and then replied, "Yes, my doll, you are right. That is why I am pushing my men so hard to get our canon to reach the enemy first and at the same time I am working with our surgeon to be ready in case this horrible disaster should befall us. Still, the repercussions could be devastating. I wish there were other options, but there are none that I can see."

Vanessa tried to smile coyly, but she didn't quite have the knack yet. "There is another alternative, sir. Have you ever thought that the squirrels and rabbits might be equally worried about your artillery shells decimating their men too? If they are, perhaps if you three generals could meet; you might find that they would like to end this war somehow and to avoid the massive casualties that are extremely likely."

"Say, doll, you just might have a point. Perhaps we have scared them into admitting defeat," he admitted. "You are as sharp as you are gorgeous."

"Thank you, sir," she managed to smile, though she wanted to kick her heels into his muddled brain instead. "I believe that I know a way that we could perhaps get their generals to meet with you. Obviously, sir, you will need a sort of neutral fourth party to help run the meeting, one that isn't directly going to be fighting should any of the three armies actually attack."

"You do?" his eyes again roamed from her legs upwards, finally lighting on her overly large bosom once more.

"Yes sir. What would you say if I volunteered to be the fourth party? I am sort of neutral. You don't expect me to put on one of your uniforms. I don't think I could fit in it, do you?" she asked coyly, moving her bright red nails in the direction of her bosom.

"Oh, no, no, certainly not! That would be very considerate of you if you could sort of act as a mediator. I know that I would pay attention," he replied.

Vanessa thought to herself, "I am sure that is not all you want to pay attention to," but restrained her thoughts. "It would please me very much to help do my part to prevent you and your handsome men from being ravaged by enemy shells. I will see if I can somehow arrange for the other generals to meet with you. Maybe they can tomorrow afternoon. If that is too soon, maybe the day after that. We should meet soon, just in case they perfect their cannons before we do, don't you think?" She smiled coyly again.

"Oh yes, yes, you are very right. As soon as we can meet — think of all our men. Yes, we must make it so, ma'am. I am so glad that we had this nice talk this evening. I do hope that you will consider joining me each evening for dinner."

"Why, thank you, sir. It would be my pleasure," Vanessa replied. "I'd better get back to my nurse's station. Some men did get minor injuries, and they may need their bandages changed yet tonight. Thank you for dinner, sir." She rose and Trina quickly joined her, putting her arms around her waist steadying her as Vanessa walked across the uneven grasslands to their tent. She felt the general's eyes watching her every motion until she was out of sight. "The pig," she finally said when it was safe. Trina chuckled. She had been totally ignored by the general all evening long, but at least she had a good meal.

Once back at the doctor's tent, Rose wanted to know how it went. Doctor Milan likewise was most interested when Vanessa related what she was planning. "That is a wonderful idea, Vanessa," he stated. "If you can get the three to talk, perhaps they can settle their differences peacefully once and for all. Heck, if they did that, then I could carry on and perhaps see if there is a way back to London. I wonder if any time will have passed while I have been here?"

Trina also nodded her agreement with his question. "Yes, if we can somehow get back to Peoria, what year will it be for us?

"When Miranda, Rose, and I went back using the emergency exit in Malbon, we found that the same number of days that we had been gone had passed," Vanessa tried to break the news as gently as possible.

"That would mean that it wouldn't be the nineteenth century anymore," Doctor Milan mused.

Rose whispered, "It is 2010 now. However, we simply do not know precisely what will happen if we can somehow find the true exit point. We might find ourselves having been only gone a day."

"Then again, I might return to find myself two hundred years old!" Doctor Milan suggested. "Well, that would finish me off in a second." Rose grimaced, recalling how she had turned into an aged man when she tried to return in Henri's body.

"Well," Vanessa hastily jumped in, as Trina gasped, "when Rose tried to return as Henri, she was fine for a few hours and then began aging like mad. We hastily returned here, and the Henri body sort of un-aged almost at once. So Doctor Milan, if we exit and you suddenly start aging rapidly, we can always get you back here fast. You too, Trina." She guessed neither wanted to die just yet.

"Now that is useful to know. Very well done, Rose. Keen observation on your part, but so risky. You are an impressive woman," Doctor Milan validated her. Rose smiled.

Albert returned from visiting his friends and gave his report. They were inducted into their respective armies but were taking it all in stride, curiosity kept them interested in learning what was going on. "Neither has been able to find out why their people so hate these humans over here. It is most strange," Albert reported, adding a slight bit of emotion in his last sentence, quite unusual for him.

"Good job, Albert. Here's what I want you to do tomorrow." Vanessa explained in detail her grand plan to bring the three generals together for a meeting that hopefully would end the war threat.

# Chapter 11 The Meeting

"Well it is all arranged. The two generals have agreed to meet with you here in your tent, General Wilhelm, but only so long as we three women are with you. I don't know why they want us three." She batted her long eye lashes. The general smiled, but he didn't dare say why he thought that they would want the women with him. Vanessa was the most attractive woman that he'd ever seen, and he was pleased that she was often near him. Too bad that she was married, he thought.

Vanessa continued, "They will each be bringing one other with them to help them with whatever might be needed." She did not mention that they would be the same two that he'd ordered drawn and quartered when they first met the general. As far as he was concerned, their stuffed bodies were sitting on his trophy shelves in a tent. "They will be coming under the universal white flag of truce. I gave them your word that you would honor that, as I am sure that a man of your stature would automatically do, right, my general?" she asked coyly.

"Oh absolutely, absolutely. What time may we expect them?"

"Around one o'clock. I would suggest that you prepare a large pot of tea and perhaps have some biscuits and honey as well. You know, put your best foot forward, and these generals may well be encouraged to end this war," she deftly suggested. He agreed.

Later that afternoon, Henri visited them in the doctor's tent, pretending to need his bandages changed. "You are doing a terrific job, my love! You are actually getting the three leaders to sit down and talk. Now that is something! Well done, Vanessa."

"Yes, but will it accomplish anything?" Rose asked. "You know men, daughter of mine, er, son of mine at the moment." Both chuckled.

Vanessa shrugged her shoulders. "Don't know, but as long as I can keep them talking, there is a chance that they can reach an agreement. Not talking will certainly never produce one."

"Smart woman," Doctor Milan interjected, much impressed with this beautiful, young woman.

Now they had to wait until tomorrow came. Vanessa fidgeted and worried all the next morning. Just what could she say to get these men to agree to end their conflict? She really had no idea at all. Around noon, the three women, accompanied by the doctor, made their slow way over to the general's tent. Doctor Milan insisted on coming along in case anyone needed his services. The general mostly ignored him, as usual, focusing his sole attention on Vanessa. From the corner of her eye, she spotted Henri, who had cleverly found some work to do nearby. He was close enough to overhear the whole discussion, and his presence bolstered Vanessa's confidence immensely. She wondered why that should so affect her, but had no answer.

They dined with the general, and then they helped set his table for their coming guests. All the while that Vanessa moved about helping Rose and Trina make the preparations, the general's eyes followed her every motion, much to her annoyance. However, she rightly continued to periodically flash him a smile. Got to keep him interested, she thought.

At last around one, the squirrel and rabbit generals began their long walk down their hills into the valley. Each carried a white flag held high. Hastily, General Wilhelm raised his high, showing them where to come. Now they waited. A half hour later, the three met at last and the introductions began.

General Franco Gott led the rabbit army. He was an elderly rabbit, dressed in a sparkling blue uniform. General Amos Slaughter led the squirrel army. Likewise, he was elderly and wore a light green uniform. "Thank you all for agreeing to meet today," Vanessa began after she and the other two women were formally introduced to the two generals. "My sole purpose in getting you three fine gentlemen together today is to see if we can find an amicable way to settle the threat of all-out war between you before any of us gets killed or worse, mutilated."

"Well, I am ready to accept your surrender, generals," General Wilhelm spoke up, brashly.

"Never going to happen. You are the scum of the Hills, but we are prepared to accept your surrender, general," General Franco declared, puffing himself up to his full height.

"Of course, you all have disagreements with each other. If you didn't, why would you three be so against each other?" Vanessa attempted to tone it down as fast as possible.

"You have it wrong, pretty woman. We squirrels have no quarrel with the rabbits, only with this vile, wicked General Wilhelm," General Amos explained.

"Say, General Amos, may I ask what General Wilhelm here has done to you and to you, General Franco, that has made you such bitter enemies? You see, I have only just arrived here a few days ago from Malbon, the great city. There, we humans and the rabbits and squirrels all live in complete peace and harmony. I just cannot imagine what has happened out here in the Hills."

"Well, he is pure evil, that's what," General Amos answered.

"No, it is they who are vile and evil," General Wilhelm retorted, not to be outdone.

"Hey, hold on a second. What exactly have you done to each other that makes you consider the others so vile and evil? I am just a pretty looking woman, and I simply don't understand this," Vanessa tried to use womanly wiles on them. It mostly failed, however. They only repeated what they had been saying about each other.

Thus, she tried a different approach. "The other day, each of you tested your new cannons, firing a salvo towards each other's hilltop."

"Yes, and we almost succeeded. Soon, we will be able to end this war permanently," General Franco pointed out. The others agreed, but from their own viewpoints.

"Yes, that is what I am afraid will be happening soon, generals. Have you considered what will actually happen once your cannon finally reach each other? Such carnage. So many of your soldiers will be killed or mutilated. Why, when you get done blasting each other, there might not be anyone left alive on any of the three hilltops. Have you considered this in your plans?" All three generals sat silently; none dare to mention this detail, which from their silence Vanessa assumed they had considered this possibility.

At last, General Franco pointed to history. "Look, gorgeous human doll, at first your general here had his soldiers attacking ours using knives. At least few died as a result. Later on, they began using swords. Of course, we had to obtain swords as well. When that failed to produce any change of power, longbows were discovered. My, that very nearly did us all in, but we all invented proper defenses against that rain of deadly arrows. After that stalemate, the general invented muskets. Admittedly, they were not so effective, but rifles soon evolved from them and those are in widespread use today. Naturally, we had to acquire rifles to defend ourselves. Now we are all inventing cannons in hopes that we can end this conflict very soon, once and for all."

"Interesting how all this developed," Vanessa replied. "It seems that as one side gets a better weapon, soon the other sides also have them. Don't you three find that coincidence the least bit curious? I certainly do. What are the odds that if the general's men here invent a rifle that almost at once, your men also invent it? Astronomical, I'd say."

"Oh no, pretty human doll. You have it all wrong. We are able to purchase these new weapons from our armaments dealer," General Amos hastened to correct her.

"Same with us," General Franco added.

Begrudgingly, General Wilhelm admitted, "Yes, we do too."

"Now *that* I find even more curious! Just who is your armaments dealer?" she asked.

All three blurted out at very nearly the same time, "Pugsley Paisley." All three were slightly taken aback, having just mentioned the same name.

"And who is this Pugsley Paisley?"

"He is a pig. Runs a huge factory about fifty miles from here," General Wilhelm explained, before the other two could. Those two nodded their agreement.

"So let me see if I have this straight. You know how sometimes a woman's mind gets so befuddled," she feigned a bit of confusion. "Each of you pays this Pugsley pig fellow a handsome sum to purchase more and deadlier weapons. He supplies each side the same weapons so that neither side ever wins?"

"Er, yes, so it would seem," General Franco agreed, pulling his whiskers thoughtfully. He obviously did not like where this was heading.

"So Pugsley the pig is becoming incredibly wealthy by continuing to supply each of you three with the same weapons, knowing that neither side will ever win and so you three will continually want to buy the newest, greatest weapons in hopes of defeating the others, and he continues to sell them to all three of you at the same time, maintaining the balance for — how long have you been battling this out?" Vanessa had dragged her tease out as long as she dared.

"For over two hundred years, lovely doll," General Amos answered her.

"My god! This Pugsley the pig has made a humongous fortune off of you three men!" She punched in her key point. Three very sober men stared at her. She added, "Well, back in Malbon, this Pugsley the pig would be hunted down and outright shot for having done such a thing! But I guess out here in the Hills, you have different ways than we city folk," she added, knowing that certainly General Wilhelm would refuse to be so different; his eyes still drifted onto her massive bosom. So did the other two generals for that matter. For a moment, she wondered if these men were even listening to what she was saying. Vanessa sighed; she had to admit that he too had stared at Vanessa when she was close to him on the Malbon Express.

Just then, a singular event occurred that totally tipped the scales. Vanessa had finally run out of ideas to get these generals to come to some agreement to end their conflict. As if right on cue, a wagon came rolling slowly up the hill, escorted by a number of General Wilhelm's soldiers. His captain rode on up and reported, "Sorry to interrupt, general, but we've just found a new recruit for you, but I think that you will reject this one. Still, we follow your orders; anyone entering the Encounter Hills must be stopped and brought before you to be recruited into your army." He saluted and backed off as the wagon approached.

Trina gasped, holding her hands over her mouth! It was her husband, Reginald Noxwood. Rose also involuntarily inhaled. Vanessa stared in disbelief. Reginald sat at a crazy angle in the driver's seat, crazy only because that was his only way to maintain his position and still partially control the two horses. He had no legs and only his right arm. He was the splitting image of how he'd left his wife, Trina, which is why she gasped and forced her hands over her mouth to keep from shrieking. He had a most difficult time trying to maintain his position and yet control the team. He barely managed to halt the team, assisted by two soldiers, one of which was Henri, who dashed up to make sure that Reginald was able to stop them.

"Greetings generals. Ladies. I have come to help you try to end your conflict. I am Reginald Noxwood of Malbon. I see that you generals are shocked by my appearance. Rightly so. I am what you and many of your men will become if you continue with your intended artillery barrage of each other's hilltops. Can someone help me down? I am unable to get up or down from here without help." Hastily, Henri obliged, lifting him down. He requested to merely be positioned on the ground. "I must show them that I am not helpless," he whispered. Using pathetic motions, he ever so slowly moved his body closer to the generals.

When they could get a full look at him, he spoke up, "Still, I have managed to come all the way from Malbon on my own to show you three generals what you are condemning youselves and your men to if you persist in using artillery barrages. Just ask your Doctor Milan there. He'll back me up. The shrapnel kills you, if you are lucky. If you are not lucky enough to die, as I wasn't, this is what results when such deadly shrapnel hits fleshly bodies. The doctors have no choice but to remove the shattered limbs. At least I still have an arm, so it could be worse for me. Take a good look at me, generals. One or more of you may look just like me in a few days, if you continue to fire your deadly artillery shells at each other. Or maybe you will only have a leg left and no arms or no arms but yet be able to walk or maybe one leg and one arm. If you are lucky, you will die outright. Let me tell you, living like this is anything but fun."

"My god! Doctor Milan, is this true?" asked a white faced General Wilhelm.

"Yes, he does exaggerate some. More will actually die of their wounds than will live like him. So the odds are that you will be killed rather than maimed like he is. I know, I treated hundreds of men under General Wellington back in 1812. So many men came in with such bad shrapnel wounds that our first action was to start sawing off affected appendages as fast as we could. Many never survived the operations. Of course those that did often looked like Reginald here, but as he says, some lacked one leg or two, one arm or two. It varied from survivor to survivor. Yet, as you can see, somehow Reginald continues to live," Doctor Milan replied. Vanessa suspected that he was also exaggerating in hopes of helping to end this war.

Reginald added a final word, "Generals, actual battles are never fun, and I am what usually results when you use artillery barrages."

"I — ah, well, I believe that we three generals ought to focus our attention onto Pugsley the pig, as Vanessa has pointed out," General Wilhelm finally headed their antagonism down a different path.

"I agree, general. We squirrels are enraged that Pugsley has been manipulating us. We are going to march on Pugsley tomorrow," General Amos added.

"Same with us rabbits. Pugsley is nothing but a criminal and must be beheaded," General Franco declared angrily.

"No, drawn and quartered! Armless and legless," insisted General Wilhelm. "Generals, what say we conduct a mutual offensive against this most vile traitor?" They agreed and promptly dismissed the women, saying that they had no further need of their council.

While Rose and Henri supported Vanessa, as she began to slowly walk back to the doctor's tent, Trina didn't quite know what to do. Reginald spoke up, "Permit me to make my own way, Trina. Allow me to walk along your side, please."

"But you can't walk," she managed to whisper, her voice choked with emotions.

"No, I can sort of move, though." He moved very slowly and the others kept him company as he worked at moving what was left of his body across the grass to the tent. Once there, Doctor Milan lifted him up onto a chair. Trina pulled another up to his.

"Trina, can you ever find it in your heart to forgive me? I am wholly to blame for all that you endured. I am truly sorry for what I put you through. If you cannot, I understand. I have so badly mistreated you that it is no wonder that you cannot forgive me," he explained to her.

"What — what happened to you?" Trina finally managed to utter.

"After you escaped from Finigan's fortress, I appeared in a boardinghouse in Malbon. All of the gold coins that we put in the wagon were my bed. I had no sheets, just the coins. My body was then just as you see it now, only I was lying there naked. When I came to my senses and realized what an awful thing I had done, I vowed to find you and at least apologize and help you to get free from this awful place. I had my landlady purchase me this wagon and I gave her all of the gold. I've been driving this wagon for days, all the way from Malbon, in search of you. I kept my last memory of you beside me in my mind as my inspiration to somehow succeed. When I entered the Encounter Hills, I heard what was happening from the soldiers who said that I was going to be recruited into his army, though I knew that would be impossible. I came as fast as I could. I do hope that I helped convince them to cease their war," he explained hastily.

Tears flowed down Trina's cheeks as she listened to his tale. Reginald then asked again, "My dear Trina, can you ever find it in your heart to forgive me for what terrible things I have done to you? I promise to never, ever do anything like that again. You are more precious than all of the gold of Finigan or all the gold in the whole world."

"I forgive you, Regi, I do," she sobbed and leaned over and hugged him. He began to cry as well.

"I think that it is time that we quietly make our departure," Henri suggested. All agreed. Quietly, they loaded up their few things onto the carriage, while Albert went to bring Sir Thomas and Herr Adelstein back to the carriage. He followed Vanessa's suggestion and had the two appear inside the carriage to avoid any suspicion on the doctor's failure to carry out the general's orders.

"Excuse me, Rose. Would you mind terribly if I tagged along with you? I do believe that my work here has come to an end," Doctor Milan asked.

Rose flushed, "Why no, please do, doctor. We would be glad to have your company. Please, sit with me. Vanessa often sits with her husband topside. First, you will have to help Reginald into the carriage, I am afraid."

The doctor lifted him inside. Though Regi tried to get himself up onto the bench seat, he couldn't manage it. Without a word, Doctor Milan lifted him up and Trina sat beside him, putting her arm around him so he could sit upright like a human again. Poof! The three friends appeared and squeezed in. "Oh, you are back. My, they have pulled off your legs and arms too," exclaimed a surprised Sir Thomas. "Did they then eat them for supper?"

Regi laughed, "No, Sir Thomas, they did not do that. They just vanished them. I don't mind as long as I have Trina back with me."

"You ready down there?" Henri called out. Rose yelled up that they were and the carriage began rolling over the hilly grasslands. No one attempted to stop them and soon he put several more hills between them. At last, Vanessa breathed a sigh of relief; they would not be pursued, she hoped.

A short while later, Rose called up, "Hey, Reginald's legs and arm just reappeared!" Vanessa and Henri smiled at each other. They had hope such might happen. Reginald had just helped prevent a war. Surely that was a worthy action. Yet, what lay ahead of them, Vanessa wondered? Her map was in her night bag back under the bench seats.

"God, I love doing this!" Henri began to level with Vanessa, that is, Miranda to Zed. "Driving the horses, like this, out on a grand adventure. You don't mind do you if I like to be controlling things? I mean you don't mind being with a woman who likes to run things a lot? I've found that men like to think they are running the universe and that they are the bosses, but I do too. That doesn't bother you, does it? I am having a ball being Henri, a guy. Here it's expected that I be the one in charge and all that."

"Not at all. I don't mind. There's an advantage this way. Two minds are better than one. With Trina and Regi, they have each got their own separate areas of life to control and they don't overlap. I think that was the way society was back in the 1850's, but history was not my best subject in high school. Found it boring. I'm wandering, sorry. My point is that when they were faced with a crisis, like with Finigan, they couldn't work together to solve it. You and I, we work together. When we first came into the world, you kept me from crashing into the ground by making the stairs to descend. Each time we work well together, and I don't think that would have happened if you were like Trina, interested only in keeping the home going properly. After all, there is so much more in the world than a mere house. I think you and I look for bigger things to interest us."

Henri leaned over and gave Vanessa a quick kiss. "I do really like you, you know," he added. "What do you think of our reversed sex roles, eh? Isn't this really interesting? No one ever gets to really experience what life is like for the opposite sex, you know, well except for those who undergo an operation that is. I've always wondered what it was like to be a man instead of a woman. I have to admit, Vanessa, er Zed, that I am truly enjoying it."

"Because you can have a free hand in being the one expected to be running things?" she asked.

Henri flushed, "Yes. Little Miss Bossy. That was my nickname in grade school. I liked tomboy better, though until I got to high school, that is."

"I bet you kicked some butt back then," Vanessa teased him. Henri chucked. She had at that. "You know, I think that there is a far simpler way of looking at all this, Miranda, er Henri. I've sort of been thinking about this ever since we first entered this world, when I was falling in the nothingness and you conjured those steps. You created the steps. Isn't all this really just a matter of Cause and Effect?"

"This sounds interesting, Zed, er Vanessa. Do go on."

"Sometimes one is Cause, and at other times one is Effect. Falling down in the nothingness, I was Effect. You were Cause, making the steps appear and rescuing me from falling. With us, we each seem to be being Cause when the other needs us to be and the Effect when the other is being Cause. We sort of naturally blend the two together, almost without really trying to do so. I was your eyes when you needed them and you were mine when I needed them.

Neither of us particularly asked the other to be the Cause, we just stepped in and did it. I think that is the way that it should be. Instinctively, neither of us has yet ever let the other down."

"You are so right, dear. That's why I am really falling for you in a big, big way, Zed, er Vanessa," Miranda replied, once again forgetting that Zed was now Vanessa. "Say, what would you have done if I had made that gold deal with Finigan? I being in this body, Henri's, and you being Vanessa."

Vanessa laughed. "Well, I surely would have tried to get you to take a good hard look at it. Can't you just decide to have money, and then let it come on in, like I did when I needed it to start my coffee vending business? After what I saw you do in your bedroom, I am certain that you could do something as easy as that. For sure, I would not have gone along with Finigan's deal. Anyone ought to have seen that he was merely playing to one's greed and avarice. I'd have tried to get you to see that for what it was."

Henri laughed. "Good dear. I thought about it too. If you were Zed and I Miranda, I would have conjured a mountain of gold and rained it down on your head until you begged me to stop." Both laughed at her imagined illusion.

"I'm sure that you would have," Vanessa added playfully. "I'd sure think far less of you if you did not."

"Same here. We seemed to be well suited for each other, don't we," Henri suggested. "Seriously though, a woman's role is often one of nurturing — their children most often, but also their family and even others. Most nurses are women, if you haven't noticed. Still, I don't want to be that limited. I hope you can accept that in me."

"Perfectly, dear. Perfectly. But you know, there might be more to all this than just Cause and Effect. Where does communication enter into it? When we communicate, one of us is Cause and the other is Effect. Cause somehow delivers something across a distance to the Effect. Right now it is ideas via speech."

"I can see that. Effect must understand what Cause sent, though. Also, both of them have to be paying attention. I've seen many people just talking away while those that they were talking to were not even paying attention. Students are awfully guilty of this in classes, secretly texting away on their cell phones while the teacher is trying to talk to them," Henri pointed out.

"Precisely. I got onto this line of thought when we were in bed making love. The man is always outflowing the particles, while the woman is always inflowing the particles, which makes man Cause and woman Effect. What bothers me is that there is no way to reverse that physical flow. It is sort of a trap. That is why I am so intrigued with what we are experiencing here in this world. We're in opposite bodies, and the flows are reversed. I have to admit that I am enjoying being on the Effect side for a while. Things balance out this way."

"Incredible observation! You are right. Wow, I'd never looked at it quite that way before. I am supposed to be the driving force as a man, but I'm not used to it at all. Am I doing all that I ought to be for you, dear?" Henri realized that this role was entirely new to him and that he may well be letting her down as a result.

Vanessa laughed, "Damned if I know, love. I am new to this side as well. I don't know what to expect or that I ought to expect. As long as we keep on really communicating our deepest thoughts to each other, I don't see how we can get into any trouble, though. It's when one party isn't straightforward and honest with the other that upsets, confusions, and problems arise. I promise you that I will always be right up front with you about everything, Miranda, er Henri. I still get confused with all this." Both laughed.

Rose called out, "Hey Miranda or Henri, Milan and I have been looking at the map. This road leads to a place called Pander Parkland. We've been discussing what might be there. Ideas?"

"Thanks mom. None yet. We'll think about it," Henri yelled back down. To Vanessa, he added, "Pander Parkland? What a strange name for a land or place."

"Maybe it is a sort of vacation spot," Vanessa suggested. "Guess we will find out soon enough. The hills are staring to diminish."

# Chapter 12 Pander Parkland

Around noon, the grass covered hills gave way to a strange new countryside. "Wow, look at this place," Henri exclaimed. Ahead of them, the road continued on, but the ground became a patchwork quilt of multicolored ground cover. Uniform six-foot square patches of one kind of vegetation and color hue stretched out before them. The pattern was completely regular as if someone had pieced together the land from quilt blocks, each six-foot square. The colors spanned the entire spectrum from deep reds to dark indigos. The colored blocks were randomly laid out. Eyes could see no pattern in the color of the layout, yet it was amazingly beautiful in a rather chaotic way. No one color predominated.

"Wow, look at those!" Vanessa pointed a long red nail to the giant toad stools that now appeared on either side of the path, replacing the scattered trees of the Encounter Hills behind them. "Their stems must be at least six feet tall. No, that one is at least ten feet. The top is large enough to be someone's table! How utterly strange. Old Montford must have had quite an imagination to have thought up this place."

"Are you guys seeing this?" yelled Rose from the carriage below them.

"Yes mom. Really unique," Henri called back. The further into Pander Parkland they rode, the taller the toad stools grew, and they became denser until one could call them a forest of toad stools!

Caught up in marveling at this utterly unique terrain and vegetation, if that was the right term, the two failed to see the occupant of a large toad stool ahead of them. If they had, they might have turned around and left. "Halt!" came a bellowing voice, taking both quite by surprise. Even more interesting, their team also came to a complete stop so quickly that Vanessa lurched forward, nearly falling off the driver's bench. Inside, half of the passengers very nearly fell forward onto their companions on the opposite bench.

Ahead of them sitting on a ten foot tall toad stool sat an enormous snake, black with brown diamonds running down its body that was at least three feet in diameter. Later, Vanessa suggested that its length might well have been fifty feet, had they measured it. The snake wore a suit jacket with a wide paisley tie done with a double Windsor knot around its neck. It wore no shirt, however. Its look was most strange, with the empty arms of its blazer hanging empty at its side. Adding to its unusual appearance was a top hat that men wore back in the 1850's. Now that the snake had their attention, its top hat rose up and then back down, as if some worthy gentleman was tipping his hat to greet Vanessa.

"Thanksss for ssstoping." Its voice had a distinctive "s" sounds and was terribly nasally in tone, as if it might have had a cold. "My name isss Becktold. Welcome to Pander Parkland. I am here to greet you. It hasss been a long time sssince guestsss have come to this wonderland. It hasss much to offer you, oh yesss. I am sssure that you will enjoy your ssstay."

"Pleased to meet you, Becktold," Henri took charge. "I am Henri Graves and this is my wife, Vanessa. Others are below in the carriage. We are on a grand vacation. Is there an inn where we might stay the night?"

"Oh yesss. A fine inn, fine indeed. Have you the toll for entering Pander Parkland?" Becktold asked.

"I'm sorry. We know nothing about the toll. How much is it?" Henri asked.

"One of thessse," he replied. A strange coin with a two-headed snake biting itself in bias relief appeared hanging in space before the two, allowing them a good look at it.

"No, I am sorry. We have never seen such coins. Where might we obtain them?" Henri answered politely.

"Not a problem. I am here to collect the toll. One coin per each perssson who isss entering Pander Parkland isss the toll. You have the coinsss within you. If you will allow me to collect them from each of you, then you may continue on your journey to the inn. You will sssurely reach there before nightfall. Sssurely."

"Well, if you must collect our tolls, then I suppose that is all right, but honestly, Becktold, we don't have these coins within us," Henri replied.

The giant snake slithered off his stool, well partially that is. His diamond shaped head appeared before the two in the driver's seat; the rest of his body formed a U-shape with much of his body still coiled on the toad stool. Henri found this huge snake's head facing him a bit unnerving. Even more so when the snake opened its mouth, revealing two needle sharp fangs. "Thisss won't hurt a bit," Becktold said. Before Henri could reply, the snake struck and bit him in his arm. One of those strange coins suddenly appeared in the air above Henri. "Sssee, I told you that you had it within you." The coin floated down and slipped into one of the jacket's pockets.

Before Henri could react to this, the snake struck a second time, biting Vanessa in her arm. A coin appeared and dropped neatly into Becktold's pocket. "Are we poisoned?" Henri finally managed to utter, shocked by the suddenness of the attack.

"Oh by no meansss no. You are not harmed. I am jussst extracting your coinsss, the toll for entering Pander

Parkland. If you will excussse me, I will get the coinsss from the othersss."

The two heard shrieks from the carriage compartment and knew that the others had been similarly bitten by the snake. Shortly, Becktold's head appeared before Henri. "You may continue on your way. The inn isss perhapsss another five milesss dissstant. Pleassse enjoy your ssstay in Pander Parkland. It isss mossst enjoyable. Everyone sssaysss ssso." He re-coiled his body back upon the toad stool and ignored them completely. Henri shrugged his shoulders and slapped the reins. The horses responded and the carriage continued on down the road in this strange land.

"Did I handle that as a man ought to have handled it, Vanessa? Ought I to have somehow stopped the snake from biting us? I don't feel any different though," Henri asked, suddenly having lost her confidence.

"You did just fine. I don't think that we had any choice in the matter. The snake was lightning fast in its strike. If we were poisoned, I think that we would be feeling bad about now and I feel just fine," she replied. "This sure is the strangest place that I have ever seen. I wonder how they get all those colorful plants to grow in such strict patterns?"

Everyone continued to marvel at this incredibly strange landscape as they rolled along towards the inn. "Inn ahead," Henri called out to the others inside the carriage. "What a strange looking village!" The road ran straight through the village. However, instead of homes as they expected to see, raised bumps of ground marked the dwellings' locations, which must therefore be underground. The slanted bump expanded to around fifteen feet tall at the edge of the road, where a huge round front door stood. "Looks like a hobbit village," Henri remarked, "like something Tolkien thought up. I bet snakes live in this village."

The inn was a single story affair, perhaps a hundred feet long and fifty wide, a large inn. It too was colorful, as various climbing vines in a variety of colors grew up its sides, partially hiding the red stone of its walls. They halted before the large double doors at its main entrance. Embossed on each door was that same double headed snake motif. As they halted, a very excited mouse stepped out from the inn. He stood nearly six feet tall and was dressed in a doorman's uniform, reminiscent of the nineteen hundreds, Henri thought. He seemed overly excited, though.

"Welcome! Welcome! Welcome to the Pander Inn! Oh my, it has been so long since we have had the pleasure of guests here! Allow me to assist you down," he said, highly emotional, as if he'd not seen humans for many years. He helped Vanessa step down and then held the hands of Rose and Trina as they stepped out of the carriage. "I am Ulysses S. Minty, doorman and proprietor of this inn. I will do everything in my power to make your stay here as enjoyable and memorable as possible. If there is anything, *anything* at all that you require, do not hesitate to ask. Please leave your baggage. I will have my son, the bellboy, bring them to your rooms. Oh, this is a Great Day indeed. Fabulous. Fabulous. If you will follow me, I will get you all signed in and show you to your rooms. Dinner will be at six. In your room, you will find a menu of the exquisite dishes that we offer here at the Pander Inn. Please mark them tonight and they will be prepared for you tomorrow. My charming wife is a most excellent chef, yes, indeed."

Stepping inside the inn felt like stepping back into time. The decor was that of a very ritzy hotel around 1800. Draperies lined the walls framing various portraits of other mice, presumably relations of Minty. They were made from velvet, Henri thought. The atmosphere gave off a fresh odor of flowers. Ah, that came from a dozen ornate vases holding numerous of the multi-colored flowers similar to those that they had seen dotting the countryside. Ulysses led them to a mahogany sign-in desk. He had each person sign their name on the roster. Unfortunately, there were no dates in the journal, merely names, Henri noted. Thus, he could not tell when the last guests had been here.

"Ulysses, this inn is fabulous. Extremely nice," Rose made conversation as she stood in line to sign in.

"Yes, we pride ourselves on having the finest inn in the world. It has been in the Minty family for many generations now. Ah, my wife and your chef. This is Missy L. Minty."

"So pleased to meet you!" the mouse replied. She was equally tall but wore an apron over her green silk dress. "I so look forward to cooking your requested meals. Please look over the menus. Do not hesitate to make your requests. I do love cooking."

"And these are my daughters, who will be your maids. Angie, Betsy, and Ginger. My son, Herman; he will handle your horses and carriage for you. Now if you will follow me, I will show you to your rooms." The children were almost as tall as their parents. The girls wore fine gowns made to look like maids outfits. Herman wore a brown uniform, reminiscent of a stable hand.

"Now this is your room, Henri and Vanessa Graves." A room later, he announced, "This is your room, Reginald and Trina Noxwood." A few feet further on down the elegant hallway, he said, "Rose and Milan, this is to be your room." Neither Rose nor Milan insisted on having a separate room. By tacit consent, they entered their shared room. Finally, he placed the three friends into a single room.

Henri and Vanessa entered their room. The floor was plush with a thick, red carpet. "Oh, this is harder for me to walk upon, dear. Thanks," Vanessa observed and Henri placed a steadying arm around her. The room smelled of wood polish. Mahogany walls gleamed. The room contained all of the furniture that one might expect to find in an expensive hotel room. However, the bed was both huge and covered with satin sheets. Presently, Mr. Minty returned with their night bag. He added, "You will find additional clothing in the wardrobes. Please feel free to wear any of them that you desire, compliments of the Pander Inn. I trust that each will be of a correct size for you. Such elegance is part of the charm of our inn. Your private bath is just through that door. You have time to bathe and dress before dinner. Now if you will excuse me, I need to see to the others' comforts as well."

Henri could not resist taking a peek into the walk-in wardrobes. "Wow, Vanessa, look at these! Silk dresses, satin, even velvet! Just feel them, incredible. And look — camel hair and suede suits for me."

"Oh do wear one of these," Vanessa suggested, feeling the soft texture of one of the brown suit coats.

"Only if you wear this red satin gown, dear," he teased her. Both agreed and headed for the bathroom to clean up.

Sometime later, Vanessa was surprised to find that the red satin gown actually fit her. "Look, it really is going to fit. I didn't think it would, what with these incredible boobs of mine."

Henri looked pleased as he zipped her up. He ran his hands over her dress, up and down her sides. "You look fabulous in this one, dear. Is there enough ease to actually walk?" He was a bit concerned because the full length dress fit her tightly all the way down to her ankles, where there was a small walking slit. They tested it; there was, but only as long as she took the smallest of steps. After Henri donned his new camelhair suit, Vanessa ran her fingers over him and pronounced him delicious. He laughed and arm in arm they headed off to find the dining room.

Rose and Milan were already there. She wore an elegant, deep red, velvet gown and he, a brown camelhair suit, similar to Henri's. "Mom, you look fabulous," Henri exclaimed, giving her a big hug. She beamed. Now that Henri thought about it, she seemed far happier than she had been since her dad died. Milan was having a good influence on her, and Henri thought that he seemed taken with her mother as well.

A bit later, Trina entered holding the arm of Regi. She wore one of the silken gowns, a conservative black one, while he wore a suede suit. Both seemed flushed and Henri suspected he knew why. Shortly, the trio entered. They too had donned some of the suits provided by the inn and they smiled broadly. Herr Adelstein said, "Sorry about vanishing like that, but we hate snakes, especially such large ones."

"Oh yes, yes. We could easily be eaten," Sir Thomas added, his body shook slightly as he recalled the snake.

"You didn't get bitten?" Henri asked. They had not. Just then, the three daughters entered with the guests' dinner, covered by stainless steel covers. Roast pheasant in a delicious sauce was the main course. Later, they sat back and enjoyed a perfectly brewed black tea. The meal was not only filling, but delighted their pallets. Missy was a superb chef, no doubt about that.

One by one the couples adjourned to their rooms. All were feeling a little tired from their journey. Once in their room, Henri took Vanessa in his arms and their passions exploded. Later, they blossomed once more, as the two began to fully enjoy the satin sheets. Soon, Henri removed both of Vanessa's corsets. She was fine as long as she continued to stay in the bed. Much later, Vanessa whispered, "I never knew that sex could be so pleasurable for a woman. That was incredible, mind blowing even, dear."

"Hey, same here. This is fantastic. I do love you, dear."
He began kissing her once more. Exhausted, they finally
drifted into a satisfying sleep.

In the morning, again, both could not keep their hands
from lovingly caressing each other's bodies. Passions
exploded yet again. "Let's skip breakfast!" Vanessa insisted.
They did. Finally, around noon, Henri began to redress
Vanessa, who had a difficult time with her highly weakened
stomach and back muscles. However once the corsets were
finally fully tightened, she was back to normal. "Somehow,
dear, I am going to have to find a way to strengthen my weak
muscles. I want to always lay naked with you, love."

"I agree. I want to feel you as well." He gave her a loving
kiss, and they were barely able to pull themselves apart to
finish dressing. At last, with Vanessa dressed, she sat before
the mirror and worked on brushing out her hair, while Henri
gave her pointers on how best to do it. They joined the others
for lunch. All three women were quite flushed, and Henri
guessed that her mother was also enjoying Milan's affections
as well.

Again, after an exquisite meal, the couples found
themselves back in their bedrooms, their passions exploding
once more. Late afternoon, Vanessa and Henri lay back, side
by side, though still holding on to one another. "I've never
felt this way before, such feelings, such passions, such, well I
don't have words to describe what I am feeling and sensing,"
Vanessa said dreamily.

"Same here, dear. It is incredible. I never want to stop
fondling you and loving you." Then Henri had another
thought. "You are making me jealous of you, you know?"

"How so?"

"Because you have the woman's body and are so enjoying
this. I can't help but wonder what you are experiencing. I
mean I'd like to have our rolls reversed and have my body

back and feel what you are feeling," Henri explained dreamily.

"Why not? I don't want to hog all of this pleasure, dear. Come, let's see if we can somehow switch back, if only for a little while," Vanessa suggested. "How do we do it?"

"Okay, thank you. I think that we just sort of will it to occur and step out of them. Let's try it." A minute later, four bodies were visible. However, Miranda asked her Henri body, "Will this be okay with you? We won't lose you will we? We have promised to get you out of this world somehow and we intend to keep our word." The Henri body nodded, and she felt that it would both be okay to switch for a time and that they would not become lost or transported back to Malbon. A bit later, Miranda stood before Zed, each looking at the other.

"This is so strange, Miranda, but I do love you." Zed gently touched her and then kissed her. Soon, their passions exploded once more as they lay upon the satin sheets.

"Oh my god! Zed, that was incredible! I've never ever felt such passion before. What's come over us?" Miranda said softly. "It's like we are stoned or something."

Zed sat up. "That's it dear! We are stoned! Pander Parkland! We are drugged, though it is a fantastic drug, I'll give them that. I could stay here and love you forever."

Now Miranda sat up, though she could not keep her hands off of Zed's body. "You are right. We are acting like we are both stoned out of our minds. Well, I do love you, but you know what I mean. The sensations, while fantastically unbelievable and exquisite, they can't be real, can they? Our sensations must be being enhanced by some drug of theirs. Man, this could be highly addictive! I just want to hold you and make love to you again and again and again!"

"I know, I feel the same way. Say, we ought to switch back to Henri and Vanessa soon. I don't want to risk losing them. We gave them our word, after all," Zed suggested. Two minutes later, the transformation was complete. Henri and Vanessa were lying side by side on the satin sheets. "One more time, please Henri," she begged him. He complied willingly. Then he carried her into the bathroom and they shared a warm bath.

Refreshed, the two headed off to the dining room for supper. Over another sumptuous meal, Rose announced, "Dear, I have the most wonderful news. Doctor Milan has asked me to marry him and I have said yes!"

"Congratulations mom! Doctor Milan," Henri exclaimed happily. "That's wonderful news indeed." Then he realized that much of their passions may well be coming from the drugs in their systems. "Mom, doctor, we need to talk. Can you come to our room after we finished eating?"

"Well, yes, if you insist, but only for a minute. We both want to go to bed soon, right Milan dearest?" Rose said dreamily. Henri and Vanessa saw that she was really hooked on this drug. So was Milan. They looked over at Trina and Regi, but they too were gazing into each other's eyes oblivious to the others. In contrast, Herr Adelstein, Sir Thomas, and Albert were in a heated discussion over the quality of the rich black tea, comparing it to their own brand of tea. Henri realized that those three seemed unaffected by the drug. Either their bodies were immune to it or it had something to do with their having avoided being bitten by the snake. He had no way to tell which, though.

A bit later in their room, Henri tried to tell Rose and Milan that they were being drugged, but neither would listen to them at all. Rose kept insisting that they wanted to return their room. At last, Henri gave up his futile attempt to reason with Rose, and the pair hastily left, passionately kissing each other as they headed to their room.

"Now what do we do?" asked Henri, perplexed.

"Undress and share our bed? Please, let's do it again before we fall asleep, my love," Vanessa suggested.

"God! It is *so* hard to say *no* to you!" Henri replied, trying hard to counter the effects of the drug on his body, senses, and mind. "I just want to ravish your gorgeous body, my love."

"It's waiting for you," Vanessa replied coyly. "I can't fight it much longer. How about you?"

"Damn! No, I can't either. Come here gorgeous!" Henri swept Vanessa into his arms and their passions exploded once more. Later they lay back and tried to reason out what they could do to counter the drug's effects on themselves and their friends.

"It seems to come in waves," Vanessa pointed out, "unless that is how it is with a woman. I am out of my league here."

"Right waves. Is it like that for a man?" Henri asked.

"Well, I do get aroused when I see a beautiful woman, but I never have had waves like these that I am feeling. Must be from the drug," Vanessa answered from Zed's point of view.

"Same here. I have to admit, Zed, I've not been with a man before you." Henri flushed, but felt that he needed to be honest with him or her.

"Me either. You are the first and I hope the only one for me. I have fallen for you totally, Miranda. You are the most fantastic person in the whole world," Vanessa replied from Zed's perspective. "How are we going to counter this drug anyway? I can feel another wave coming over this body again."

"Same here, I am having to fight to keep my hands from touching your gorgeous body right now. What's really weird is that I really do want to love you again, independent of what the drug is dictating to me," Henri pointed out.

"Same here. I want to make love to you anyway. The drug is just lowering my barriers to getting on with it. I think that's how it works — lowers your inhibitions to just do what you would naturally want to do in the first place. Does this help us?" she asked.

"Hum, I wish I knew something about drug addictions, dear, because we surely are getting addicted to all this sensualness rather quickly. God, do I ever want it," Henri gushed. "We got to fight it I think and not do it anymore, that is, if we can."

An hour later, they again lay side by side. "Well, my love, that fight lasted all of five minutes," Vanessa pointed out. They both laughed. "Guess we will have to do better this time."

Over breakfast the next morning, Herr Adelstein asked, "Henri, when are we going to continue our journey? We three are now getting a little bored. If we are staying longer, can you ask if it is safe for us to go outside? It's the snakes, you see. We fear that we will become their dinner." Sir Thomas shook rather violently at the mention of dinner and nearly spilled his tea. Albert just looked bored and said nothing.

"I'll ask," Henri agreed and went in search of Ulysses. "Ah, might I have a word with you?"

"Oh yes, yes! What can we do for you?" the mouse replied, seemingly eager to help in any way possible.

"It's our friends. They were wondering if it is safe for them to go outside. We assume that the large snakes live in this village and they do want to be eaten. Neither do we for that matter."

"Yes, yes, it is safe. The snakes do live here, but they are very peaceful; they dine on the toad stools, not us. Oh my no. Otherwise, we rodents would not be here. Perfectly safe outside."

"Well, that is good news. Say, another question. It seems that we are under the influence of some kind of drug that is heightening our senses. Are you putting it into our food?" He thought about mentioning that the trio were not being affected, but thought better of it.

The mouse squirmed a little. "I suppose that it is all right to tell you, since you have nearly figured it out. Sort of. You see, it is a combination. The snake injected the catalyst or so I am told. Whenever you eat a meal, part of the meal then acts as that which heightens your pleasures. Please, don't worry. The effect wears off in about a week, though I must say that many of our guests in the past have asked to stay on here for far longer periods of time. We were so hoping that you would find this so enjoyable that you would stay a while. Are we not doing such a good job for you?"

"Oh no, no, sir. We are truly enjoying the experience. It is, well, quite something else. Rather, it is that we are needed elsewhere. Perhaps when we have finished our business there, we could come back and stay longer, if such is permitted."

He brightened up. "Yes, of course, it is permitted. Please do come back. We will welcome you with open arms. We do try to do our very best to make this inn the finest in all the land."

"Well, for our money, you certainly have succeeded, Mr. Minty. This is most definitely the finest establishment that any of us has ever stayed in, bar none." He looked very pleased, and Henri returned to explain what he'd learned to the others.

"I don't believe you," Rose commented. "I am not drugged. We are just having the best time of our lives, right Milan?"

"Right, dear."

"So it is safe out there," Herr Adelstein asked again. "Would you two perhaps like to accompany us this first trip outside, just in case, you know?"

"Sure we can, can't we, Henri?" Vanessa felt a surge of sympathy for their three friends who were not experiencing such fantastic sensations.

The five headed outside into the fantastic colored world. It seemed safe enough. Arm in arm, Vanessa and Henri strolled, albeit very slowly as she was wearing her high heels as she always had to do. Suddenly, the two seemed to be in the air, flying above the ground, swerving in and out and around the toad stools. The multi-colored patches became a swirl of colors. Henri's voice sounded strange to his own ears and even weirder to Vanessa. "God, I think that we are tripping or something!"

"This is unbelievably cool, dear. Look at me! I'm flying, I think," Vanessa exclaimed. The two continued their "trip" until suddenly she felt someone tugging on her arm. Pulled back mostly to reality, Herr Adelstein finally got her attention.

"Whatever are you to doing?" he asked.

"Tripping, I think. We had better get back inside," she said and began pulling Henri with her. The rabbit made sure that the two got safely back inside the inn, before returning for his walk with his two friends, grumbling something about silly 'umans.

"My god, what a trip!" Henri gushed as the two headed for their bedroom. "We better not tell the others about this or they will want to do it too. We might have really gotten lost out there!"

"I know, I know, but right now, love, I need your hands all over my body. Please, I can't wait any longer," Vanessa pleaded.

As the days stretched out, the six experienced many other wild sensations. They took a walk in the atrium hall, filled with exotic flowers. All six "tripped out" on the flowers. Another time, they found the swimming pool which very nearly ended in disaster, as far as Vanessa and Henri were concerned because the other four suddenly wanted them to join in an orgy. Her monster breasts had commanded the attention of the other four, including Rose and Trina, who wanted to get their hands on them too. The two had a narrow escape, dashing off to their bedroom to avoid partaking of the orgy.

Finally, their seven days ended. All six felt utterly exhausted as they made their way to breakfast. "Boy, am I ever dragging!" Vanessa commented. "You best hang on to me, love. My legs feel like mush."

"My head feels like mush," Henri replied.

Rose moaned and groaned as well. "I feel like an old woman."

As they sat down to dine, one of the giant snakes came slithering into the room. At once, the trio vanished, poof! "Well, guestsss, how do you like your ssstay in Pander Parkland? Isss it not the bessst? Have you thoroughly enjoyed yoursssselvesss?"

"Yes, of that, there can be no doubts whatsoever," Henri took charge, since he had been their initial contact with the snake on the toad stool.

"Excellent. I have come to asssk you if you wisssh to ssstay another week? Mossst guessstsss do, you know."

"No, I am afraid as much as we have truly enjoyed ourselves, we must be on our way. We have business to handle. Perhaps when we finish we can return and enjoy this inn once more. Such is permitted, is it not?"

"Oh yesss. Yesss it isss. Pleassse do come back. We have not had sssuch fine guessstsss asss you in a long, long time," the snake answered.

"I just wish that you had told us that you were drugging us," Henri hinted. "We are so worn out now."

"If we had, would you have come?"

"Perhaps," Henri replied.

Vanessa had a flash of insight. "Say, if a guest keeps on staying here, allowing you to bite him or her each week, surely their bodies cannot take that much stimulation. What happens to them?"

"Ah, a sssmart one you are. I am obligated to anssswer that direct quessstion. Bodiesss do wear out, and you have sssseen many of them asss you entered Pander Parkland. We put what isss left of them when they are burned out to good ussse. Our toad ssstoolsss."

Vanessa shuttered. All those toad stools had once been a person! "Thank you for being honest with us. We will be leaving today, but we may well return when our work is finished."

"We better return," Rose declared. "I for one want to stay on now, but you are being so insistent that we get on with whatever we are supposed to be doing that Milan and I will follow you. Just make darn sure that you bring us back here when your business is done!"

"Yes, we insist on coming back as soon as possible," Trina added her desires to Rose's.

"We will look forward to your return then." The snake slithered on out of the inn. The somber crew finished up their meal and headed to their rooms to pack. Henri and Vanessa wanted to get out of there as soon as possible. While their bodies craved to stay and at least rest up a few days, they knew that they dare not risk it.

They did stay for lunch. Henri had their map spread out, examining their proposed route. "It looks like Causeland is next. I wonder what is there?"

Ulysses overheard him and spoke up. "Oh dear me. You are not going to go to Causeland, are you? I would not recommend that anymore."

"Why? What do you mean? It sounds harmless enough."

"Many years ago, yes, Causeland was extremely powerful and beautiful. We rodents came from there several centuries ago. However, these days, it is not safe. We used to get many guests vacationing here from Causeland. Not any longer. Why, I can't remember when we last had guests from there. No, I would not go there if I were you. It is not safe."

"Okay, why isn't it safe, Mr. Minty?" Henri probed for more information. Neither he nor Vanessa had a good feeling about this next destination. Clearly, it was on their route and they had to follow the route if ever they were to find the true exit.

Ulysses squirmed a little and fiddled with his long whiskers before answering. "Honestly, we do not know, only that it must be bad since guests have long ago stopped coming here for a visit. It is ruled by Duke Leo Tarsus and his wife Duchess Marla. Beyond that, we cannot say for sure. I do wish you would reconsider."

"Well, we have to go there. Perhaps, if we find out what has gone wrong there, we can help put it right. Then, guests may start returning here for visits," Henri attempted to put the mouse more at ease over this situation.

"Oh, now that would be wonderful, wonderful indeed. If you can, we would be especially honored if you would return for a stay. In fact, allow us to give you some of the clothing that you were wearing as a token of our appreciation for what you are attempting to do for us. Such is only fair, you know." Ulysses would not take no for an answer. Hence the rest of the afternoon was spent with Ulysses and Missy hovering over the six men and women helping them choose the best outfits to take with them. In the end, each woman now had six more complete outfits and the men, two each. Even the trio left with one new fancy suit, which pleased them considerably.

They stayed the night and fortunately slept very soundly. Henri and Vanessa felt much better in the morning, as did the other four. After breakfast, they said their farewells and climbed back into the carriage. This morning, Milan insisted on sitting with Henri, though Reginald also wanted to sit topside as well. The men intended to protect the women from whatever threat lay in this new Causeland. Hence, the three men squeezed into the driver's box and off they went.

"Do you think that we are again heading into difficulties?" asked Herr Adelstein. "We seem to be running into problems wherever we go. Curious, isn't it? Why, we never had any serious problems where we live."

"But, but, Herr Adelstein," Sir Thomas nervously pointed out, "we did. The Enforcers. We were always being hounded by those — those — those monsters." He finally got it all said, and his body shook slightly adding a bit more emphasis.

Albert added his protest to that of the squirrels. "He's right, you know. Many times I had to duck for cover. I am amazed that I was never stepped upon — I always worried about that, you know. You fellows popped up into your houses, but me, while I ducked into mine, there it sat on the ground — an accident waiting to happen."

"Small matters, small matters," Herr Adelstein attempted to make less of their protests.

"You would not think so if you were squashed by a million pound Enforcer," Albert countered.

"Look, guys. So far, we've not let anyone harm a single hair on your heads," Vanessa pointed out. "Wait a second,

Herr Adelstein. You just said something that might be significant. What did you say about problems?"

The rabbit puffed up, exonerated, and replied, "We seem to be running into problems wherever we go."

Vanessa replied, "You have a valid point, Herr Adelstein. Problems seem to be everywhere. However, think about this whole universe or world or whatever this place is. Sorry, Rose, I really don't understand all this any better than I do. If I understand Miranda correctly, this Able Montford somehow made all this way back when. At least we know it was in operation when he was alive in 1850, though it may have begun earlier. Unless the guy is immortal or inhuman, he has to be long since dead, given that he was say maybe fifty at that time. Now, he'd be over two centuries old, and it is a very rare one of us that makes the century mark."

"Yes, yes, Vanessa," Rose complained. She was still greatly annoyed at not being allowed to stay on at the inn and was still groggy and exhausted. "So what's your point, if there is one?"

"My point is if the Creator of this world is long dead, that means he has not been around for quite some time to keep things fixed up properly and running well. Think of the world as my coffee kiosk truck. If I don't keep it maintained, over a long period of operation, it runs down, breaks down. Small things at first; then larger and larger things go wrong, until even the motor won't start. I think that's what we are seeing happening all over this world. Things are going off the rails because no one has been tending all the small details of maintenance. Henri and Vanessa are examples. Look how long Trina and Regi were trapped in our bodies. They ought to have been able to continue their trek through this game world long ago, but were stuck there for a century and a half."

"It was awful," Trina whispered. "We'd rather not think about that anymore."

"Right, I think that what we are seeing is a world that is slowly breaking down because it has not been properly maintained," Vanessa concluded.

"So what does that mean?" asked Herr Adelstein. Rose, who ought to have been paying close attention to this, wasn't, her head throbbed and wished that she could somehow just doze off. Trina wanted to forget it all and just go back to the inn. Vanessa suspected that Trina got more enjoyment from their week at the inn than she could ever have imagined possible. Instead, of all them, the rabbit was listening intently to Vanessa's ideas.

"I am not sure, but when you couple this idea with what Mr. Minty told us about things now being somehow all wrong in Causeland, it starts to make sense of all this. We should expect trouble ahead, if only because folks have stopped coming over to Pander Parkland from Causeland. Now we should ask ourselves: why would the people suddenly stop coming over here? You see, most people would enjoy Pander Parkland greatly."

"And get themselves addicted. Don't forget that! Brrr. I would not want to become a toad stool!" Sir Thomas shuttered even thinking that these toad stools passing by the carriage windows were once people.

"I suppose someone ordered them not to leave Causeland," put in the somber voice of Albert. "But then, I am probably wrong again."

"Maybe not, my friend," Vanessa tried to cheer him up a little. "You might be right. Something drastic must have happened in Causeland to force folks who would ordinarily enjoy and desire to come to Pander Parkland for a vacation to abandon ever going again."

"Sounds rather ominous, doesn't it?" Herr Adelstein commented.

"Yes, it does, my friend. That is why the men are a bit worried this time." Vanessa bit her lip. What were they heading into this time? The war, while threatening, was handleable. A whole country or land? That seemed to her to be rather formidable. It would help to know what Causeland used to be like, she thought to herself, but there was no way to know that unless there was a book on life in Causeland back in the Count's study in Malbon. No way did she wish to return there to check on it.

Instead, much to the relief of Rose, she and the trio contented themselves to watching the colorful patchwork quilted countryside roll slowly by them. The day seemed warm to her and Vanessa dozed off as well. While she didn't want to admit it openly, her body was exhausted as well.

# Chapter 13 Causeland

Late afternoon, the multi-colored landscape of Pander Parkland yielded to the grasslands of Causeland. A large river formed a natural barrier between the two countries or lands, but Vanessa was not sure of the proper designation. A quaint stone bridge over the river lay ahead of them, and Milan, who was now driving, halted before it. Henri climbed down and opened the carriage door. "Well, there it is ahead of us, just over the bridge. It is getting late. Do we sort of camp out here beneath the toad stools or do we go on across and gamble that we can find an inn ahead of us. Of course, we might run into trouble as well. What do you think, dear?"

Rose was about to speak, when Henri cut her off. "No, mom. We are not going back to the inn in Pander Parkland just yet." Rose frowned and Henri winked to Vanessa.

"Sleeping in the carriage is going to be tough, but it might be better than heading into trouble when we are all tired and hungry. We still have a bit of leftovers from the inn that might tide us over until tomorrow. On the other hand, there might be an inn not too distant from here which may be just fine for us. I wish we knew more about the location of the inns around here."

"True, it would make sense for travelers to have an inn not far ahead. We've made average time today. If there used to be a lot of traffic between these two lands, more than likely, there ought to be an inn not much further. Of course, we don't know what to expect there," Henri suggested.

"Oh *do* find us an inn, daughter. We can't sleep in this carriage," Rose complained. "Besides, I am hungry."

"Perhaps we should go a bit further," Vanessa decided and Henri agreed. A minute later, they rolled up and over the quaint stone bridge and into Causeland. Initially, they saw tall grasses that rolled gently from the barely perceptible breeze. Off of the path, the grasses rose up some three feet tall in places, while on the road, which was heavily rutted, grasses grew perhaps a foot down the center, leaving a clearly marked path to follow, though obviously not used much in recent times.

Before long, everyone was gazing out of the windows. To their right, an enormous swarm of butterflies took flight, thousands of them. Dazzling colors sparkled against the green of the grass and blue sky. To their left, a dozen rainbows arced over the land, but their positions seemed random, unlike rainbows that Vanessa saw on earth. "I wonder how many pots of gold there are out there," Rose said dreamily.

"Don't even mention that word!" Trina said curtly. Vanessa grinned.

A few miles further on amid swarms of butterflies, a small village appeared. As they drew near, an ominous silence greeted them. No one was out on the streets; no smoke curls rose into the sky from the chimneys though there ought to have been since it was suppertime or nearly so. They entered the village accompanied by an eerie silence. Ahead, Milan spotted the inn and halted before its main entrance.

"Queer. It seems deserted. I'll go see if we can at least obtain rooms," Reginald suggested. He jumped down and entered the building. It was a single story, brownstone building. The grasses had overgrown the streets and even pushed up in the sidewalks leading to the inn. While the others climbed out of the carriage and looked at the village around them, Reginald stepped back outside. "It seems completely deserted. I could not find anyone inside. Dust is thick on everything. Come on in and see for yourself."

"Spooky," Vanessa said as she entered the inn, holding onto Henri's arm. The main dining hall and bar was filled with tables and chairs, all covered in a thick layer of dust. The place had been abandoned for a long time, she concluded.

"Here's the hallway that leads to the guest rooms. Come on; let's see if we will be able to at least sleep here tonight," Regi called out, sounding hopeful.

The rooms were not as dusty as the dining area. "Well, we can sleep here. I don't suppose that we can find a change of sheets, but look, they are clean underneath the covers. This will be fine," Rose pointed out. "Now how about some food? Surely we can find something that isn't spoiled."

Minutes later, they found the pantry. All of the food was inedible. Rose groaned. Meanwhile, Regi and Milan continued their explorations, while Henri and Vanessa headed back to the carriage to fetch what remained of their left overs. "Sure is strange. I wonder what happened to all of the people?" she asked.

When they returned with their meager rations, Rose and Trina had the tea water boiling and found some clean dishes. Trina was already setting a table for them, having dusted it off. Just then, Herr Adelstein wandered back inside from a rear door. "There is a nice overgrown garden out back. Lots of tasty vegetables. Carrots are super," he said, revealing a bit of carrot stuck to his teeth.

"Excellent, Excellent. Show me, I'll get us something from the garden," Rose insisted.

An hour later, they sat back from the table, sipping their tea. All were full, though mostly from fresh garden produce, which suited the women mostly. They speculated on what had befallen the village, but no one had any substantial clues, save the people all vanished and probably all at nearly the same time.

"It is ominous, I'll give Mr. Minty that point," Vanessa said as she and Henri crawled into their bed, being careful to minimize the disturbance of the dust on the covers.

"I don't like it. Something awful happened here, but what?" Henri answered. "Perhaps, we will find out more tomorrow, dear."

When they entered the dining room in the morning, they found Herr Adelstein sitting back picking his teeth. "Such a fine meal. Why there is no finer meal than carrots, cabbage, and strong black tea for breakfast!"

"I prefer acorns, though," Sir Thomas squeaked. "Still, we are full. Help yourselves. There is plenty to go around. Albert is out sampling the grasses. He says that they taste better than they look. Me, I never eat grass. Bah!"

An hour later, they headed off once more. A mile further on, a giant flock of birds rose up from the tall grasses, startled by the sound of the carriage and horses. Not long after that they encountered another giant swarm of butterflies. Vanessa counted at least a dozen different varieties, assuming that each color represented a different type. The dozen rainbows continued to arc in the sky off to their left or north, though there did not appear to be a cloud in the sky. Still they saw no living person or mammal.

By late afternoon, they were becoming more and more edgy. "Hey, a large city is just ahead!" Henri called out hopefully. An hour later, they halted at the outskirts so that those in the carriage could get out and take a look.

"Wow! Spectacular," Vanessa commented. Others expressed similar feelings. Here was a city. Towering spires, some reaching a hundred feet tall, rose throughout the city, which covered perhaps a five mile circle. "Something like a cross between the domes of Moscow and the spires of an

Islamic city," she suggested, trying to make sense of the wild architecture before her eyes.

Every color of the rainbow was represented, and many of the towers were banded as if emulating the rainbows. Various flags fluttered gently in the soft breeze that waved the tops of the tall grass fields that stretched to the very edge of the city. A large sign, black lettering on a grey background, announced: Heartland, Duchy of Causeland. From here, paved streets headed into the city.

"It's laid out like some giant wheel. See, there is the rim road to our left and right. Our path keeps on heading towards the center of Heartland," Henri pointed out for the women's benefit. The men had already seen this detail from their elevated driver's box. "Still don't see any people, though."

They had not gone but a few feet into the city when suddenly they were forced to stop. From all directions, matchstick men riding matchstick horses and carrying matchstick guns swarmed their carriage. Hundreds of these matchstick men appeared from seemingly out of nowhere! They stood seven feet tall, with a red dome at their top. Their body, arms, legs, and feet, if that's what one could call them, were matchsticks! Imagine laying wooden matches out forming a body and that's what they looked like, only they were seven feet tall. The matchstick horses looked similar and both walked stiffly and with a strange gait. However, they moved fast, five times faster than Henri could run! They fired off several warning shots from their matchstick guns, each shot detonating in a flashing, loud explosion. Even more shocking, they spoke!

"Halt! You are under arrest and will be brought before Duke Leo Tarsus at once. You will follow us now or we will incinerate you, your carriage, and your horses," one matchstick man ordered, though Henri could not see any mouth from which the voice came. They had little choice but to obey; the explosions were most convincing.

Even more frightened, Herr Adelstein and Sir Thomas attempted to pull their usual vanishing act, disappearing into their homes. However, the voice said, "That will not work here in Causeland. You cannot escape by hiding, rabbit and squirrel." Both looked shocked when their bodies did not vanish. Sir Thomas became so nervous that his legs began knocking against each other, completely unnerving Rose, who begged him to stop, but he couldn't.

Finally, as they began to move, the squirrel's legs at least stopped banging together loudly, somewhat appeasing Rose, who was still in an ill humor, an aftereffect of the drugs and intense physical activities that she'd done for a whole week. "What are we being arrested for?" yelled Vanessa up to Henri.

"We have no idea. The matchstick man didn't say. I don't like the way that this is going, though," Henri called back. She then told him what had happened to the rabbit and squirrel. "What? They cannot disappear? What is going on here?" he added. No one knew, however. For the time being, they could only peer out the carriage windows at the magnificent buildings and hundreds of these matchstick men on their matchstick horses escorting them down the spoke road. "I still don't see any people or creatures, other than these queer matchstick men."

Around suppertime, they finally halted before the largest and tallest building spire in Heartland. A sign read: Royal Palace. Here, the matchstick men insisted that everyone vacate the carriage and follow them into the palace. Hundreds of these guards forced them into the building. Reginald tried to resist, testing the strength of the matchstick men. One gave him a shove forward. So strong was his push that Regi very nearly fell over from the push. "They are very strong," he whispered after regaining his balance.

They walked into a long hallway on a red carpet that did show signs of heavy usage. More matchstick men stood guard at the end of the hall, before a large pair of double doors. Each door bore a crest that showed a rhinoceros head. As they approached, two matchstick guards opened the doors wide, while their escort continued to usher them on inside. Here was a small throne room, perhaps forty foot square, bare of furniture, save a large throne.

Sitting on the throne was a huge rhinoceros, an enormous crown perched on his head. He had purple robes draped over his huge bulk. "Prisoners sir. Found them entering the city," a matchstick man announced. The party was shoved before the throne, and the matchstick men stepped back.

"I am Duke Leo Tarsus, ruler of all Causeland. Ah, some women. That is good. There have not been new women for ages. Take the women to the Duchess. She will be most pleased to have them. Take the men to the dungeons."

"Hey, don't we get a trial? What have we done to warrant being thrown into a dungeon?" asked Henri, growing very worried at the rapidity with which this was evolving.

"My word is the law around here. What I say goes. I say take the men to the dungeons. I think that is very clearly said, don't you? You are here and that is that."

"No, it's not clear at all. Why are we being imprisoned? What crime are we guilty of?" asked Henri, trying to make even some slight sense of all this.

"Crime? You need to be guilty of a crime? Ha!" Duke Leo snorted as if this in itself was a major affront. Then he seemed to relax a bit, "Oh, I am sure that I will invent one soon enough. Around here, I don't need a crime to send someone to the dungeons. So without further wasting of my valuable time, take the men to the dungeons! The women will become the duchess' dolls."

Without further words, the matchstick men began pushing the males in one direction and the three women in an entirely different direction. The men were taken down a long, circular stairs, far below the main floor on which they had entered. Henri tried to count the steps, but lost count; it was well over fifty. Finally, they reached the dingy dungeon. Poof! Duke Leo appeared before them once more, materializing out of thin air. This time, he was dressed in a jailor's costume.

"Ah, we have prisoners once more. So glad that you could come and stay in my dungeons here. They have been vacant for far, far too long. Now then to ensure that you cannot escape," he waved his hand and a rod appeared in his paw. He tapped it severely, perhaps making sure that it was still operational. Apparently, he found it so and then he waved it. Poof!

Nothing could have prepared the men for the result. Suddenly, each man found himself barely an inch tall! From way down there, the rhinoceros and the matchstick men appeared as giants. Carefully, the matchstick men lifted up each and put them into the dungeon cell. All were being housed in the single cell. From their viewpoint, the lock on the door seemed impossibly far above them. The jailor, Duke Leo, called out, "Beware the rats."

"Good god! What has happened to us? Rats? If we are this size, a rat will be humongous!" Henri pointed out, fearfully. This was playing out very badly, he thought. Thrown into a dungeon without having even committed a crime went against his very fiber of justice.

"Now we are all dead," Albert moaned. Sir Thomas sat down in a corner and curled up in a fetal ball, waiting for a rat to devour his now tiny body.

Meanwhile, the three women were escorted into a side waiting room, where what appeared to be a matchstick woman stood, her arms crossed. Her head, instead of having a red patch on it, had a bit of hair or at least what seemed to be hair. Her voice was feminine, though.

"Ah, new toy dolls for the Duchess. My, oh my, will she ever be pleased with you! However, I do know her wishes. How many times have I heard her yell out: 'Ceramic their arms!' Why, a thousand if not once. Well, it is my duty to properly prepare you for the Duchess Marla." Several more matchstick women entered. To these, she said, "We must ceramic their arms. You know our duchess. The last time that my predecessor failed to do so, she ignited her head. Oh my. Watching her burn up was ghastly! Terrible beyond words! I have no desire to incur the wrath of our charming Duchess Marla. Ceramic these three at once, while I prepare proper apparel for them. Anyone visiting the duchess absolutely must be properly attired! That has been the rule for many, many centuries. I well remember the temper tantrum that she threw when Agnes entered her presence dressed much as these are! Oh was our duchess affronted! She had Agnes beheaded, be-armed, and be-legged. As I recall, Agnes didn't survive that though. I am sure that you three do not want to be beheaded, be-armed, and be-legged all at once. So it is up to me to make you three presentable to our charming duchess."

To the waiting matchstick women, she barked, "Well, what are you waiting for, ceramic them!" Two matchstick women grabbed Vanessa's arms, pulling them straight down at her sides. She felt something cold touching her shoulders but could not see what it was. Suddenly, her arms and hands felt terribly cold! The freezing sensation quickly vanished, replaced by a total loss of all sensation in her hands and arms. What were they doing to her? She couldn't see because another matchstick woman continued to hold her long, lush hair forward over her front side, blocking her view. Try as she might, she could not move her arms the slightest. She did pivot slightly to watch what was happening to Rose and Trina. In doing so, she got to see that their arms looked a ghastly white now. Her stomach knotted in a wave of panic.

"There, now you cannot use your arms in the slightest, just as the Duchess Marta prefers. They have been turned into ceramic arms. Of course, I cannot emphasize enough for you three to be very careful and not take a bad fall. Your ceramic arms are easily broken. If they break, I am sorry but they cannot be mended. You will just have to then have rubber arms attached to your shoulders and those simply do not look anywhere near as good as these original ceramic arms. As you know, all quality dolls have fine looking ceramic arms. There now, at least the duchess will not outright have you three slain. Now to get you three presentable to her." At this point, the matchstick women began removing their clothing. However, when they discovered the corsets of Vanessa, the matron added, "My, at least this one already is wearing the proper foundations. That is something. Get the others done up quickly. The duke has already told our charming duchess that she is about to have some new toy dolls, and you know how excited our duchess will be. Hurry up, hurry up."

The matchstick women fastened impossibly tight corsets on Rose and Trina, who both gasped and protested, but to no avail. Then, similar black nylon hose were slipped onto their legs. At least they didn't have to do any of this to Vanessa, for she already work similar stockings. However, they did remove her heels, replacing them with black oxfords which they then tied with a double knot. "This way, you cannot slip them off by accident and they cannot become untied. If they did, how would you be able to retie them? See, we are thinking of your future needs." Vanessa breathed a sigh of relief. The heels were the same height as she normally wore, and she didn't have to beg them if they had tried to put lower heels or flats onto her feet.

Next, a huge hoop skirt was tied around their waists. It billowed out six feet in front of them. "What about my panties?" Rose complained.

"Oh, you must not wear them. How will you ever go to the bathroom if you are wearing panties? This way you merely squat down. It really is better this way." Then they proceeded to finish dressing the women, who found that they were now wearing very fancy ball gowns quite similar to those worn in the royal courts of Europe centuries ago. Vanessa did like the fact that they were satin and was able to obtain her choice of color, cherry red. At least they had some slight choice in their apparel. Rose requested a deep blue and Trina asked for a light blue dress.

The matchstick women then brushed the three women's hair a bit, arranging it properly. "There now. Three very presentable human toy dolls for our charming duchess. If you three will follow me, I will take you to the Duchess Marta Tarsus. I cannot begin to tell you how very, very pleased she will be to see you three! No indeed! She will be thrilled to death. You will see."

At least the floor was stone and level, Vanessa thought. Henri was gone and she had no support. Rose and Trina were already having a most difficult time walking, unused to such heel heights. Fortunately, their matchstick matron walked slowly for their benefit. She tried to keep track of all the twists and turns, but soon got lost. Worse, they then came to a spiral staircase! "Please go slowly, ladies. I don't want you to take a tumble and damage yourselves or break your new ceramic arms. The duchess will ignite my head if you do!"

As the three very, very slowly felt their way up, step by step, the matchstick matron came behind them, prepared to catch them if they lost their balance or footing. All three women found ascending this stairs a frightening experience and went up very slowly. How far? Vanessa had no idea, but it seemed an eternity to her, a scary eternity, and she hoped that she would not have to descend the stairs later! She longed for the steadying arms of Henri or at least the use of her own arms. She glanced down and looked the useless, dangling ceramic arms and shuttered.

At long last, they took a hallway to their right, though the stairs continued upwards as far as she could see. Their heels clicked on the hard stone as they traversed the hall. Various portraits of elegant women lined the walls. Perhaps previous duchesses, Vanessa thought to herself. At last, the matron opened a pair of wide doors.

As they entered the Duchess' Throne room, the matron called out, "The Duchess Marla Tarsus of All Causeland. I present your duke's new presents to you. I hope Your Majesty will enjoy them." To the three, she whispered, "Walk up to her majesty and curtsey."

The three had little choice but to advance into the room. It looked more like a child's playroom, Vanessa thought. However, sitting on a throne was a human woman, dressed in a yellow ball gown, much as they were wearing. Hence, their attire seemed appropriate, she thought. However, the woman was the ugliest woman that Vanessa had ever seen. She had stringy brown hair tied into a bun rather carelessly. She had two ugly warts on her nose and misshapen teeth; two were quite yellowed. The duchess appeared to be in her twenties, perhaps, if the age of the body was even correct. She later suspected that it was not.

"Oh goodie, goodie! Three new toy dolls! How utterly marvelous!" she spoke in a childish way. "Oh great! They have the most beautiful ceramic arms! Wonderful, just like the pictures. Dears, please be extra careful not to fall and break them, please. My other ones have all broken theirs, and I had to replace them with rather ugly rubber ones. They just are not the same at all."

"Excuse me, I am Vanessa Graves. What is going on? We just. . ."

"She speaks!" shrieked Duchess Marla in a high, piercing, shrill voice, so loudly that Vanessa instantly ceased mid-sentence. "Ring them! Ring them at once! Ring them!" she continue to shriek as though the very world was being threatened by some incredible disaster.

At once, several matchstick women appeared so fast that Vanessa blinked. They moved at least ten times faster than a man could run. Before any of the three could respond, their mouths were forced open and a huge O ring inserted between their teeth, forcing their mouths to stay open as wide as they could possibly open them. A harness was attached to the ring, and the matchstick women secured the harness around their heads. Vanessa saw at once that there would be absolutely no way that they could possibly undo the straps unless they could somehow get their arms restored. What was going on here? Once more, panic began to swell in her stomach! She realized that they were now securely under the control of sadists!

"Oh for heaven's sake! They are drooling on their new dresses!" the duchess cried out barely a minute later. "Neck them! Neck them at once! I will not have my toys drooling all over themselves. It is highly unseemly! Perhaps it is not even healthy to drool so, don't you think so, Matilda?" Vanessa saw that she'd missed seeing a small kitten in the duchess' lap. Apparently, it was named Matilda, and it seemed to be a mere kitten, nothing more. The matchstick women once more appeared in a flash. This time, they fastened neck braces around each woman's head and tightened them up. It forced Vanessa's head upwards so that her opened mouth no longer drooled saliva. However, her head was pointing slightly upwards, and she couldn't bend it at all, let alone turn her head. She was forced to move her body instead of moving her head. Things were only going from bad to worse by the minute.

Once the matchstick women finished securing them, they again made a hasty exit. The duchess rose, still carrying the kitten. "Matilda, let's introduce our new dolls to our other dolls, shall we? Dolls, if you will please follow me?" To the kitten, she said, "See, now that they are civilized, I can speak in a civilized tone. We are civilized around here, if nothing else, aren't we, Matilda." Bravely, the three women followed very slowly behind the duchess, who led them out a side door and down another hallway. Vanessa had never felt so completely helpless in his or her life. Unable to move her neck, she constantly moved her eyes to see as best she could, but hoped and prayed that there would be no steps to ascend or descend!

None of the three were prepared for the sights they soon saw. Entering what was possibly at one time a child's playroom, they saw another dozen young women much like themselves. All had arms that appeared to be made of rubber, dangling lifelessly at their sides. All wore similar satin ball gowns. At least none of the twelve women's dresses was the same color as the three newcomers' dresses. Quite why Vanessa had that thought, she didn't know. What a funny notion, she thought. All twelve were also wearing a head harness which held O rings securely between their teeth. However, they were not wearing the awful neck braces, Vanessa noted. Further, all twelve seemed to be somehow hanging or suspended from either side wall. Their feet had to be at least a foot above the ground. Twelve pairs of eyes looked at the three new women dolls. She knew instinctively that none of them could possibly have gotten down to the floor by themselves or up on the hooks for that matter.

"My pretty dolls, see what I have brought for you? Three brand new dolls! Aren't they very pretty, especially this one with the really big tits. Now you have more company. I think that we ought to play some today, don't you my dolls?" Several of the hanging women uttered some strange sounds, unable to speak properly. "Matchsticks, please get my dolls down for me," she ordered. Instantly, twelve appeared, and each hastily lifted a woman down from her hanging perch. All twelve seemed greatly relieved with this, at least Vanessa thought so from their eyes.

"Ladies, let's have a *tea* party. Come with me to my tea room, please. Oh, *do* show my new dolls the way, please," Duchess Marla said very politely. "Oh, we should introduce everyone. I am not minding my manners, dolls. If you each would be so kind as to tell my three new dolls you names please. Thank you *so* much," she said most politely. Vanessa grimaced. How could they possibly speak intelligently? Several of the dolls gave the newcomers a sympathetic look, and then they began making ah'ing type noises, completely unintelligible. "Now it is your turn," the duchess said to Vanessa. She tried to say her name, but it sounded mostly as an "ah" sound. Likewise, Rose and Trina did the same. "There, now you each know each other's names. It is not polite to forget someone's name. Now here we are: my tea party room."

The room looked like a little girl's doll house only on an adult's scale. Five quaint tables, probably mahogany, and one throne sat in the middle of the room. A small stove and sink with cabinets overhead lined a wall. "Now you dolls help yourselves to seats. Perhaps you can assist each other sitting.

Oh do make sure that your dresses are not messy when you sit. I will make the tea for us."

Vanessa, Rose, and Trina watched the others to see how they managed this. The dozen moved slowly to a chair. Then, they pushed into it with their hoops, sliding it out a bit. After turning around and making sure that their dresses were falling right and that they were in the proper position, they sat down as carefully as possible, trying hard not to lose their balance and take a tumble.

In their heels, huge hoop dresses, and with their arms quite immobile, this was a huge challenge. One young woman in a light red gown missed her chair slightly and fell helplessly to the floor. Vanessa saw the woman fighting wildly to use her rubber arms to arrest her fall to no avail, they didn't move in the slightest. The duchess looked up from her tea preparations, "Oh dear me, Lucinda has taken a fall. Well, a proper lady must also know how to get herself back up as if no calamity has happened. Hurry up, dear Lucinda. You can show our three new dolls how it is done properly."

Vanessa's heart went out to the young woman, whose long blonde hair now got in her way as she struggled mightily to get to her knees. Once there, she finally managed to get onto her feet, but her hair was now disheveled. As Vanessa watched, the woman tossed her head to the left and right until her hair finally draped back over her back. Then she pushed her chair back into position and successfully got herself seated. Now it was the trio's turn to sit down. With their necks held immobile and their heads looking somewhat upwards, it was all that Vanessa could do to get her chair positioned so that she could sit down. At last, she gave up and sat down, hoping and praying that she didn't fall and break her ceramic arms. Luckily all three women got themselves safely seated without a mishap. Rose and Trina's faces were pale; Vanessa sensed terror coming from the two. As they watched, several of the dolls wiggled a bit and managed to slide their chairs in close to the table.

Soon Duchess Marla carried a tray of cups and the steaming pot over to the table. She properly sat the table and poured each doll a cup of black tea. Then she returned to her own chair, sitting down properly and demurely. "Now then, my pretty dolls, it is time for our tea. Oh dear me. Our three new dolls will be unable to join us with their collars. Matchsticks, please Un-neck our three new dolls." Instantly, three of the matchstick women came swiftly into the room and unfastened the collars from the three, much to their great relief.

"Now then, my three beautiful new dolls, if you *continue* to drool on your pretty new dresses, I will have no choice but to put your Necks back on. *So* please, act like refined ladies and do not drool. Okay, where were we? Oh yes, dolls, would you be so kind as to show our three new dolls how to drink their tea properly?"

Several dolls made an ah sound. Vanessa watched them carefully, figuring that there was no way possible for them to drink their tea. However, the others leaned over and used their tongues to lap at the tea. Vanessa emulated them and found this a laborious process. Very little tea stuck to their tongues unless they sort of curled them a little. It was the most frustrating tea Vanessa ever had. Meanwhile, Duchess Marla chatted away.

"Now at High Tea, it is proper that we ladies chat. It seems that I am doing all of the chatting. Lucinda, what have you to say?" The woman who had fallen began making numerous "ah" sounds, trying to talk, but mostly it sounded like noise. Apparently, this didn't matter to the duchess, who occasionally added, "Oh?" "Well, yes, I would agree." "You don't say!" "How interesting." She played along with the imaginary conversations. Finally, she ordered, "New dolls, why don't you tell us how you got here? I am sure that we are all most interested to hear all about yourselves. Let's begin with you," pointing to Vanessa. "I swear that you are my prettiest doll, and I do love your huge breasts. Tell us how you came to be so well endowed?"

Vanessa had no choice but to make noise. Instead of trying to speak, she simply made "ah" sounds. This seemed to satisfy the duchess. Apparently, the duchess cared little for their true story. After a while, the duchess seemed to tire of the tea. A gong sounded. "Oh dear me. Time is up for today. My duke is calling me for our dinner. Dolls, your dinner awaits you. Will you excuse me now? You can lead our three new dolls to your dining room table and show them how to dine. Thank you. We will play again tomorrow. I think that we may play games instead of just having tea. Think about it and let me know your ideas tomorrow. Night, night my pretty dolls." She rose and left the room.

Vanessa saw what had to be relief on the dozen women's faces once the duchess had left the room. Only then did they begin to rise. Vanessa, Rose, and Trina followed suit. Lucinda nodded to Vanessa, as if saying "follow us." Thankfully, the dozen walked very slowly and very carefully. None wanted to take a tumble. Now Vanessa knew why, if she hadn't already guessed. It was nearly impossible for the women to get up after a fall.

They went down a different hallway and stopped before another pair of large double doors. Vanessa realized that all of the doors had been built with women in their wide gowns in mind. When opened, their dresses cleared the opening easily — when opened that is. The dolls found the doors shut. Lucinda, who was in the lead, was clearly annoyed that the duchess had not had the doors open for the dolls. At last, she made some noises and soon another woman caught on to what Lucinda's head nods meant. The two of them pressed their bodies into the doors, opening them. Both then stood still, holding them open for the rest.

Inside, again there were five tables, each with four chairs, more than enough for the fifteen dolls. Vanessa saw that there were fifteen places set, and the three newcomers allowed the other dolls to take their places before Lucinda nodded to them to come and sit at her table with her. Once more, the fifteen took their time and got seated without mishap this time. Still, it did not alleviate their fright. Vanessa watched Lucinda closely to see how they were to eat. A plate of liquefied food sat before them along with a tea cup. Once more, Lucinda leaned over as best she could in her overly tight corset and dress and used her tongue to lap at the food on the plate.

It took the dolls nearly an hour to finally finish eating their supper. Vanessa found this utterly frustrating, though the liquid food did taste quite good. The dolls then relaxed and lapped at their tea for quite some time. Lucinda tried to explain something to the three, but soon gave up. No way could she make herself understood. Vanessa saw that she was terribly upset over this, but could do nothing for her.

Vanessa wondered how long the women would sit here lapping at their tea. After an hour, fifteen matchstick women entered and ordered them to rise. One announced, "It is time for bed, dolls." Vanessa wondered where the beds were at and how she could sleep with her arms so immobile and useless. She followed close behind Lucinda, who she now regarded as a friend. They went down several halls and again Vanessa lost track of their location. They came back to the very room in which the dolls had been hanging on hooks!

Quickly, the matchstick women twirled each doll around and lifted them up. There was a loop on their backs and this was then slipped over a hook, leaving each doll hanging with her feet about a foot above the floor! "We sleep like this?" Vanessa exclaimed, though her words came out as a series of "ah's."

Lucinda moved her head towards her and nodded as if she understood what Vanessa was asking. Then, she made a series of noises. Shortly, Vanessa heard her peeing on the floor. Now she understood. This just cannot be happening! Yet it most certainly was and her chest began to throb from the hanging pressure. She turned her head and saw Trina sobbing and fought back her own tears as well. She couldn't see where Rose hung, but turned to look at Lucinda and discovered that she was looking at her. From Lucinda's eyes, she knew that she wanted desperately to communicate something, but only unintelligible "ah" sounds could any of them make. The young woman slowly kept closing her eyes and Vanessa got the idea. They were supposed to go to sleep. She wanted to thank Lucinda, but had to settle for "ah" instead. Not long after that, the lights went out, leaving the fifteen hanging dolls in utter darkness.

For a time, Vanessa thought about Henri and what had happened to him. Had he encountered sadism himself? Where was he? Surely if he were not a prisoner himself, he would rescue them. Since she had not seen him the whole evening, she made the assumption that the men had troubles of their own. Somehow, I have to get myself and these women out of this incredible sadistic mess. Thinking of this, she finally fell into a miserable sleep.

# Chapter 14 Games

Sunlight trickled in from a distant window, rousing Vanessa. Her chest which had been aching now was merely numb. The sleep did wonders for her. Her mind was clear, though her mouth was terribly dry. She turned her head from side to side and saw that Trina and Lucinda were still asleep. Good thing; stay sleeping as long as you can, she thought to herself. What do I know about this situation? The only people that we have seen in this whole place are the dozen dolls, plus the duke and duchess. Everyone else around here is a matchstick creature.

Where could all of the people who once lived here have gone? From the size of the city, there must have been tens of thousands of them, she guessed. Surely they all had not gone to Pander Parkland and died there. Yet there were a large number of the toad stools, but they could all not have been people, surely! This idea, Vanessa discounted as unlikely. True, the drug was addictive, but to keep on staying there week after week until your body died from total exhaustion — that was not likely. For some, yes, but the entire population of Causeland? No, she made that assumption.

Okay, if the people here didn't die in Pander Parkland, where did they go? Where are they now? She reflected on the various places that they had seen. Nowhere had they seen an overabundance of people, as a mass migration might suggest. Well, they had not yet seen all of this world. Vanessa could not entirely discount a mass migration of Causeland's population, though she could see why they might have done that if the duke and duchess were acting back then as they were today. Most people would flee from a pair of sadistic rulers.

If they didn't die and they didn't migrate, then what did happened to the tens of thousands of people? Vanessa felt that she was at a dead end on that one and turned her attention to the matchstick men and women. What were they? If nothing else, they were the strangest life form she'd seen. Giant squirrels and rabbits — she could cope with them. Even the large rhinoceros duke she could comprehend. Cat women, talking lions, giant mice — again strange, but not mind blowing. Stick people. They did not seem to need to eat or sleep; they were simply made of wooden, albeit enormous, matches. They could move extremely swiftly and even talk, though they had no lungs or voice boxes that she could see. They knew how to dress women in their fancy gowns and were dexterous enough to tie shoe laces and strong enough to tighten corsets. If I was blind, I might have thought that the matchstick men and women were the real men and women of Causeland, Vanessa thought to herself. Of course, their heads could be ignited, which apparently killed them by burning.

Then a frightening notion struck her. What if these matchstick men and women *were* the people of Causeland who had undergone some *horrific* alterations of their bodies? There were a rather large number of them, at least it seemed that way when they first saw them in the city. Of all her theories, this one seemed more plausible simply because of the sheer number of the matchstick people that were here in the city. What kind of horrific spell had so drastically altered their bodies? Such certainly *had* to have happened long *after* Abel Montford had ceased coming to his own world. Mr. Minty had not indicated that the people from Causeland were matchsticks. Somehow she could not see the drugs having any impact on these creatures whatsoever. No, their transformation into matchstick people must have occurred sometime ago. It may well correlate with the sudden cessation of Mr. Minty's vacationers from Causeland. The more that she thought about it, the more plausible this theory seemed to her, ignoring entirely how such an awful transformation could have ever come about. She wished that she could talk to Henri and Milan about her theory, but of course could not.

Meanwhile in the dark, damp dungeon, the six took stock of their situation. A little light came into their dungeon chamber from the torches which were kept burning just outside their cell. They looked around and saw a large rat hole in one corner. There was a patch of straw which was big enough for all of them to use as beds. A pudding bowl held drinking water which they could reach if they stood on someone's shoulders. A pie tin held food as well as a number of very tiny forks and spoons. No knives, however.

"Right now, a knife would be useful," Henri said sourly.

"What for? We haven't any meat to cut up. It's all sort of a mush," Reginald asked.

"To defend ourselves from the rats and perhaps to dig our way out of here," Henri replied.

"I have a number of them in my house," Herr Adelstein suggested, growling, "only I can't apparate any longer to get into my house."

"Me too," squeaked Sir Thomas, growing more nervous with each passing minute. His eyes never left the rat hole.

"I have a pocket knife in my house, which I always have with me. Only now it is awfully small. I don't suppose that it will be useful though," Albert said mournfully.

"Albert! You are a genius. Yes, it will be useful. Please can you fetch it?" Henri asked, becoming more hopeful. The tortoise ducked into his shell and returned with his pocket knife.

"See, it is now very small indeed."

"Look, Albert. If it was its natural size, then as small as we are, we could not even lift it, let alone use it," Henri pointed out.

"Oh! I see that I am wrong again. I believe that I feel good about being wrong this time." The others grinned and Henri opened the knife blade, examining it.

"Okay, let's search our cell and see if we can find anything else that we could use to defend ourselves from the rats," Henri suggested. He knew that he needed to get them all actively doing something useful or depression would set in and all would end up in a total apathy. The six scurried about the cell, which was quite large, considering their size. Henri himself was now one inch tall.

They found a paper clip, a rusty nail, and a hair pin for their efforts. Milan and Regi bent the paper clip into a long spear. Now armed with four potential weapons, Henri felt a bit more secure if a rat should appear.

Next, they examined every inch of the joints between the walls and their floor. Henri was looking for any possible way that they could get out of the cell. "Our first objective is to get out of this cell," he explained. Unfortunately, the thick stone of the walls sat solidly on the stone flooring. The door itself was incredibly thick wood, considering their size and their tiny pocket knife. It would take an eternity to cut their way through the wood. At last, sleep overcame them, but Henri insisted on posting a guard to watch for rats.

Dawn came and thus far, no rats. A matchstick man dumped a bit more water in their bowl and slopped more food onto their pie pan plate. He reached his hand in through the barred window and didn't open the door, much to Henri's disappointment. He'd hoped that they'd at least open the door occasionally. After helping each other up to eat, they sat back on their straw. Apathy began to seep into their minds, all except Henri's that is. He began to worry about Vanessa. What was happening to her? Was she in another prison cell elsewhere? If not, could she possible sneak down here and open the door for them? Even if she could, their size difference would cause problems. Still, she could rescue them and drive the carriage. Maybe later on they could find a way to reverse the shrinkage magical effects.

Do I wait and hope that Vanessa can somehow get to us and free us or do I keep on trying to find a way for us to get out of the cell and go in search of her? Such thoughts swept through Henri's mind until at last he too sat back down on the straw. What could he actually do? Even if the door was opened, how could they even climb up one step? Each step represented Mount Everest to someone who was barely an inch tall. Escape seemed hopeless. His head sank into his hands and knees.

The matchstick women suddenly appeared. One stood before Vanessa and gently lifted her down, carefully setting her on the floor. It even waited until she found her footing. Reactively, Vanessa said, "Thank you." She immediately regretted it, only weird "ah" sounds came out her open mouth, now parched and dry. She fell in line with the others and noticed that most had gone to the bathroom. Just as they began to slowly make their way after the matchstick woman, she noticed others began scrubbing the stone floor, cleaning up after them. That was needed, she thought.

Before long, the fifteen women again struggled to get seated without falling down. Unfortunately, Rose missed her chair and fell hard onto the floor. Vanessa headed for her wishing to somehow find a way to help her get back on her feet. Also, she feared that Rose might have shattered her ceramic arms. No, Rose's white arms were undamaged, a tiny relief, but she could only stand by and watch her pathetic attempts to get to her feet. Seeing that Rose was not succeeding, Lucinda purposely squatted down in front of Rose and then managed to fall gently to the floor. Lucinda made some "ah" noises and got Rose's attention. She showed Rose how to manage it by eventually getting her knees up under her while her head rested on the floor. From there, she sat up and then carefully got to her feet. At long last, Rose managed to get back up, gasping for breath from her overly tight corset.

Not long after that, the matchstick women entered and fixed the fifteen their breakfast plates of a thick liquid. Vanessa suspected that they ran the food through a blender to get it into this consistency. Again, the women bent at their waists and leaned over the tables, then bent their heads down to the plates. Tongues licked into the food bringing a small layer into their mouths. Often, they'd have to lean back to swallow though. Eating took considerable time, and Vanessa was starving and cleaned up her plate before tackling the tea, which took forever to drink, one lick at a time.

She guessed that eating their breakfast had taken perhaps two hours of very frustrating effort on their part. As they finished up, she wondered what would happen next. Would they be taken back and hung up on the wall waiting the next time that the duchess desired their company? She suspected that this was often the case, but had no way to ask the others.

Just then Duchess Marla came waltzing in, humming a cheerful tune. "Good morning my pretty dolls. I've come to play with you all today, especially my new dolls. I dreamed of you, I might add. Good ones. Now then, we have enough dolls to play a game of checkers. If you all will come with me, we will have lots of fun playing together today. I just know it. I have thought of a whole lot of fun things that we can do together. Come on, up and at it. Follow me, though I will go slowly. Don't fall down now. Dolls are not supposed to fall down." One by one, the dolls got to their feet and fell into a line, two abreast, behind the duchess. She was wearing a bright yellow gown this morning. Vanessa stood beside Lucinda, who nodded to her, the best that she could do to show that she appreciated her being beside her.

Then began the long walk to her playroom. Unfortunately for the dolls, they had to ascend one of the circular stairs. While the duchess lifted up the front of her enormous hoop skirt, the dolls could not. For a moment, Vanessa panicked. She could not see her feet beneath the twelve foot in diameter gown and could not lift up her hoop. She gave Lucinda a panicked look and Lucinda moved a little ahead of her showing her how to do it. Feeling carefully with her feet, she found the step and carefully put one foot up. After bringing the other one up, she inched forward until her toes touched the next one and repeated the process. At least the duchess gave them time to make their extremely slow ascent and didn't harass them as Vanessa thought she might.

At long last, they entered another playroom. Again, there were tables and chairs. The duchess had moved most of these back along the wall. The floor was a black and white checker board, eight by eight. She now realized that the dolls would become the checkers — at least for one side anyway. The duchess moved Vanessa over to one square in the front. "Now this is your starting square. Lucinda, you are on the next one, here." Dutifully, Lucinda moved to the indicated square. In a few minutes, the duchess had a dozen of the dolls properly arranged. Three were lucky and got to sit on the chairs.

"Now to get my pieces on the board," the duchess explained, talking to the dolls as if they were just that, a child's play toy. She put four-foot tall chess pieces, all pawns Vanessa guessed from their shape, onto her dozen squares. "Now I move first, because I am the duchess. It would be unseemly if I did not move first. Royalty always goes first, you see, because you are just my dolls. There. Now when it is your turn and if you want to take one of my pieces, you have to fight it and knock it over and push it off of the board. If my piece takes one of yours, I get to push you over and off of the board. Okay, it's your turn. Vanessa, make your move. And so the game began.

Before long, Vanessa saw an opportunity to jump one of the duchess' pieces and did so. "Oh that was a good move, my pretty doll. Now you have to fight the piece that you are taking, go ahead, fight it and knock it over." Vanessa wanted to scream, "How?" but thought better of making a sound. She pushed her billowing dress into the piece and eventually bumped it hard with her leg, toppling it over. "Now you have to push it off the board, please." That was far harder to do, but she kept pushing it a little with her shoe, being very careful not to lose her balance, which she very nearly did three times. She was determined though not to give the duchess the satisfaction of seeing her fall. At last the pawn was off the board and she resumed her new square.

As the game progressed, the duchess jumped over a doll and purposely used the pawn to knock the helpless doll over. Unfortunately, she also bumped into two other women who fell as well. The poor women struggled mightily and after several frustrating minutes finally got to their feet. The "taken" woman gladly took a seat along the wall, relieved that her duties were over.

Vanessa decided to see if she could possibly beat this sadistic duchess. Soon she saw her chance and jumped over three, became a king and took another two. The duchess screamed and ranted like a little child, and Vanessa suddenly wished that she had not antagonized her so. Now she had to knock five pawns over. Unfortunately, she fell herself twice, but was extremely careful to twist her body enough so that her ceramic arms didn't take the brunt and crack. She had two very awkward struggles to get back on her feet. By the time that she was done, she was gasping for breath. Her corsets bit into her and she nearly fainted. The duchess then cheated and took Vanessa, knocking her over for a third time. After another five minute struggle to get to her feet and gasping for air, she took a seat beside Lucinda, who nodded appreciatively and blinked several times. It was clear that she approved of what Vanessa had done.

"Well, game's over. I win again. This is boring, don't you think. You are supposed to agree with me, so nod your heads yes." Fifteen dolls nodded; none dare defy her openly. "See, I am so glad that you find it boring too. We need more action. I have just the thing. Badminton!"

Several dolls made what sounded like a protest or groan. Vanessa wondered how on earth the dolls could play badminton without their arms. Perhaps, the duchess would let them free for a while. This sounded very plausible to her, and she rather began to look forward to the game. Unfortunately, they again had to ascend the stairs to the next floor and on the way, one woman lost her footing and fell. She was crying from the pain, but managed to somehow get to her feet and continue on up the stairs. Vanessa began to dread going back down them!

The room was all set up for the game. A net, far lower than regulation play, divided the room. Again, a lot of chairs were against one wall. It was only a two-player game. "Let's see, which doll wants to play against me today. Vanessa looked at the others now sitting in a row and saw what could be construed as panic on their faces, and she didn't understand why. "Ah, yes. It must be my new, gorgeous doll," she pointed to Vanessa. "Come on, out onto the playing field."

Vanessa rose and walked slowly onto her side of the net and stood waiting for her arms to be turned from ceramic back into flesh and blood. To her dismay, that did not happen. Instead, the duchess ordered, "Matchstick woman, please fix her racket for her now." A matchstick woman appeared and came over to Vanessa. She unbuckled the O ring that forced her mouth to open as wide as possible. For a moment, Vanessa's jaws ached and she wiggled them around, glad for the freedom of her jaws.

That was short lived. The stick woman inserted a thick rubber mouthpiece that filled her mouth completely, forcing her to bite down on it. Attached to the end not in her mouth was the shaft of the handle with the racket net at the far end. She was holding the racket between her teeth! The stick woman then secured the mouth piece to her head harness, and Vanessa could not remove the racket assembly if she had wanted to. "Ah, thank you. There you go my prettiest doll. Now you have your racket and we can play. You can't serve at all well, so I will always be the server. Are you ready to play? Nod your head."

Thus began the strangest badminton game Vanessa had ever played or seen! She nodded, with the racket bobbing in front of her face. The duchess served an underhanded tap that arced up and over the net. Vanessa had to watch it come and then turn her head to the side and try to then swing it back so the racket would hit the shuttlecock. She missed. "Mark one on my column," the duchess called out to Trina.

Rose and Trina now had rubber corks inserted into their O rings. A felt marker stuck out of a hole in its center. A white board was divided into two sides, one marked

Duchess, the other Doll. Trina moved her head up and down making a vertical mark on the duchess' side. Vanessa had played a lot of badminton when he was a young boy and became determined to succeed. First, the duchess was just underhandedly lobbing the shuttlecock over the net. Second, she wore similar restrictive clothing and could not move fast either. Third, she didn't really know how to play, but Zed or rather Vanessa did. After missing another one, Vanessa finally hit one, but the shuttlecock went straight and thus into the net. She realized that she needed to bend her neck a little to get the racket angled up slightly. Further, she guessed that if she actually got the shuttlecock back over the net, the duchess would not be able to return it. After five marks were drawn on the duchess' side of the scoreboard, Vanessa finally hit one back over the net and the shocked duchess could not get to it. "What?" she exclaimed and looked at the scoreboard. Already, Rose had obeyed her orders and drawn a mark on the Doll's side. The duchess glared and walked over to the shuttlecock and squatted down to pick it up.

The duchess again lopped the shuttlecock over the net and again Vanessa timed it right, returning it just barely over the net. If the duchess had been wearing sneakers and pants, she could have dashed forward and retrieved it. However, she could only move very slowly just as her dolls and was frustrated that she could not even get close to it. Again and again, she continued to miss Vanessa's returns and grew more and more angry. She moved up closer to the net and lobbed the next one way over Vanessa's head. She turned and made a big deal out of having Trina mark another score on her side. "See, dolls, this is how you win at badminton!"

Vanessa backed up and was ready for her next serve. She got it over the net and the duchess swung wildly, smashing the shuttlecock straight into the net. Rose marked another line on the Doll's side before the duchess could interfere with the score keeping. Rose was now rebelling, at least a little, Vanessa thought. The game progressed in a similar fashion. The duchess grew angrier and angrier. Yelling loudly, she screamed in her high shrill voice, "No, mark that one on my side. She cheated. I wasn't ready!" Rose looked blankly at her. Even if she wanted to obey the duchess, she had no way to erase a mark that she had made, which only infuriated the duchess all the more. Lucinda and the other dolls continued to blink their eyes and nod their heads toward Vanessa. They were doing their best to cheer her on, and Vanessa suspected that until now none of them had ever bested the duchess in one of her games. Before long, the dolls were making all sorts of "ah" sounds, overtly cheering Vanessa, risking retribution from the duchess, who was growing angrier with each serve.

Just as Vanessa thought that the duchess was about to strike her with her racket, the duke entered the room, lumbering slowly across the floor. His weight vibrated the floor slightly; Vanessa felt the flooring moving slightly beneath her heels. "Calm down my dear duchess. What is going on? I could hear you clear down in my throne room."

He looked at the scoreboard. The Doll side had thirty marks while the duchess side had only fifteen. "Duke, my new doll isn't *letting* me win," she wailed.

"Dear duchess, it would not be a game if you *always* won. It seems to me that from the scoreboard, your new doll has won several times over. Doesn't the game go to twenty-one points?" he pointed out.

"But the duchess is *supposed* to win. It isn't *polite* for the dolls to *beat* their duchess," she protested.

"Dear duchess, didn't you want the dolls to play a game with you?" The duchess squirmed a little, rocking her hoop skirt to the right and left a little bit. He continued, "If so, it isn't a game if you always win, now is it? I admit, dear, that I don't see how one of your dolls could have beaten you. You are such a *good* badminton player. Still, you should *reward* your dolls for their victory. You know, give them something *special* like a trophy or a ribbon. Meanwhile, I think that you have played *quite* enough with your dolls for today. Put your racket down. Let's get some lunch, and then you and I will go rainbow riding this afternoon."

The duchess brightened up. "Can I go sliding down the rainbow, dukey, please, please, pretty please?" Vanessa thought that she was acting like a little girl and not an adult. Strange.

He laughed a deep bellowing sound. "Yes, my dear duchess, you may. Come, let us run free among the tall grasses of Causeland and then ride the rainbows. Matchsticks: take care of the duchess' dolls. See that they have their lunch too," he ordered. He and the duchess hastily left the badminton court room.

Several matchstick women entered and one undid the fasteners and removed Vanessa's racket. She wiggled her very sore jaws quickly before one re-inserted the awful O ring once more and fastened it to the head harness. Well, I got my jaws loosened a little bit, she sighed. Already two of the matchstick women had removed the rubber corks from Rose and Trina's O rings. Now they had to follow the matchstick women down the stairs, far more treacherous than going up!

Going down nearly blindly was scary, their hoop skirts totally obscured the steps. Feel, feel, feel, Vanessa kept saying to herself. An eternity passed before they finally reached their floor, and she was very glad to finally be able to sit down. The matchstick women already had their lunch waiting for them, more of the thick liquid on their plates. As before, it took the dolls nearly two hours to eat their lunch and drink their tea. When they finally finished, the matchstick women led them to their hanging wall. Before any could really protest, they were hung back up on their hooks and left alone once more. Lucinda turned her head to Vanessa. She blinked and nodded her head. Vanessa replied in kind, she suspected the woman was thanking her for standing up for the dolls.

Hanging there was incredibly boring. Most tried to doze. On the other hand, Vanessa tried to think. What had happened to the men? Surely they had not been killed outright, but why had she not heard or seen the men? Were they being kept somewhere else? If they were trapped, perhaps they were depending upon the women to come and rescue them. That, she found a chilling thought. She couldn't do any such thing, not any more. Vanessa began to feel quite miserable and hope began to fade, especially as the dolls merely hung on the wall all afternoon!

Just when her stomach was growling, they were again taken down, led to their dining room, and allowed to lap up their supper, before being taken back and hung up for the night. Vanessa groaned as she was once more hung up on the wall. The matchstick women ignored her strange sounds. Left alone once more, Lucinda made a noise and Vanessa turned her head to look at her new friend. The poor woman was trying her best to communicate something to Vanessa, but Vanessa simply could not grasp what. Eventually, Lucinda sank into apathy and gave up, shutting her eyes. Vanessa saw tears trickling down the woman's cheeks, but she could do nothing to help. Where are the men, she thought. What is keeping them from helping us?

The next morning while the dolls were finishing up their breakfast, the duchess made her appearance again. Evidently rainbow sliding had raised her spirits. Vanessa was curious about what that involved but had no way to ask. "Ah, my pretty dolls. Today, I have decided that we will play ballet. Let's put on a ballet. I have a recording disk of music and I will direct you in our ballet. I'm going to call it the Doll Dance. Now of course, you will all need the proper footwear. I want you to know that I have done my research on the ballet most properly. I spent all of last night in our library studying how humans make the proper footwear. I found it in an unusual catalog of boots. Yes, I know that is not where I ought to have found them, but they do look fabulous. So I have had the matchstick women make each of you a pair for our performance today, along with some really fine costumes to go with them. I just know that you are going to love them. We will have such a fun time. Now come on, follow me, please."

They rose and fell into their usual two abreast line behind the duchess. Vanessa thought that perhaps her mood had indeed changed. How much trouble could they get into with a simple ballet? Had she known, she would have likely protested as would have all of the dolls. As they slowly shuffled along behind her, the duchess added, "The duke is right. I should give you all a prize for winning the game yesterday. That's why I have gone to all this trouble to have us a wonderful ballet this morning."

They climbed up another three flights of stairs, and Vanessa began to wonder just how many floors this spiral tower had and what was on all of the floors. In another time and other circumstances, she would have loved to go exploring this unusual building. As it was, she had to pay strict attention to her invisible feet and heels, feeling for each successive step to avoid a very nasty fall.

The room that they entered had indeed been decorated, resembling a stage. Again, there was one chair facing the stage which contained several fake-looking trees. She supposed that it was to represent a forest setting. Along one wall were the chairs for the dolls, and the duchess had them all sit down. "Now then, matchstick women, come and remove my dolls heels and put on their new ballet boots. Here, this is what they look like. Aren't they just magnificent? You will be walking on the tips of your toes, just like the ballet dancers do. These also have really tall heels which will help you keep from falling over. That's why I chose this kind. The catalog said that by making them thigh-high and lacing them very tightly, that will take some of the pressure off of your toes. I suppose that they know what they are doing. Anyway, matchstick women, make sure that they are really tight. Oh, dear," she noticed that once Vanessa's had been fully tightened, she could barely bend her knees any longer. "Well, I guess don't fall down if you can't bend your knees any more. Yes, that must be right," the duchess decided.

Vanessa panicked a little. How could she possibly stand in these, let alone walk? She glanced at Lucinda and saw panic in her face as well. Evidently, the duchess also sensed the growing terror from her fifteen dolls. "Don't worry, the ballet dancers always manage to dance on their toes. I am sure that you will soon get the hang of it, but let's get you into your costumes." At least they no longer wore the huge hoop skirts. Vanessa, chosen to play a leading lady role, was dressed in a form-fitting leotard with a pink crepe tutu. At least she could see her feet now, but walking and standing were awful. Lucinda was dressed in a man's suit with top hat, playing the leading man's role. At last, the duchess had all the dolls stand and take their places on the stage, directing each doll to her assigned location.

Wildly wobbling and wiggling, the fifteen frightened dolls hobbled pathetically to their spots. Stumping might have been a better description, for none of the dolls could manage to keep their balance and be graceful at the same time. "Straighten up, dolls, this is a graceful ballet. Here's the music." She started an ancient gramophone which had a speaker cone and a windup motor which the duchess cranked several times before placing the cone's needle on the recording disk.

Quickly, the duchess saw that her grand ballet was a total disaster. None of the dolls could actually dance. All were wiggling and wobbling, trying to just stand up and at last several did fall. Because of the overly tight thigh high boots, none could get to their feet. "Up, up," the duchess demanded of the struggling women. Vanessa, wobbling like mad, decided that she needed a crane hoist above her to hold her up. Poof. An invisible line hooked on to the loop on her back which normally was hooked onto the wall. Her invisible hoist supported her fully and she relaxed. Lucinda was faring little better, and Vanessa hastily created another invisible hoist to hold her up as well. Lucinda looked over at Vanessa, who blinked and nodded. Lucinda tried to smile, but couldn't, nodding back instead. The significance of what she had just done didn't register with Vanessa for some time, though.

"Oh this isn't working at all right! Cancel! Matchstick women, undo the dolls. Put them back into their usual outfits. Darn it anyway. It was *such* a good idea. Oh well. Why don't we all go outside for a walk? It is a very pretty day. Let's!" the duchess decided. She certainly took this fiasco well, Vanessa thought.

An hour later, greatly relieved, the dolls began descending the dreaded steps. This time, however, Vanessa again created her invisible hoist to keep herself from falling should she make a misstep. She also created one for the other women, who suddenly felt a strong supporting pull on their back hook. More than one tested its strength to see if it would actually hold them if they stumbled. It did. Several turned to glance at Vanessa, who merely nodded. The duchess was oblivious to this, as she led the way down the many flights and then on out the main hallway. Vanessa recognized this as the hall in which they had first entered this spiraling tower palace.

Fresh air and warm sunlight! How wonderful it felt to be out of doors once more. She saw a tremendous relief on the faces of the dozen other dolls and suspected that it had been a very long time since they had been outside. The duchess seemed in good spirits and led the parade down a block and then back again. All moved at their slow speed, of course, but it made quite a sight, sixteen women wearing enormous ball gowns parading along the main street in front of the Royal Palace. Vanessa still saw a lot of the rainbows just north of the city, and it was not raining. How strange, she thought once again.

"Well, it is time for lunch again. Back in we go, my pretty dolls," the duchess announced. Again, Vanessa created fifteen invisible hoists, supporting the dolls as they struggled up the circular stairs to their floor. She canceled them once they began walking down their hallway. A matchstick woman led them to their dining room as usual.

A couple of hours later, they had finished, and the duchess once more appeared. "I have had another great idea. This afternoon we can all play ball. Here is the rule book. It says that there are two teams of players. One player is the pitcher and he or she tosses the softball to one of the opposing teams who tries to hit it with a bat. If they miss, it is called a strike. Each player gets three strikes before he is called an out. Each side gets three outs, you see; then it is the other side's turn to bat. If they hit the ball, they run to first base. If a player gets all the way to the fourth base, where the batters stand, that is called a run. After taking nine complete turns, the team with the most runs wins the game. Doesn't this sound like a whole lot of fun?"

Well, it did, but the duchess was missing a key point: the batter needed their arms and hands to hold and swing the bat. Perhaps, she would transform their arms back so they could play this game. Vanessa became rather hopeful about all this, and she willingly marched along to a floor five floors above their private dining room. She thought that this might be the break that she needed. Getting her arms back would go a long way to allow her to find out what happened to Henri and the men.

The room was laid out like a baseball diamond. The duchess had done a fairly good job with this, except for its dimensions. First base was only twenty feet away, as were the others. Eight chairs lined one wall and another eight lined an opposite wall. Vanessa suspected that there would be eight on each side and she was right. "I will be team captain and my big boob new doll will be the opposing captain. You stand over there. That is your bench, chairs really. I choose a doll first and then you choose one." Vanessa's first choice was Lucinda. She also had Rose and Trina on her side as well.

The duchess continued, "Now then since you dolls will be unable to pitch, we will both use an impartial matchstick woman to pitch to us. Okay, we bat first, of course, but I must change into my baseball costume. You can sit down and wait for me." The duchess slowly walked out of the room.

Not long after that she returned wearing what looked like an early baseball uniform from sometime in the late 1800's. She wore sneakers but not spikes. "Don't I look fabulous? Just like the pictures in the rule book. Okay, I don't actually know what a *soft*ball is, so I made some from the duke's old socks. They are certainly soft. I suppose that is so we do not get hurt when someone hits the ball. Now I have a real bat, but I have had one made especially for your O rings so you can hit too. Okay, your team goes out there. When we hit the ball, you need to get the ball over to first base before we run there. If so, we are out. If not, we are safe and the next one gets to bat. This is going to be a whole lot of fun, don't you think? You are supposed to nod your heads," she declared flatly, her hands on her hips. Dutifully, the dolls nodded, and Vanessa led her team onto the playing field. Suspecting that hardly anyone was going to hit the balls any real distance, she had her women in fairly close to the impartial matchstick pitcher, while she stood on first base. The game began.

The duchess missed the first two pitches but clobbered the sock ball on her third try, sending it out past the pitcher. The duchess dropped her bat and raced for first base. Lucinda moved as fast as she dared in her heels to where the sock ball landed. She had no idea how to get the ball over to Vanessa and eventually tried to kick it over there with her heels. Of course, her heels were invisible beneath her twelve foot wide hoop skirt and it took her several tries to get it sliding across the floor. It took her two more tries to finally get it to Vanessa. By now, the duchess had long since reached fourth base and was cheering that they had a home run. "One to nothing," the duchess happily announced.

Vanessa made an adjustment to her dolls' positions and a doll came to bat. A matchstick woman had jammed the conical end of a stick into the woman's O ring and a long batting stick extended out nearly two feet. She would be batting it by swinging her head; pathetic, Vanessa thought. Two dolls swung three times and missed all three times. The third doll actually made contact on her third swing. The sock ball flew perhaps five feet. Now the doll began to run to first base. Walking in such high heels was most challenging, but running was nearly impossible. She moved as quickly as she dared, trying hard not to fall. Meanwhile, Lucinda got to the sock ball and began kicking it towards Vanessa. "Safe!" called an enthusiastic duchess.

The next doll struck out and now the teams traded sides. Vanessa noted that the dolls liked to bat because it meant that most could sit down for a time. She decided to bat first. After the funny bat was wedged into her O ring, she walked slowly to the base. At least the pitcher was impartial and continued tossing the sock ball the same way that she had done to the duchess' team. She missed the first two, but timed the next one right. She swung her head and hit the ball which flew a whopping five feet. She knew that running was impossible, but moved as quickly as she dare. Meanwhile, the duchess was screaming orders to her team members to kick it to her on first base. Vanessa got there long before the sock ball. A stick woman pulled the bat out of her O ring and then inserted it securely into Lucinda who batted next.

Vanessa could not resist attempting to influence the game. After Lucinda valiantly tried to hit the ball twice and missed both times, Vanessa decided that she would hit the next one. She did. Vanessa decided the ball would go twice as far as hers had. It did and she moved as quickly as she could to second base. All the while, the duchess continued to scream orders to her dolls.

Rose struck out as did Trina. The next doll, Vanessa again decided would hit the sock ball and she did. Now the bases were loaded. Vanessa once more decided that the doll would hit it, and as the woman actually touched the sock ball with her stick bat, Vanessa decided that the ball would fly ten feet instead of dropping there at the plate, which it ought to have done. It did and when she crossed home plate, her team members jumped a little and made loud "ah" noises. It was one to one now and the next woman missed completely, never getting the hang of how to swing the bat with her head.

The game continued to progress. The duchess was rather annoyed that none of her dolls ever seemed to manage to hit the sock ball. Still, whenever she batted, there seemed little that Vanessa's team could do to prevent the duchess from running all around the bases, scoring another run. When it was Vanessa's team's turn, she continued to help her dolls hit, deciding where and how far each hit ball would travel. The sock ball obeyed her decisions unerringly. Still, Vanessa was now fully aware of the duchess' temper and carefully kept the score tied and never tried to get ahead. Thus, when the nine turns finished, the score was tied.

"Now that was fun!" the duchess declared, "but it is time for supper. I am late and the duke will be annoyed with me. Matchstick women, take care of my dolls for me please." She dashed out of the room. Vanessa's feet were killing her, as were those of the other dolls. All were very happy to finally sit down for their supper. Two hours later, Vanessa's body was again attached to the hook on the wall, her feet dangling a foot above the stone floor. It did feel good to be off her feet though.

The next day, the duchess did not come to play with them. Vanessa and the others remained hanging on the wall, save for the three mealtimes.

With all this time just hanging, Vanessa began to think hard. Obviously the men were having at least as hard a time as she or they would have found some way to contact her before now. It was up to her to get the rescues going, but how? What have I learned so far? She forced her mind down a constructive path, trying hard to ignore her chest which was holding her up on the wall like some coat. I know that I was able to manipulate the soft ball game. I got some of them to hit the ball when I know darn well that they would have missed it. I know that I was able to push the sock ball much farther away than we were actually hitting them. What would Miranda do in a situation like this, she thought?

I know, test my limitations! Let's see. I want this damnable O ring out of my mouth. Begone O ring! Nothing happened. Well okay, I want down from here. Down! She focused her attention and really intended to be let down. Nothing happened. Okay, I want my arms back to normal. Now! Once more she did her best to alter it with no result. She sighed and thought a bit more. Looks like I cannot go up against the postulates of the duke and duchess which have imprisoned me so to speak. The other things that I was altering were not those of my direct imprisonment. I wonder if that has anything to do with it?

I know, let's see if I can free Lucinda. She worked at that for several minutes but once again she had no effect upon her new friend. She slumped into an apathy for a time. It must be that I am allowed to change things that are not undoing what they have done to us directly. Hanging on the wall, she couldn't see much to impact at all.

The next day, the duchess appeared as they finished their morning tea. "Good morning, my pretty dolls." The fifteen looked up. Vanessa wanted to moan and complain, but thought better of it. Best not to get the duchess angry again and fire up her sadistic streak. "You are *supposed* to say good morning back to *me*, dolls. Let's try this again. Good morning my pretty dolls," she said. The fifteen responded with unintelligible "ah" sounds which seemed to please the duchess.

"Much better. You should always be polite and respond correctly, my dolls. Now then, this morning I want to play cards. So we are going to have a fun time with it. What do you say? Don't you want to play cards with me?" Again, she forced a series of unintelligible sounds from her fifteen dolls. She led them up two flights of stairs and down a hallway into a room that she'd prepared for them.

"Now you all stand over there by the wall. Four can play at one time. Since none of you can deal or shuffle the cards, what with your rubber and ceramic arms, I will do it for you.

Now then, we are going to have a contest and see who the best card player is. Four of you will play until one of you wins. Then another four will play and so on. I will play with the last three. When this first round is over, we will have four winners. Then the winners will play to see who the champion is. Oh, I nearly forgot, the card game is called poker, though I am not sure where in the game you are supposed to poke each other. I think that we will skip that part. You, you, you, and you, my big boobed new doll, you four will start. Come have a seat. The rest of you stand and watch. No cheating now, dolls."

She pulled up a fifth chair and shuffled the deck and dealt out five cards to the four dolls. "Now you are supposed to not let the other players see your hand. Since you don't have hands, I guess that I'll just turn them all face up. Let's see, you can ask for up to three new cards, if you get rid of up to three that you don't want. I know, you push the ones you want to discard over towards me with your tongues. Here we go. How many do you want, Lucinda?"

Lucinda struggled against the constricting corset to bend over enough to use her tongue to push three cards over a little. "Lucinda takes three," the duchess declared importantly, picking up the three discards and flipping another three over for Lucinda. "She has two pairs. That's a pretty good hand." She handled the other two dolls and finally came to Vanessa.

Like the others, it was terribly hard to bend over enough to reach the cards, but she finally did. She thought a second, made a decision that the duchess would spot her two more Aces. She used her head and tongue to push two cards slightly towards the duchess. "Big Boobs takes two. I do like that name, Big Boobs; yours are the biggest that I've ever seen. Oh my! Look, she has three Aces. Big Boobs wins! Goodie."

She had these four stand up and got another four to sit down. After shuffling, she dealt the cards once more. This time, Vanessa decided that Rose would get three Kings, which she did and thus won the hand. The next four took the seats and the game continued. Naturally, each game took some time, for the dolls were quite slow on moving the cards. Vanessa decided that Trina should win by having three Jacks. Amazingly, she won as postulated. Finally, the last three dolls joined the duchess. Vanessa thought better than to interfere and force the duchess to lose. Naturally, the duchess won.

"Okay, Big Boobs, you, and you, come. It is time for the championship round. Whoever wins this one is the big winner!" the duchess explained, shuffled the cards, and dealt them out. Of course, the three doll's cards were all in plain view of the duchess, while she held hers in her hand so that the dolls could not see what she was holding.

Vanessa made a decision. She wanted to see how the duchess would handle losing the card game. Besides, it was about the only way that she had to create an effect upon her tormentor. She decided that she would get four Aces. "Oh wow! Look at what Big Boobs just got! Four Aces! Darn, I only have two pair. Big Boobs wins. The cards are getting sticky because you are all getting them wet with your tongues. That's why I can't shuffle them well at all. If I could have shuffled them really good, I would have won, you see. This isn't working very well is it?" She looked at the dolls who sat quietly looking at her. "I said, this *isn't* working very well is it?" Fifteen dolls made their "ah" sounds once more. "I am *so* glad that you agree with me. Well, it is time for lunch. Matchstick women, take my dolls off to lunch please."

Around two in the afternoon, just as they were licking at their tea, the duchess entered their dining room once more. "Dolls! I have a wonderful surprise for you this afternoon.

We are going to have a pretend Royal Ball. The duke is letting us play in the Royal Hall where dances are held! The matchstick musicians will be playing for us. This will be a formal ball, so we must all look our very best, you know. Since I will be dancing with all of you, I don't want you drooling on my new ball gown, so I am going to have to Neck all of you. Besides, at a Royal Ball, you must always have perfect posture, if you are to look your very best. Matchstick women, see that they are Necked properly and get them dressed in Royal Ball Gowns please, the really fancy ones. Then, bring them down to the first floor Royal Hall, please. I have to go change into my new ball gown now and get everything ready. Dolls, we will really have some fun this afternoon!" She dashed out of the dining room.

The matchstick women appeared and a flurry of action occurred. The fifteen dolls had their dresses removed, including the large hoop skirts. However, they then redressed them with an even larger hoop skirt. Vanessa groaned, this one was eighteen feet across. Next, they were redressed in a fancy velvet ball gown. The sheer weight of this new dress doubled their previous satin gowns, containing far more and much heavier materials. Once their gowns were on and adjusted, each had their hair brushed out and draped attractively. Finally, each was given a matching cone shaped hat with a veil that covered their faces, though they could still see through its fine gauze. It fastened securely to their head harness so that they couldn't accidentally lose their hats. Satisfied with their appearance, the matchstick women then produced the highly restrictive neck collars that Vanessa hated. Once again, her head was forced upwards slightly so that she could not drool out of the O ring. Worse, she couldn't bend or twist her neck. Thus, the dolls would have to turn on their feet to change even slightly the direction that they wanted to see.

Vanessa thought that she'd like to see how she looked. Surprisingly, the matchstick women then brought in full length mirrors and adjusted them so that the women could see how attractive they looked. She noticed that their neck braces were also covered in matching velvet, completing their total outfit's look, detracting nothing from their look. They were lined up in pairs and followed one matchstick woman down the long hallway.

As they walked, Lucinda pivoted slightly to look at Vanessa. From the corner of her eye, she saw her and also pivoted on her feet slightly. Lucinda made a little noise, but Vanessa could not decipher or guess what the woman wanted to communicate, unless it was fear. Then came the dreaded stairs. This time, they had to descend five floors. Vanessa moved very slowly, feeling for the edge of the first step. In frustration, she again decided to have the invisible hoists attached to their hanging loops, holding them all up in case one stumbled.

They were half way down when stumbles began occurring. Her invisible hoist worked, saving first one and then another from a disastrous fall. Then she too lost her footing and stumbled. Her hoist kept her upright and she frantically felt for the step, regaining it at last. Once on the main floor, many turned to look at Vanessa, a questioning look in their eyes. Vanessa did her best to nod by bending at her waist slightly, since her head was immobile now.

A bit later, they entered the wide double doors, designed for women in their fancy ball gowns. The Royal Dance Hall was huge. She estimated that at least five hundred couples maybe more could have attended a dance here. Vanessa also wondered when the last time a real dance had been held here. The fifteen stood around; the duchess was not yet here.

Vanessa noticed that there were large golden banners or plaques arcing across the top of the walls. Great velvet curtains hung from the walls as well, and she took this time to move around and read them. There were no chairs on which to sit so she had little else to do at the moment. Curiosity reined for a while.

With her head already held slightly upwards, she had little difficulty reading them. Causeland's Royal Dance Hall. Duke Leo and Duchess Marla Tarsus. She noticed a pair of portraits hanging just below them, and she was shocked to see two normal looking humans, dressed much as they were now staring beneficently at her. The portraits had been placed perfectly for this illusion, she noted. "They don't look at all like the current duke and duchess," she said without thinking. Of course, she heard only a stream of unintelligible "ah" sounds.

She continued moving around looking at the banners. She read some. "In times of great trouble comes the Appointed One." "The highest purpose is the creation of an effect." "Any effect is better than no effect." Each one's letters had to be a foot tall, she mused.

"Ta da. Welcome my pretty dolls. You do look positively stunning in your new dresses. What do you think of mine?" the shrill voice of the duchess broke in on her reverie.

A random chorus of "ah" sounds echoed around the room, apparently satisfying the duchess. Vanessa turned to look at her host and saw that she too wore a yellow velvet gown even larger across at the floor than theirs. Hers was likely twenty feet across. "Okay, everyone, pair up, find a partner for the dance. I will dance first with Big Boobs. Musicians, time to play." Vanessa would have laughed if she could have. Ten matchstick people appeared holding instruments and the music began, though the "musicians" did not seem to be doing anything at all but standing there.

Vanessa cringed involuntarily as the really ugly duchess came up to her and put her arms on her shoulders. She was glad that her eyes were looking over the head of the shorter duchess. She had no idea how to dance and allowed the duchess to mostly push her about the dance floor. Soon the duchess tired of her and moved on to another partner, and Vanessa found herself with Lucinda as a partner. She wanted to tell her to make the best of it, but the two could only exchange knowing blinks.

The combination of much heavier dresses and being constantly on her feet attempting to dance soon had her feet aching. Even Lucinda was occasionally stumbling slightly, and she suspected Lucinda's feet were also taking a beating. Before long, all fifteen dolls were more than ready to have the dance end. "Well, haven't we all had such a fine time? I know I have," the duchess ended the dance at last. Several "ah" sounds seemed to agree with her, and she ordered the matchstick women to take care of her dolls while she headed off to change.

An hour later, Vanessa and the dolls were back in their usual gowns and licking at their liquid supper. Two more hours later, the dolls were hung back up on their hooks in the doll storage room. Vanessa's feet appreciated the relief and now she had something to ponder. She could not get the portrait images out of her mind, nor the plaques' sayings: "In times of great trouble comes the Appointed One." "The highest purpose is the creation of an effect." "Any effect is better than no effect." Why did the current duke and duchess look so vastly different than their portraits? Who was this Appointed One? Well, Miranda had told him about creating effects; she was really good at it. Hey, I am getting better, she thought, reflecting on the card game and the screwy softball game. Those were effects and I created them, Vanessa mused.

It was full dark now, though torches provided a little light. Strange, the torches never went out and never seemed to consume themselves, she thought. More effects, she thought. I wonder how far I can go with creating effects? I really ought to see if I can find the men. They must be in a really dire situation to not have even contacted me yet. Well, I have to get down from this hook in order to do anything at all. I wonder if I can lift my body up and off the hook like the matchstick women do?

Hey, it can't hurt anything to try, she thought. I can use my invisible hoist. Let's see. Up and out and gently down! Vanessa concentrated on the desired effect and found her body being lifted gently up, clear of the hook, and then lowered to the stone floor. Her heels felt the wooden floor and she got her balance. She moved out from the wall and looked back at the other fourteen dolls hanging from their hooks. Most had fallen asleep. Lucinda had not and her eyes were wide open, staring at Vanessa. She nodded rapidly, as if saying take me down too. Okay, Vanessa thought, I'll do it. She focused her intention and had the invisible hoist lift Lucinda up and then lowered her safely to the floor. Once she too had her feet securely on the floor and her balance, she nodded vigorously, as if thanking her.

Now what? I need to see if I can find where the men are being held. She used her head to motion to Lucinda that she wanted to go this way to the stairs. Lucinda nodded and slowly they made their way down the hallway. At the closed doors, she halted. Now what? No one had apparently heard the telltale clicks of their high heels on the floor so far anyway, but how to turn the door knobs? Again, Vanessa imagined that she had imaginary hands and went through the motions with them. Sure enough, the knobs turned, and she pushed open the doors with her body. Lucinda nodded her approval, and they entered the circular stairway.

She decided to go down. Dungeons are always in the basements, she recalled from what she'd heard about medieval castles. Though the lighting was dim, they could see, and the two began their extremely cautious descent of five floors to the main floor where they had been earlier at the dance. Nevertheless, she kept her invisible hoist on both their bodies. If they fell, no one would notice or come to help them if they needed assistance. As they stood at the entrance to the first floor hallway, Lucinda nodded a little as if asking what now? She replied by nodding towards the basement.

Down they went into an unexplored part of the building. Down the two descended, very slowly, very carefully feeling each step before taking it. She expected to soon find another hallway, but none appeared, only more steps. On they went. She lost count of the number of steps. Finally as her knees were about to give out from the exertion, the stairs ended in a hallway. Cautiously, the two peered into the dimly illuminated hallway. No one was around.

Vanessa led Lucinda into the hallway and shortly began seeing prison cells! They must be down here somewhere, she thought, but where? The cells were open, doors ajar. Well, she thought, look for a locked cell. That made sense. They walked on and near the far end, she saw the only cell whose door was shut. She struggled to get a good look through the barred window. The cell was empty and her heart sank. Lucinda, curious too, took a look after Vanessa backed away. She gave Vanessa a questioning look, but neither woman could communicate what they wanted to say. Together, they headed back up the many flights of steps. Vanessa's heart was heavy.

# Chapter 15 Dungeon Days

Henri took the last watch and used the time to think. There had to be a way out of here somehow. He tried to increase his own body's size. Nothing. He tried to increase the size of the others, one by one. Nothing. Try as he might, he simply could not create an effect to undo that which the duke had done upon the six. He sighed and looked at the sleeping five. *Now what?* he thought. Nothing came to mind.

A while later, he studied the rat hole in the wall. Evidently, the dungeons had vermin, but probably no one cared enough about them to eradicate them. He looked again at the small knife and wondered if it would really be effective if a rat came out of the hole and attacked them. While he had said nothing to the others, he doubted very much if such a tiny knife would do much of anything to ward off a rat. After all, they were barely an inch tall and a rat ought to be vastly larger. Well, perhaps their luck would hold and the rats would ignore them. Henri hoped so.

But what about the three women? They had been taken off to some other part of the palace. What had happened to them? Were they all right? Surely the duke would not harm women. Then again, nothing that the duke had already done made any sense. His actions were more like that of an insane man. Had the duke gone mad? If so, when? Why? Henri had far more questions than answers. Still, he kept coming back to the three women. Somehow, he had to find a way to get out of here and find them.

Later, Milan woke and took over guard duties. "Any sign of the rats?" he whispered. No sense in frightening the others needlessly, he correctly thought.

Henri shook his head. "Nothing but a total silence down here. I'm getting some sleep, Milan. I am really worried about the women though. Somehow we have to get out of here and find them. Lord knows what kind of trouble they are in right now."

"Yes, I agree on that one. Rose needs me. I can feel it. I'll think on it while you sleep," Milan offered. Henri smiled and laid down in the straw. He soon fell asleep. Curious, he thought as he drifted off to sleep, these tiny bodies seem to need a lot more sleep than before.

After two more days of utter boredom and total isolation, the captives were getting rather impatient for an escape. "We have to get out of here. So far, we have been phenomenally luck that the rats haven't yet found us," Reginald said while Henri held him up so he could eat his portion of their breakfast.

"Hey, you are heavy. Hurry up and eat. We can talk when you get down," Henri grumbled.

After Regi got down, he added, "I simply must find my wife. I am sure that she really needs me. I will not abandon her, even if I am stuck in this dungeon. There must be a way out of here."

"The only way out that I see is to fly up to the barred window there," Milan pointed out the obvious.

"Or that rat hole," Henri suddenly suggested. "I wonder where it goes? Maybe it connects to other cells. If so, maybe we can walk over to another cell and get out that way."

"But, but, but what about the rats?" Sir Thomas blurted out.

For once, Herr Adelstein agreed with Sir Thomas, "He has a point. We are so small and a rat will be so big!"

"Hey, the flies around here are almost as big as us. Is that a problem too?" asked Albert, swatting a fly buzzing around his face. Herr Adelstein glared at Albert as though he had lost his marbles.

"Er, there are no lights in the tunnel," Reginald pointed out. "I guess we can feel our way along the walls, I suppose."

"But, but, but the rats! What do we do if we run into the rats?" asked Sir Thomas, feeling that everyone was ignoring his scary question.

"I've got Albert's knife and Milan has our make-shift spear. We'll keep any rats at bay, Sir Thomas," Henri promised the nervous squirrel. He looked at Henri's small knife and then at Milan's bent paper clip and shook his head. To him, they didn't seem like much protection at all. "Besides, if a rat comes after us, you can stay at the rear and run back here while we try to hold the rat off," Henri added. That placated the squirrel.

Sir Thomas then said, "I — I — you — you — look!" Everyone was looking at Sir Thomas, but he was looking at the gaping rat hole, terrified. His legs knocked together like a tympani in a lively orchestra piece. The group turned around and saw a large rat peering out of the hole at them. Large, well, it was normal rat size, but he stood ten times taller than they. He was dressed in a nice looking suit and was sitting on his hind legs, his front legs were scratching his head, while holding a bowler style, black felt hat, staring at the one inch tall people. Henri whirled and held the knife up, and Milan readied his paper clip spear, ready to a battle to the death, surely theirs.

"I say, tiny people. Haven't seen tiny people in, well, let me see," he continued scratching his head as if that would jog his memory somehow. "Nigh on to half a century, I expect. Oh, do forgive me. I am Phillip d'Groot, ex-captain of the palace guards and bodyguard of the late Duke Milo Masters." He bowed.

Henri lowered his knife. "Sorry, we thought that you were here to dine on us. I am Henri Graves," he replied, introducing the others in turn. "Yes, we entered the city from Pander Parkland a few days ago. As soon as we got to the city, these strange matchstick men captured us and brought us before the rhinoceros, a Duke Leo Tarsus. He immediately convicted us of some crime of which we know nothing about, took our women companions away, shrunk us to this size, and locked us in this dungeon cell. We fear that our three women companions are in bad trouble, but as yet we can't figure a way to get out of this cell. Perhaps your tunnel leads to another cell whose door is open?"

"Well, yes it does. However, how will you ascend the steps? Each one is ten times your height," Phillip asked.

Henri chuckled, "We had not got that far. We've been focused on getting out of this cell first; then we have to find a way to rescue our womenfolk."

"Well, good luck on that one," the rat replied.

"Say, do you know what is going on here in Causeland? Where have all the people gone?" Henri tried a different approach: get information.

Phillip sat down; a sad look came over his face. "Yes, I am doomed. I do indeed know what has happened, though it has been some one hundred twenty years ago. It is a long story. Would you care to join me for a tea and I can tell you my whole pathetic story?"

"Tea? Yes, that is the magic word. I haven't had a good cup since we got here," Henri replied. The others agreed and Phillip turned on his pocket flashlight and led the small folk into his tunnel. After some ten feet, a very long way for the small ones, they entered a well illuminated cubbyhole, which Phillip had fixed up rather nicely.

His guests sat on a long couch — okay, it was really a small stick, but it served them well. He had obviously been raiding the pantry of the duke and had all manner of food stocks including a lot of black tea. He heated up the water on a hot water pipe and soon produced thimbles for the small folk, serving as cups for them. "You must have had other small folk here before," Henri suggested.

"Yes, from time to time, Duke Tarsus throws others like yourselves into the dungeon. I have rescued them, well somewhat. I hope you enjoy the tea. It really is quite good. Let's see, I should start at the very beginning, shouldn't I?" Henri nodded. After a sip himself, Phillip launched into a lengthy explanation.

"It all began one hundred twenty years ago now. Duke Milo and Duchess Minni Masters had run Causeland for quite some time. I was his bodyguard and Captain of the Palace Guards. I was 6-6 back then, a force to be reckoned with, I might add, unlike now. Anyway, that fateful day, I admit that I was lax on security. It was their daughter's birthday, Lucinda Masters; she was twenty-one, and they wanted to have a grand party in the City Park to celebrate her coming of age."

"You see, here in Causeland, everyone goes about creating all manner of interesting things. It falls to the duke and duchess to put right anything that goes astray or that is threatening to Causeland, whether by accident or by intent. In order that his create can out-create what must be set right, he was given a powerful rod which boosts such powers. By commandment of the founder of Causeland, the duke must never be without it on his person, just in case of an emergency. Well, that fateful day, he did not want to bring the rod with him, suggesting that he might drop it or lose it in the festivities. That, of course, would have been a disaster. So I agreed. Woe is my lot for ever having done that. Hence, the last hundred twenty years of horrors is all my doing, my responsibility." Phillip sighed heavily; the weight of all Causeland was on the poor rat's shoulders.

"Anyway, a disgruntled rhinoceros, Leo Tarsus, had come to Causeland from the Greenway some time before then and had evidently carefully noted the importance of the rod. During the celebration at which thousands of our people came to pay honor to Duke Milo and Lucinda, the wicked Leo, having just stolen the rod, suddenly trampled and horned Duke Milo killing him. He also trampled the duchess as well. I tried to stop him, but I was too late and was knocked out by his huge horn for a minute."

"As confusion reined, he used the rod and turned all of the people of Causeland into those matchstick people whom you met. They are mere ghosts of themselves. They do not need to eat, sleep, or think. They simply do as the wielder of the rod orders. He ushered me and several others, including Lucinda, into the main Royal Dance Hall, where he declared himself the new Duke of Causeland. I was powerless to stop him. He held the rod you see."

"He also had a young child with him, Marla. He declared her the new duchess, and he turned Lucinda and nineteen of her girlfriends into Dolls for Marla to play with. You see, Marla wanted to have a human body form, and with the rod the rhinoceros was able to do that for his child. To keep the young women from causing problems for Marla, he immobilized their arms by turning them into ceramic arms and found a way to prevent them from speaking. They are kept in a Doll Closet, hung up like a child's toy dolls, when she is not playing with them. It is ghastly. Over these many years, several of them have taken bad falls down the circular stairs and died. There are only a dozen of them left now. At one time or another, they have all fallen and broken their ceramic arms. The duke replaced them with rubber arms."

"He then shrunk me to the tiny size that I am now and imprisoned me in the very cell that you were in. However as he did so, there in the Royal Dance Hall a new banner or plaque suddenly appeared on the wall! It said, 'In times of great trouble comes the Appointed One.' Well, that really spooked him! After ordering his new matchstick men to imprison me, he then issued orders to bring all visitors to Causeland to him immediately. I spent years digging my exit tunnels. Now I have ways into the main stairs and have looted his pantry. However, I keep my eyes open and ears peeled."

"More so at first than now, visitors did come to Causeland. Fearing the Appointed One, the duke shrunk them to your size and imprisoned them in the dungeon, just as he did you. When I found them, unable to undo what he had done to them, I helped them escape from here. I have a passage way that leads to the outside world. They were quite grateful and fled from here on foot. I have never heard from them again. I do hope they somehow survived in the wide world."

"If you like, I can take you out of this dungeon and tower. Then, you can be on your way," Phillip offered.

"Thanks, but we can't abandon our three women. We are going to have to rescue them and somehow put this mess to rights," Henri replied.

"But you are not the Appointed One are you? I mean you are under the duke's control now and are barely a inch tall. Even if you could get to the rod, you are too small to wield it," Phillip countered.

"I don't know anything about this Appointed One, but we must rescue our women and undo our size reduction. We won't take anything less," Henri stated categorically. "Now where is this rod?"

"Duke Leo keeps it on him at all times. It is wherever he is. However, it is not safe to walk the stairs and halls during the daytime. The matchstick people may spot us and come after us. I have had numerous close encounters with them over the years. At night, it is much safer for us to travel about this tower," Phillip explained.

"We should try the obvious first," Regi suggested. "Let's get out of this tower and back into the city. Then, see if we can return to our normal sizes. Once we do, we can reenter and go about rescuing the others." While Phillip doubted that would happen, the other five were encouraged by his suggestion and it was adopted.

"If you walk, it will take you days to get outside. Permit me to carry you on my back; it is the very least I can do for visitors to Causeland," Phillip volunteered. Saving days sounded terrific to the six and they agreed.

While they waited for nightfall, Phillip began arranging boxes and cartons so that the small people would have a way to gain enough height to get to his back. Once the evening had come, one by one, the small figures climbed up the stack and got onto the back of the rat, clinging tightly to folds in his sports jacket. Once they were all aboard, Phillip headed down a side hole, using his long whiskers to feel his way. It was dawn when he finally brought the six safely out of the tower.

They arrived outside beneath a colorful yellow and orange canopy. "Here you are," Phillip announced. Carefully, the group slipped off his back and onto the ground.

"Okay, let's see if we can get back to our normal size," Regi suggested. All six made strong intentions to have that happen, but nothing occurred. They grit their teeth and tried again and again, growing more and more annoyed and antagonistic about their inability to counter the duke's intention that their bodies were so tiny.

The orange and yellow canopy moved a little and a deep voice said, "Trying to get larger and free, I see." The canopy spoke. Startled, Henri and the others looked up at the strange looking eyes of one of the butterflies. "Mortimer Hammersworth, at your service. Would you like me to fly you somewhere? I have flown several small people from here in the past."

"Er no thanks. If we can't get big again, we will have to go rescue our three women who are being held captive inside," Henri answered, thinking it a bit strange to talk to a butterfly. It was huge compared to himself.

"As you wish. The dew upon the morning glories doth call to me. I must take flight and partake of the golden nectar." With that, the six were knocked flat by the air gush coming from his enormous wings as Mortimer took flight.

Dusting himself off, Herr Adelstein grumbled, "The nerve of that butterfly. He ought to have given us prior warning that he was going to create a whirlwind!" Henri smiled; how strange.

"Well," Henri concluded, "Phillip is right. Just being outside isn't going to do it. Looks like we are going to have to get that rod from the duke."

"But, but, but, but he's so incredibly huge!" Sir Thomas countered, his knees clacking together in fright once more.

"Can't be helped, Sir Thomas. You don't want to be miniaturized forever, now do you?" Milan asked.

"Well, no, of course not, but," the squirrel countered.

"Come on. Let's get back inside and make some new plans," Regi suggested. "Oh dear!" The problem now was how to get back onto the rat's back. Try as they might, they could not scramble up on their own. At last, Phillip began lifting each one up and sitting him on his own back, giving them time to grab on to his jacket before lifting the next companion up. It was dinner time when they again entered the rat's den. He offered to fix dinner for everyone and they accepted. The food was twenty times better than what the matchstick men were providing them.

Over after-dinner tea, they discussed what to do next. Everything hinged around this rod. As tiny as they were, all knew that it was useless to go to the women. They could do nothing to help them. They had to get the rod first. However, the only feasible way to get the rod would be at night while the duke was asleep and that meant getting to his bedroom. Phillip did know where that was, on the forty-second floor! With the height of each step being ten times their own height, Henri moaned at the sheer number of impossible steps just to get to the bedroom, perhaps five hundred of them.

"Ah, yes, I see your problem. It is the same with me," Phillip consoled Henri and his companions. "While I am much larger than you, still, it is a huge effort for me to ascend a step. That's why I usually only go up three floors during one night. Far too fatiguing to attempt anymore. I've made myself little burrows on strategic floors, you see, and when I am up there, I stay in them during the daytime. That's why I didn't see you all for several days. I was seven floors up, exploring one of the duchess' playrooms seeing if I could find anything useful there. I have been doing a little counter-espionage over the years."

Henri gave him a curious look, and he continued, "Oh, over these many years, the duchess has become terribly bored and has been rummaging in the adult material files that someone once brought here. She is a sadist, you know, the duchess is. Anyway, considering how badly she treated her dolls, I began to get suspicious and discovered that she'd uncovered piles of those magazines. Over the years, I have been duty bound to remove them. She is or was rather a child. However, she occasionally finds another one, and they put strange ideas into her head which she then uses to torment her dolls. While she finds that entertaining, the dolls do not. Several have died as a result of her sadistic streak. I keep finding and hiding those magazines, and she keeps hunting for them. For your women's sake, I do hope that she doesn't find another one."

"Well done, Phillip. I expect that Lucinda greatly appreciates what you are doing for her and the other dolls," Henri validated him for his good efforts. He knew that they just had to put an end to this somehow, but how? It would take the rat two weeks to ascend to the bedroom where the rhinoceros slept!

"We don't have much choice," Regi declared, fearing the worse for his wife, "we have to get that rod from the duke. So bright minds, how are we going to accomplish that?"

After some discussion, Phillip came up with an idea. "If I tie this bit of string around my chest, I can scale one step and lower it down to you. You can grab on to it and I can pull you up to me. It will be slow, but we ought to be able to make three floors per night. I do have food stuck away in my hideouts along the way, but I've never ventured above the twelfth floor. Beyond that, we will have to pack our food supplies with us as well as find a place to lay low during the daytime hours. Still, it will be risky."

"Good plan. It will work; it has to work," Regi exclaimed. "Let's get to it. We've a tower to scale!" Henri wondered how long his enthusiasm would hold up. This seemed an impossible task which they had set for themselves.

That night, they began their ascent of Mount Palace, as Milan jokingly began calling this spiral tower. Poor Phillip really had to exert himself just to make it up one step and after that first night, the six fully realized what they were asking Phillip to actually physically do. They slept in an unused closet that day. However, they heard the voice of the duchess talking to her doll collection, and the three men just had to peer out from beneath the door. They were small enough to fit under the closed door. They gasped when they saw how the women were being mistreated.

"My god, they are helpless like that! The duchess ought to be shot, drawn and quartered, boiled alive, roasted until well done and carved up for dinner," Regi exclaimed. Fortunately, their voices were so soft that none of the dolls even heard them. "We should follow them and see what they are up to," he added.

"Oh good god! I heard what the duchess said to them." Regi repeated what she had said, ending with, "That's why I have gone to all this trouble to have us a wonderful ballet this morning."

"What's the matter? It sounds perfectly benign," Regi inquired, seeing an awful look on Phillip's face.

"She's found one of those adult magazines again. It has pictures of these awful boots which force the wearer to stand and walk on her toes. Torture, torture, torture, I am afraid. Oh dear me. Tonight when it is safe, we must find where she has put it and hide it from her again!" Phillip explained. "Now, we must sleep. I am exhausted from all that climbing." The six slept ill, imagining all manner of tortures that their women were enduring.

That night, they crept out long after dark and saw the dolls hanging suspended from the wall and groaned once more. However, the women were asleep, and they headed off for the stairs, more determined than ever to get to the rod. The rat stopped on the fifth floor and hastily scampered around the room, returning with the magazine which advertised such things. He hastily shoved it into one of his holes. "She might not find it in here. Come on; we have stairs to ascend," Phillip explained.

In the middle of their third night of climbing, they reached the tenth floor. Phillip explained that many of the next floors contained the matchstick people. "Hundreds can fit into one room, for they take up very little space. We must be extra silent from now on."

On the twelfth floor, they camped into a cubby hole that Phillip had made. While eating their cold breakfast, they heard the duke's voice coming from the room closest to his hole. The three men decided to take a peek by squeezing beneath a closet door which lay between Phillip's hole and the room. The duke was building something, but they couldn't tell what it was exactly. They looked like soccer goal nets. Regi spotted the golden rod lying on the floor where the duke had placed it while working. "Come on, here's our chance to grab it."

Henri doubted it, but went along with him. The three men scooted out from beneath the door and crept silently across the floor to the rod. The duke was totally engrossed in his construction project, humming merrily to himself. From his bits of conversation to himself, Henri figured that he was devoted to his daughter and was trying his best to please her with her latest request. They got to the rod which was about a foot long and an inch in diameter. All three tried to pick it up but it was far too heavy. Next, they tried to all three get on one end and lift it. Still nothing. At last in frustration, they tried to roll it. Heaving together, they managed to rock the rod slightly. Even rolling it was out of the question. Henri signaled them, and they quietly crept back to the door, laid down on the floor, and scooted under it. Soon, they were safely back in Phillip's hiding place.

Regi looked like the whole world had collapsed upon him. "We can't budge it! All is lost! We are doomed!"

"Well, the barriers that small people face are now very real to me," Henri commented. "Whatever are we going to do now?" He looked from face to face in the dim light; all looked hopeless.

"We should sleep," Phillip suggested. "Perhaps after a good rest, an idea will come to us." Henri doubted that but he was tired from the long night's climb.

Over breakfast the next evening, Henri suggested, "Perhaps we can stop in one of the duchess' playrooms and experiment with moving objects. Surely we can find something to make a lever or crane with which to lift and move the rod, a dolly perhaps or something." Considering no one had any other real ideas, this was adopted. They spent two days rummaging through the duchess' playrooms, but came up with little that was useful.

At last, they decided to see if they could talk to the women and tell them what had to be done. The night that they finally made it back down to the third floor, they were shocked to see that the hooks for Lucinda and Vanessa were empty! Henri began to panic. Were they dead? Had they taken some terrible fall and crushed their heads upon the stone steps?

Phillip then noticed the floor beneath the two women's hooks. "No, look there. If I am not mistaken, and my nose seldom is, they have gone to the bathroom recently, and the matchstick women have not yet cleaned the floor. Perhaps they have found a way to escape."

Henri took heart. "If they have, I bet anything that Vanessa trying to find us! She'll probably be heading to the dungeon and we are up here! Oh no, she'll think that we are dead when she doesn't find us."

"There, there, lad. Perhaps not. If she is wise, she will likely be returning to this doll store room before dawn comes. That means she and Lucinda must come up the very steps that we must go down! Come on. Let's get descending, fellows. We will run into them. Gosh, I hope that they do not step on us!" Milan pointed out.

"Genius, Milan. You are right. Come on; descend fellows; descend!" Henri called out.

It was three in the morning when the rat heard the telltale clicks of the women's heels on the stone stairs. Even though the two were being as quiet as they could, their steel heel tips did make a little noise, as well as the constant brushing of their hoop skirts against the steps. The group halted, and Phillip adjusted his lantern so that the women could clearly see him and the six small ones. Now they waited.

Vanessa let her tears trickle down her cheeks as she climbed slowly back up to the doll storage room's floor. The three men and their three companions were gone. She'd seen a rat hole, but nothing else in the dungeon cell, and she assumed the worst. Suddenly, she spotted a faint light coming from above them. She halted and listened, Lucinda, likewise. Had the matchstick people discovered their absence? No, no footsteps, just that pale light. Emboldened, she felt for her next step and continued climbing the circular stairs towards the faint light.

Before long, she had rounded enough of the stairs that she could see a small lantern shining on a well-dressed rat, who had a string tied around his upper chest. How strange, she thought. The rat was directly in her path, but she continued, figuring that it would move out of the way as she got closer. Now Lucinda also sat the rat and began making a bit of noise, "ah" sounds of course, through the O ring in her mouth.

When the two got close enough that her billowing dress nearly touched the step on which the rat sat, Phillip spoke up. "Please, ma'am. Stop before you step on your men. They are here beside me, but they, like me, have been shrunk by the duke. I am Phillip d'Groot." Lucinda made even more noise through her O ring, recognizing the former captain and bodyguard of her deceased father. "Duchess Lucinda. Good to see you are still alive," he added. Lucinda made more unintelligible noises, as Vanessa did likewise, finally seeing Henri and the five others, who were barely an inch tall, shorter still since they were sitting down on the step.

"As I said, the duchess is a real sadist. They cannot speak at all, which is the way that they duchess wants her dolls to be," Phillip pointed out the obvious to the six.

"We have been trying to rescue you," Henri said to Vanessa, who made an "ah" sound through her O ring. "Okay, don't try to talk. Here is what is going on and what we have to do." Hastily, he outlined everything that Phillip had told them. "Somehow, someway, we have to get the rod from the duke and put things right here. The best chance is when he is sleeping in his bedroom on the forty-second floor." He outlined their failed attempt to obtain the rod a few days ago. "We cannot budge it if all three of us try together. It is far too heavy for us now. I really, really hate to even suggest this, but do you think that you might be able to pull it off?"

Vanessa nodded her head vigorously. At last she knew what had to be done! Henri asked, "Dear, can I come with you? I can perhaps crawl up and sit in your hair. I am able to crawl underneath closed doors so I can go in first and make sure the duke is asleep."

While she really liked the idea of having Henri close to her, considering the awful things that the duchess had been making them undergo, she thought better of it. If she should dislodge him, he could be discovered or even stepped upon by the other women. Reluctantly, she shook her head no and hoped that Henri would guess why. He did. "Too dangerous?" She nodded.

"We best get down fast, it will be dawn soon. We must not let the matchstick people find us," Phillip cautioned them all. Reluctantly, the two groups parted, the rat and six squeezing tightly against the side of the stairs while the women in their wide skirts brushed past them. Henri sighed; how could Vanessa possibly get the rod from the duke? She was almost totally helpless. No, wait, he thought. Somehow she had gotten herself and Lucinda down from their hooks. A faint hope flickered in his mind as he shimmied down the string to the next step.

# Chapter 16 The Appointed One

Vanessa got Lucinda hooked back up and herself as well with only a few minutes to spare. Her feet ached, and she was dead tired when the matchstick women entered and took the dolls down, leading them off to breakfast. At least she was able to sit for two hours, while she pathetically licked up her liquefied breakfast and then had her tea. While she hoped and prayed that the duchess would not desire to play with her dolls today, she sighed as the ugly young woman came into their dining room, her heels clicking rapidly on the hardwood floor.

"Good morning my pretty dolls. Guess what? Well, even if you can, you can't speak, as good dolls can't, I'll have to tell you. The duke has just finished making us two fancy goal nets so that we can play a game called soccer. You see, there are two teams, and there is this white ball that gets kicked or knocked around. The objective is to score a goal by kicking it past the opposing players and into the goal net. The other team tries to stop you, of course. Lots of players do lots of fancy head knocks of the ball. None of us are allowed to use our hands. That won't be a problem for you dolls. See, I am trying hard to find a game that suits you the best. I think this will be great fun. We will divide into two teams and kick and head butt the ball and score goals."

Vanessa wanted to tell her that soccer was a rough sport with lots of running, which would be impossible for them, but could not, of course. "There is just one little problem, though," the duchess frowned. "You see I have been trying it out yesterday. With our pointed heels, it is terribly difficult to kick the ball and make it go where you want it to go. So last night I decided that if we all wore our new ballet boots with their flat front, why, we could kick it straight, making the ball go where we want it to go. Please don't groan so," she said with a huff. Several dolls made "ah" sounds, which she correctly interpreted as protests.

"I've had them put some metal stays in them around the knees so that knees don't bend at all. That should help us all stay on our feet better, since we can't bend them much. Also, I will help each one of you dolls learn to walk in them. I'll use my arms to support us both, since I have to learn how to walk in them too, you see. It will be fun. Once we have that down, we can play a really fun game of soccer. You will see; it is perfect for you dolls; no arms are ever allowed," she repeated what she thought was the clincher idea.

Lucinda looked at Vanessa, her eyes pleading for Vanessa to do something. How to stop the duchess from executing her childish sadism? Then Vanessa had an idea. Well, that ought to stop anyone, she thought to herself. Concentrating, she focused her intention and delivered her postulate. Shortly after that, the duchess belched and grabbed her stomach. "Oh! I don't feel so well. My breakfast is coming up!" She dashed out of the room, leaving her dolls standing there wondering what had happened. Lucinda nodded to Vanessa, who nodded back adding an incomprehensible "ah," echoed by Lucinda.

With the duchess gone and without her having given the matchstick women any orders concerning her dolls, the women found themselves alone in their dining room. The three women and the other dolls as well were free for the first time since the three had entered the city — free in the sense that they were not subsequently hung back on their hooks after eating or being led away to "play" with the duchess.

Looking at the dishes on the table, Vanessa spotted a ladling spoon that the matchstick woman had used to dip out their breakfast into their plates. She had an idea. Tonight when the duke was asleep, she fully intended to sneak into his room and steal away the rod. The only barrier was just how was she to pick up the rod and carry it away? While the ladle didn't much resemble a rod, Vanessa decided to experiment and see if she could somehow find a way to transport the rod once she found it. She could will doors open and get them up the stairs, but could she get the rod carried away? Everything depended upon that. Hence, she decided to experiment with the ladle. She used her chin to maneuver it over to the edge. That alone took some doing on her part.

Lucinda saw her actions and stared at her, trying to grasp what she was attempting to do. Then it struck her. Vanessa would have to carry the rod out of the duke's room somehow. She was trying to get the ladle into her O ring and hold it with her tongue. She moved over beside Vanessa, pushing their large hoop skirts together. Using her chin, she pushed the ladle a little, and Vanessa got the idea. She repositioned herself, and Lucinda was able to push the end on through the O ring. Using her tongue, Vanessa was able to hold it and walk carefully around the room carrying the ladle partially protruding from her mouth. If the rod was not too heavy, she could do it the same way. Both she and Lucinda began to laugh, though it sounded extremely unusual to the others. Together, they nodded to each other, a sign that both understood what they would have to do this night.

Around noon, the matchstick women entered, carrying fresh plates and a pot of lunch, along with a tea pot. Vanessa could not tell if they were surprised to find the dolls already here or not. The matchstick people were void of any and all expressions. Yet, they were incredibly strong, able to lift them up easily. Strange, Vanessa thought as she watched the creatures going about fixing them their lunch. It was hard to believe that they had once been living people like herself and Lucinda. What had the rogue rhinoceros done to them?

Like clockwork two hours later, the matchstick women ushered the dolls back to their doll room and hung each one up on their hook. The duchess was too indisposed to play with her dolls this day. Vanessa chuckled again as she was hung up on the wall once again. Now she and Lucinda dozed, catching up on their much needed sleep. They were awakened at suppertime, fed, and then rehung up for the night. Vanessa waited until she was sure that the hour was late before she carefully intended for her hanging body to be lifted up and sat down gently on the floor. Then, she did the same for Lucinda. Already Rose, Trina, and the other women had fallen asleep. Stealthily, the pair headed for the doors that led to the circular staircase.

Once there, Vanessa looked up. The forty-second floor seemed impossibly far, but they had to get up there. Worse, they had to not only get up there, snatch the rod, but also get down to a place of safety before dawn came and the palace became filled with activities once more. Slowly, she began feeling for the next step as usual. Her billowing hoop skirt prevented her from seeing her feet, much less the steps within almost six feet from where her feet were currently. After climbing several flights, her knees were aching. At this rate, by the time she got to the top, assuming that her legs didn't give out, she'd be utterly exhausted and the whole venture doomed.

She paused catching her breath. Looking at Lucinda, she didn't need words to know that Lucinda was also aching. Vanessa looked up once more and got another idea. She focused her intention once more and then delivered her postulate. Presto, she and Lucinda began rising. Her invisible hoist was lifting them up! Lucinda's wide eyes expressed what she could not say in words. One floor went by, then another and another. Vanessa focused on counting the floors, hoping that she had not miscounted and then enter the wrong room.

Around one in the morning, the two finally halted at the forty-second floor and stepped into the hallway there. Well, there was no guessing which door led to the master bedroom. There was only one door at the end of the hall. As quietly as they could manage with their steel tipped heels, the two crept to the door and listened. Hearing nothing, at least they could see a little in the dimmed torch light. Vanessa took as deep a breath as she could, which wasn't all that much and focused once more, causing the door to open a little. The two peered inside.

Here was a regal bedroom! The huge bed held the enormous rhinoceros, who was snoring peacefully. A dim lantern acted as his nightlight, though much of the room was in deep shadows. Lucinda had been in this room many times as a child and knew precisely where the night stand was located. She nodded to Vanessa and tried to go in first. Vanessa tried to stop her by pushing against her hoop skirt. Sensing that, Lucinda turned and nodded rapidly to Vanessa, who got the message. The young woman was familiar with the room, and Vanessa allowed her to lead the way. Tip toeing in extremely high heels was tough for the two, especially with their arms immobilized, yet they did the best that they could.

Close to the left side of the bed was the night stand, and the golden rod lay on top of it. As they had practiced, both women moved to their respective positions. Vanessa crouched down and got her O ring and mouth close to one end of the rod, while Lucinda got into position to push it with her chin. It took quite a bit of doing, but the rod finally began to slide in through the O ring into her mouth. It felt cold. Lucinda pushed it in as far as she dared, not wanting to cause Vanessa to gag and wake the duke. Just as Vanessa began to hold it firmly with her tongue and rose up, the duke began to stir and wake up. She focused her intention and thought, "Go back to sleep." The duke rolled over and did so.

Holding her head upwards helped keep the rod inside her mouth and O ring. Slowly, the two made their way back to the door. Once outside, Vanessa decided the door should close and it obeyed her decision. Now for the stairs.

This turned out to be even more dangerous than either had imagined. Before, they constantly stared downwards, trying to get a feel for each step's location hidden beneath their hoop skirts. Vanessa dare not look down for the rod would simply slide out of the O ring and her mouth. Her tongue could not hold it that secure. She had to make a decision and did so.

She turned and pushed the rod towards Lucinda's mouth. After giving her a questioning look, Vanessa nodded slightly and aimed the protruding end of the rod towards Lucinda's open mouth. A minute later, Lucinda was trying to hold the rod with her tongue and keeping her head upwards slightly. Free to use her head, Vanessa concentrated and postulated her invisible hoists once more. Down the two went, their huge skirts opened up like some hot air balloon as they descended from the forty-second floor.

Partway down, from behind them, the duchess, who was still feeling ill, had come out of her room and was heading for the duke's room when she saw the two women moving down the stairs. "Hey, dolls. What are you doing out here?" Lucinda and Vanessa halted and turned around to see the duchess, holding her stomach standing on the landing not ten feet from them. "Hey! That's the duke's rod! Give that back right this minute! That is an order," she screamed in her high pitched, shrill voice. "Match. . ."

Both young women knew what the duchess was about to say. Matchstick women, help or something akin to that. They would respond in seconds, and they knew that there would be nothing that they could do to stop them from taking back the rod. Lucinda acted, aided now by the rod in her mouth. Vanessa blinked. The duchess suddenly returned to her original form, that of a small, baby rhinoceros! She bellowed hideously and lumbered on up the steps to fetch her father, the duke. The two women headed on down, only now Vanessa began to wonder how they could stop all of the matchstick men that the duke would shortly summon to his aid.

As they reached the first floor, Lucinda made some noises and nodded her head to their left, indicating that she wanted to go down the hallway here. Vanessa couldn't read Lucinda's mind, but decided to go along with her. She canceled her invisible hoists and followed after Lucinda, but she heard many footsteps coming down the stairs that they had just descended. She knew that the duke was roused and had summoned his matchstick men to retrieve his precious rod. Vanessa's heart sank, as she slowly made her way after Lucinda. Any minute now, the powerful creatures would accost them and simply pull the rod out of Lucinda's mouth. She didn't want to imagine what would happen to them after that!

Lucinda opened the doors into the Royal Dance Hall and headed straight for the small throne on which the reigning monarch officiated at the dances. As Lucinda carefully turned and sat down on the throne, Vanessa moved slightly in front of her. If nothing else, she'd use her body to protect Lucinda from the matchstick men as long as she could. She prepared for the worst and rightly so. At that moment, hundreds of matchstick men poured into the room, moving at an alarming speed straight towards the two women.

Lucinda acted. Vanessa blinked. The entire group of matchstick men suddenly turned into their original forms, men dressed in various types of clothing. They stopped and appeared stunned, feeling their arms and legs, then looking at their surroundings and then at Lucinda. "Your Majesty," one man said, getting down on one knee. Quickly, over a hundred men followed suit.

More matchstick men tried to push their way into the room, shoving the now-human men out of their way. Quickly, the humans dashed out of the room, using the side door. As before, when the newly arriving matchstick men got about halfway to the throne, they reverted back to their original bodies, shocked and surprised. Seeing those before them racing to the side exit, they hastily bowed to their monarch and ran to the door to avoid being trampled by the still incoming matchstick men. Mass confusion arose.

Just then, the duke, followed by the duchess, came down the stairs, following behind yet another batch of the matchstick men. "Seize my rod!" he screamed above the noise. However, at that instant, the hundreds of men who had been restored saw him, and they reacted with one hundred twenty years of pent up anger and hatred.

"Kill the duke! Rip his legs off him! Blind him! No, torture him slowly in a vat of boiling oil!" The vat appeared, steam rising from the boiling oil. "Fry him and feed him to our dogs!" yelled another. Promptly, a bonfire with a huge spit appeared. More and more men added their viewpoints to the din of utter confusion. All had one intent in common: the torture and annihilation of the duke for what he had done to the entire land. Lucinda acted. Before any of the mob could actually reach the duke and duchess, both of their bodies shrank to only a foot tall. Both shocked animals were lifted up by invisible hands and floated on down their stairs. Unseen by Vanessa at the moment, they were deposited in an unused dungeon cell and the door secured. She had prevented their complete destruction by the mob, even as she continued to undo the incoming matchstick men.

Not long after that, Henri, Milan, Regi, Phillip, and the trio came dashing into the room. Lucinda had restored them to their proper sizes. The second that happened, all seven dashed up the stairs only to see the shrunken rhinoceros floating down into the dungeon. Phillip stopped and made sure that they were placed into a cell and that the door was securely locked. Then, he raced to join the others.

Pushing and shoving, Henri and the others finally made their way to the two women. Hastily, Henri undid the head harness and removed the despicable O ring from Vanessa's mouth. She moved her jaw, which ached and thanked him. "Massage please." Meantime, Phillip did the same for Lucinda, being careful not to dislodge the precious rod from her mouth. Unfortunately, she had now had that ring in her mouth for over a century and her jaws barely worked at all now.

Her words, though hard to understand, were grasped, "Summon all of the matchstick men and women here, Phillip, so I can restore them quickly."

"As you wish, Your Majesty," Phillip bowed. "You heard her. Start fetching the many rooms of matchstick people down here. One room at a time. Come on you men. Get with it, hurry up!" Phillip made an effective administrator; men jumped at his orders, racing back up the steps. Indeed, Vanessa later learned that the entire population of Causeland had been turned into thin matchstick people and housed in the many chambers above the tenth floor.

"Phillip, you know where the dolls are kept. Take some men and rescue them; bring them here too," she said, barely understandable with the rod in her mouth. Milan and Regi insisted on going with him so they could rescue their womenfolk.

Still more and more matchstick people entered the room and were changed back into their natural forms. Vanessa just could scarcely believe what she was seeing, such a gigantic mass transformation. The rhinoceros had really very nearly destroyed Causeland. "Has this kind of thing ever happened before?" Vanessa asked Lucinda, during a lull between rooms of matchstick people entering, being changed, and leaving.

"Never," she replied. "Can you take the rod from my mouth and stick it between my breasts? It will work from there just as well." She had to repeat it twice before they grasped what she was saying. The woman's jaws and mouth were still not operational. Henri did so. "That's better. I can't close my mouth yet, but I can talk better this way. Here comes another room of them."

A half hour later, Regi, Milan, and Phillip led the rescued dolls into the huge room. Rose and Trina were still wiggling their jaws about, relieving the stiffness, Vanessa noted. She'd love to have her hands restored to massage hers some more too, but that would have to wait, because another batch of matchstick women rushed in past the slow moving women in their fancy gowns and heels, only to be changed back into their natural body forms. "Wow! They were people?" exclaimed Rose, shocked by the suddenness of the changes that were occurring.

A woman just behind her said, "Yes, the duke changed everyone here into those abominations, except a few of us who became toy dolls for his young daughter, the duchess." Rose and Trina began to understand the situation better.

An hour later, one man called out, "Your Majesty, that's the last of the matchstick people."

"Thank you. Phillip, I want you to scour every inch of this tower and make sure that we have not forgotten a matchstick person. Now, Vanessa, let's restore your ceramic arms." She used the rod again and feeling came back into her arms and hands. Both were stiff and sore, but they were back to being flesh and blood once more. Rose had a bruise where she'd fallen on hers, though. Lucinda requested. "There, now will someone, please make us some tea and breakfast."

"If Your Majesty will follow us to the Royal Banquet Hall," one older woman, who Vanessa suspected might once have been in charge of such things, replied.

"Ladies, my dear friends, please come with us," Lucinda requested. "It's on the second floor." She rose and the others bowed briefly. The large party moved slowly across the huge dance hall and out into the hall. At the stairs, someone assisted each of the "dolls" to manage the stairs safely. Henri refused to let Vanessa walk without his supporting arm around her waist. Likewise, Rose and Trina were held by Milan and Regi. Other women helped Lucinda and her fellow dolls.

Once they were seated in the long unused banquet hall, one of the dolls said, "My jaws don't work right. How are we going to chew? Will they ever work right again? At least we can talk now. Are you the Appointed One, Lucinda?"

"I don't know about our jaws. Mine are so numb that it is hard to speak clearly. Maybe they will in time. Let's hope so. No, I am not the Appointed One. Vanessa here is the Appointed One. It was she who made all this possible." Suddenly, Vanessa was the center of conversation, praise, and a growing adulation. She was also besieged with questions and was grateful that their breakfast and tea arrived. The women set the table, placed ornate silverware beside their fine china plates, and poured their tea.

"I'm afraid that we might not be able to chew our food, ladies, but let's give it a try," Lucinda explained.

"Won't you need someone to feed you?" asked Trina.

Lucinda and her friends giggled. "This is Causeland, and we are now free from the suppression of the rhinoceros. Make good decisions and they will work. Like this," she explained. Her fork moved as if controlled by invisible hands and then lifted a small bite of pancakes up and into her mouth.

The other young women followed her example. It had not before when they were under the control of the duke. As expected, Lucinda and her girlfriends couldn't get their jaws to fully close, but managed to get softer foods handled anyway. "It will be a while before I can eat a steak again," Lucinda observed.

Once they finished and sat back sipping their tea, cups magically floating up from the table to the women's lips. Lucinda asked, "Well, can I ask one of you to please pull these silly rubber arms off of our shoulders?"

"What do you mean? Can't you change them back into your regular arms?" asked Henri.

Lucinda sighed, "I am afraid not. You see, our arms were changed into ceramic ones. Over these many years, most of us have fallen and broken them. Mine shattered into a zillion pieces on the stairs. The duke replaced them with these dumb looking rubber ones. I'm afraid that we twelve simply don't have any arms any longer."

While Vanessa gasped, as did several others, the three men began doing as she asked. Indeed, a slight tug and the rubber arms simply popped off of their shoulders. Henri examined one and saw that it has been held onto her shoulder by a suction cup. "That's better. Thanks, Henri," Lucinda said, relieved to no longer be seeing the ugly rubber things hanging at her sides.

She then asked, "Well, now what do we do, Vanessa? I have saved the rhinos from being slaughtered by the people of Causeland and have the people back to normal. Who is going to run Causeland now?"

"Oh that is simple, you are, Lucinda. You and your friends here, along with Phillip, have more than earned the right to lead your people," Vanessa replied without hesitation.

"Then, you are not staying here?" she asked.

"No, we are just visiting," Vanessa answered her honestly.

"All hail the Duchess Lucinda Masters," Phillip called out regally. Everyone gave Lucinda a cheer and toast.

"Then, as my first act as ruler of Causeland, I hereby appoint you, my fellow dolls who have endured so much sadism from the ex-duchess, to be my cabinet members. Later, we will figure out what posts you would most like to have. You will be my court. Phillip, you will resume your post as Captain of the Palace Guards and my personal bodyguard."

"Thank you, Your Majesty. I am honored, though I am not fit, not after having failed your parents and all Causeland," Phillip replied humbly.

"Not so. It was dad who insisted on not bringing the rod with him, Phillip. Without it, no force could stand against the wielder of the rod. You have no blame. Indeed, did I not see you from time to time checking on we 'dolls?'" she asked. He flushed and replied that she had.

"Now then, we all need a long, long bath. I can't believe that we have gone one hundred twenty years without a bath!" Lucinda stated factually. The matchstick women only occasionally washed off their bottoms. After all, they had only been a child's dolls all that time. She added, "Time is again moving for our bodies. It has been stopped all the while the duke had us being his daughter's dolls. Dolls don't age, you see, well not like people. Now at last, we can resume our lives."

Milan came up to Lucinda to examine her shoulders. She said, "In time our jaws may get back to normal, but our arms, well, we anticipated the worst. Still, please don't worry, doctor, we can easily get by without them. This *is* Causeland."

After the last woman was freed from her rubber arms, Lucinda said, "Come on, ladies. To the Royal Bath! I think that I shall soak for hours and hours!" Several giggled, heaven had arrived.

Phillip led Vanessa and her group to the sixth floor guest suites. Already, some of the servants had prepared hot baths for all, and the three couples helped each other into their private baths, while the trio decided that they stunk like the dungeon and took a rare bath themselves. Interestingly when they dried off, all found that their clothing had been thoroughly cleaned and pressed. "This is more like it," Herr Adelstein declared, donning his spotless suit once more.

"Hey, my pocket knife is back to its normal size," Albert commented, though no one paid any attention to his declaration.

When they had finished their long baths, the three women found new dresses waiting for them. Gone were the awkward ball gowns. In their place were form fitting dresses that fell to just below their knees. "I will look like an office woman now," Vanessa teased Henri.

"Far more practical, dear, but do all office workers wear satin dresses?" Both chuckled as he helped her into her new dress.

"I didn't want to mention this to Lucinda," Vanessa commented as Henri zipped her up. "After wearing those heels and corsets for so long, they are going to be like me.

Our leg muscles have altered and our feet can't go flat. They are going to have to continue to wear them just as I am. Plus, I bet they are also going to have to continue to wear their tight corsets as well. Still, they have their lives back. That is something. How did you like being a tiny person?"

"Let's not go there, dear! I will say this, I have a newfound respect for size, and I have never, ever felt so utterly helpless in my life," Henri admitted. She smiled, knowing what he meant.

"You got me the information that I had to know in order to pull off our rescue. That's something, dear."

Just then, Phillip knocked. "Her Majesty will be in her bath all this afternoon. She has requested that I take you all for a ride on the rainbows. In time, many of the other attractions of Causeland will be back in operation."

"This is incredible; what a view," Vanessa exclaimed. Already, the four others had taken their first rides down the rainbows. She was still constrained by her heels, and she and Henri followed after the others at their leisurely pace, allowing the others to get far ahead of them. Now with Phillip beside them, they were at the top of a rainbow, gazing for miles in all directions, particularly back at the towering spires of the city.

"You sit and slide down. Do not worry about falling. Even if you try to fall off, you will not be allowed to do so. While you will gain speed as if this were a huge sliding board, your body will decelerate at the right time, landing you gently on your feet at the bottom," Phillip explained. Henri held her hand as she sat down on top of the rainbow. When he let go, she began sliding, slowly at first and then the acceleration took hold. As she flew down the arc, the wind blew her hair out behind her, much like a roller coaster ride, she thought. As the ground came up fast, she grew worried but that faded as she felt herself slowing down. As Phillip said, she landed gently on her feet. Henri and Phillip soon landed beside her. "Now was that fun or not?" he asked.

"Okay, again. Got to do it again," she teased him. They went for another dozen rides before heading back to the tower. The streets were filled with people this time, going about their enormous tasks of re-establishing their lives.

The Royal Banquet Hall was decorated in gay colors, reflecting the newfound freedom of all Causeland. Fireflies illuminated the ceiling in many colorful patterns while they dined and later culminated with a flashing message that read: Thank you, Vanessa Graves, the Appointed One. Lucinda and her court also wore satin form-fitting dresses, much like the one that Vanessa wore. She noticed that they were also again wearing their corsets and heels and knew why.

Over dinner, Lucinda answered Vanessa's question, "Well, many did die. One was my boyfriend, Carl. Guess I have to rediscover love once more. I promise you that I will choose wisely, since he will become our duke. I've had all of the sadistic leaders that I ever want to see. Still here in Causeland, we women can create in place of our missing arms, so it is no big thing for us, mostly just annoying. I still haven't decided what to do with the prisoners. Some of the doll women want Marla to experience the torture that she inflicted on us, but I am vetoing that. Honestly, no one should suffer as we were made to suffer. Still, I just cannot let them go free. They'd just do it again elsewhere. At times like these, I wish my dad were here. He'd know what I ought to do. Vanessa, you are the Appointed One. What do you think I should do?"

"Hey, look at me," Albert called out from high above them. He was floating in the air doing graceful somersaults among the fireflies.

Herr Adelstein was not amused. "What *are* you doing up there, Albert?"

"I'm creating. This is Causeland. I've always wanted to do this," he yelled down.

Henri grinned, "Go for it, Albert!"

Before long, Sir Thomas took flight and joined him. "Whee, I have always wondered what it was like to be a flying squirrel like some of my distant cousins. This is fun. Try it, Herr Adelstein," he called down. The rabbit pretended to ignore them both.

All this gave Vanessa time to think of how best to answer Lucinda. "I think that you are doing the right thing by keeping your people from torturing them back. That isn't going to solve anything nor is just killing them. Perhaps keeping them in prison until they change their ways is the best option, occasionally giving them a chance to prove to everyone that they have reformed."

Lucinda smiled, "Okay, thanks. I will do just that with the rhinoceros."

After a thoroughly enjoyable evening, back in their bedroom, Vanessa commented, "You know, if Able Montford had not died and left his universe creation here unattended for a century and a half, none of this might have happened. It is as if he left his world running sort of on automatic. When something unanticipated happened, his world could not adjust and handle it."

"I think you have a valid point. I suspect that is just what has happened in this world of his," Henri validated her observations.

"Another thing, I sure am glad that Duchess Marla was actually a child and not a full grown woman. Do you realize the sexual things that she could have done to all of her 'dolls?' We were quite at her mercy, which she seldom showed, if at all. We could have had a vastly worse time of it." That was a sobering thought.

"I think that they both became bored of the whole thing. I wonder what will happen to them now?" Henri mused. "Lucinda saved them from being tortured and killed by her vengeful subjects, but what will she do with them now?"

Vanessa shrugged her shoulders; she had no idea. "She'll keep them in the jail for now. We should probably be thinking of continuing our journey, looking for the way out of this world and back to ours."

"Where's the map?" he asked.

# Chapter 17 Musicland

That afternoon someone knocked on their door. The knocking sounded a bit on the soft side and unusual. Henri answered it and saw one of the ex-dolls standing there. She looked a bit different, but he didn't see what at first. She said in a soft voice, "May I come in and speak to you and Vanessa in private, please?" Henri beckoned her inside, indicating that the two were alone. The trio was off on an exploration of the entire tall tower.

Vanessa came out of their bedroom having brushed her hair. "Oh hi there. You were one of us though we haven't been introduced formally. I'm Vanessa; this is my husband, Henri Graves. You look really good today." She wore a new dress similar to Vanessa's, but hers was light blue in color which blended with her very blonde, long wavy hair which fell to just below her shoulders.

"Thanks. I am Mia Tynara. I feel lots better now that they have removed my silly rubber arms and had that long, long bath. Thanks for the compliment. I really do need it about now."

"I am so sorry for you; come, sit. We can talk," Vanessa replied, pulling out a chair for her and taking the other one. Henri had to sit on the sofa where he could see both women.

"Yes, I wanted to talk to you both in private. I was twenty-one when I came to this world, but I don't know what that may mean now. Time seems so altered here. Lucinda looks twenty-one same as I am, but she's been a prisoner for a hundred and twenty more years. So confusing."

"Yes, I think it had to do with what the Rhinoceros created. That is, a child's doll doesn't age," Vanessa replied.

"What did you want to talk to us about?" She attempted to direct the conversation to what interested her. Why the private talk?

"Perhaps. Yes, I don't know how else to say this, but you two — you are not really Vanessa and Henri Graves, the Count and Countess of Malbon. You can't be. I was there; I met you both but failed to solve the crime on the Malbon Express. You said something like I wasn't supposed to be alone. Now, I think that you are both outsiders, travelers like myself. I want you to take me with you when you leave here. Please, you must; you have to. I know that I will very likely be a burden on you, but I don't have any choice. Who are you really? I've not mentioned this to anyone else. Your secret is safe with me. I promise."

Henri fidgeted. Vanessa answered in a non-committal manner, "What do you mean that we are not really Vanessa and Henri Graves? Do we look different somehow?"

"Oh no, no, you look exactly like I remember you looking. How can I ever forget seeing the most gorgeous young woman ever with such impressive breasts and dressed most elegantly? No, it is not your physical appearance that is in question. It is you. I don't know how to say this. Just call me a dumb blonde, if you like. You don't think or talk quite the same. You don't use the same shallow words. You both seem vastly more intelligent than the real Vanessa and Henri Graves. You are travelers or something, just like me, right?"

Vanessa looked at Henri and made up her mind. "You, Mia Tynara, are a very observant young woman. Yes, we entered this world, or whatever it actually is, to find Miranda's mother, Rose. That's Miranda Whitney. Rose is her mother, who foolishly entered this world alone and became trapped in here. I am Zed Osmund, a friend of Miranda's. I know, we are in opposite bodies, due to the way the apparent game works. We are currently trying to help Vanessa and Henri also escape from this world."

Mia brightened up. Her face was that of an enchantress, captivating and charming, especially when she smiled as she did now. "I knew it! I knew it! Okay, let me tell you my story and then maybe you will agree to help me. I was a fashion model in London. It was 1990. I was living in a flat in London, a converted old Victorian mansion. They were doing restoration work on my floor, and I had to temporarily put up with the construction mess. Anyway, that day the workers found a strange window with two doors on it hidden behind an old wall. Really, it was my fault that I am here. After they left work, I opened the doors and looked in to see what they were. It was so strange. I couldn't find anything that the windows could have opened to reveal except another wall. Then, I was falling and landed on a grassy knoll and very nearly died."

"I sort of meandered around and somehow got onto the Malbon Express, hoping to return to some place that I could recognize, like Leeds or Manchester. But no, Malbon was totally foreign — all those weird animal people and such. I wandered around for a long time and found the Badlands. It didn't seem too promising, but a cat woman once told me that many visitors go there, so I did. I thought that I would die there in the dry canyon, but I found this inn. Only that night I had an awful nightmare, which has now come true." She flushed, perhaps revealing something more than she had intended.

"Yes, we both have been through the Badlands. At the inn, one experiences ones worst fears. We both did," Henri spoke up. "I was blind and in great pain while giving birth, terrified that I was dying and couldn't do anything about it. Zed was afraid of being in a war battle and having his arms blown off, leaving him helpless with little, short arms. It was very real and very scary."

Mia smiled again, "Then you do know what I mean. Well, I don't know how I managed, but I got out of there and ended up in a land of drug addicts. As a fashion model, I get paid for looking my best. No way was I going to do drugs. That has to be what that was all about. Well, okay, I did try a little pot when I was a teen and that's what it seemed like to me. I fled that place after one day. When I got here, the duke turned me into another of the duchess' dolls the very minute that I got here. Much later, I fell down the stairs and shattered my ceramic arms, and the duke put those ugly rubber ones on me."

"I really want to get back home, though I know that my modeling career is over. You don't see models without arms. Still, I have some savings. I will find a way to get by somehow. I just want to get back home to London or somewhere on earth. Will you help me, please? If you want, I can give you all my savings."

"We don't want your savings, Mia. Okay, we'll take you with us. Regi and Trina are also from earth — same city as us," Henri answered her, "Peoria, Illinois, USA. We are trying to get them back with us. Milan is also going to try to get back too. He got stranded here in this world. The three of them came here somewhere around 1850 or so. We just don't know what is going to happen when they get back. Will they suddenly age and die? Will their lives just pick up where they are now at? We have no idea."

"What year is it now?" Mia asked quietly. Her concern came through.

"2010," Henri answered.

"Gosh, that would make me forty-one maybe," Mia said, her voice sinking.

"Maybe and maybe not. We'll have to see."

"Thank you both. I will try not to be a burden for you. Here in Causeland, I am able to move things just by thinking about them hard enough, but that is probably only because we are here in this place. I know that I'm going to be pretty helpless, but I just have to find my way back, and I can't do it alone anymore, not like this. Our feet now have to wear these heels, and we have to wear these tight corsets because our waist and back muscles are so weak. It is really awful, but I promise you to do all that I can possibly do," Mia pleaded.

"No problem, Mia, we'll take you with us. We have no idea how we are to actually get back home ourselves, but we will take you if we can find a way to do it," Henri explained, sympathetically.

Just then Milan came by. "I say, Rose is anxious to get moving again. How soon are we planning to leave here? She's ready to travel now. Rose is really anxious to get home."

Mia informed Duchess Lucinda of her plans. After that, Lucinda gave each of the four women three complete outfits and five pairs of heels. The men all got a spare suit and a small bag of gold to help defray future expenses.

"So where are you traveling to next?" Lucinda asked Vanessa over supper.

"The next place on our map is called Musicland. Do you know anything about it?"

"Not much. They do everything to music, I've heard. They have music to accompany everything in life. I hope that you like music," she told them all that she knew of the land.

"Well, that sounds delightful. What possible trouble can we encounter there?" Rose declared and asked rhetorically. Vanessa kept her opinion to herself. So far, everywhere they went, trouble followed them, though she found it hard to believe that they could get into trouble in a land where everything was accompanied by music.

The next morning, after saying their farewells, Henri assisted the three women climb into the carriage. When Mia's turn came, she said, "Please, let me try it on my own. I am going to have to learn to adapt. I don't have an arm for you to hold and steady me." Henri held his hands out around her waist, ready to catch her if she fell. Mia bravely took her time and did it herself. Then the trio gaily hopped inside, followed by Milan. Henri and Regi volunteered to share the driving duties this day. Tomorrow, Milan would replace Regi. Henri was reluctant to merely be a passenger, not that he didn't trust the other two men.

As they started out, Mia volunteered with a sigh, "Well, I get to live my worst nightmare every day now."

"I'm sure that you will somehow make the best of it, Mia. You still have your youth and beauty and mind. That's something at least. Tell me about your modeling career, unless even thinking about that is upsetting to you now," Vanessa asked, curious about fashion models. Mia was only too eager to chat. She'd been forced into total silence for many years by the ex-duchess; thus she relished the chance to simply chat with others.

"I bet my accent gives me away," Mia said. "I'm originally from Edinburgh, Scotland. When I was seventeen, I got my big break in modeling and soon after moved to London and the fashion zone. Not long afterwards, I fell in love with that old English Victorian home and was lucky enough to get an apartment there. I was always teased on the sets because of my Scottish accent, and I did work hard to London-ize it, you see. Of course, if I can ever get back, I don't know what I can now do, not like this," she shrugged her empty shoulders.

"Well, I think that you can do pretty much anything that you set your mind to doing," Vanessa replied. "I've heard that there is a young woman in Phoenix, Arizona, who was born without arms and who flies light airplanes solo."

"Are you kidding? Really? How?" asked Mia rather taken aback.

"We can fly here. What's the big deal?" asked Sir Thomas. "Of course, we can only fly here in Causeland, unless you are a cousin of mine. He's a flying squirrel."

"We humans don't fly by ourselves, Sir Thomas. We have these machines which transport us in the air," Vanessa attempted to explain an airplane to the squirrel, but gave up that notion. "She uses her feet — at least that's what I saw in the photos." The two continued chatting.

"When you get back to London, will you have someone who can help you with things? Your parents perhaps?" Vanessa asked.

The enchantress face soured, and Vanessa wished that she had not asked such a personal question in front of the others. "I lost dad two years ago — well, I don't exactly know what the years mean now. Before I was pulled into this world, I lost him. We, my family, we were close. Dad had always been there for me. He called me his Little Spring Angel. In fact, he helped get my started in my fashion modeling career. I took a couple of weeks off when he passed and helped mom deal with it. It was so awful going through all his things and tossing the worn out shoes and stuff. We donated as much as we could to the World Relief Organization to help others in need. Dad would have wanted that. Still, our home was so lonesome without him. I hated to leave mom there in the empty cottage." Mia sighed.

"You know what they say about close couples, when one goes the other is not far behind them. I ought to have seen it coming, but I had just gotten my new apartment in that elegant Victorian mansion. I did go see her during the winter holidays. I almost gave up my career when I saw her. Mom had lost a lot of weight. 'What's the use of eating now? Dad's gone,' she'd say. She used to call him dad when we kids were around. Never knew why she did that. Her mind was going. I cried myself to sleep each night I was with her. Some holiday, eh?"

"You must have been great comfort to her," Vanessa consoled her, wondering what else she could say.

"I suppose I was. Alzheimer's the doctors said. It was just awful. At least three times a day she would ask me when Phil was coming home from practice. 'Don't forget to set a place for Phil, dear. You forgot dad's place too,' she'd say at meal time. Phil was my older brother. He died in a polo accident when I was seventeen. He was always hyperactive, on the school's polo team. He took a bad spill and broke his neck. They said that he died instantly. Mom kept thinking that he was still with us, you know; she was sort of living in the past. When I tried to tell her that Phil had died four years before then and that dad died last year, she'd break down in grief for an hour, sobbing her heart out. Soon, I just stopped telling her about that; I couldn't take her reliving our painful losses over and over. It was so weird. An hour later, she would tell me all about dad's funeral, as if I'd missed it entirely. Maybe I should have stayed there with her and not returned from the holidays. I got a call from the bobbies a month later that she had passed away in her sleep."

"I spent a month back there at the cottage in Edinburgh, crying my eyes out. Now I had to get rid of all her things too. The neighbors suggested an estate sale and that helped a lot, but it was so hard to see all of her things and what was left of dad's being taken away by total strangers. I kept crying. They probably thought I was a basket case. Anyway, with the neighbor's help, we got what was left carted away to the World Relief Organization. I had to sell the cottage, though, to cover all of mom's doctor bills and some of dad's too. She had not paid some of them. I guess she just forgot about dad's bills. I took a few things back to London with me, our photo albums mostly and mom's rocker."

"So no, Vanessa. I am twenty-one years old, and I have no family left. I am really totally alone now. Fashion models really work hard, and I have never had time to make any real friends. I have no idea what I can do now, but I do have some savings. Somehow I will manage, though I must be honest with you. I am terrified of it. I had nightmares about being like this when I was a little girl. Dad would always sit up with me in my small bed and read me stories until I calmed down and fell asleep. I wish that I could just wake up and find all this has been a really bad dream, but that's not going to happen is it?" Mia asked.

"I honestly don't know, Mia. We have promised to help get you back and we will. If nothing else, you can stay with me or perhaps with Miranda," Vanessa offered.

"Shoot, honey, you are more than welcome to stay with Miranda and me. I've a large older home with plenty of room," Rose added, most insistent. "In the end, who do we really have? I lost my husband and spent years moping about over it. Until I met Milan here, I was a hopelessly lost, middle-aged woman. I think that we must treasure those who are around us in our lives and keep our memories of our lost ones alive in our minds and honor their memories. I realize now that my late husband would have wanted me to find another man to share the joys and sorrows of life and not become an old maid spinster, which I darn well almost became. Vanessa, just don't tell Miranda that she was right about me, mind you. She's hard enough to live with as it is. Hardly a day didn't go by without her telling me to get on with my life, but it was so hard to do that. Maybe it was a huge blessing that I foolishly came here."

"Okay," Vanessa chuckled, "I won't tell her, Rose. Just remember, I've fallen for Miranda and when we get back I will be courting her. You aren't going to get rid of me easily. Miranda is the greatest woman that I have ever met."

Rose chuckled this time. "That is a good thing. It is high time that she settles down, but I hope that you can keep up with her. I never could. Only her father could, so maybe you have a chance."

"Well, I aim to keep up with you, dear Rose," Milan grinned mischievously. "I don't plan to let you out of my sight, my pretty rose." Rose gave him a little hug, and Vanessa smiled as did Mia.

Mia's enchantress face returned. "So you are in love with Miranda or Henri?" she asked Vanessa.

"Yes, I am. Big time. I first saw her standing beside a building watching me serve out coffee to others, brightening up their early mornings. I've been trying my best to keep up with her ever since."

"Now that's a pretty tall order, Vanessa! I certainly never could," Rose laughed. "Just you wait, Mia. I am sure that soon some handsome fellow will sweep you off of your feet. If it can happen to this old maid, it most certainly can happen to a beautiful, young fashion model!"

Mia flushed and decided to open up to them. "I hope it doesn't. I really don't like men much. I prefer women."

"Oh!" Rose exclaimed; her face felt hot. She didn't press her point any further.

Vanessa picked up on her hint too. "In that case, I am sure that some gorgeous young woman will sweep you off your feet, Mia." Both women smiled at each other. Mia didn't say that one already had done just that. It was too personal.

"Well, all this might be fine for you humans, but I for one am not ready to do that yet," Herr Adelstein grumbled. "I'd have to get a permanent burrow, and then there is all that work maintaining it. Think of all the work and hassle looking after all those little bunnies, to say nothing of having to provide for the misses and all them little bunnies. Oh no, that is not the life for me! You humans can have all that, right Sir Thomas?"

"Er right, right. I'd be terribly afraid that I would completely botch it all up and get kicked out of my own nest," Sir Thomas answered, growing nervous just thinking about such things.

"Oh, I wouldn't mind it so much, I suppose, but then maybe I'd just be wrong yet again, and I wouldn't like it at all. Then, maybe that would be wrong too, and I would like it. Oh bother with it all anyway. The countryside is changing again. Now that interests me, but then maybe that is wrong too, and it should not be interesting me. What do you think, Herr Adelstein? Should I be interested in the countryside or not?"

"Well, Albert, that all depends on whether you like it or not. Let me see; get your big head out of the way. Oh, well, this is different. I may like this Musicland." He saw men cultivating large fields of carrots and cabbages.

How strange, Vanessa thought. She saw a number of men working the fields, hoeing, but she also saw several large rabbits and a human playing guitars and flutes nearby the men. They were too far away to hear the music. Well, at least they are being entertained while they work, she thought.

Henri called down, "Village ahead. Sign says Bittersdorf. We'll stop here for the night." Vanessa smiled; Henri or Miranda did love to be in charge of things. For a second, she had a flash of what it had meant for Henri to have been an inch tall in the rhinoceros' dungeon, unable to take charge, let alone do anything really useful to help out.

A few minutes later, they rolled into the quaint cobblestoned village of Bittersdorf. It looked like something from Bavaria. Zed's mother had a coffee table book of Bavaria, and he'd often looked at the pictures in it. Mia's startling comment brought her out of her reverie, "How strange! Look at their faces!"

There were a few humans walking in the streets this late afternoon. All had zippers across their mouths. Lips had been somehow replaced with zippers. Worse, a small padlock kept them zipped closed! At least half of the humans must have had bad accidents. Many had full-leg, white casts on their left legs. Some also had their left arm in a cast as well. One man lumbered along on two broken legs and a broken left arm, Vanessa observed and concluded.

Usually behind the working men and women, a group of musician played marching style tunes as if the very music would inspire the workers to work harder. The musicians were mostly rabbits with an occasional human as well. How unusual, Vanessa thought. They halted before an inn which looked rustic and inviting. A large sign said Welcome. The men dismounted and proceeded to assist the women stepping out onto the paved walk.

"I can't seem to cause anything anymore like I used to be able to do back in Causeland. Can you help me get down, please," Mia sighed and asked rather apologetically of Henri.

"Of course, Mia. You don't have to apologize for needing help," he replied softly, lifting her carefully down from the carriage.

The group entered the inn. As they entered, a loud speaker played a formal fanfare as though they were royalty entering some fancy court. They saw the pub and dining area was nearly deserted except for a young woman who was cleaning the tables. She looked up at the newcomers. They stared at her; her lips were gone, replaced by a strange zipper, securely locked shut. She shook her head wildly and pointed to the very door that they had entered. Then she tried to push them back outside. The party stood there rather confused by her antics.

"Ah, guests. Agata! Cease your silly antics and get back to cleaning your tables. Welcome human strangers. Will you want rooms for the night? Yes, I insist upon that. No charge at all," the innkeeper declared. He was a six foot tall rabbit, dressed in a Bavarian costume befitting a wealthy innkeeper. "Come this way. I will show you to your rooms," he gestured.

Henri wanted to ask a lot of questions, but as the rabbit's back was turned to him, he saw Agata wildly shaking her head with her hands on her zipper where her lips once had been. Unable to grasp what was going on, Henri and the others said nothing but followed the rabbit down a hall. As they walked along, music from some form of crude speakers played a triumphant march and seemed to follow them down the halls.

As he approached a room, he opened a door and motioned for some to enter, though he said nothing. Each room had a single bed, enough for two, possibly three. Rose and Milan quietly entered the first room. "Dinner will be announced," the rabbit then said, motioning for the others to follow him. Regi and Trina took the next one. At the next stop, Herr Adelstein and his friends started to go in, but the innkeeper hastily pulled him back. "Oh no. Let them take this one. I have the royal suite for you, sir. Name?" he asked the surprised rabbit.

"Herr Adelstein."

"Ah yes, Herr Adelstein. Nothing is too fine for you, sir. Nice catch that you have brought us. Here, take this one." He opened a door on the opposite side of the hall. Inside was indeed a royal suite, three times larger than the other rooms, elegantly done. Gaping at the luxury, the rabbit stepped in and headed for his own personal bar. Meanwhile, the innkeeper opened the next door on the opposite side, allowing Henri, Vanessa, and Mia to enter this one. The innkeeper promptly shut the door. Even more alarming, they heard him lock their door with a key!

Henri turned and tried the door. It didn't open. "We're locked in. What the devil is going on around here?" If that wasn't enough, just then music began to play, coming from a cone speaker attached to the tall ceiling. "That sounds like a funeral dirge. How gruesome," he added.

"Thank you for helping me and letting me stay here with you. I know that I cannot manage much of anything anymore, not since we left Causeland," Mia said, holding back her grief which had been slowly building.

"Dear, she and I talked a lot about her life. I ought to tell you about Mia," Vanessa said, sitting down on the bed beside her and putting her arms around the young woman. She related Mia's life story to Henri. Mia just continued to sob, however. Only now was the awful reality of her situation driven home to her. She was naturally in grief.

Before Henri could say anything, the somber music changed. "Hey, that's Wagner, I think. <u>Ride of the Valkyries</u> perhaps," he called out over the rousing fanfare overture. Then a voice akin to that of Herr Adelstein spoke loudly.

"This is Kaiser Wilhelm von Himmelhagen, Supreme Leader of Musicland. You humans must recognize that you are the inferior race! We rabbits are the Master Race! Humans are here to server the glorious Master Race and the Fatherland, Musicland! Humans must never speak unless spoken to by us rabbits!" Each pronunciation was highly emphatic in sound and emphasis. The voice continued, "Enforcers exist to ensure that the inferior race follows the Master Laws and do their part to server the Master Race! Music must accompany all actions! To act without music is to commit unthinkable heresy! If a dog can be trained, so can a human! Humans exist to serve, never to question! To question is to beg for enforcement!"

The music of Wagner ceased, replaced once more with the funeral dirge. "That sounded more like a bunch of disjointed platitudes," Rose exclaimed.

"It sounds more like some madman," Henri added.

"Who is this Kaiser fellow? Does he run Musicland?" asked Mia.

"I'm worried about the Enforcers. What exactly do they do?" Vanessa asked.

The three chatted a bit, but didn't hear the innkeeper talking into a crude microphone. "Yes, yes, I have a whole bunch of new humans here at my inn. Herr Adelstein brought them here for processing. Yes, he is to be rewarded. Get here soon. I don't know how long I can keep them locked up! Yes, yes, of course. All hail Father Kaiser!"

"God, I wish they'd play something besides the funeral dirge," Henri exclaimed, growing annoyed with the constant repetition of the same dreary piece of music while they waited for dinner. "Perhaps we will get some answers then," he suggested hopefully.

At long last, a voice called out over the dirge, "Dinner is served." They found their doors were unlocked, and they walked together down the hall to the pub and dining room. Conversation was inhibited by the still playing, loud funeral dirge.

As they entered the dining room, they saw a dozen rabbits dressed in military fatigues, camouflaged colored in browns, greens, and greys. Each carried a handgun, crude by modern standards, reminiscent of antique guns Henri had once seen in the museum. One stepped forward accompanied once more by the sounds of an overture of Wagner. "By orders of Kaiser Wilhelm von Himmelhagen,

Supreme Leader of Musicland, all humans are to be zippered. You will step forward and be zippered or you will be shot! Not you, rabbit!" He shoved Herr Adelstein back.

Henri stepped forward first; after all, he had appointed himself their leader. What was going on here? An enforcer came up to him and touched a device to his face. He felt his lips vanishing and his hands felt his face. A zipper, closed at this point, had replaced his lips, just as he'd seen on Agata and the people in the streets. One by one, the others were zippered shut.

"Now then, you may open your zippers to eat your supper. Once that is done, we will lock them securely in place until breakfast. After breakfast, you will be taken to the Court of Kaiser Wilhelm von Himmelhagen, Supreme Leader of Musicland, for disbursement to your assigned working stations. Remember, you humans are here to server the glorious Master Race and the Fatherland, Musicland! Humans must never speak unless spoken to by rabbits! We Enforcers exist to ensure that the inferior race follows the Master Laws and do their part to serve the Master Race! Defy us and we cast your limbs at each infraction of the Master Laws!"

He continued spouting the platitudes, "Music must accompany all actions! To act without music is to commit unthinkable heresy! If a dog can be trained, so can a human! We will train you humans! Humans exist to serve, never to question! To question is to beg for enforcement! We enforce without mercy or hesitation! Remember that! Now go eat your supper." He motioned them to the tables on which their dinner had been set for them.

Herr Adelstein was handed a large money pouch and treated as an important person, dining with the Enforcers. Henri unzipped Mia's mouth, and Vanessa helped feed her. None dare say a word. However, as the meal progressed,

Agata came in to clear some of their dishes. Henri could not help notice that her left leg was now in a full leg cast, causing her to walk terribly awkwardly. Her eyes were red; she'd been crying. It was clear to him that she had gotten into serious trouble for even trying to communicate to them earlier. His heart went out to her as she hobbled awkwardly on the stiff, immobile leg. He hoped that her broken leg didn't hurt her badly. Only later did he realize that if her leg had just been broken and put in a full leg cast that she'd be in so much pain that she certainly couldn't stand on it, probably not for weeks. What was going on in Musicland?

All during dinner, they could not have spoken if they had wanted to because the same loud funeral dirge continued to blare at them, drowning out all attempts to even whisper. Clever these Enforcers, he thought. Once they had finished their tea, an Enforcer came by, zipped their mouths shut, and fastened a tiny padlock on the zipper's pull strap. Now they could not undo it themselves, prohibiting any conversation. Henri hoped that he didn't get ill and need to throw up! They were marched back to their rooms and locked in once more.

At least the music changed. Now a different, very sad, somber string quartet began playing. The same piece played over and over all night long. Evidently, they played music even when sleeping. After all, sleeping was an action, he thought. He helped Mia and Vanessa undress partially and decided to sleep on the floor. Vanessa helped Mia into bed and crawled in bedside her. Mia rolled over and leaned her head on Vanessa's shoulder. In turn, she put her arm comfortingly around the woman. Slowly they drifted into sleep with the sounds of the somber quartet still ringing in their ears. When they awoke, they all felt in an ill humor. Henri wanted to yell out, "That's a nice quartet, but if I hear it one more time I will scream!" Of course with his mouth shut, he could only make a little noise.

He helped the women back into their dresses, and Vanessa quickly brushed out their hair a little before the music changed back into the familiar funeral dirge. A voice spoke, "Breakfast in five."

As before, the Enforcers ushered them to the dining room, where they again saw poor Agata hobbling around, barely able to move with her leg cast. After each was unlocked, an Enforcer said, "You may now unzip and eat your breakfast." They did as instructed.

After they finished, Henri said, "Can you please tell us what is going on here, please, Mr. Enforcer?"

The head Enforcer screamed angrily, as if Henri had just committed the worst possible crime imaginable! "Zip him! Cast him now! Humans must never speak unless spoken to by rabbits! Humans exist to serve, never to question!" Three Enforcers rushed to Henri, zipped him shut and padlocked him. Meanwhile, three others carried a large machine into the dining room. They forced Henri into the machine which was roughly human shaped. His legs were forced a little apart and outward as were his arms. The machine closed in on him. He felt something happening to his left leg, and then it became uncomfortably warm. Finally, they opened the machine and dragged him out. His left leg was in a full leg cast, wholly immobile. Henri was ordered to sit back down and wait for the carriage. Moving as awkwardly as Agata, Henri struggled to move back to his chair. Even sitting down became a challenge with his straight leg. He was fuming, but could say or do nothing about it.

A few minutes later, the carriage was ready for them, and the Enforcers ordered them up and out to the carriage. Vanessa lent her shoulders to Henri as he painstakingly tried to walk. He moved even slower than she did now. Still, he assisted a panic stricken Mia up into the carriage before trying to figure out how to get himself up the steps. Milan and Regi were ordered to drive the carriage, while Herr Adelstein was asked to ride with the Enforcers in their regal carriages.

The same funeral dirge accompanied their day long ride to the capital city of Wasserburg. The Enforcers had mounted another speaker in the ceiling of the carriage, and the music only increased their fears. How long can one listen to the same funeral dirge before their will cracks, Henri wondered.

His leg did not feel broken, just encased in a plaster cast. Well, that was something. Surely he could somehow break the plaster and get free of the damned thing, he thought, trying to raise his spirits a little. At last the music changed to the somber, sad second movement of Beethoven's Seventh Symphony, a piece Henri truly liked. It fit his mood, beautifully sad.

From time to time, they spotted men and women working the carrot and cabbage fields. All were zippered as far as they could tell. More than one had at least one cast, and one man had both legs and his left arm in full casts. He was sitting and cultivating with his right hand. What the devil was going on, Henri wondered.

At last they arrived at their destination, the Capitol of Musicland in Wasserburg. My god, it is a miniature replica of Washington DC, he thought. So did several others. Mia had only seen photos of the domed structure on the BBC Nightly News. Still accompanied by the sounds of the Second Movement of the Seventh Symphony, the group disembarked before the capital's main entrance, surrounded by numerous Enforcers. At last the music changed to another of Wagner's overtures as they led the slow moving party inside.

# Chapter 18 In the Land of Music

Inside sitting on a huge makeshift throne sat a plump rabbit dressed as if he were Abraham Lincoln, complete with stovepipe top hat. As they approached him, the music lowered. A voice called out loudly, "All hail to Kaiser Wilhelm von Himmelhagen, Supreme Leader of Musicland!" Thousands of disembodied voices cheered, and then the Wagner music continued in the background.

The plump Kaiser's eyes were a bit glazed over, Henri noted. He spoke as disjoined as he had sounded on the pre-recorded speeches they'd heard last night. "I am Kaiser Wilhelm von Himmelhagen, the Supreme Leader of Musicland. I am. You are human rats, vermin of the world, multiplying everywhere, ruining the land. My land. My people. My dome. My Enforcers. My carrots. Where was I?"

He scratched his head and continued, "Ah, you humans must recognize that you are the inferior race! We rabbits are the Master Race! Who won the race, the tortoise there or the hare, I ask you that? Ah. Obvious. Humans are here to server the glorious Master Race and the Fatherland, Musicland! Ah, the Fatherland! Best place in the whole world, if only humans were extinct. No, that's genocide. We of the Master Race cannot condone genocide. We are the ones who are civilized. We have no wars here, none at all."

"Oh yes, humans must never speak unless spoken to by rabbits! Zippered nicely, I see. Well done, my Glorious Enforcers, well done indeed! You see, we need my Enforcers. Enforcers exist to ensure that the inferior race follow the Master Laws and do their part to serve the Master Race! You must be trained and forced to serve properly. My advisors say that if a dog can be trained, so can a human! Enforcers will make that happen. Let's not have genocide or patricide or matricide or herbicides either. Do we need herbicides? No, I think not, whatever they are. Oh where was I?" he looked positively annoyed with himself.

"Oh yes. Humans exist to serve, never to question! To question is to beg for enforcement! Oh, I see one of you has already begged for enforcement. That is as it should be. Would more of you like to be enforced right now? I am sure that my Glorious Enforcers will be very pleased to accommodate your request. No? Can't talk, eh. As it should be. As it should be. Seen, worked, but never heard. That is the best way to deal with the human infestation. Say, we have an infestation of ants in the pantry, Enforcers. Deal with them! No, after we deal with these here!" He had to stop three Enforcers from running off to deal with the ants.

"Now where the blazes was I anyway? I do so hate to be so distracted. I've memorized this speech many times, but that's the way with memory. It comes and goes, and I think that it has gone right now. No, here it comes again. Yes, music must accompany all actions! To act without music is to commit unthinkable heresy! We punish heresy here in Musicland. First a leg, then an arm, and then the other leg. If still spouting heresy, then it's to the Detention Center for as long as you live, which, I'm told, is not all that long. I suppose that I ought to inspect the Detention Center. When was I last there? Oh no matter. Where was I?"

"Oh yes. What to do with these humans? Young, fit. Yes, take them to Farm One Hundred. Let them hoe our carrots and cabbages. Now take them away to serve the Fatherland! Be gone, vile humans; out of my sight. I have seen enough of your kind today. Where's my pipe? Has anyone seen my pipe? I had it when I came in here? Maybe the herbicides ran off with it! Maybe I should make a new law: No more herbicides allowed."

The Enforcers moved to the group, intent upon carting them off to Farm One Hundred. Just then all chaos broke loose. Henri saw a can rolling their way. Boom! The can exploded. Boom! Boom! Three more detonated, releasing large clouds of smoke, obscuring all vision. Boom! Boom! Two stun grenades exploded behind the Enforcers. Henri thought he heard the rabbits falling to the stone floor, but he could not be sure. An arm grabbed his and began pulling him away. With his leg in the cast, he could not effectively resist and had to hobble along as best he could — either that or fall down.

He wanted to yell out for the others, but could only make a muffled noise. Damn zippers, he mentally cursed. A few feet later, he saw that a man had dragged him out of the smoke and confusion. A male rabbit had also dragged Milan and Regi away as well. A rabbit woman, accompanied by Herr Adelstein, had pulled Sir Thomas and Albert out as well. They were being led further into the building. Henri tried to protest. The women, the women! Then he saw two human women leading Vanessa and Mia towards them; they had been pulled the other direction from the smoke and were moving as fast as possible towards them. Two other rabbit women were bringing Rose and Trina with them. Henri relaxed and allowed himself to be assisted by the man.

They took a side passage and finally the man spoke, though Henri could barely hear him. His ears were still ringing from the blasts. "We are rescuing you. Come, hurry!" Down one corridor they went and finally into a stairwell. The man lifted Henri up and, carrying him, led the way down the stairs. The others followed more slowly, especially Mia and Vanessa. Where were they going? Deeper into the bowels of the capital building they went. Ahead, darkness loomed.

The man sat Henri down for a minute and turned on a flashlight. "Here, you hold this." He did so and the man lifted him up again. Once more, he was carried rapidly down a long dark hallway. In contrast to the white marble above, this basement, if that was what it was, was crudely made. Then, ahead he saw a large hole. "Rat hole. Point it into the rat hole," the man asked. Henri complied.

As they approached the rat hole, six rats stepped out, armed with the same type of guns that the Enforcers had. "All go as planned, boss?" asked one tall, fat rat, dressed in a business suit, wholly out of place Henri thought.

"Perfectly. They move too slowly. Make sure that we were not followed, please." The man continued walking into the rat hole. Now the sides turned into what Henri expected to see inside a rat's burrow, crudely dug walls, rounded at the top. Because the rats were as large as he, the humans had no problem moving through their tunnels. At last the man sat Henri down. "There, I can't carry you any longer. From here, you are going to have to walk. Come on; it still isn't totally safe." He took the flashlight from Henri and led the way. Henri glanced behind him. Everyone was still there in a long line.

Henri hobbled along as best he could, hoping and praying this would end soon. His legs were finally giving out when they entered a cavernous room, well illuminated. Soft, cheerful music was playing in the background. Henri suspected it might be one of Vivaldi's Concerti Grossi. There were a number of chairs, obviously stolen from the White House above sitting against one side, and the man motioned them to have a seat. "Not followed, Lynn?" he asked the young woman bringing up the rear. She nodded negatively. "Okay. Let's get their padlocks off of their zippers first."

"Allow me," a rabbit woman teased him. She wore a man's pants suit and came up to Henri first. To him, she said, "I'm their best lock pick. Less than thirty seconds for these pathetic excuses for locks." He liked her attitude. She was right; it took her only seconds to pick the lock, tossing it in a small wastebasket. "Unzip yourself," she said, moving on to the next person, Vanessa. He did so.

"Thank you for our timely rescue. We have only just arrived in Musicland and have no notion what is happening to us. Can someone please tell us what is going on?" Henri asked, finally relieved to be able to ask what he desperately wanted to know.

"I am Alex Woods, my wife, Lynn. Maggie Fields." They were humans; the next three were rabbits. "Brunnhilde Dietrich, Elsa Rike, and Herr Aksel Brekt. We are the Freedom Fighters. We've rescued you from a nightmare of servitude and slavery at the hands of the Enforcers and the mad Kaiser Wilhelm. This is one of our safe houses, wholly unknown to the powers that rule our land now. We had to bring you to this one of necessity. There was no other way to get you all safely out of their hands. Now then, who are you and what the devil happened to her?" He pointed to Mia, whose zipper Vanessa just opened.

"We are travelers in this world. I am Henri Graves, my wife, Vanessa, our friend Mia Tynara. Rose Whitney, Doctor Milan Ward, Reginald and Trina Noxwood. Our companions, Herr Adelstein, Sir Thomas, and Albert. We are most grateful for your timely rescue," Henri replied.

Mia spoke up, "An unfortunate accident, sir." Mia did not want to talk about what she'd endured there in Causeland, certainly not at this moment.

"Well met, friends. We got word that travelers had come. Agata warned us, though she got caught doing so and it cost her a leg. Well, we plan to rescue her in the near future," Alex explained. "Now then, first thing, let's get that cast off of your leg."

Maggie did it using a saw. She was gentle and careful not to cut into his leg. A half hour, Henri's leg was free. "Thank you, Maggie. That was awful. I don't know how all those others can get by like this."

"It is very hard on them, but they have no choice. It's get by or the Detention Camp for them," she replied. "No one has ever come out of that place. We fear the worst has happened to them, but it is too heavily guarded for us to get in there to see. The rats, though, are nearly finished digging a tunnel in there. We hope soon to get inside and see what we can do there."

"How come you all don't have zippers?" asked Vanessa.

"We did at one time," Lynn answered her. "We have Herr Aksel here to thank for our timely rescue. Yet it was Brunnhilde who found a way to remove the zippers. You see, here in Musicland, our lives are attuned to music. Play the right piece for the right action, she says. Well, it works. We're going to begin the removal process now."

Brunnhilde, a rather rotund rabbit woman, said, "Ah yes, Vivaldi's Four Seasons ought to do it. Mind you, listen to the music. It will take a while though, so do not be impatient and listen please." She retrieved a gramophone disk and placed it on the crude player. Soon the familiar sounds blared in the cavernous room. Henri recognized the music at once, though not the players. While they sat and listened, the others went about their own activities, replenishing their packs with more stun and gas grenades and such. Lynn also got a pot of tea brewing, bringing a smile to Vanessa's face. She was glad it was not coffee. Even though he sold it from his truck, he much preferred a good cup of tea. Spring, Summer, Autumn, and then Winter played in succession, though Brunnhilde had to change disks four times before it finished.

"Incredible! My lips are back," Henri exclaimed. "Brilliant, Brunnhilde, brilliant!" The others were equally satisfied, and the rabbit woman looked quite pleased with their praise.

"Now then, shall we take High Tea? Or would you prefer lunch?" Lynn asked. "We don't know whether or not you've had lunch. It is still a couple hours before supper around here."

"Tea will be fine," Vanessa replied politely. How very different their rescuers were compared to the hostile rabbits above ground.

Over tea, Alex began his lengthy explanation. "You see, it all began over twenty years ago. I was the President of Musicland then, and it was election time. I have served my two full terms and am not eligible to run again. Herr Aksel was running along with Wilhelm von Himmelhagen."

"Back then, Wilhelm had a silver tongue. He promised the rabbits everything they could possibly desire: free carrots and cabbage, a chance to run the country. No work; let the humans work for us this time. On he went, promising them every imaginable thing and all for free."

"How could I compete with that?" Herr Aksel lamented, shaking his head.

Alex went on, "You couldn't. The people foolishly believed everything he said. He was a most eloquent speaker back then. A silver tongue can charm the devil himself it is said. Anyway, he won the election by a landslide. Power corrupts some, and it did Wilhelm. Some of his promises he eventually kept, once he had installed the Enforcers to enforce his made up laws. Before anyone had any real idea of just what was going on, the humans were enslaved, zippered, as he calls it. Without the ability to communicate what was happening, other humans in Musicland had no idea until the Enforcers came to their town or village. By then it was too late. Within two years of taking office, he proclaimed himself Kaiser and Supreme Ruler, thereby abolishing elections."

Humans tried to rebel many times and that's when he began subduing the population with funeral dirges and all manner of depressing musical pieces, chosen to subdue the human will when played over and over and over, endlessly. Still, many tried to counteract, and he then began putting full casts on the offenders. Let me tell you, if you are forced to have both legs in full length casts as well as one arm, you are darn near helpless. Even one cast makes life almost unbearable, since it is never removed. Yes, they do sometimes break, but the Enforcers just remove it and put a new one on. Once an appendage receives a cast, it is never removed, further crushing the will of the people," Alex explained. Henri breathed a sigh of relief. Had he not been rescued, he would have had that cast on all the time.

Alex continued his story. "After Lynn and I got a cast on our leg for civil disobedience, we were rescued by Herr Aksel here, and together we formed the Underground Freedom Fighters, the UFF as the Kaiser calls us. Other rabbits and all of the rats have joined us now. We've been working on freeing those that we can get to, but it is pathetically slow going. Besides, we have to steal all our food and supplies, so we cannot handle huge numbers of people down here."

"Then last night, we got word from Agata of your arrival and began making our plans. Herr Adelstein spotted Herr Aksel and begged him to help him find a way to rescue all of you. He told Herr Aksel a pretty wild story about Causeland. Anyway, we did as we planned."

Just then a rat in battle fatigues entered. "Yes, Captain Melvin?" Herr Aksel asked.

"Just reporting in, sir. As you predicted, the Enforcers assumed that we took their prisoners out the front doors. They are scouring the city for any signs of them. All is well." He saluted and left.

Brunnhilde put on another disk. Henri recognized Beethoven's Violin Concerto at once, a particularly beautiful piece, she thought. Henri asked, "Say, this music comes from composers from our world. How is it that you have them here too?"

"Who knows?" the rabbit replied. "They have always been here for as long as Musicland has been here." Henri suspected now that Able Montford had brought them with him when he created this place. Interesting point, he thought.

Henri volunteered, "Alex, Herr Aksel, we'd like to help you free Musicland from the clutches of the mad Kaiser."

"You help is accepted. Yes, you are right. Over the years, Wilhelm has indeed gone completely mad. He is only semi-coherent these days. Still, it is the Enforcers who wield the real power over us all. Come, we ought to get dinner going and get you all a place to sleep. Mind you, there are few comforts here," Alex explained, a little ashamed of this. He had been President and was now forced to live in dirt tunnels beneath his country.

Later, the three sat on the cot provided for Mia. Each had a small cot nestled in a small side niche. Vanessa said, "Henri, Mia and I are going to be pretty useless helping you on this one. In our heels, we can barely walk on this uneven dirt floor."

"I'm always going to be useless now," Mia added, still in grief over her own situation.

"That's fine. Music is my thing anyway. You look after Mia for me; that will be help enough, dear," Henri replied. Vanessa grinned and gave him a brief kiss, then helped Mia into her cot bed. The underground chamber was filled with the soft sounds of a beautiful piano sonata, which Henri recognized as the Moonlight Sonata. He felt very much empowered by his recognition of most of the music that he had heard thus far. Music was everything in this land. Surely amongst all the musical offerings lay the answer to the Enforcers and the Kaiser.

Over breakfast the next morning, Mia offered, "You know, music moves the soul sometimes. It often helps make me happy and cheerful and vibrant, and other times the wrong ones can echo my sadness and grief. Perhaps it is that way here, Brunnhilde."

"Oh yes, yes, very much so. Music reflects us and we reflect music. Personally, I am attracted to the pieces which so accurately reflect a beautiful sadness, for I often see great beauty even in sadness," she admitted. "Just so you know, not all we rabbits are behind the Kaiser any longer. In fact, after his Enforcers began casting humans, many of us totally altered our position, politically, that is. They are wholly unworthy of our support in any way. Still, they have the guns."

"True, but a gun wouldn't do me much good anymore," Mia said softly.

"Too true. I am sorry that you had such a bad accident. Still, I have just the music for you to hear, Mia. It is named the Double Concerto by someone named Bach, the slow movement." She headed off to find that disk. Before long, the intertwining of the two violins echoed in the cavern. Mia was indeed moved greatly by the music.

"Hey, that's Bach's Double Violin Concerto, isn't it?" Henri called out. Mia nodded. He then left with Herr Aksel and Alex to "get the lay of the land" as he explained to Vanessa.

Left alone for the day, Mia and Vanessa chatted about music with Brunnhilde, who never seemed tired of their questions. She played many excerpts and examples for the two. "What kind of music dissolves the zippers?" asked Mia.

"Music of great beauty and passion, but it also helps if it also has a good, recognizable rhythm to it, dum, da, dum, da, dum," the rabbit woman explained, "or da, die, dum, dum, da, die, dum, dum."

At suppertime, Henri returned enthused. "You know, this place, this country is incredible. They have somehow wired every home to a central music Distribution Center. From there, we can play just the right music to dissolve everyone's zippers at one time."

Alex didn't look as cheerful. "Yes, but that center is heavily guarded by the Enforcers. We couldn't possibly take that many of them out."

Mia pointed out, "You wouldn't have to if you could somehow get them all to go to someplace else."

"Brilliant, Mia," Henri validated her enthusiastically. "You've hit upon it. Alex, all we have to do is to get most of the Enforcers in one place, far from the music Distribution Center, and we have solved everything. We can kill two birds with one stone."

Alex complained, "Yes, but how do we kill that many Enforcers, assuming that we can even, as you suggest, get them all in one place?"

"Okay, okay. I can take a hint. We've only just begun to solve the whole problem. Still, we've made significant progress today. Now we just need to figure out how to immobilize the Enforcers. I don't think killing them is the answer, Alex. Probably they do need to stand trial for their crimes, but killing isn't the answer."

"Thank you," Herr Aksel added, greatly relieved. After all, they were his own kind, rabbits.

"Ah, we need music that will make them stand still and weep and weep and do nothing else," Brunnhilde spoke up, thinking aloud.

"Yes, but you know that these rabbits are the worst of our kind — minds full of hate and such," Herr Aksel countered.

"Our Scottish tune, Amazing Grace, always bring tears to my eyes," Mia volunteered. "It always reminds me of the funerals of my parents."

"She's right. I will test it in the morning," Brunnhilde added, growing a bit more hopeful.

"Hey, that one is on the Outlawed List at the Distribution Center," Elsa spoke up. "I used to work there for a time, before things got really bad and out of hand. I bet that is why that one is outlawed, because it impacts the Enforcers too badly."

"Okay, we'll test it out tomorrow. I am planning to rescue Agata. Fix us up a bootleg player, and we'll see if it works on the two Enforcers stationed around that inn," Herr Aksel replied.

"Okay, he'll be gone two days. Meanwhile, Henri and I will work on a way to get the Enforcers away from the Distribution Center," Alex added.

"Oh that is an easy one," Mia spoke up again. "They seem to slavishly follow the Kaiser's orders without even thinking about them, vis-a-vis that spiel about the ants. Just give them some pretend orders from the Kaiser ordering them to go to the Detention Center at once."

"You are brilliant, Mia. Yes, that's the answer, Alex. Tomorrow we'll work out how we can best deliver those orders. Brilliant, Mia," Henri heaped praise on her. Well, she really needed a morale boost, he thought. Besides, she was being very helpful in ways that she could contribute.

For a short while, Mia's face returned to that of the enchantress that he'd seen before. However, it faded fast as they struggled with getting ready for bed.

"How about Handel's Water Music or Royal Fireworks?" suggested Henri. They were meeting to discuss the best music to help undo the mess in Musicland. "Or perhaps his Hallelujah Chorus?"

"Or perhaps the ending of Beethoven's last movement of his Ninth Symphony," suggested an animated Brunnhilde. Never before had she met someone as knowledgeable as Henri was of their music.

"And we could get their total attention with the first movement of his Fifth Symphony," Henri added. "Then, launch into the zipper removers, ending with the Ninth Symphony, climaxing the restoration of Musicland to its people."

Mia, Vanessa, Henri, and Brunnhilde were standing in the Musical Archives, surrounded by shelves and shelves of the gramophone recordings. Against the opposite wall were even more shelves filled with sheet music copies of these many selections. These were their master copies, from which anyone in the land could request a personal copy at any time. Elsa had sneaked them in here, bribing a guard and keeping him occupied.

"Okay, I'll make us copies now along with Mia's suggestion. Give me ten minutes," the rabbit woman said. All this had brought new life into her world. She rushed over to the duplication machine and began punching in the numbers as Henri called them out. Sure enough, in ten minutes, she wrapped up the precious recording copies, and they headed back outside where Elsa was waiting for them. The guard was asleep, having devoured an entire bowl of fresh carrots. Quietly, they left him snoozing.

The Enforcers were still combing the streets, but they were above ground for only a minute before ducking into another rat tunnel. Here, the two women slowed their progress considerably, and Henri had his arms around both

Vanessa and Mia, helping them traverse the mile of uneven tunnel floor. All the while, Brunnhilde and Elsa hummed marching music to accompany their action, as fitting life in Musicland.

"Now all we have to do is to figure out how to deliver two separate music concerts at the same time," Henri continued to plan the attack as they walked along.

"Can't you use the delivery system to play the rescuing music to everyone?" asked Mia, wobbling slightly over the uneven ground and silently cursing her helplessness once more.

"Yes, that we will do, but we need a separate system to somehow play Amazing Grace over and over to only the massed Enforcers," Henri explained. Mia bit her lip; she knew she couldn't answer that one.

"We can use our portable gramophone," Brunnhilde replied instead, "but how do we get it over them without them being able to stop us? It will take time for the music to affect them, you see, and they have guns."

"Yes, but the range of their guns is not far. If we could be up in the air a ways, their weapons wouldn't hit us," Henri answered, wholly unable to envision how they could accomplish that feat.

"Hey, leave that to me," Elsa spoke up. "My invention can get us up say five hundred feet. Will that be far enough?"

"Very likely, but how can you do that? Do you also fly here?" Henri asked.

Both rabbits laughed. "Oh don't be silly. Rabbits don't fly," Elsa finally chastised him, though still laughing. "I've invented a balloon that can lift us up. It is really a big one, but I have had to fly it only at night. Can't let the Enforcers see it; they'd want to steal it from me."

"Cool. Can we see it?" Henri asked.

"I suppose, but it is a long walk from the cavern where you are staying. Perhaps you and I should go later on," she answered, rather pleased that her invention would play a role. Until now, the others merely teased her about her strange invention.

That evening, Vanessa, Henri, and Mia sat around a crude table sipping tea and relaxing. The others were going about their own affairs. Rose and Milan, for example, were in her niche discussing their own private matters. Henri suspected that her mother was getting quite serious about marrying Milan when and if they got back home. Vanessa brought up an observation that she had made during the day.

"You know I think that I have figured this out. Miranda or Henri rather, is really good at creating her own illusions, so real that others can see them. Like when I first met you, you invited me into your room and the whole place seemed upside down." He described it a bit for Mia's sake. "Your intention behind it was really strong, and you allowed no counter-thoughts of counter-ideas to interfere, like 'that's impossible,' 'lights don't hang upside down,' 'ceilings are always up,' and 'gravity always pulls things down.' I can see now that when I intend for things to happen, a whole lot of those kinds of ideas, counter to what I am intending, pop into my thoughts almost at once. Those, of course, then keep my intention from occurring."

"Yes, Zed, er Vanessa, that is exactly right. Allow one counter-notion to enter and that alone can keep one's intention from bringing your creation into being," Miranda, Henri rather, replied, quite seriously. "That is why you have to focus and keep those counter-thoughts and ideas from popping up just after you decide on something and intend for it to happen."

"Right. Yet, in Causeland, something there materially kept such counter-notions from instantly appearing. That's why Mia was doing so well there. Mia, remember — your spoon sort of levitated up to your mouth when you were feeding yourself. Your tea cup rose up to your mouth. All manner of similar things happened easily. Duchess Lucinda and her friends are not having the slightest bit of difficulties managing life without their arms. I think that is why."

"Look Mia, right now see if you can't lift your own tea cup up and take a sip instead of having me do it for you," Vanessa asked.

"Why? It isn't going to do it," Mia replied sadly.

"Right. Because you are convinced that you need arms to lift the cup up, right?"

"Yes, that's rather obvious, isn't it?" Mia retorted, becoming slightly hostile that she would even say such a thing to her.

"Yet, in Causeland, you didn't have such thoughts, did you?"

"Well, no, not really. They were all doing it, and I just went along, and it did work somehow," she replied. "For some reason, it didn't seem so impossible to me then."

"Right Mia, it didn't. Miranda and Mia, I think that we are supposed to be learning something from these encounters! Why else would Able Montford have created this whole universe? Some sadistic joke? Well, I kind of thought so at first, but now I think that I am seeing a pattern in all this. We are supposed to be learning something about ourselves and our true abilities and their nature. It's not just for the solving of problems that we are here. I think that he is trying to show us something about life. Look Mia, I want you to decide to move the spoon there on the table an inch to your right. Go on, decide the spoon is going to be an inch to the right."

"Well, okay, I did and it didn't move, did it? See, I can't do it," Mia replied a bit testily.

"Right, you made the decision and had the intention to have the spoon an inch to the right. What I realized today is that we make our own barriers to our own decisions and postulates and that we often fail to simply push them on through to completion, to a done. I'll show you what I mean. Mia, use your nose and push the spoon an inch to the right where you had decided it should be located. Come on. Do it."

Mia looked at her, but went along with Vanessa's request, moving the spoon an inch. Vanessa then said, "See, you pushed on through the barriers that appeared after you made the decision to have the spoon an inch to the right. That's what I think that Able Montford is trying to show us. We make a postulate, and it is up to us to push it on through to completion, despite all objections to the contrary that might arise."

Vanessa continued, "Mia, in your case, I think this is the most vitally important thing for you. You've suffered a horribly debilitating loss. You can go through life being helpless or you can intend for things to get done and back them up by doing whatever you need to do to get those things, those actions, actually done. I believe that Able Montford is showing you, Mia, that you have a critical choice to make in life now and that choice is truly yours to make. I think that he has shown you and us the way and that it is up to us to follow through on it."

"Yes, I can see what you are saying, but it is so impossible like this," Mia shrugged her shoulders, the best gesture she could now make.

"I think you have used the wrong word, Mia. How about 'so difficult like this?'" Vanessa gently attempted to push her down a different path. "Impossible implies that there is no conceivable way that it could happen. Difficult only implies that it will be a challenge, not that it is impossible. I think that we all agree that it will be difficult for you, but I for one am unwilling to go so far as to say impossible, Mia. Where there is a will, there will be a way, if only one is bright enough to invent or find it."

"You are right, Vanessa. I really do mean difficult, not impossible, though I admit at times I do feel like it really is impossible," Mia admitted.

"Good girl. That's the spirit," Vanessa validated her.

"I think that I would be better able to find or invent ways if I was finally back to our world," Mia suggested.

"You'll get no argument from us on that point!" Henri finally spoke up. He'd listened to Vanessa very much impressed with his grasp of the situation. Indeed, there did appear to be some logic behind all of this world and their experiences within it. He'd overlooked that entirely up until now. That night when they went to bed on their cots, Mia insisted on tucking herself in for the first time. Using a combination of her teeth, legs, and a bit of wiggling, she succeeded, which pleased her considerably.

Late the next night, Herr Aksel Brekt returned. "Total success, Agata has been rescued and has fully recovered. She is staying with her brother and older sister, whom we rescued last year. They are with the rats, safe underground. How goes everything here?" he asked after reporting on his mission.

Alex outlined each step of the grand plan. The only remaining detail was the coordinated time for each action. Herr Aksel suggested, "Well, our spies in the Kaiser's employ say that he always takes an hour-long bath around ten each morning. I think that the order to the Enforcers should be given shortly after ten, say tomorrow morning. Give them an hour to congregate around the Detention Center. I know that it might be more like a day for all of the Enforcers from the outer towns to get there, but all those here in the capital will surely be there within the hour." The others agreed with the rabbit.

He continued, "So at eleven we nullify the Enforcers while freeing the rest of Musicland. Sounds simple, but we are going to need to have a force in hiding, ready to come out and confiscate the Enforcers' guns just as soon as it is safe to do so."

Promptly at 10:05 the next morning, Henri spoke into the giant microphone that Alex had hot wired into the public address system, temporarily halting the endless flow of music to the entire land. He did a perfect imitation of the Kaiser and his voice. "Attention all Enforcers in Musicland. An emergency has arisen at the Detention Center. All Enforcers everywhere are hereby ordered to go to the Detention Center here in the capital immediately! Yes, drop everything else that you are doing and get there! Now!" He flipped it off. Brunnhilde replaced the usual music with the rousing Wagner's Ride of the Valkyries, the Kaiser's theme song, before releasing their temporary hook up to the address system.

She, Maggie, Vanessa, and Mia then made their final preparations, organizing the chosen disks to be played at eleven o'clock, which they hoped would undo all of the zippers throughout Musicland. Then they headed to the Distribution Center.

Meantime, Elsa Rike, Henri, and Lynn prepared Elsa's balloon for its critical flight. Lynn had the portable gramophone player ready, while Henri had the disks. They would try Mia's suggestion first, Amazing Grace. If that didn't work, they had several more to try. Shortly after Henri's address, he hopped into the wicker basket of Elsa's hot air balloon made from various multi-colored fabrics, and Elsa fired up her heat generator. Henri prayed this would work.

Not far from the Detention Center, Herr Aksel gathered a hundred freedom fighters, a collection of men and rabbits. While they had guns, they didn't want to actually use them if they could avoid it. He carefully hid each man and rabbit; then they waited patiently. All wore special earphones which would play the rescuing music, drowning out the debilitating Amazing Grace or the other possibilities. It would not do for them to also be affected by the music.

Slowly the gay colored balloon filled out and gently began to rise. Henri relaxed a little. Now if it would only go high enough and would move over the Detention Center, all would be well. A half hour later, it was high enough, but it wasn't drifting either in the right direction or fast enough. Henri acted, intending for a bit of wind to come and blow them back on course. He focused and concentrated. "Hey, we are heading in the right direction now!" Elsa exclaimed. She had no idea this was Henri's doing, merely accepting their good luck. She was playing the Hunt Section of Autumn of Vivaldi's Four Seasons just for them as they moved along in the balloon. Elsa presumed it was the music which was propelling them on course. "We are now riding to the attack," Elsa proudly proclaimed to the winds and sky.

Around eleven, the balloon floated just above the Detention Center. Below them some five hundred feet, they could see a confused group of Enforcers standing around trying to discover what the dire emergency was all about. "Now," Henri called out. Precisely at eleven, Lynn began the gramophone. The sounds of a bagpipe playing Amazing Grace very loudly from a speaker attached below their basket began, though of course, those in the basket wore their headphones and were listening to Brunnhilde's rescuing music. Henri, Lynn, and Elsa watched the Enforcers below them for any reactions. Henri kept his fingers crossed. Would this work?

All throughout Musicland, at eleven o'clock, the somber funeral dirges ceased playing. Da, da, da, daaa. The rousing opening notes of Beethoven's Fifth Symphony demanded everyone's full attention! Everywhere humans, rabbits, and rats stopped their tasks to listen to this incredible change in music. This was quickly followed by selections from Handel's Royal Fireworks and then key sections of Vivaldi's Four Seasons. When those selections finished, Brunnhilde followed that with a portion of Beethoven's last movement of his Ninth Symphony. She ended with the rousing Hallelujah Chorus from Handel's Messiah. Once that ended, she punched in the automated daily play list which had been the normal music played during the day before the Kaiser had taken office, back when Alex was their elected President. Finally, she waited for news of what had happened.

Meanwhile crouched in their hiding places, Herr Aksel and his group suddenly heard the beginning of the Fifth Symphony in their headsets. Adrenaline began to flow, and it was all the rabbit could do to keep his forces from attacking that very instant. "Wait! Wait! Wait!" he continued signaling his men. The large mass of Enforcers, some two hundred of them, began holding their hands over their ears. All knew that this music was on the Outlawed List. Brunnhilde had the volume cranked as high as the machine would go, and the rabbits below were unable to keep from hearing the wailing bagpipes. Soon, they began crying and not long after that many began dropping their guns onto the ground so they could use both hands to wipe the tears from their eyes. It was so sad, so mournful.

At last, Herr Aksel gave his hand signal. His hundred men and rabbits dashed out of their hiding places and began grabbing up the guns of the Enforcers, who continued to cry and wail along with the music. Over and over Brunnhilde played it. Would it ever stop, they wondered, so sad, so hopeless. With the guns confiscated, Herr Aksel left half of his force guarding the enforcers, while he led the remainder inside the Detention Center, a huge building. None knew what to expect. No one had ever managed to get past the Enforcers to see inside this most heavily defended building in the capital.

"Oh dear god!" Herr Aksel declared as he entered and saw the sights before him. Hundreds upon hundreds of human men, women, and children were being held prisoner here. Each one was encased in a full body cast with only their heads not held immobile by the white plaster. Wires from the ceiling held them up, and they were spaced closely together, with just enough room for someone to come by and feed them and mop up the floor beneath them. All were upright with their arms and legs spread out a little. However, here inside the freedom music was working; their mouth zippers were slowly melting away; mouths and lips returning to normal. Tears of happiness trickled down many cheeks.

A dozen of the encasement machines lined one wall just beside the door. Herr Aksel ordered his men to bring the Enforcers in and encase them for now. Others were asked to go fetch saws with which to free the prisoners. Finally, he sent runners off to signal the others of their success and to bring help and saws! When the music returned to the daily music, Herr Aksel took off his headset and called out to the hundreds of prisoners. "We have rescued you. Please be a bit more patient while we get you sawed out of those casts."

By noon, Henri, Vanessa, Mia, and the others all arrived at the Detention Center. After their initial shock passed, all volunteered to help. Mia, carrying a water ladle between her teeth, went from encased person to person, giving them a much needed drink of water. This she could awkwardly manage by herself. Vanessa, Rose, and Trina gave massages to the women as they were finally cut out of their plaster casts. At the very least, they needed their circulation restored. Elsa and Lynn headed up the cooking detail, providing a good, hot meal for the rescued folks. However, it was full dark before the last human had been freed and fed.

A very tired group finally headed back to their underground cavern for the night. It was too late and too dark to try to find other accommodations. "Hey, what about the Kaiser?" Henri asked. He and the others had completely forgotten about him. Last they knew, he was taking his morning bath.

Herr Aksel replied, "I am truly sorry, but during all that action and confusion, a number of humans who were freed turned him into rabbit stew and ate him. I only found out about that an hour ago. Sorry."

Herr Adelstein said only, "Brrrrr." He shook his whole body as well. Henri didn't inquire further.

As Henri fell asleep, he heard Alex and Herr Aksel talking intensely in low voices, but he could not hear what they were saying. In the morning at breakfast time, over the countrywide network, Alex's voice interrupted everyone's meal. "Good morning everyone in Musicland. This is your ex-President Alex Woods speaking. The terrible reign of the Kaiser and his brutal Enforcers is over. If anyone still is wearing casts or still has zippers, please report to the capital at once. You will be freed immediately. New elections will be held a month from now. In the meantime, Herr Aksel Brekt is our new President. I give you our new President Aksel."

The rabbit then spoke, "Greetings everyone. Yes, we are finally free of the wickedness of the Kaiser and his Enforcers. At this time, most of the Enforcers are being held at the Detention Center. Those still at large are being rounded up and will also be held accountable for their treacherous actions. After the elections are over, our new President will handle whatever punishment these Enforcers deserve.

Meantime, my responsibilities lay in getting us all back to normalcy once more."

"Our miraculous rebellion would not have been possible without the timely aid, advice, and assistance of three visitors to Musicland: Mr. Henri Graves, his wife Vanessa, and their friend Mia Tynara. We in Musicland owe these three our eternal gratitude and thanks for helping us recover our freedom. Henri, Vanessa, Mia, we will never forget what you have done for us. Now then, let us all spend this day in celebration. I've asked Brunnhilde to arrange for a day of musical celebration. Let us all enjoy our newfound freedom from tyranny and oppression."

Happy and cheerful music played all that day. Henri found their carriage and things, and the group moved into one of the fanciest inns in the capital, compliments of the new President. "Where to now?" asked Herr Adelstein. "We are getting rather bored of all this music."

"Well, let's dig out our map and see where we must go next," Henri suggested. Everyone crowded around the inn's table to see for themselves. Its label read: Prosopopoeia.

"Whatever does prosopopoeia mean?" asked Mia.

"I've never heard of such a word. Maybe it isn't even a word," Henri pointed out.

"Hah, daughter of mine," Rose spoke up with confidence. This once she knew something that her daughter didn't. "Prosopopoeia means a figure of speech in which an abstract thing is personified. It could also be an imagined or absent person that is represented as speaking — like personification."

Henri merely made a "Hurrumph" noise. Vanessa said, "I don't get it. Must be a strange place."

Alex returned from business to relax and chat with the visitors and had overheard them. "I went to the edge of

Prosopopoeia once. Talking trees. Way too strange for me, so I left. I don't think that you will find much there."

"Wow, talking trees?" Mia exclaimed. "I've never heard of such things, only in fiction, like <u>The Lord of the Rings</u>, where he had talking trees; ents, they were called."

"Cool! You've read that one too. Great books. Have you seen the movie version? Oops, I'm sorry, it wasn't made until the 2000's, sorry. Well, if you come back with us, Mia, we'll show you the DVDs," Vanessa suggested.

"What's a DVD?" Mia asked. Thus went their conversation. However, Alex did point out that it was a day's ride to their easternmost town, Easton. From there, they could enter Prosopopoeia the next morning. Plans were made over tea and biscuits.

The ride in their carriage was pleasant enough. Herr Adelstein was most pleased to have nothing but silence and the horses hooves in his ears. "I've had enough of all that music to last me a very long time."

"But I thought it was pretty," Albert countered hopefully, but then slumped. "Oh, I am always wrong. I see, Herr Adelstein."

"Hey, Albert, don't listen to him. It is perfectly fine if you liked the music," Vanessa countered. The tortoise smiled and raised his nose to the rabbit.

The day was a particularly fine one, cool, breezy, and sunny. Everywhere that they saw rabbits and humans out tending their fields, the locals waved to them, and the party waved back. During the afternoon, a gust blew in and flipped Mia's golden shoulder length hair over her face. Instinctively, she used her hand to drag it back in place, only to discover that nothing happened. A bit startled by this, since she had had her attention focused on the beautiful countryside rolling past them, she looked annoyed. Then, she tossed her head first one way and then the other and her tresses slipped back over her shoulders.

Vanessa whispered, "See, I told you so."

Mia smiled, "Yes, I do see what you mean. Find a way to carry out your intended action. It works, but only if I can figure out a way to get it carried out if it doesn't happen."

"True, we can work on that when we get you back to the real world."

"Isn't this the real world?" asked Sir Thomas. "It seems real to me."

"Sometimes far too real," cautioned Herr Adelstein. Sir Thomas nodded, agreeing with him.

"Yes, your world here is real too. I mean our world, which is different from your world," Vanessa corrected herself.

"On our world, rabbits don't talk and are about this big," Mia pointed out, trying to use her hands to indicate the size. "Oops, as big as my head, I mean."

"What? How utterly preposterous! The size of your head? Why, those cannot be real rabbits! Here, a really small rabbit might only get as tall as four feet and would be considered a dwarf rabbit. I am sure that I don't want to visit such a world at all. Honestly, teeny tiny rabbits who cannot speak? Rubbish!" declared Herr Adelstein.

"How about we squirrels?" asked Sir Thomas.

"They don't speak either and are even smaller, I'm afraid," Mia said politely.

"Brrrr. Count me out on that too!" Sir Thomas agreed with his rabbit pal.

"Suppose tortoises are the same too," Albert said somberly.

"Oh no. Some tortoises are as large as you, Albert, but they don't talk either or walk upright as you often do," Mia answered him.

"Hum, well, that is something. We tortoises are big everywhere then. See, Herr Adelstein, we are big wherever we are. That's something," Albert said with a slight hint of personal pride. The rabbit merely looked out of the window, trying to ignore the tortoise.

# Chapter 19 Prosopopoeia

The carriage halted just across the border of Musicland. Ahead was a very dense forest, and Henri could see no way for them to continue. "Okay, everyone out. We've hit a barrier to our travel," he called out. Milan assisted the women down this time, as Regi and Henri were handling the driving.

Ahead of them lay a dense, tropical forest. "I don't see how Mia and I could possibly walk through that, not in these heels," Vanessa whispered to Henri.

"I say old chaps, why don't we get a machete and chop a path through for the carriage," Milan expressed his opinion.

"How *dare* you even think of wounding us!" a large bush in front of him bellowed out in a deep bass voice, filled with righteous indignation.

Startled and quite taken aback, Milan apologized, "Er, sorry, speaking before thinking again." He whispered, "What are we going to do?"

The bush continued speaking, though in a normal tone this time. "I am called Bush. I am here to inform you that your carriage is now waiting for you in Prosopopoeia City at the center of Prosopopoeia." The surprised group turned. Sure enough, their horses and carriage had mysteriously vanished! They turned to face Bush once more. "I told you so. Humans. Never believe a word I say. Ah well. There is a patch of jungle first. After that comes the Desert of Desolation, a very nasty place, dry with sand everywhere, wholly unfit for any life. I personally would return to from whence you came. That is an option. I dare say most do choose that avenue. If so, your carriage will be returned hence forthwith."

"No, I'm sorry, we must continue our journey," Henri dismissed that option. Obviously, Alex must have taken advantage of that choice.

Bush continued, "As I was then saying, there is a big patch of nasty desert to cross. It leads to the giant lake. I do hope that you all are very excellent swimmers and are in very good shape for such a lengthy swim."

"But, but, but I can't swim," Sir Thomas whispered, his knees knocking together once more.

"Cross the lake and in its center lies Prosopopoeia City, your carriage, and safe passage on your journey," Bush continued its explanation. "You will travel in pairs, as always expected in this world." What happened next occurred simultaneously, though at first glance, it did not seem that way.

Bush asked each simultaneously the same question, but the bush did not say the words out loud. The words appeared in their minds as did their immediate answer. Henri heard, "With whom of these present do you wish to make said trip?" All of the others heard exactly the same thing in their minds.

Herr Adelstein asked, "Say, all we have to do is to get to Prosopopoeia City?" Sir Thomas echoed him as did Albert.

Bush replied to them, "Yes, isn't that what I just told you? Honestly, pay attention here!"

"Oh, that's simple," the rabbit said. Nodding knowingly to his two friends, he and they went Poof! All three vanished and appeared in Prosopopoeia City, standing beside their carriage.

"Well, that was easy. I wonder what is keeping the others?" Herr Adelstein asked.

"Dunno. Maybe they are slow at Poofing," Sir Thomas attempted to answer his friend's question.

"Maybe they are walking here," Albert tossed in his opinion, knowing that it was in all likelihood completely wrong. "I guess we should wait for them. Tea anyone?"

"Good idea, Albert," Herr Adelstein replied. "Table. Two chairs. One rock." Poof, the four items appeared.

"I'll get the tea. Albert, you manage the tablecloth. We must be civilized about this. No wait, you get the tea, and I'll manage the tablecloth. I still have it in my house," Sir Thomas corrected himself. Shortly, the three friends sat down for tea.

Rose and Milan suddenly found themselves wholly alone, apparently abandoned by all of the others. Similarly, Regi and Trina were by themselves. However, Vanessa, Mia, and Henri looked at each other somewhat confused. Mia had indicated that she was with Vanessa, as did Henri, while Vanessa suggested that she was with both Henri and Mia, unwilling to leave Mia on her own. This unexpected turn confused Bush.

"Where did everyone go?" asked Henri, baffled by the sudden disappearance of everyone else.

Bush replied, "They are on their way already. This is a bit confusing to me." Branches moved this way and that, as if Bush was scratching its head, though it obviously did not have one.

Henri took this opportunity to ask, "We are supposed to go from here to the island at the center, Bush? As simple as that?" Accidentally, Henri intended just what he said. To his utter amazement, everything completely vanished. He was standing on a perfectly flat plain. Far off in the distance, he saw the carriage and horses standing, waiting for them. He also thought he saw the trio setting up a table for tea. Confused, he began running across the featureless plain towards the three. By the time that he arrived, they were just taking their first sips.

"Ah, here comes Henri. I suppose he will want a chair too," Herr Adelstein commented to his friends.

"I'll fix him a cup," Sir Thomas volunteered.

"Perhaps the others will be coming soon, and we won't have time to finish our tea," Albert suggested. Herr Adelstein computed that and then went ahead and conjured the chair, figuring that they would therefore have a very long wait.

Henri vanished, leaving Vanessa standing beside Mia. Both women looked startled. "Where did he go?" Mia whispered, a bit fearfully.

Bush now spoke more decisively. "Okay, you two. You must get through this jungle, then somehow cross the desert, and then cross the wide lake to get to your carriage and the others. You are to work together as a team to get yourselves across. Now then, the rules. You have to get there together or not at all. Each of you can have one change of form and only one; yet you will have to get each other across all three barriers. Use your form changes wisely."

"Excuse me, Bush. What exactly do you mean by form change? And is it permanent?" Mia asked. She would have crossed her fingers had she any.

"For example, you might decide to be a snake and slither your way through the jungle. Once you have used the form to get across that barrier, you will return to the forms you now have. Each can only change form once," Bush replied.

"But I don't know how to change my form," Mia protested, growing worried that this would be beyond her skill.

"Easy. You simply declare the form that you want. Be as explicit as possible. Just saying that you want to be a snake is not necessarily sufficient, for you might end up being one that is three feet across, which would make moving through this dense jungle most challenging."

Bush went on, "You may talk to whatever you find along the way, and they will answer honestly, but they will not tell you what form you should be using. That would be cheating. No cheating is allowed. Further, between you, a single form may be used only once. So if one of you chooses to become a snake, later on, the other cannot then choose a snake form."

"Is there a time limit on how quickly we must get there?" Vanessa asked, trying hard to think of all the key points that needed clarification.

"No, though I suspect humans will get hungry if you take days to do it," Bush replied a bit sarcastically. Vanessa got the idea that Bush didn't have too high an opinion of humans.

"Where are all our other friends?" she asked quickly.

Bush replied somewhat bored, "They are either on their way or have already arrived." Vanessa's heart sank a little. Already there? They must have worked out this puzzle incredibly swiftly! "Remember, you both must get there together. Let the challenge begin now." Bush ceased speaking, and the animated foliage returned to normal, indistinguishable from all of the other vegetation before them.

"We should take our time and think this through," Mia said cautiously, with just a trace of fear in her voice.

"You are right. Think this through. We can't possibly walk through this. He suggested a snake, but if we did that, we'd both have to be a snake, and we only have one change which ends when we get through the jungle. That cannot be the right choice," Vanessa declared.

"Right. That won't work." Mia looked around her hoping for some inspiration. "We could maybe fly over it if one of us was a really big bird."

"Great idea, Mia. I'll go first and carry you over the jungle. Then we can figure out what to do next. It seems odd, though. Three barriers, but only two changes of form. Can you swim?"

"Yes, er when I had arms. I don't know about now and not in these clothes. Heck, we can barely breathe as it is," Mia answered, growing more afraid by the moment. What had they gotten themselves into this time?

"Let's walk a bit and see if we can find a path or trail through here," Vanessa suggested. "Since we are allowed only two changes, there must be an alternative way through one of these barriers, don't you think?"

"That makes sense, Vanessa," Mia admitted. She looked at the ground a moment and then steeled herself and spoke up. "Vanessa, in case something bad happens to me and I don't make it, there is something that I wanted to tell you. I, I love you. You are fabulous, and I have fallen head over heels, madly in love with you. I know that you are married to Henri and all that. Plus, I don't understand the Miranda-Zed thing. I just know that I love you and I wanted you to know it. I'd do anything for you."

Wow! That was unexpected, Vanessa thought to herself. She still thought of herself as Zed, not a woman, but he knew that Mia was speaking from her heart and knew that she'd better answer both honestly and sincerely. "Thanks for telling me, Mia. I am growing rather fond of you too. Maybe we can all sort this out when we get back to our world? Who knows, you might find someone better than me, and I wouldn't want to stand in the way of your happiness, Mia."

"Okay, we can wait. I just wanted you to know how deeply I feel for you, just in case I don't make it. I do love you, Vanessa, very much so. Okay, what are we looking for anyway?" Mia replied, thinking: she hasn't rejected me and she did say that she was fond of me. Maybe I dare hope.

"Honestly, Mia, I don't know. Hang on. I've got us. High heels aren't made for hiking in a jungle. Honestly," Vanessa growled, wobbling wildly, but still supporting Mia as well. "Go really slowly."

"I did a lot of hiking in the woods near Fondulac Reservoir back in East Peoria. There were always deer trails through the woods. Perhaps we can find something similar here," Vanessa suggested. The two continued moving slowly along the edge of the jungle.

"Look there!" Mia exclaimed, "you were right, my love! There is a trail. Can we walk it?"

Indeed, a deer trail appeared and the ground looked passable. The two headed on down it, moving into the jungle. If only the trail went all the way through, Vanessa worried, though she didn't mention this to Mia. The poor woman was being challenged enough at the moment. Time passed, but the meandering trail continued. At long last, the jungle thinned and the sandy desert appeared.

"Will you look at that?" Mia declared. Thick sand stretched out seemingly for miles ahead of them. The dunes rose and fell, as if some unseen winds had long ago formed them into their current state. Not a single blade of grass or living plant could be seen. Heat waves distorted their vision of the horizon.

"We should look for the footprints of the others," Vanessa suggested. The two did, but saw nothing.

"We took all sorts of twists and turns back there in the jungle," Mia pointed out. "How do we know which way we need to go to cross this desert?"

Just then, a section of the sand arose and spoke, "The direction that you need to go is that way. I am called Sand, by the way. And you are?" A protrusion of sand pointed in a specific direction.

"I am Mia and this is Vanessa. Thank you, Sand. Is there any water out there that we could drink along the way? It looks terribly hot. An oasis perhaps?"

Sand replied, "Yes, it is one hundred twenty degrees out there. We enjoy the hot dry climate. We are sand, after all. None of that sticky water stuff. It makes us all cling to each other. I don't know about you humans, but we sand don't like to cling to every other sand without any choice in the matter. So no, there most certainly is not any water out there, thank goodness."

"Neither do humans — like to cling to just any other human. Only those that we love and respect," Mia replied politely.

"Good point, Mia, dear, good question. We certainly can't walk across that desert. We would never make it. The sand will fill up our shoes as soon as we take a step or two. I think that one of us is going to have to fly the other over it. I'll go first, Mia. Okay, I want to have the form a giant bird, big and strong enough to fly across the desert and carry Mia with me."

Poof! Vanessa found herself morphed into a giant eagle, whose wing spread was thirty feet from outstretched tip to tip. It took some doing, but she finally got a good grip on Mia and began flapping her wings to get airborne. "I forgot to say that I also should know how to fly!" Vanessa exclaimed as she frantically tried to figure out how to use and manipulate her new body shape. She almost dumped them both into the searing sand before she got them airborne. "This is incredibly hard work, Mia. I can hardly breathe. Keep an eye on our direction for us please."

Slowly the desert sands passed beneath them. Still the uprising heat was sweltering. Mia began sweating and she was just a passenger. Slowly Vanessa's strength began to ebb. Gasping between words, she said, "I forgot to add with enough endurance and strength to get us across the desert!"

"Keep going. You are doing fine, my love. Just fine. I can see the end up ahead. Keep going." Mia continued to shout encouraging words to Vanessa, hoping that would be enough. Slowly Vanessa's strength gave out, and bit by bit, in spite of her flapping, the two began descending. "Just a little more, dear, a little more."

The two landed in a heap on the soft sand, close to the lake's edge. Vanessa's form returned to that of herself, but she was exhausted and passed out, beyond fatigued from the heat and exertion. Mia struggled and got to her feet by herself. "Well done, my love. Oh, no. Well, I did get myself up by myself, like I intended. That's something. I guess that we have to rest a while." She looked out at the clear waters of the lake. Far off in the distance she thought that she saw an island, their destination.

As she stood looking, she thought, Well, I can't be a bird and fly us across since Vanessa used that one. So what can I be to get across? She said aloud, "Are there any boats around here?"

A section of water rose up before her and spoke. "Hello there. My, you look like a fashion model."

"Yes I am or used to be. Not anymore. I've lost my arms. I am Mia."

"I am called Water. Not very inventive a name, I know. I have always cursed my mother for being so ludicrous when naming me. How about Charles or Peter? Something sensible. But no, she had to call me Water! Incredibly stupid of her, don't you think? I certainly do. Anyway, you still look like a fashion model to me. Oh, I am supposed to answer your question. No, there are no boats around here. And thank goodness for that! Honestly, how would you like someone placing a big, heavy wooden boat on top of your pretty body? Just awful, don't you think? I certainly do."

"I agree with you. I would not like a boat on top of me either. Still, we need to cross the water to yonder island. That is where we are supposed to get to, right?" Mia asked, wanting to be very certain of their objective. It was now up to her and her alone. Her love, Vanessa, was utterly exhausted and unconscious, probably from the heat.

Water replied, "Yes, that is where you must go. You cannot fly there, you know."

"I know. Vanessa flew us over the very hot desert. Now I have to get us over you, Water."

"Interesting. And how do you propose to do that, my fine looking fashion model Mia?"

"You really think that I look that good as a fashion model still?" she asked, becoming slightly distracted, but curious.

"Yes, I most certainly do. Your dress is most attractive. Your appearance is, shall I say stunning, though your companion is perhaps more so, what with her enormous bosom."

"Thanks. Okay Water, I have to think this one through," Mia flushed a bit from his compliment.

"Okay, I have it. I want to be a great big dinosaur that can float and swim across using its four big, long legs, the kind that have the long necks so that I can keep Vanessa safely on my back, and have enough strength and endurance to swim us across the lake to the island," Mia declared, trying to picture the whole thing in her mind. Poof! She found herself a huge dinosaur, standing on her four legs. Her head was far above her body down below.

She lowered her head and carefully lifted Vanessa onto her back, being careful not to bite her too hard. Then she walked out into the lake. She began to float. She kept her head bent around to her back to make sure that Vanessa was above water. She was. Slowly, she began using her big legs to dog paddle her way along. It was working, but still tiring. Remember, I did ask for enough endurance and strength to get us across, she reminded the invisible world around her. Sometime later, she arrived at the shore of the island. Poof!

She was back into her normal form, with Vanessa still lying beside her. She saw Henri and the trio sipping tea and called out to him, "Henri, a little help here. I am sort of stuck in the water with Vanessa."

Henri looked up. There was Vanessa and Mia lying on the flat ground which stretched out the whole way that they had come. "Hey, look you are on a flat plain. There is no water there. Poof! Mia found herself lying on the flat plain with Vanessa awaking beside her.

"What?" asked a confused Mia, who tried to sit up on her own. Vanessa sat up too and looked around, trying to grasp the situation.

At last, Vanessa chuckled, "Well, honey, it looks like Mia and I took the long way here."

Henri came over and helped the two to their feet. "Yes, it was just an illusion. Care for some tea, compliments of Sir Thomas and Albert?"

"Yes, I seem utterly parched," Vanessa replied. Herr Adelstein conjured two more chairs and added an extension to his table, while Albert extended the table cloth, though he made the extension purple instead of white, much to the annoyance of the rabbit. Sir Thomas poured the two nice cups of tea.

A while later, Rose and Milan came puffing up to the group, and even later Regi and Trina finally joined them, laughing all the way. Regi said, "Well, we were kind of dumb about it. I plunged by brute force a path for Trina to follow through the jungle. I got so pooped. I've never been that pooped before. I must be terribly out of shape. Tea? Wonderful, lots of sugar, please, Sir Thomas."

Rose and Milan didn't say how they managed to cross the course, only that they had had some interesting conversations with amazing things along the way. After they finished their tea, they climbed into the carriage to continue their journey.

Poof. The world changed again and they found themselves on the other side of the land called Prosopopoeia. However, it was nighttime. "I guess that we ought to rough it a bit and sleep in the carriage. No good traveling blindly," Henri decided. They agreed and tried to do just that, though it was both crowded and uncomfortable. They had already eaten all of their meager food supplies that they had brought with them. Stomachs also growled, making sleep even more difficult for the group.

# Chapter 20 Land's End

Dawn came rousing the tired companions who slept rather ill. "Gosh, I sure am hungry," Mia said as she pushed with her legs back into an upright position. "I am a bit stiff."

"Same here, Mia," Vanessa agreed. "I'd like bacon, eggs, some orange juice, milk, and then a hot tea to round it off."

"Look! Out the window! There it is, just as you asked for, only it's on a table," Mia exclaimed. That got everyone's attention, and they all piled out of the cramped carriage, stretching their legs.

Vanessa walked over the grassland to the table, sat down, and tasted it. "Hey, it is the real thing, I think."

"Well, my jaws are working better," Mia said. "I'd like two pancakes, buttermilk ones, two strips of bacon, one egg sunny side up. I suppose I ought to have a small glass of orange juice as well. Oh, and tea of course." Poof. Her order appeared, sitting perfectly arranged on another table.

At once, everyone else began asking for their desired meal. Poof. Tables appeared right and left, the orders filled exactly as requested by each. Henri scooted his chair over to Mia, who had managed to get herself seated, but no further. Here was just what she wanted, but had no means to partake. Outside of Causeland, she was unable to lift the silverware or cups. Vanessa's heart went out to her again, and she nodded to Henri, who began to feed her, taking care to ask what she wanted first.

A half hour later, the satisfied companions sat back sipping their tea, quite contented. "I wonder where we are?" asked Milan. Instantly, a large sign appeared, something like a sign post from the nineteenth century in style. It read:

Land's End. "Ah, Land's End. I wonder what that means exactly?"

"Perhaps it is the end of our journey, and we can all go back home," Rose spoke up saying what she most desperately desired. She had had all the adventure that she wanted.

"I wish that we had a better map and a better idea of where to go next," Henri stated his viewpoint. As leader, their next move was up to him. Poof! A scroll appeared on his table.

"What the heck?" Mia exclaimed. "That wasn't there before. What's it say, Henri?"

He unrolled the scroll. It showed a grasslands area and a dotted route clearly marked to a large X. "It seems that someone has been kind enough to show us the route to follow," Henri called out for everyone's benefit. "Shall we?"

Everyone rose and headed back to the carriage. As he supported Mia while she was ascending the three steps to get inside, she turned her head and asked, "What should we do with all those tables and chairs out there? We ought not leave them cluttering up such a pristine landscape."

"True. I wish the tables, chairs, and dishes would go back to from where they came," Henri said clearly. Poof! They vanished entirely. "Cool!"

"I wonder if we get whatever we ask for?" Milan speculated. "I wish for a Cuban cigar and a match." Poof. They appeared in his hand. "Don't worry, my love, I will smoke it in the driver's box, not inside."

Rose smiled, "That you'd better do!" Both grinned.

"I wish that I had a bag of acorns to munch on while we travel. Now that would be quite nice indeed, don't you think so, Herr Adelstein?" Sir Thomas stated. Poof! His requested bag was in his hand. "Well, I'll be! So here they are! Amazing."

"I wonder how far we can go with this?" Vanessa asked, suddenly inspired. "Mia, ask for your arms back. Let's see if that can happen."

"I wish that I had my arms back." Mia held her breath, but nothing at all happened.

"Okay, I didn't think that would happen, Mia. Now ask for a yellow ribbon for your hair. That way we can tie it back and keep it from slipping over your face if the wind picks up," Vanessa suggested. Mia did so and the ribbon appeared draped over her shoulders. While Vanessa tied up her hair with it, Henri began thinking hard.

"You know, it seems that our wishes are granted if we ask for simple things. If we ask for something complex, like new arms, it doesn't happen. Most curious. Well, let's get going," Henri suggested. Soon, they were rolling over the prairie lands on a pretty, sunny day. The temperature was perfect, neither too hot nor too cool.

They stopped around noon and asked for a lunch. Once more, they received precisely what they asked for, including Henri's T-bone steak, medium well done. However, they all noted the peculiar absence of all other living things. Only the gently rolling grasslands could be seen in all directions — a strange land indeed.

Late afternoon, they arrived at a very large, black X emblazoned upon the prairie lands. Yellow buttercups grew in a circle around it. Henri pulled the carriage to a stop, and all disembarked to examine the curious land feature. "Well, we are here. Now what?" asked Rose.

"Don't know, mom," Henri replied, scratching his head. Until now, they had to deal with all manner of situations to be allowed to progress further. Here at Land's End, nothing, nothing at all. No people, no towns, no animals, just rolling grasslands with the occasional patches of buttercups in full bloom.

"Well, I wish to go home," Rose stated firmly, a trace of annoyance in her voice. Poof!

An image of Able Montford appeared in the center of the X, startling everyone, even more so when Herr Adelstein put his hand through the image. "It's not real," he muttered, rather startled by his own discovery.

The image flickered a lot and then began speaking in a broken manner. "You — you — you have — you have reached — reached — the — the — the — end." The image flickered again and died out.

"Well that thing sure is broken!" Rose declared angrily. "We come all this way only to find that the exit mechanism has broken down! Honestly, this takes the cake!"

"Calm down, dear, we will work it out," Milan consoled Rose, putting his arm around her lovingly.

"Well, it does make some perverted sense," Henri began, rubbing his face with his hand in a rather exasperated manner. "Able's world has been running sort of on automatic for well over a century and a half now. Machinery does need routine maintenance, right Vanessa?"

"Right, I need to have the oil changed on my truck at least twice a year. Tires do need replacing when they get too worn, to say nothing of replacing brake pads and such. Machines definitely need to be maintained. I wonder where the control room is for this projection? Maybe we can fix it," she suggested. "Show us the entrance to this image's control room, please," she stated firmly. "We are here to do maintenance." Poof!

A doorway appeared; the door was ajar. It seemed peculiar to all to see a door standing there in the middle of the prairie. "Okay, let's see where this leads," Henri called out. "Well, done dear." Vanessa smiled. Everyone looked inside the door. Steps led far underground. Henri made a decision. "Gang, the space might be a bit cramped down there, and we do not know what kind of machinery is there. Why don't Vanessa and I go down and see if we can figure it all out and fix it? Mom, you are all thumbs with mechanical devices, and Milan, you are a doctor, not a mechanic."

"Hey, that's fine with Trina and me," Regi added hastily. "We don't know anything about such things as these. It is all pure magic as far as we are concerned."

"You won't get us to go down there," Herr Adelstein added. "It looks much too dangerous. It might explode or something."

"No need, Herr Adelstein. If we really do need help, we'll let you know," Henri suggested.

"What about me?" asked Mia. "I know that you think that I am just a blonde fashion model, but I did use to help my brother fix his motorcycle. I know a few things about machines."

"Sure, come with us, Mia. The steps are too narrow to go two abreast. I'll go first and you ladies watch your steps," he explained and headed down them. "It's a bit cool down here."

A few minutes later, the three crowded into main underground room. They gazed around at the various unusual looking pieces of machinery, though they had no idea of their purposes or uses. "We ought to get some lights turned on," Mia suggested. "We should look for signs of obvious damage first. Have any of you ever seen anything like all this?"

"Nope, not a clue," Vanessa replied, "but I see lots of lanterns. Let's get them on shall we? Darn these long nails. Henri, be a good dear and light them for us please." A few minutes later, he had the dozen lanterns burning brightly. Now the three could see very well, almost as if sunlight were shining into the room.

"Don't touch anything, but do as Mia rightly suggests; look for signs of obvious damage," he suggested, again taking charge. The three fanned out, looking closely at everything.

Before long, Mia called out, "Over here. Water has corroded this connection thing." An hour later, they had covered the entire chamber three times, spotting four instances of water corrosion on connecting plates made from copper. "Well, it seems to me that some form of electricity runs this thing. Pretty advanced for the 1850's, but electricity needs a good connection. Perhaps we can find a way to replace these four connecting plates."

"I do believe that you are precisely correct. It is the obvious thing to fix first," Henri replied.

"How dear?" asked Vanessa. "We could always try scratching them off a bit, but two are very nearly gone, not much metal is left."

"Good point. Let's use our brains first. I have it. Back in a bit." He headed back up the long stairs, the two women were thankful that he hadn't asked them to go back up and then down again, especially Mia, who now found taking stairs in her high heels very daunting.

Above ground, Henri was besieged with questions and spent a few minutes explaining what they had found. Meanwhile, the others had conjured tables and suppers for themselves. Henri then spoke clearly wishing for replacement copper parts. He was very careful to make his requests very specific, particularly with the dimensions of the four parts. Poof! Four replacement bars appeared in his hands. He dashed down the stairs once more, greatly enthused.

It did not take too long for him to replace the corroded strips with his new ones. "Now will it work?" asked Vanessa.

"If I might make a suggestion?" Mia broke in. The two turned to her.

"Absolutely, always, Mia," Henri replied.

"Well, we ought to have the others try to activate it and see if they can go home, while we watch all this machinery down here. If more repairs are needed, perhaps we can see what part of all this is malfunctioning. Get some clues, perhaps."

"Mia, that's brilliant!" Henri exclaimed and gave her a big hug. "Back in a minute." He dashed up the stairs. "Okay, mom, we are ready to try this again. I want you to request the machine to send you back to our house. See if you can take Milan with you."

"Wait a minute," Regi interrupted him. "What about Trina and me? If we return to our time, we'd be dead for over a century."

"I understand, Regi. This is the great, big unknown factor. We have no idea what this machine and what this world does with time in our world. My best guess is to have you return with Rose. If we are in luck, you will arrive in our house as you are. You will have your whole lives to live, but yes, it will be culture shock at first. So much has changed since your time. Still, I'd rather deal with that than risk having you both end up dead."

Regi breathed a huge sigh of relief. This very problem had been on their minds for days now. That Henri agreed with him and was offering them a chance a life was all that he and Trina could desire. "Okay, dear, I'll see if we four can return to my home. When will you three be coming?"

"We are going to observe the machine in operation. If it malfunctions again, we hope to be able to see what part of it is failing and maybe get more clues on how to fix it. If it does work, we will be along as soon as we can, mom. Don't worry; we have no intention of staying behind."

"Well, you had better not, dear. Okay, yell when you want me to try this," Rose said, eager to get this going. Henri dashed back down the stairs. All three of them stood in a triangular position, sides to sides, so that they essentially had a three hundred sixty degree view of the machinery. Henri yelled up to Rose and the three watched and listened.

Above ground, the image of Able Montford appeared. It spoke, this time the fluctuations were gone. "You have reached the end of your journey. I hope that you have indeed learned something about yourself and your abilities. Do you wish to return to your home now? If so, state your name, destination city, and the number of people in your party to be returning there. Declare that now. If you do not wish to return, speak the word No."

"Rose Whitney. Peoria, Illinois. Four in my party."

"One moment while the connection to the doors is made. Connection made. Step through the doors now, one at a time, please. You may carry anything back with you that desire as long as it fits in your hands. Thank you for visiting Montford's Portail Mystique d'Univers." A large, shimmering door appeared.

None of the four had or wanted anything to take back. Rose walked up to the door and stepped boldly into the shimmering light, vanishing from Land's End. Milan followed her, then Trina. Regi made sure that Trina was gone before he too stepped through the door. After he vanished, the doors disappeared, and the machine shut down, becoming dormant once more. Henri headed up the steps to see what had happened.

"Yep, they are gone," Herr Adelstein stated formally as Henri's head appeared coming out of the ground by the doors. Henri had him describe what the three had seen. Satisfied, he headed back down the steps.

"Did it work right?" Vanessa asked.

"As far as we can tell, it worked perfectly. They had the chance to take back with them anything that they could carry in their hands. Do you ladies want to take the gifts that we've been given back with us?" He need not have asked. They did.

"Dear, Mia has made another discovery while you were up there. Show him, Mia."

"Over here, see. There is a button labeled Maintenance. I think that we should press it and see if anything else needs to be done before we leave. What do you think?" Mia asked.

"Blondie, you are a genius!" Henry pressed the button. Another image appeared of Able. This time, his mood was serious.

"Accessing images. You are not Able Montford. Has Able Montford become deceased? Reply 'Yes' or 'No' only, now."

"Yes." Henri stated firmly.

"Data accepted. Montford's Portail Mystique d'Univers needs a new caretaker to watch over the universe. Do you have someone who will do that? Answer 'Yes' or 'No' only, now."

Henri thought fast. He smiled. "Yes."

"Accepted. State name or names and race."

"Herr Petr Adelstein, rabbit. Sir Thomas d'Lyons, squirrel. Albert Rose, tortoise."

"Accepted. Please have named caretakers stand here to be recognized and scanned into the system."

"One minute while I go get them."

"Waiting."

Henri dashed up the stairs again, while the two women backed out of the way as much as possible. The space was going to be cramped with six down here. "Guys, it is time for you three to get your reward for helping us. This universe needs a new caretaker, since Able Montford is long gone. I have made you three the new caretakers. You three will control this entire universe."

"Oh dear me. Does that mean we will be like gods?" Sir Thomas asked, astounded with this sudden promotion.

"Absolutely. You will be running things everywhere, though I hope that you three will do an honorable, ethical job of it," Henri replied. "The machine needs to have you tell it your name. I think that it will be making a record of your voices so that it can recognize you in the future and all that. Come on down, please."

With chests very nearly bursting out, the three proud fellows followed him down the stairs. Their eyes nearly popped out at the sight of all this strange machinery. Henri had them stand before the machine where he had stood. One by one, they stated their full names and the machine replied, "Accepted Caretaker Herr Petr Adelstein." So it went with the other two.

"Please have originator of this maintenance cycle stand here again." The three headed up the steps, more than a little intimidated by the machine. Henri retook his position once more.

"Recognized. Thank you for your timely service. Maintenance is long overdue. Can you perform this action? I will direct you on what needs to be done."

"Yes, I would be honored to perform the maintenance for you. First, can we have a few minutes to eat supper?"

"Yes. Thank you. Say 'Activate' when you are ready."

Henri and the women headed up the stairs. Outside, they requested a turkey dinner, with mashed potatoes, gravy, and peas, but only one table with three chairs. As expected, it appeared as desired. The three had a delicious meal. The women then began collecting their dresses and gifts from the carriage, preparatory to their return, while Henri headed back down to handle the maintenance. It took him nearly two hours to do it all. The poor machine had not had any servicing in a hundred fifty years and was in dire need of it.

Finally, Henri climbed up and the doors vanished, leaving the prairie grasslands in a pristine condition once more. It was late evening now, the sun had just set. Both women had their bags near themselves and were waiting patiently for Henri. "All finished. Quite a lot to do down there actually. Are you both ready?"

"Yes, we got our things with us and your new suit too. All set on your end?" Vanessa replied. It was.

The three hugged their three new "gods" of Montford's Portail Mystique d'Univers. For the three, it was a tearful farewell. "Please come back and visit us," Herr Adelstein said, wiping the tears from his eyes. "We will miss you 'umans. I never ever thought that I would say that."

A minute later, Henri spoke solemnly, "We are ready to go home. Peoria, Illinois. Three to go." He and Vanessa held onto their many packages and waited. The door appeared once more, shimmering with its peculiar lights. "Okay, you go first, Mia. Just step through the door. Vanessa, you follow her. I will bring up the rear."

Mia did as asked. Holding her breath, she stepped into the shimmering light. Vanessa was right behind her. Henri waited to make sure both had truly vanished before he stepped through as well. The trio watched with tear-stained eyes as the door vanished before their eyes. "I do hope that they come back to visit," Albert said sadly. "I am rather fond of them, even though they keep changing body forms on us."

"Come, fellows. Let's go back to our green lands. This time we control things. Nothing to ever be afraid of again, Sir Thomas. We control everything now," Herr Adelstein explained.

"I am powerful now, aren't I," the squirrel said, before he vanished from Land's End with his friends, appearing where they'd first encountered Zed and Miranda falling down from the sky.

As Vanessa began falling though space, a voice appeared in her mind. "Mia made a wish that I was not able to fulfill at that time. She wanted arms back. Vanessa, are you willing to give her your arms? Answer 'Yes' or 'No.'"

Vanessa had but seconds to make her decision. "Yes." Later she would have to explain her reasoning to Henri, but she felt this was the right thing to do. Give Mia a chance for a real life after her long years of imprisonment. After all, she had not intentionally entered this world as had Rose or they, for that matter.

Mia was falling, exactly as she had when she entered this world so many years ago. This time, she focused and concentrated on the room that was appearing before her. Then she found herself landing, though tumbling off her feet. She reached out and caught herself with her arms, breathless. "Oh my god! My arms are back." Mia stared in disbelief at her arms and hands and then noticed that she had three inch long cherry red nails, just like Vanessa had.

Vanessa focused her will as the room appeared. I am going to step out gently and not fall down. I am going to step out gently and not fall down. She did exactly that, stepping out gently onto the floor before the small double door window that she'd use to enter the strange world. Mia was just getting up from the floor in front of her. However, the many bags that Vanessa had been carrying with her came tumbling out onto the floor. Vanessa looked at herself and was not at all surprise to see that her arms were entirely missing. She looked at Mia and saw her staring at her new arms and hands with her long red talons. Vanessa smiled and stepped a bit out of the way, as Henri came stepping through, carrying even more bags.

"Look at me!" Mia exclaimed, turning to Vanessa, but then gasped as she saw Vanessa was now armless. Instantly she realized that she now had Vanessa's arms.

Henri saw his armless wife standing before him, her bags scattered over the floor and Mia standing with her arms back and gasped. "My god! What happened? Did something go terribly wrong?"

More confusions occurred, as the bodies of Miranda and Zed came tumbling onto the floor. "We made it!" Miranda exclaimed and then saw the others and gasped. "Oh!"

# Chapter 21 Home Confusions

"Everyone, we are in my house. That part is fine," Miranda took charge of the very confused group. She and Zed were still wearing the clothes that they'd originally worn when they first entered the portal, tee-shirts and jeans. Mia just held her new hands in front of her mouth, terrified of saying anything.

Henri exclaimed, "My god, I thought that I'd never get back into my own body! I've been stuck in my wife's body for over a century. Vanessa, how can I ever thank you enough for caring for me all those years? I'm sorry about your arms. You see, Zed and I were given a choice as we came back. Mia? This is so confusing. When are we?"

Sheepishly, Henri added, "Zed and I had a choice, dearest. We heard Able's voice, I think. He said, 'Mia made a wish that I was not able to fulfill at that time. She wanted arms back. Vanessa, are you willing to give her your arms? Answer 'Yes' or 'No.' Zed and I both agreed and said 'yes.' I hope you understand, dearest. Mia has no one to come back to and you have me."

Vanessa grimaced, "My arms weren't yours to give, Henri." Mia's face crimsoned; her elation faded rapidly. "But," she added, "had you asked me, I would have agreed with you and Zed. We have each other. Besides, I've had my fill of being a man! Gosh, this is awkward, isn't it? All of us and me with no arms. Mia, you are most welcome to my arms. I'm more than happy to have my own body back again. Honestly, I hated every minute that I was stuck in your body, Henri. Now, you get to look after me. That's going to be a very pleasant change. Zed, Miranda, thank you for rescuing us from that awful world!"

Mia began to relax. Vanessa didn't hate her for taking her arms. Still, she was confused, and asked, "Who is who?"

Zed laughed, "Better ask who was who and when? It was me in Vanessa's body, Mia, well most of the time. Miranda was stuck in Henri's body. We promised to rescue them both and we've done that. The year is 2010, I hope. The next question is will Vanessa and Henri's bodies suddenly age a hundred fifty years?"

"But I don't want to become fiftyish," Mia protested. "Oh, I see. They'd be nearly two hundred years old." Her voice trailed off as she realized what that would mean.

"Don't worry. If you start to age, we can send you back through the portal. That should undo the aging process. At least it did with mom," Miranda explained, hoping that none of them would age.

Vanessa commented, "Well, I sure hope that we don't age. I'm so glad to be back in my own body!

Just then, Rose walked in, "Oh, what's happened to you two? Oh, five of you?"

"Mom, this is Zed. We got our own bodies back, but Zed and Henri donated Vanessa's arms to Mia on the way back."

"Well, this is confusing. Just like a man to give away his wife's arms. But I'm glad to finally meet you, Zed. You are not quite what I imagined, but then if Miranda is happy with you, I won't complain. Anyway, we four all got back in one piece. Domino's is here. Come on. Pizza is waiting for you."

Vanessa said, "I would have given Mia my arms, Rose, if they'd asked me. She needs them more than I do. Pizza? I'm famished." She teased, coyly saying, "Okay, Henri darling, you get to feed me."

Rose declared, "Well, that is the most generous thing that I have ever heard of! Just leave those bags for now. Pizza is getting cold. How come you took so long to get back here? We were starting to get worried about you three," Rose chatted away as she led the five to the dining room, where Regi, Trina, and Milan had finished their pizza and were sipping tea, having turned down Cokes, not knowing what they were. Once more, Vanessa had to explain why she didn't have her arms and Mia did.

"You somehow gave her your arms?" Trina asked in disbelief. "That's, that's so unbelievably kind! Did it hurt?"

"Didn't feel a thing, besides, she needs them more than I do. Now, Henri can feed *me* the pizza instead of her." Everyone chuckled at her tease. Mia could only cry. No one had ever been so kind to her before; the gift was unimaginably important to her.

"While you five finish up, I am going to get our guests fixed up for the night. Tomorrow, we can sort this all out. They are going to have a lot of catching up to do," Rose explained. She led Regi, Trina, and Milan off to show them the bathrooms and the spare bedroom for the couple.

Still crying, Mia said, "Vanessa, how can I ever, ever thank you for these? I do love you so! I will always be faithful to you, I promise."

"I know, Mia, I know, but it's going to be complicated. You see, I wasn't in this body when you fell in love with me. Zed and Henri were. So now, you might not be in love with me. Gosh, this is terribly confusing, isn't it?"

"Understatement," Henri declared, sampling the pizza and wondering what the red and white cans contained. He'd never seen them before, but then most everything around him was foreign to him. Well, the table and chairs looked functional, but a far cry from such things back in 1850.

Vanessa declared, "You are sleeping with us tonight, Mia. Tomorrow we will have to sort all this out." Later, Vanessa,

Henri, and Mia went into one of Rose's spare bedrooms for much needed sleep.

Mia helped Vanessa get ready for bed. "So I was in love with Zed?" she whispered to Vanessa, "because he was being you?"

Vanessa answered, "Using my body might be a better way of putting it. I was in Henri's body with Miranda, but she was dominant. I think Henri and I were mostly resting quietly in the background. We could see what was going on around us, but couldn't do anything about it. So it was probably Zed."

"But I don't really like men, just women," Mia admitted. "And that means, Zed — no, this is just too confusing for me."

"No kidding. Come on. Help me into bed and snuggle up to me," Vanessa ordered. Mia complied, her mind struggling to grasp what had happened to her.

"Rise and shine in there, you three, breakfast in ten," Rose called out.

"So soon? I could sleep for a week," Vanessa said sleepily and tried to sit up, before she again remembered that her arms were gone.

Mia was right there though. "I have you, my love." Mia got Vanessa dressed and hastily brushed her very long light brown hair for her, while Henri slipped Vanessa's Oxford style heels on her and tied them. Quickly they dressed themselves. Then, the three stood looking at each other, looking for signs of rapid aging.

"Vanessa, Mia, you both look as beautiful as you did last night," Henri declared. "So far, so good." Both women looked relieved and headed off to join the others for breakfast.

After sitting down at the crowded table, a confused Trina asked, "So Zed here was Vanessa and Miranda was Henri?" Milan and Regi also looked just as confused.

Miranda answered, "Precisely. You see, Vanessa and Henri were also victims of Montford's Portail Mystique d'Univers, back around 1850 or so. They too ended up in opposite bodies of the then current Count and Countess, thereby freeing them so that they could continue going through that universe, rather like we did when we got there. But they got trapped, because hardly anyone ever came to the universe after that, excepting Mia and then years later Rose, Zed and me.

Milan exclaimed, "Confusing, but the real point is that we are now all back, safe and sound. We owe everything to Zed and Miranda."

"It all seems to have worked out," Miranda admitted, though she didn't mention she was still worried about them prematurely aging.

"After breakfast, I am taking everyone on a tour of Peoria and then out to the mall to get them some new clothes," Rose pronounced decisively. "Time to get them into the twenty-first century. What are your plans, Miranda?"

"Not sure yet, mom. Mia is only a few years behind the times. Say, what day is it? How long have we been gone anyway?" she asked. The present time slowly returned to her awareness.

"According to the morning news, it is the fifteenth of July now. I've been gone nearly two months," Rose answered, smiling that she knew something that her daughter did not.

"I think that we're going to stay in and rest some today. Long baths and all that," Miranda declared. Zed smiled; his girl did like to make the decisions, and he flashed an approving grin her way. It was not that she was overly bossy; rather she knew what the others desired and simply went ahead and saw that such happened.

After breakfast, Miranda showed Mia how to use her laptop to surf the Internet and left her exploring Google. She and Zed headed for the bathroom and a much needed soaking.

"Wow Zed. Your beard. It's growing!" Miranda commented. "Wait, my nails are growing!"

He looked into the mirror. "You are right. While we were there, my beard didn't grow any. How strange, but then everything there was strange. Say, look at it. It's growing almost as I look at it. Perhaps it is making up for two month's stunted growth. Oh god! I wonder if this is the aging process going again. Regi, Trina, Milan, Vanessa, Henri!" Miranda had a freakish grimace that Zed had never seen before.

"Good lord! I hope not. I'd better text mom about this. Back in a minute, where's my cell?" She returned a bit later looking very much relieved. "Mom says their beards are growing, but they don't seem to be aging. Trina's nails and hair are growing, too. I am beginning to think that it's only going to be hair and nails that are going a bit berserk. Mine seems to have stopped growing now. Come on. Let's get our bath done."

Dressed in clean jeans and tee-shirts, the two headed back to Mia in Miranda's bedroom. She looked up at the two and said, "Blimey, you do clean up okay, I guess. Come here and see what I've done." Pride radiated from the young woman. "Oh these darn nails. Look at them; how they have grown! They are six inches long — and my hair. It's down to the small of my back, like Vanessa's. Anyway, look." She switched tabs in her browser. "I've found my old bank accounts. Checking and savings. Look at what twenty years of accumulated interest has done! I'm rich, two hundred thousand pounds! Incredible. I've got them re-certified as mine, and they are sending me new checks, passbook, and debit card, which is like a charge card, if I followed it right. Plus, look here," she tabbed again. "My passport. It's being re-issued. I filled out a lost passport form, and a new one will be mailed here. I cheated a bit and looked at your mom's stack of mail to find the address. I hope that's okay. I'm rich, gang. That's a relief."

"Mia, that's fantastic. You are adapting well indeed. Most encouraging."

Mia giggled, "Well, as long as I don't suddenly age to fifty."

Later the others returned from their shopping. As soon as Vanessa entered, Mia went to her and brought her to Miranda's computer. "You have to see what I've just found for you, Vanessa. Oh Vanessa, look at your gorgeous brown hair! It's now down to your knees," Miranda pointed out."

"If it doesn't stop growing," Vanessa joked, "I may end up walking on it." The women giggled and made their way to the bedroom.

Mia explained, "I did a bit of research for you. If you exercise a bunch, you can get your muscles built back up. After we bathe you, we'll begin your workouts. Your goal is to no longer *have* to wear those corsets. I do love your look when you wear them, but realistically, it has to be our choice when to wear them. I think it will much more difficult to get your legs stretched enough to wear flats again. I think not having to wear the corsets are far more important the heels. What do you think?"

"I agree. I don't mind the heels anywhere near as much as the total restriction, particularly now, Mia. Show me the exercises, *please!*" Vanessa said emphatically.

While chatting, Miranda helped Mia undress. She faced the same weak mid-section muscles problem that Vanessa did, though far, far less. She had only endured twenty years of the tight corseting of the duchess' dolls, while Vanessa, as the Countess of Malbon, had endured it for a century and a half. While Miranda said nothing about it, she suspected that Mia would soon be free of the corset, but probably Vanessa never would.

When they finally finished their baths, Mia went through the battery of exercises with Vanessa, though she found them easier to do than Vanessa. That done, they tackled their hair. Finally, they dressed in the fancy outfits that they had been given. As Miranda expected, Mia would be making rapid progress on toning up her back and waist muscles, Vanessa was not, though she didn't tell them her observations just yet. Best let them come to their own realizations in their own time, she thought.

When Rose returned with the group and Mia whisked Vanessa off, Miranda noticed that Milan looked a bit flustered and harried, but Regi, Trina, and Henri looked ghastly. Yes, the men now sported beards, and Trina's hair and nails had grown significantly as well. Miranda noted that her mother's hair and nails were longer than she usually kept them. Still, she saw no signs of the terrible aging process that had happened to her Henri body and that of Vanessa when they had returned using the Emergency Exit. That is a relief, she thought.

Over supper, Chinese takeout since Rose was too tired to cook, Miranda began to get a sense of how the culture shock had gone with the five who were so out of their own time, the 1850's. Milan was adjusting somewhat. Miranda thought that his extensive travel background, beginning with serving with Wellington over in Europe in the early eighteen hundreds had something to do with how he was adapting. On the other hand, Regi, Trina, and Henri were not doing well at all.

"Things are so utterly different now," Regi tried to put his fears into words. He had to; Trina was miserable and he knew it. He could see it in her face. "Everything that we know and everything that we know how to do — none of this has any real relevance in your modern world. We are like fish out of water. We can't see how we can possibly fit into this world of yours. It is impossible to go back to our own time. We'd be long dead if we did." He sounded pretty distressed and hopeless, Miranda thought.

Rose also felt his intense worry. "Why don't you sleep on it all? Give yourselves time to learn new things, new ways. I know things must seem terribly different and foreign to you right now, but give yourselves time to adjust. I know that you can do it." Well, she didn't know it, but was unwilling to say so.

They agreed and retired for the night, as the sun set. Once they were gone, Doctor Milan spoke up, "My dear Rose, those four might not make it. I've seen those looks on faces many times before. Young men about to head into a battle for the first time often look that way. They know that they are about to die. I fear for them, I really do. We should keep a sharp eye on them."

"Oh dear, it's worse than I was admitting, isn't it, Milan?" Rose slumped in her chair. "What can I do? Surely there must be something we can do to help them adjust." Silence.

Milan broke the awkward quiet, "Sleep may help them. Let's see how they feel in the morning. Things are so different in your world, Rose, so different, and yet, the same. How funny. After all these many years, some things never change. Amazing and interesting too. I hope I can learn quickly enough, dear."

"Oh you are doing superbly! Come on. Let's take a hint from them and retire. Daughter, you can clean up. Night." Rose hugged her daughter and took Milan's offered arm, heading off to her bedroom.

"Did you see how awful Regi and Trina looked?" Mia pointed out, as the three sat sipping their Cokes. They did and it was sobering. Vanessa and Henri soon joined them.

"Hey, I like this, ladies," Vanessa teased them, as the three set about cleaning off the table and putting the dishes into the dishwasher. "I don't have to deal with the messes. No arms." Both women laughed at her jest.

"Hey dear, you are going to have to learn new ways to do things. Remember what you kept telling me," Mia teased her back. Vanessa flushed, yes, she recalled how Zed had tried to drill that into Mia's head. Now it was coming back to haunt her.

"Okay, okay. I'll work on it," Vanessa agreed, though at the moment, she had no ideas.

With the dining room handled, the five headed to the living room to watch some movies. As promised, Miranda started the Lord of the Rings series of movies, which Mia greatly enjoyed watching. They only got through the first one before they were too tired to continue and headed off to bed.

The next morning, Miranda very carefully examined Mia for signs of rapid aging. She found none. She and Zed also checked on Vanessa and Henri and found them unchanged from the day before, save Henri had stubble on his face and needed a shave. "This is going to be really annoying, having to shave every morning," Henri declared flatly. "I got so used to not shaving." Zed chuckled and Mia smiled.

At breakfast, Regi and Trina looked a little more composed. He said, "Trina and I have been talking about things last night. We've decided that we really don't belong in this century. We just cannot relate to anything here. Is it possible for us to go back into Montford's Portail Mystique d'Univers? At least we felt very comfortable living there."

"Sure, Regi, Trina. If that is what you truly want, you certainly can," Miranda spoke before anyone else could. "I am sure that Herr Adelstein, Sir Thomas, and Albert can find you a great place to live and enjoy your lives. Perhaps, you can help them run the place."

The relief on both their faces was enormous. "Thank you! Thank you! That would be wonderful for us!" Regi gushed. At last, both had their charming smiles back. "We really appreciate all that you have done for us, we really do."

"I know, the modern world is so vastly different than when you left it," Miranda replied. "We all do truly understand. Can you wait to return for a few hours? Zed and I want to get a couple of presents for the trio. You can give them to Herr Adelstein, Sir Thomas, and Albert when you see them next." Both agreed and Zed and Miranda hastily ducked out to do some quick shopping. They got each a fancy Buck knife and a compass, nicely gift wrapped with a card thanking them for all their aid and support.

When they got back, Henri and Vanessa took them aside. "Zed, Miranda, Vanessa and I have been discussing our situation. You see, neither of us belongs in this modern world either. Everything is so utterly strange. Besides, it is so difficult for Vanessa here. If we could go back and live in Causeland, then Vanessa could live normally."

She spoke up, "He means that I can do things that I can't do in the real world. Honestly, we both would be far better off living the rest of our lives in Causeland, if that's possible."

"Absolutely," Miranda replied. "Regi and Trina are going back shortly too. I'm sure that Herr Adelstein can get you safely there." Zed watched Vanessa's face carefully and saw that she was totally sincere; he knew why she wanted to go back. In Causeland, her lack of arms and hands would only be an inconvenience, as Lucinda claimed.

Around noon, Regi and Trina stood before the magical doors in the wall, holding the small packages. Again, the two thanked everyone, and then they leaned into the shimmering light. As the group watched, their bodies seemed to be sucked into the window, vanishing from the room. "So that's what it looked like when I got accidentally sucked in there," Mia said, finally witnessing what must have happened to herself twenty years ago.

"Okay, now it's your turn," Miranda said to Vanessa and Henri. After hugs, Henri put his arms around Vanessa, and they leaned into the portal and vanished as well.

Mia sighed. "There goes the love of my life. Say, whenever you two decide to pay a visit to that world, let me know and I'll join you if I can. Anyway, I'm going to visit the Grand Canyon before I go back to London. Care to join me?"

Zed looked at Miranda. She replied, "Sure, why not?"
The End.

# Other Books by Vic Broquard

Without Warning (fantasy)
The Trident Series: (fantasy)
      Volume 1 The Trident and the Book
      Volume 3 The Trident and the Scepter
      Volume3 The Trident and the Resurrection
The Adventures of Elizabeth Stanton Series: (science fiction)
      Volume 1 The Evolution of the Path
      Volume 2 The Great Messiah
      Volume 3 Of Kings and Queens and Troubadours
      Volume 4 Chaos in the Aftermath
      Volume 5 Power Plays
      Volume 6 Age of Exploration
      Volume 7 Abducted
      Volume 8 The Emperor and Empress
      Volume 9 A Job Worth Doing
      Volume 10 Degradation
      Volume 11 The Second Crusade
      Volume 12 When Worlds Collide
      Volume 13 Dark Ages

The Lindsey Barron Series: (fantasy)
      Volume 1 The Rod of the Apocalypse
      Volume 2 The Board of Governors
      Volume 3 The Crown of Moses
      Volume 4 Dominus for President
      Volume 5 The National Health Care Program
      Volume 6 States Justice
      Volume 7 Cross and Double-cross

Zoran Chronicles Series: (fantasy)
  Volume 1 A Dragon in Our Town
  Volume 2 Dragons, Power, Courts, and War

Planet of the Orange-red Sun Series: (science fiction)
  Volume 1 When Kingdoms Fall
  Volume 2 Dark Ages
  Volume 3 Age of the Towers
  Volume 4 Difficillis Exitus
  Volume 5 Age of the Lords
  Volume 6 The Renegade Tower
  Volume 7 Rebellions
  Volume 8 The Aliens Return
  Volume 9 Power Struggles
  Volume 10 Guilds, Genetics, and Gods
  Volume 11 Magi, Witches, Swords, and Superstitions
  Volume 12 The Voyage of the Eagle's Seed
  Volume 13 Justifications
  Volume 14 Responsibilities

The Return of the Wizards: Twelve Companions – The Making of Wizards (fantasy)